The Unnamed

The Unnamed

Cover Design: Stefanie Saw @designsbyseventhstar
Interior Illustrations: Jawaad Mohiuddin @radartist.md
Map Design: Marta Riva @marta.intotheforest
Editing: Alexandra Moyer @alchemy_edit_ | Joyce Fernandez @ rejoyceliteraryediting
Book Design and Typesetting: Enchanted Ink Publishing

The text type was set in Sabon LT Pro

ISBN: 979-8-9935359-0-6 (E-book)
ISBN: 979-8-9935359-1-3 (Paperback)

WWW.MSMASOODBOOKS.COM

For those who refuse
to let their stories be erased
and their names forgotten.

The Song of Fallacy

ENTERED 1,000 YEARS AGO

The greatest fallacy we can create,
The biggest lie we can then believe,
Is that the land belongs to us.
As do the sky, the mountains, the sea.

The land belongs to no one, my love.
It is we who belong to the land.
It is we who come from its heart, my love.
It is we who will return to its hand.

So do not praise it when it gives in abundance,
Only to blame it when it gives but few.
Does a guest demand from his host?
Beware the ones that do.

The land belongs to no one, my love.
It is we who belong to the land.
It is we who come from its heart, my love.
It is we who will return to its hand.

Those who attempt to take without being given,
Who own and steal and claim,
Who attempt to come without welcome,
Then the land will do the same.

It will withhold its love, my love.
It will taint all you take with hate.
It will turn your soul to stone, my love.
Filled with hunger you can never sate.

The land belongs to no one, my love.
It is we who belong to the land.
It is we who come from its heart, my love.
It is we who will return to its hand.

Koors Dësërt

Thë Citadël

Këëp

Sakoon Sës

Vuor

The Unnamed

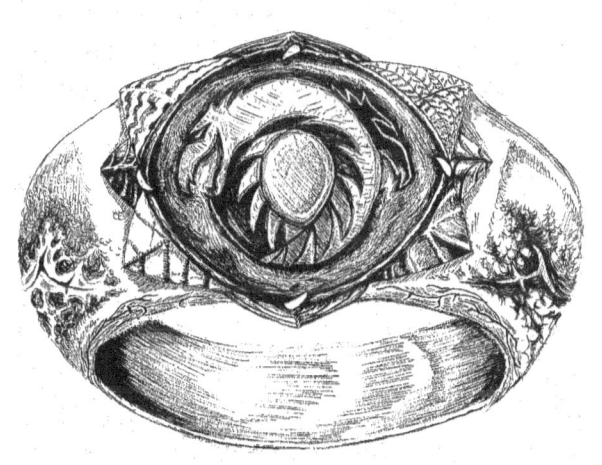

M.S. MASOOD

SOME STORIES START AT THE END, LITTLE GAZELLE," Baba begins from behind me, lacing my midnight hair through his sure, slender fingers as he has every morning for as long as I can remember. Parting the strands into nine equal lengths, he weaves the first three into long rows of tight knots against my scalp and down my back in the intricate pattern of our mighty warriors of Vuor.

"Some stories can only truly be *heard*, be completely understood, when you know how everything turns out." His quiet words pound in my ears, in my *heart*, like the calling of the imperial war drum. While his deft hands work over the crest of my skull, the spicy plumes of blackwood incense from the castle healer's earlier visit sting my eyes, forcing me to shut everything out.

Forcing me to *hear* him, just as he always asks.

Just as I always comply.

"An ending could tell us the good things." His voice tangles with my strands of hair. "Whether the hero saves their kingdom . . ." *Pull.*

"Or weds their beloved . . ." *Twist.*

"Or dies an honorable death . . ." *Knot. Repeat.*

"Or it could tell us of our catastrophes—of those crucial moments in our stories when we should have done something differently. Something that would have altered the very course of our lives." His fingers falter in their primal rhythm, the feathering so slight, it would have been easily missed had I been anyone else. "Or of the ones we love."

My eyes remain closed as my senses wrap tentative tendrils around that last word, holding it tightly to my chest.

Love.

Love, like his tugging, scraping, smoothing of braid after braid, row after row, akin to the almazi groves the farmers of Canton One sow.

Love, like his fingers, made of calloused, gnarled roots from our kingdom's history of battle and blood. Prosperity and growth.

Love, like his voice's cadence—an unyielding force like the solid walls that protect our precious land.

"For instance, the end of our story could have come one day in the midst of the wet season. A clear day. A beautiful day where the women could finally take their baskets of wash and relieved smiles to the rolling fields of wild blooms to gossip and hang their sheets, their worries, their colors."

Loop. Twist. Twine.

"Or on a day when the sea was calm, the waves still and sparkling, beckoning the men to unmoor their cedar vessels and row into their welcoming lull. To feed their people with their hearty catch, their own souls with their tales of battles waged and won."

His hands still, the gentle pressure of his weaving fingers vanishing from my head. A clawing grip snatches my shoulders in their stead. I snap my eyes open, whipping my confused gaze over my shoulder only to collide with his cold, distant one. The one he wears not for *love* . . .

But for *war.*

"Or the ending could have come on a day when a father was braiding his beloved daughter's hair, intertwining the story of her people and her land into her very soul with every knot. Trusting her to remember it. To protect it."

His eyes lock with mine in the mirror at my front as his hand does the same to my hair from behind.

I can't look away.

Wouldn't dare.

"But. It. Didn't."

His words are so quiet in a pause so long, I question whether I pulled them from my imagination.

And then he lets go.

His eyes soften again to the rust color of the sand dunes shifting with the setting sun, his touch passing over my bound locks not like a father reassuring his daughter, but like a king donning a helmet over his High Commander's head.

"And do you know why that is, little gazelle?"

I swallow past the suffocating power of his presence. Force myself to shake my head, in awe of the gravity of his attention.

This great, selfless, brave man is confiding in me.

Trusting me.

"Because, you see," he murmurs, tilting my chin up so my eyes lock with his own unwavering gaze, "knowing how a story ends tells us how to stop it from beginning."

Chapter 1

15 YEARS LATER

A BEAD OF SWEAT TRACES THE VALLEY BETWEEN my shoulder blades beneath my leather armor as I adjust the strap of my sword sheath across my back. I hate summers in Vuor, especially in Canton Two.

Hate the overwhelming musk of perpetually filthy bodies steeped in sweat and sun. The busy yet somehow silent streets of sand and dust, where the raggedy dwellers of this canton amass in droves every single morning to drag themselves to work. To be divided into groups and loaded onto wooden carts to earn their keep in the baluur mines.

But most of all I hate the ever-changing labyrinth of dilapidated mud buildings, potholed streets, and strangled alleys meant to serve as death traps to ajnoob.

Outsiders. Like me.

The only refuge from this oppressive heat is the fluttering shadows of the phoenixes that flit and soar above our heads, delivering messages fastened to their ankles from within the kingdom and beyond.

A particularly bright one boasting plumage of emerald and gold but no parchment swoops down, locking its fiery eyes with my muddy ones just before it ascends once again.

Just before my boot sinks ankle-deep in a heap of garbage.

I look down, but the putrid smell reaches me first. That is *definitely* not garbage.

I curse under my breath.

"Come now, Reim. Not the scowl again." The low, muttered words skim the shell of my ear.

I swat at their source like a buzzing gnat while scraping my boot free of the khur, which only serves to turn the grumble into a chuckle.

Grinding my teeth, I push past the much larger body in my way, not knowing which reaction annoys me more.

"Hey, hey, hey," Tamir, my second-in-command and the captain of our forces, swings in front of me, walking backward as I continue my punishing pace. The sooner we finish patrolling, the sooner we can leave this disgusting place. "You know I'm right. You don't need the khasir to mistrust us any more than they already do."

I roll my eyes. "Yes, because my smile is going to change their selfish ways."

My response makes *his* easy smile stretch wider, a single dimple curving like an archer's bow in his right cheek. "Well, it has mine."

A different kind of heat envelops my body at his words. One that snatches my gaze up to collide with his cerulean one, the color matched only by the sparse oases scattering the Koora Desert beyond Vuor.

In their depths are our past five years together under not only the sweltering sun, but also the star-riddled sky—the first heartbeats of attraction punctuating the endless days of training and the sleepless nights that followed.

Not that we would act upon it. Not that we *could*.

These thieved brushes of the in-between are all we'll ever have, me being who I am.

Ameera.

Princess.

The heir to the Iron Crown.

I look away, focusing my surveillance on a narrow alley to our left while every other part of me remains acutely attuned to his proximity. Tries to forget what it never had.

As much as I detest these patrols, I understand the need for them. Especially in the Burrow, where just last week there was a surprise attack on another patrol, leaving three dead and four in the healing ward of the castle. And for what? The khasir perpetrators were rounded up, interrogated, and then executed. Their families, now forever under the Crown's watch. Their futile purpose buried with their quartered corpses.

Fate, why can't they just be grateful? They have reliable work, the protection of the Jirga, food, water, and shelter. Why is it in their nature to be forever unsatisfied, always creating chaos?

Something suddenly shifts in the alley's shadowed depths. Stops immediately when I do the same. Seems to hold its breath in anticipation of my next move in order to make its own.

"What is it, Reim?" Tamir whispers, pecking at my concentration, my honed training to hunt.

To capture.

Distracting me from the niggling thought that this time, I don't feel like the hunter, the seasoned warrior. But rather the prey.

I shake the feeling loose, signaling for him to stay as I creep across the cracked cobblestones, winding through the drudging citizens too old or too young to work the mines, through their piecemeal carts of wares, through their ingratitude for the king's insistence for their safety by sending his elite guard to protect them. Too often, from themselves.

I continue my prowl, but whoever is tucked into the sliver of black is plotting too. I can tell by the switch from mirroring my movement to the careful immobility they assume as I approach.

Whoever they are, they are choosing to confront.

Bracing themselves to fight.

I pause perhaps a yard from their position, letting out a breath in the measured way Baba taught me when I was young and wild, interrupting his morning meetings with my incessant need for his attention and approval.

He would make me stand—as I was never one capable of sitting still—and command me to ... just ... *empty.*

"Empty your mind, little gazelle," he would instruct in his steady baritone, the voice of my dreams, of his enemies' nightmares. "Gutter that fire, deprive it of air."

At first, I would be so eager to do it right that I'd pass out from literally depriving my lungs of air. It would be many failed attempts until I understood it to mean trading my flaming unpredictability for icy precision. Exchanging my innate curiosity for practiced control.

I close my eyes.

Gutter that fire, I breathe, emptying the ashes of my feelings of distaste for this place and its people, the sputtering embers of pointless attraction for my comrade, my friend.

Deprive it of air, I mouth, drawing my sword from its sheath along my spine.

Snapping my eyes open, I relish the sudden pulsing power surging through me fueled by years of training and control. I become one with the sheer instinct of it as I lunge.

A muffled shriek slices through the space between us as my sword meets mortar not an inch from my target's head.

My eyes acclimate to the alley's gloom, the late afternoon sun filtering through drying laundry strung above us, outlining in turn a pair of wide black eyes under a mop of dusty chestnut braids, mud-streaked cheeks, blushing tapered ears, and thin cracked lips.

As my calculating gaze takes in the scrawny Unnamed street urchin, his brazen one takes me in too.

My brow cocks up.

"Quite bold of someone at death's door to stare into the eyes of its guard."

But my words just make him raise a brow of his own and I wonder if he even understood them when–

"Quite stupid of its guard not to finish the job," he returns in a voice just a tad lower than his earlier squeak as he looks me over once more. "Or maybe it's not that you're stupid," he drawls. "Maybe you're just bad at it."

I almost smile, *genuinely* smile like Tamir suggested, at this kid's daring. Doesn't even come up to my shoulder but acts as if he's as tall as the Ma'asa Mountains.

"You were following me," I cut to the chase.

He looks at me for a long moment, as if measuring his answer on an internal scale, unsure which side weighs heavier. He looks so much older in that instant, and I wonder how. Wonder why. And I *never* wonder anything about the khasir.

And then he jerks his head in a reluctant nod, like he's wondering about me too.

I swallow, my pulse quickening under such open scrutiny. I'm the one who's supposed to be doing the interrogating, yet it feels like the roles have reversed.

"Well, out with it. Why?" I ask two questions with one.

"Not so fast, ajnoob." He puts up a hand in my face as if

I'm the one with the honed blade an inch from my neck and not him. "What do I get if I tell you?"

My mouth pops open at his unexpected parry.

This kid.

"To keep your life," I say without any heat, continuing our dance, though he seems to be the one leading it.

He glares at me like he doesn't believe me.

Or . . .

My stomach sinks.

Or like he doesn't value it.

"You're so dramatic, ajnoob," he sighs as if he read my mind. Then, puffing up his chest, he straightens his rags. "I'm talking about coin. A man has to eat."

And this time, I do smile. Wide.

I'm searching my mind for my next quip, enjoying this senseless sparring much more than I would an actual fight, when familiar footsteps approach, only their cadence isn't its usual meandering beat.

It's thundering.

"What is going on here?" Tamir barks, the echo of his anger ricocheting off the narrow alley walls. I snap my attention his way only to find his piercing rage, along with his equally sharp sword, aimed at the boy.

Something inside me twists.

"You. Boy," Tamir calls again, and the kid blanches, the spark in him from moments ago sputtering before my eyes in the presence of Tamir's intractable ire.

"P-please. I—I didn't do anything wro—"

"Then start talking, khasir filth," Tamir orders. "Or would you rather I finish what the High Commander started, right here, right now? Let you bleed to death in this fateforsaken alley? Let the damn rats eat your rotting corpse? I doubt anyone would even miss you."

The boy's hands start to tremble, and my tongue feels heavy from holding back my objection. My heart from indecision. Why does this time feel different from the hundreds of past Burrow patrols? Why does this time feel almost *wrong*?

The boy glances at me so quickly I almost miss it. Almost miss the beseeching plea in his eyes, the desperation of someone with nothing to give, nothing to lose.

In the next breath, I seize his wrist, halting his tremor, propelling my protest.

"The offense was against me, so the punishment is mine to give, Captain," I declare, my voice full of authority, knowing I'm abusing my rank and Tamir's feelings for me for my own perilous whims.

My heart races.

What am I doing? I never do this. This isn't supposed to be personal. It's supposed to be about Order. Safety. Security. What I'm doing violates all three.

Tamir whips his attention to me for the first time since he approached us, confusion and caution muddying his brilliant eyes.

"Reim—I mean, High Commander," he lowers his voice. "Your word will always be obeyed, but Order . . ."

Is being broken. And there is nothing above Order.

I let the unspoken words thump onto the sewage-slicked stones between us. He's right. Of course he is. This boy *was* watching me. He said it himself. Though he may not be aware *who* he was watching, he did not insist on his innocence of the act itself.

I turn away from the boy's fearful gaze and face Tamir's confused one, jerking my chin down in a curt nod as I drop the boy's wrist.

"Yes, Captain. Order above all else."

Tamir's shoulders lose their rigidity, his brows smoothing in relief at hearing the familiar adage. The conditioned warrior's mask slips back over his features as he turns his attention to the boy, grabs him by the collar, and drags him away.

I half expect the boy to barter or even plead with Tamir. Almost want to beg him to. But he doesn't. Instead, he leaves a sticky, unnerving silence in his wake.

Leaving me to hold, to *cut* myself on, all the broken shards of what strangely feels like my betrayal.

T HE SUN IS JUST STARTING TO DIP BEHIND THE jagged peaks of the Ma'asa by the time I return to the Keep. The behemoth guard stationed on the overpass atop the massive iron-gated entrance to the equally vast boundary wall between the Citadel and the cantons glowers down at me, his eyes narrowing when he doesn't see Tamir at my side. Not because he gives a khur about the Captain, but because I'm alone.

Unprotected.

I wait for his usual gruff chastisement of "The Maliki won't like this." Meeting his angry gaze with my own, I dare him to say it after a day like this.

To just try me.

Our standoff ends when a grinding sound behind his gritted teeth begins, rivaling that of the cranking gears that lift the heavy bars of the gate and begrudgingly grant me admittance.

I dip into a theatrical bow before slipping under the still-rising lattice, earning a hiss from him when I come too close to the sharpened heads of the iron portcullis.

It's unfair to goad him like this, but I'm livid and can't even decide who my anger is directed at.

The gravel crunches beneath my boots, and though I usually relish the thought of the Burrow's grime being scraped away, today the filth feels as though it has seeped beyond my leather armor, pierced through my very skin, contaminated my very marrow. That no amount of scraping will ever be able to remove it.

Who was that boy?

What did he really want?

Khur, why do I even care?

That last thought troubles me the most as it calls into question everything that defines my role as High Commander, as the expected heir to the Vuorian throne.

"There is an infinite difference between us and the khasir, little gazelle," Baba *murmurs as he blots the bleeding gash slashed through my left brow after my first patrol. After an Unnamed child struck me with an errant stone. The savage burn of the open skin lessens to a tolerable sting with each pass of the whiteclove-oil-soaked gauze.*

He grips my jaw, lifting my anxious gaze until it meets his stalwart one.

"You have now seen it for yourself. We fight them because we must, to protect ourselves. They fight us because they blame others for their unhappiness instead of helping themselves."

Taking a deep breath, I walk through the Citadel and also take in the capital's bustling market square, its ordered streets, homes, and shops. Take in the smiling citizens of Vuor with their pressed clothes, easy strides, and civilized demeanor returning to their homes after a productive day of work and learning, hoping perhaps to remind myself of my purpose to serve them, to protect them. Willing the reminder to lessen the tightness, the *suffocation* pushing at my ribs that still hasn't let up since earlier this afternoon.

Rubbing my chest as I approach the castle grounds, I watch the servants fill the torch posts lining the various barracks and turrets of the massive limestone edifice with baluur crystals before lighting them as twilight encroaches upon the kingdom.

Guards, scribes, and advisers pass me by, debriefing one another as they head toward the castle's Jirga chambers. Some with kind smiles, some with sour frowns. Some with no expression whatsoever, their eyes blank, their faces unreadable.

I plaster a small, flat line across my own mouth and follow them in the direction of the castle's ornate entryway.

For all the unease of the day, walking under the castle's carved arch embedded with intricate mosaics depicting the story of our people's glorious rise affords a sense of familiarity, if not exactly comfort. As does the grand, open courtyard I trudge through next, its bubbling fountains reminding me of how thirsty I was in the bone-dry Burrow. As does the general opulence of the gilded staircase to my right, the mural-covered ceilings above, and the solid carved wooden doors of the Jirga chambers I stop in front of, which emit a slow roll of thunder as they are heaved open by the royal guards.

Just as I belatedly realize I'm still wearing my patrol leathers, too lost in my thoughts to have bathed and changed as is the custom to come before the king.

Perfect, as if the people filling this room needed one more reason to find me lacking.

But my self-criticism disappears when I step across the entrance, when I sense *his* presence.

The Maliki of Vuor.

My father.

Baba.

He stands at the head of the large obsidian table, tall and proud, his thick silver mane of hair pulled back into three braided rows tied together at the back of his neck representing the cantons of Vuor, while a simple iron-plated diadem symbolizing his rule encircles all three of them atop his head. Long bronze fingers brace the stone ledge as he stabs his undivided attention at each of us as we enter. His eyes are still pools of ocean, deceptively calm on the surface, an infinite secretive depth just beneath.

Until they land on me.

And then something in him yields; his cool gaze warms to the color of desert dunes under a blazing sun, a fissure forming across his granite cheek in what is meant to be a smile.

A smile just for me.

I take my place three seats to the right of him, the muck still coating the bottom of my soles now soiling the pristine rug beneath the table when someone tuts their disapproval, guttering the lick of joy I let ignite under my father's loving gaze. Making me pick at that scab of shame I always carry inside instead.

Not worthy. An abomination. A curse.

I bite the inside of my cheek until I taste metal. I let it coat my tongue and throat, swallow it down, and imagine the iron forming an impenetrable mask that clings to my face once more.

"Let us begin," Vuor's Maliki booms across the table as he lowers himself to sit. But neither I nor the other Jirga members, I imagine, miss his trembling grip on the chair's armrest, or the forced exhale when he is finally seated.

"Sire, if I may start us off." His vizier bows from his seat at the king's immediate right. Wiping a cloth over his sweating hairline, he narrows his eyes at all of us as if daring us to say anything of the king's physical weakness we just witnessed. "I'd like to table the usual agenda and prioritize some pressing matters."

"By all means, Basteel."

The man jerks a nod. "As many of us are already aware, there has been an increase in frequency and intensity of insurrectionary activity throughout the three cantons. Cantons One and Three have fallen back in line with their newly appointed Vuorian governors, who have increased tithe and surveillance after the last khasir attack. However, Canton Two, or the Burrow, arguably the most degenerate of the three, continues to be a cesspool of freeloaders and criminals. Heretics who are nothing but veritable parasites on the Iron Crown."

Adamant fists thump in unison on the table's polished surface in agreement, only Baba and I refrain from Vuor's Jirga room custom out of deference to our higher positions.

The king finally raises his fist for silence. "So it should come as no surprise that last week's attack was not the end of their delusional deviance," Basteel continues. "That they have just *today* been found to be raising their offspring not only as thieves and vandals . . . but also as spies!"

The room erupts in a voracious roar.

"*Enough*," Baba thunders back before whipping to Basteel. "How did you come to know of this?"

A sense of dread trickles down the same path along my spine as the droplet of sweat from earlier today. Every inch of me it touches already knows the answer to that question.

"The spy's scheme was found out just this morning by our High Commander herself," Basteel says, chin tilting in my direction. He seems proud, but I've known him long enough to understand the gesture is more likely accusatory.

The same look is reflected in every Jirga member's eyes as they turn to face me too.

I swallow thickly, choking on their impossible expectations, their unequivocal judgment, before standing.

"I encountered a young Unnamed boy watching me from an alley during patrol," I begin as the murmurs start anew, conclusions being drawn and quartered before I get past the first sentence.

"He was there, yes, but it is unclear his purpose," I insist with a confidence in my voice that I do not feel in my heart. "It is my honest opinion that to call him a spy would be premature at best and a grave injustice at worst."

By the time I finish, the fiery whispers have evaporated into a frigid silence.

I hesitate before bending forward to take my seat—

"Stay standing, Reim," the king orders, and I readily obey. "I admire both your empathetic nature and desire for justice, even when it's for those who do not deserve it, but the clarity of his purpose is not in question here."

He holds up a hand, halting my protest. His perpetual tremble suddenly, *dangerously*, absent.

"It is a simple matter. He was following you, was he not?"

Was he? He said he was. But did he know who I really am? There is more I need to know. That I need to find out.

"Yes," I say instead. A commander responding to her king's query. Not a daughter appealing to her father.

His outstretched fingers relax.

"Order above all else, Reim. Order was the reason for our ancestors' victory over the Unnamed during the Nihaya. And Order is what continues to ensure our safety, our very *survival*, today."

Order. Which means unyielding commitment to original law. Law that dictates interrogation, conviction, and . . . execution for its violation by the Unnamed.

"If we leave room for exceptions, we leave room for our destruction," he goes on. "Remember, if our ancestors didn't stop the Unnamed two hundred years ago, we wouldn't be here today. Allowing their kind to remain here at all is a mercy they would never have given us."

My own throat feels the constriction of the gallows as the other members utter their consent. Consent I have given in countless cases myself.

So why can't I do so now?

"Then, the matter is settled," he says when I don't oppose.

Basteel presents him with the execution edict, drips hot red wax over the parchment, and recites the blessed benediction when the Maliki stamps it with the signet ring on his left hand, which bears Vuor's seal, the two-headed dragon. The wax cools as my father's eyes blaze.

"My most trusted advisers, we must not cower. Remember what was foretold. What is our destiny," he says with such potent conviction, I almost forget my sudden lack thereof. "Victory will not come for those Unnamed."

"Victory will not come for those Unnamed," the room echoes his vow.

I STARE AT THE GAPING COPPER MAW OF THE DRAGON HEAD knocker welded to the king's chamber door. It's been a few years since I've been able to look it straight in its ruby eyes, rather than looking up at it, imagining it coming to life and diving down, devouring me.

But dragons, or dahaka, as our books name them, have not walked our earth, flown our skies, or burrowed in our sands since before the Nihaya. Before the Great End, when we brought the end to the chaos of the Unnamed and brought the beginning of Order to Vuor.

So why Baba made them our sigil and kept this old relic

is beyond my understanding. But so much about Baba is just that.

I know the Jirga feels it too, this sense of awe at his leadership, his righteous ancestry that can be traced back to the beginning of our great kingdom, but also a shaky hesitancy with his choices. A slippery discontent.

Especially when it comes to me—his heir.

I swallow the sudden dryness in my throat, lift the copper ring grasped between the dahak's unforgiving bite, and let it strike against the wooden door.

Once. Twice.

My knuckles follow in the same number, the same cadence. The same way I've done it all my life.

The internal latches release with a few familiar clicks and creaks, and my gaze collides with eyes the color of desert midnight, swirls of black and violet shot with silver, that are as capable of crinkling with hidden mirth as igniting with righteous indignation. That have been known to fill with catastrophic worry when I ended up in the healer's wing after an unlucky patrol, and with honeyed tears of pride when I achieved my current rank of High Commander.

"Mori—" I barely breathe her name in greeting when I'm enveloped in her doughy arms, her loving embrace. My face pressed into the dip of her neck, forced to inhale her steeped cloves and cinnamon scent that's infused in the healer's scarf she always has tied over her head.

And then I'm pushed away, held at arm's length to be scrutinized just as ferociously.

"What's wrong?" she says it like a statement, not a question. A demand she doesn't want to know the answer to.

"Nothing," I lie too quickly, too easily. Her hard-set mouth pops open to object, but a rattling cough from behind her steals the words from her lips.

"Reim," my father welcomes me with a lilt of curiosity and affection coating the single syllable of my name. All traces of the firm king I saw earlier are tucked away with his diadem and armor. He stands in just his linen night robes between his massive four-poster bed in the center of the otherwise practically furnished room and even bigger limestone balcony behind him.

Relief courses through me at the cool evening breeze the balcony's open doors let in, at his warm greeting, his approachable appearance. It plants a seed in my heart that perhaps what I have come to discuss in private will be met with reason, and it rips the roots of caution that were starting to take hold at his admonishment from earlier.

But then his smile is hacked away by another cough, this one deep and strangling as it powers out of him, causing his stalwart spine to bend in a way no enemy ever could. When he recovers, he turns away from me, but not before I see the crimson-tinged spittle he wipes from the corner of his mouth.

I'm livid, the relief and hope from moments ago evaporating in the sudden heat of my frustration. Does he really think I can't see what's happening? That I don't see that Mori, the Citadel's High Healer, is here more often than the healer's wing? That his Court appearances and edicts have become more urgent over the past year? I storm forward, Mori's desperate clutching at my arm doing nothing to hinder my determined approach.

"What is happening, Baba?" I plead, the worry outpacing my anger by the time I reach his side. I leave the question deliberately open to interpretation, willing to take whatever answers he is willing to give me.

He nods at Mori to take her leave before walking through the open balcony, a silent invitation for me to join him. The bedroom door snicks shut with her departure as he lets out a long exhale through his nose, his gaze fixed on his realm as the veil of night slowly cloaks it. Clutching the limestone balustrade, I watch the lights awaken across the Citadel, while the cantons beyond the Keep remain in darkness.

"Can you believe that when my great-great-grandfather discovered this land, it was but a barren waste?" he scoffs, shaking his head as he takes in the now-thriving kingdom. "The tribes of khasir who squatted in this area were neither intelligent nor capable enough to understand its potential. But they somehow had 'gifts'—the ability to call upon everything and anything created between the earth and sky and use it as they saw fit. The only explanation for it was Fate having pity on them, but they were thankless, relying on their long lives, their *gifts* to solve their problems, having tasted nothing of the world's cruelty. Of its affinity for destruction. They didn't know what it was like to have to strive, to barely survive as we once did."

His eyes harden, his lips set in a thin line as he pins his stare on the shadowy squalor of the Burrow, his lasting failure.

"They didn't value Order," he whispers. "So Fate showed them chaos—took their longevity, their gifts, their names—when we defeated them. Leaving only their truthful tongues as punishment so they can't fool us again. Yet, instead of working on themselves, helping themselves, they still blame us for it."

"I know all of this already," I snap, impatient, desperate, though I have yet to discover why. "I know how ungrateful the Unnamed are. How Vuor gave them shelter, work, and purpose, yet they remain aloof, unsatisfied. How they leech from this kingdom instead of contributing to it, and how they continue to tell themselves tall tales of Fate returning their names—even of one among them who has supposedly retained a 'gift,' when there has been no evidence of this *ever*. I deal with them every *damn* day. But what I don't know is why you're speaking of them at all. The Unnamed are a nuisance, but, Baba, you are the Maliki. They are no match for your prowess, your enduring rule."

His faraway gaze whips toward me, and my pulse starts galloping.

"Tall tales. A nuisance. My enduring rule." He rolls my words over his tongue like one of his foul-tasting tinctures before his lips curl in a small ironic smile. "Oh, little gazelle—once again you are listening, but you are not *hearing* me. You cannot be so dismissive. Of them or of this."

He sweeps his hands down his front, and I take a good look at him for the first time today: his parched lips, his hollow cheeks, the jaundiced pallor shading his brown skin, the thinness of his shoulders and waist when divested of his many layers of authority and armor.

"This sickness I've been carrying in my body is as old as the mantle I wear on my shoulders as Vuor's king, though I've never let it be an excuse to absolve me of my responsibilities. *But . . .* make no mistake, Reim. No ruler is 'enduring.' Death is coming for me. Maybe not today, or tomorrow, but it's coming. And you will have to be ready, for it will be *your* rule you must rely on soon. Not mine."

I back away as if struck.

No. This can't be.

"B-but you've been doing better. You haven't missed a single Jirga meeting this past month. You know what's going on in the cantons even before the reports are read from Basteel's ledger," I tell him, though I was just telling myself the exact opposite a few minutes ago. "You are *fine!*"

"I am not!" he thunders. And the strike of his words is enough to turn mine to ash. He rounds on me, forcing me backward into the room until the back of my legs hit the back of the little mahogany apothecary table next to his bed, and the various herbs and salves, the small vials and incense burners on top of it, start to tremble like my fingers.

Gone is the patient father who once trained me in sword and strategy—who always sent me secret smiles during meetings and shared meals with me during feasts. In his place is the infallible king once more, the heir to the resilience of our ancestors. And I now understand how he did it. How he fooled me, fooled the entire kingdom into thinking he's fine. His very essence evokes unquestionable authority, a self-composed power. Even as his mortal body fails him, his presence has always seemed transcendent of mere mortality. He is the kingdom. His kingdom is him. That is why he is Maliki.

That is why I never can be.

"You don't understand, Baba," I say, my voice breaking alongside my heart. "Our people don't see me like you do. They don't see me as Vuor's queen, as their Malika. They barely see me as one of them."

He says nothing, which makes my stomach plummet even more. But his eyes don't dart to the unusual taper of my outer ears either—neither like the sharp ridges of the khasir nor the rounded hills of the Vuorians, but something in-between—and I try to be grateful for that.

But I fail.

"And if truth be told, their barbed whispers of me being an-an *abomination* make me wonder if they ever will."

I can't believe I'm telling him this deep-rooted insecurity. But he's the one who decided to eviscerate me with his own devastating truth first. I wait for his response. His validation or denial of the rumor he must know, a rumor he must abhor as much as I do, if not for my sake, than for his. For what would it mean for the king's daughter, his heir, to be a shadeed, a curse?

I wait and wait, but so does he. His eyes, which often convey more than his lips, are hard as rocks and just as impenetrable. I will get no answers from him today, but I feel a painful sort of victory when he turns away from me first.

"Why did you come here tonight, little gazelle?" he murmurs as he points his stare back toward the balcony once again.

And now I'm the one having trouble meeting his eyes. My confusing concern for the Unnamed boy from earlier today feels like self-incrimination, evidence of the incompetence I feel as Vuor's future ruler.

He doesn't need another problem right now. Doesn't need to question whether his trust and faith are in the wrong person, a person who came here to question Order, the very basis of our people's survival, the basis for everything. No. He needs to save his energy for his body, for his very life.

"To be with my Baba," I say instead. Not the complete truth, but also not an outright lie. I want to be with him today, tomorrow. But most importantly, I want *him* to be with *me* too. I want him to be with me forever.

He opens his arms to me, and I don't hesitate to enter his embrace.

To let the tears fall.

THE MOON IS HIGH AND FULL WHEN MORI KNOCKS on the king's chamber door. Baba and I had spent the last few hours speaking of lesser subjects as he held me through my premature grief, my ear listening to the steady beat of his heart as my tears dried on his chest. Tiny wrinkles forming on the white linen beneath my wet cheeks in the hours we sat side by side in front of his crackling hearth talking about my latest training regimen, my opinion on last season's harvest, *my* health, *my* sleep, *my* days. My. My. My.

Because he didn't want to talk about himself anymore. Not when I reacted the way I did. Not when he didn't want to see what I see of myself—what *everyone* sees of myself—that I'm weak. Incapable.

A curse.

The door creaks open, a shard of flickering light from the hallway peeking in before admitting Mori into the darkened chamber. I look back to Baba, now sleeping on his bed, and my eyes trace the tortuous strands of his thick silver beard, the intricate weave of his three braids that lay nestled in the long mane that drapes his pillow like a crown. He is a king even in sleep. And he will remain one, even in dea—

Warm fingers close over the curve of my shoulder.

Rub.

Mori moves my own hair and overlaying braids over the other shoulder while dipping low to whisper in my ear.

"Come away, Reim. Let him rest even if you won't let yourself do the same."

I stiffen, the wild and untamed part of me telling me to stay right here, telling me that time is slipping away, and what if . . . what if I leave him and then . . . he leaves me.

Gutter that fire. Deprive it of air.

Baba's mantra of control is a ferocious *whoosh* in my ears. He's right. This isn't the place or the time for my inability to control my emotions, my hysterics. Baba trusted me with news he did not trust anyone in his Jirga with—his vulnerability about his kingdom. His vulnerability about his own life.

A deep breath in. A deep breath out.

I reach back and cup her fingers. The wooden chair on which I've sat hunched by his side groans with protest as I rise.

Mori tries to pull me into one last embrace, but I rip away and charge for the door, knowing that if I give into her comfort, her *pity*, I would feel only that much more incapable of handling what lies ahead.

I make it only a dozen determined paces into the dim hallway when I nearly barrel into a wall made of armor and flesh.

"Reim," Tamir breathes my name in relief. And perhaps something else. Something that would have made my own breath catch just this morning, but suffocates me in an entirely different way now. In a way I fear I will never be able to return from ever again.

I step back as he steps forward, my mind too tired, too overwhelmed to navigate yet another uncertain relationship.

He sees my withdrawal, if not in my person, then in my lowered gaze, and mercifully matches it with his own.

"High Commander," he tries again, and the tension sluices off my shoulders. The perfunctory title, the one thing defined, the one thing solid in my life right now settles over me, protecting me like its own kind of armor.

"Captain," I return with a nod of my head. He smiles, encouraged, if not a bit saddened at the formality.

"Were you . . . were you waiting for me?" The question bursts from me even though I'm not sure I want to hear the answer.

His silence answers me anyway.

I start walking, an unspoken invitation for him to walk with me too. It seems that, despite my desperate need for the day to be over, it won't let me go just yet.

"I wanted to apologize for what happened earlier today . . . in the Burrow," Tamir begins.

My attention whips in his direction at the mention of it, unable to believe that I forgot about it, forgot about the boy's precarious life in the new knowledge of my father's.

He mistakes my stunned regard for irritation with him and hurries to amend it.

"For questioning your decision-making in front of the khasir boy."

And then something does rankle inside me at this.

"But not for *your* decision-making *about* him?" I snap. His next step falters, his brows cocking up into his hairline.

"What do you mean?"

"I *mean*, Tamir," I spit, "you know the sentence for spying on the Crown—spying on *me*—is death. How could you tie the noose around him so quickly?"

And he looks nothing more than an injured street dog protecting his open wound as he snarls back, "And how could *you* not? You, who know Order better than all of us. Who knows that if you give *them* an inch on that rope, they will not only find a way to escape it, but have it around your neck before your next breath."

I have the decency to look away at his blunt but accurate assessment. The Unnamed uprisings have been not only more frequent, but also more precise. Their goal seems to be shifting from inciting fear to disrupting the intricate operations of governance.

"He's just a boy," I whisper, whether to him or to myself I don't know. And I want to tell him even more. Tell him the boy is different somehow. But I don't even know how, let alone how to explain it.

Tamir shakes his head, shaking off his justified frustration in the same motion.

"They're not like us, Reim," he insists with a small sigh, turning me toward him by the shoulders but keeping me at arm's length. "They're not *just* anything. Their ages don't matter when they aren't raised like us. Their intentions don't matter when they don't act like us. They are chaos. We are Order."

My mistake is looking up into his eyes when he says the word *we*. Because though he used it in the general sense, the lowering of his voice as it cushions the space between us implies an intimacy of a different kind. The intensity in his gaze as it drops to my lips crosses the line beyond implication entirely.

It would be so easy to take what he's offering—the comfort, the escape from . . . *everything.*

Even for just a few moments.

So, one by one, I weave Tamir's fingers on my shoulders with mine and bring them to link behind my neck. Fold my arms in the same way around his waist, rest my face on his chest . . . and *squeeze.*

Then let them go.

Let *him* go.

Because even if it would be easy or feel good, I can't seem to care about any of those things anymore—not when a few moments given to him would mean a few moments taken away from thinking about Baba. Thinking about the millions of moments ahead without him.

Tamir looks at the sliver of space I created between us as if it's a chasm. His face warring between denial and acceptance of the finality of my decision before he offers a stiff bow and marches away.

Before I let my clenched fist at my side unfurl and feel the small iron key I unhooked from the ring around his waist drop into the cradle of my palm.

Because though Tamir may still be right about the boy, about *everything*, if I am going to be Malika, I need to know it for myself.

THE SMELL HITS ME FIRST. SO RANK THAT I ALMOST GAG, almost forget to catch the heavy wooden door before it slams home, alerting everyone to the Ameera sneaking into the Citadel prisons with uncertain purpose and an even more uncertain plan.

I pull at the swath of cloth I wear around my neck and wrap it over my nose and mouth as I descend the slick stone stairs. The salty stench of the day's sweat clings to the fabric—a poor reprieve for my senses, but it allows me to better blend with the gloom.

As my boot touches the bottom landing, I try to assess the

pitch-black tunnels ahead of me. If I thought the Burrow was tortuous to navigate, it holds not a single sputtering flame to the twisted arteries of the castle prison. Its convoluted design meant to thwart even the most astute escape attempt.

I scuttle into a damp alcove as heavy tandem footsteps approach from one of the tunnels ahead.

Guards.

I hold back an inappropriate laugh born of exhaustion and incredulity. I am the future Malika, and here I am hiding in the shadows of my own castle's prison.

The footsteps stop two paces from my position, because *of course* they do.

"He's been sick for ages and everyone pretends it's nothing but a sandblasted head cold." The broader warden of the two holds the torch in one hand while adjusting his breeches with the other, spitting on the dank stone floor in emphasis.

My pulse rockets.

Baba. They're talking about Baba. They have to be.

"Well, not everyone, I suppose," he amends, and the slighter one, who by the look of his vacant expression has heard his comrade talk of this subject one too many times, perks up.

"What do you mean 'not everyone,' Laiq?"

Laiq looks around the dim landing more for his own aggrandizement, for having something that someone else values, than for actual security of the conversation.

"Well, you didn't hear it from me, but there's talk that he's not only sick, but *dying,* Sethi." When his friend says nothing at this piece of information, Laiq hurries to continue, "And that leads to the question of succession."

Sethi huffs in annoyance.

"That's no question at all. It's going to be the Ameera . . . despite the shadeed that she is."

"But that's just it, you fool. We're not the only ones within the Citadel who think she's a curse. There is reason to believe we may see her . . . *challenged.*"

"The Maliki wouldn't stand for it." Sethi waves a dismissive hand.

"But that's the thing, isn't it? If he's dead, he won't be here for his opinion to matter. And what's more, if he refuses to enter death's door soon, then there are those in the Jirga who don't mind nudging him through it, if you know what I mean."

My pulse crashes in my ears until I'm afraid I'm going to give away not only my location but my identity—give way to my murderous impulse that's tired of having been caged all day. Not because of what they said about me, but what they're saying about the Jirga. About what they're possibly planning.

A coup.

"You mean the purity-zealot vizier? Bastian or Basteel or something?" Sethi raises a brow. "I know his Janoon sect is a bit obsessed with purging Vuor of the khasir, but that would mean we'd have no one to mine baluur or work in the Groves. And . . . that kind of labor is just beneath me."

I don't hear what Laiq says next, my entire focus honed in on my fingers curling around the blade's handle strapped to my back, channeling my rage—both displaced and justified—into one singular purpose: protecting the Crown. Protecting Baba.

But right as I am about to unleash, a familiar churlish voice calls from somewhere in the gloom.

"You squawking phoenixes done gossiping yet? Some of us haven't eaten anything all day."

The Unnamed boy.

I let go of the pommel, squinting into the shadows to pinpoint his exact cell, patting my pant pocket while praying the key I stole from Tamir is the right one.

"Why do you have to eat, khasir," Laiq yells in his direction, "when it's just going to come spewing out of your strung neck tomorrow on the gallows for all the other swine to see?"

Keep talking, kid. Keep talking so I can figure out where you are. Keep talking so we can figure this khur out.

The boy's exaggerated yawn grates the air.

"Listen, if you already ate it, that's alright. I won't tell."

Wet chuckles and dry jeers come from the other cells until not even the darkness can hide the splotches of red embarrassment spreading across Laiq's pudgy cheeks. Sethi wisely says nothing, though the lip caught between his teeth is the sole thing restraining his own mirth.

With a murderous growl, Laiq charges toward the furthest-right tunnel before disappearing down its inky corridor, leaving Sethi to silence the delinquent chorus of prisoners. I squeeze my eyes shut in desperate concentration, listening for turns . . . *a right and two lefts* . . . counting his echoing footfalls . . . *Eleven . . . Twelve . . . Thirteen . . .* until they come to an abrupt halt.

My eyes snap open at the sharp grunt of a body being hauled up against the iron bars of a cell. The sizzle of burning flesh and the victim's unwilling whimpers as he's held there for endless, agonizing seconds brand themselves into my soul until he's thrown to the ground with a heavy thud at last.

"You still hungry, you streak of khur?" Laiq snarls. "I'd be happy to serve you some more."

When the question is met with silence, my mind starts blaring.

Oh no. No. No. No. He can't be dea—

How am I still standing here when . . . when—

A wheezing cough comes from the pitch black, and my lungs expand at the sound, as if taking a much-needed breath for the both of us.

"C'mon, Laiq. You made your point," Sethi calls down the tunnel, his alarmed voice a direct contrast to his previous boredom.

Throwing one more curse over his shoulder at the boy, the larger guard reappears at the tunnel's mouth, smug and self-satisfied.

And then it hits me: How is *this* Order? How is one man's actual words about harming the Crown from within the Citadel less treasonous, less punishable than the mere conjecture that a khasir boy may have intended to do the same?

I admit I didn't know what I was going to do when I found the boy, my inexplicable sympathy for him and the need to have more information, my main driving forces before now. Well, I do have more information, just not from the person I was originally seeking.

The guards soon move down another corridor, and I wait for their barking threats to the other prisoners to grow fainter before I escape from my pocket of shadow. Before I creep down the one that leads toward the boy.

One right and two lefts. One right and two lefts.

I beat the directions in my head so the booming beat of my heart won't drown them out, then count the thirteen steps in the dark as I skip from one stone to the next until my back is against a narrow wall that separates the cells. Packing my lungs with what little air is left in this hell mouth, I pray that the cell is his and try to stop myself from regretting this endeavor if it isn't.

This is impulsive.

This is dangerous.

This is wrong.

A small moan slices through my warring thoughts, and I exhale a breath I didn't realize I was holding.

No, this is right.

Swinging my body just enough to peek inside the cell, I find the boy crumpled in the center. He's breathing though, alternating between harsh wheezes and strangled whimpers. But he's alive, and that has to be enough for now.

"*Psst*," I hiss while peering into the cells on either side of his to make sure they're unoccupied.

He manages to lift himself halfway onto his knees, squinting at me crouching behind the bars. And then he falls back into a heap.

"Oh, it's you."

I resist the absurd urge to smile, to admit to myself how easily his dismissive response after such a cruel assault eases something strung tight in me. To admit that perhaps I even like this kid.

The iron key, which I assume fits his cell, burns in my pocket. Granted, when I stole it from Tamir, the plan was to dangle it in front of the boy to get more information and then return it just as I found it. But . . . but since the traitorous revelation from the warden and the contradiction I can't get past about the boy's sentence for treason . . . my mind is confused. Contemplative. Considering a treachery of its own.

"Yes, it's me," I answer redundantly.

"The reason I'm even in this mess," he quips.

"The reason I'm going to get you out of it," I shoot back before I can stop myself.

Khur. There goes my mouth again.

He pushes himself up onto his scrawny elbows more resolutely this time. Looks at me. Really looks at me.

And I let him. I'm sure a khasir kid like him that walks those deceptive streets of the Burrow can detect a trap when he sees one. And I need him to trust me if the hasty plan in my head is going to work.

"Whyyy?" He draws the word like a sword through the

sheath of his throat. His sharp eyes like twin blades he keeps for reinforcement.

"Because something is still not adding up about what you were doing in that alley earlier, kid," I confess, breaking away from his suspicious gaze at last.

But not before I catch his eyes widening at my answer. At which mine narrow. *His first tell.*

I busy myself with digging for the key in my pocket. "There's something you're keeping from me, and I need to know what it is."

"And I'll ask you again. What do I get if I tell you?" he demands, defiant as ever.

I jam the thing into the lock, both of our attentions consumed by the moment of truth as I attempt to turn it. And then—

Click.

The iron gate swings into my waiting grip.

"Your life."

Chapter 4

ITH THE WAY I CAME TOO RISKY, MY STEPS too heavy to go unnoticed by patrolling guards, I haul the injured boy into my arms and carry him deeper below ground, which makes him stab me with a suspicious glare. I shoot him one of my own just as I round the corner, and the distant sound of rushing water comes to greet us from the darkness ahead.

"The sewers?" he scoffs, his eyes narrowing further. "*That's* your brilliant plan?"

"As opposed to literally *dying* tomorrow? Why, yes," I mutter back.

Lowering him onto the damp floor, I go about lighting sconces in the small round hall, deciding now is as good a time as any to have the conversation picking at my mind all day.

"So, what *were* you doing in the Burrow earlier today?"

Fate, was it seriously just earlier today?

"Minding my business until two ajnoob who weren't minding theirs decided to assault me."

"You swear you weren't trying to spy on me?"

Another scoff.

"You even going to believe me if I tell you no?"

I snap my jaw shut. Grind my teeth. He's not wrong. Order insists that we consider any suspicious activity as if it were a crime already proven. Any suspicious talk as if it were treason. I am at once reminded of the talk between the two prison guards. Reminded that Order didn't seem to matter within the walls of the Citadel. Only in the streets of the cantons. Only when it comes to the Un—

I snap my head to the side to shove the festering thought away.

Do I believe him? The Unnamed can't lie. Their teeth snap down on their tongues if they even try to. But that doesn't mean they don't have other ways to bend the truth. To manipulate it. Mold it into something unrecognizable, even beautiful, if they wanted to.

"Now, my turn," he rasps as he rolls onto his back.

"Fine," I snip over my shoulder, though I regret my irritation once I catch another look at his blistered skin.

"Why did you come back for me? Why risk your neck for mine?"

My laugh is short and humorless as I walk back to him, crouching so he can see my eyes. "Believe me or not, my risk is nothing compared to yours."

His acute perusal carves up the hollow of my cheek and holds for a full minute. What does he think of me? And why does it even matter? It shouldn't, so I stare at him in return, attempting to put us back on equal—if uncertain—footing. Instead I am struck by a sudden sadness at how young his face appears, maybe ten or twelve at most. Yet the expression he wears, the words he speaks, testify to a longer, heavier life. One that can perhaps understand my own burden.

Maybe that's why I look away, why I shed the weight I've been carrying all day and place it with him.

"My father is dying." The words spill from my broken lips, my bleeding heart. "And I am to take his place on the—take his place in our line of trade."

He says nothing, but I can feel him still watching me in that way that feels like he's picking my words apart, searching for the things I'm *not* saying. So I jolt to my feet and return to lighting the rest of the torches. "And I don't want it. Don't want anything more than for him to live."

To not leave me the kingdom. To not leave me at all.

"So, I guess that's what drove me to release you instead of interrogating you. I want—" I sigh. "I *need* someone to just . . . live."

Again, the silence between us stretches, but I dare not look back. Who knows what my reckless tongue might divulge next.

"Well," he says at last, "among my people, what you just did for me requires an exchange."

"An exchange," I parrot, not understanding his meaning.

"It means I owe you."

With the last sconce lit, I turn back to the boy, ready to dismiss his insistence on "exchanging" something when he likely has very little to begin with, and expect him to be huddled on the floor like when he was in the cell nursing his wounds. Like he was mere minutes ago when I brought him here . . .

But he's not.

He's on his feet, frowning while he brushes off the dust of the prison as if there's a vast inferiority between it and that of the Burrow's streets. As if his body wasn't branded, wasn't *charred* by being pulled against the iron bars just an hour earlier.

I stare at his clothes that still bear the prison gate's vertical burn marks, but behind the sooty torn fabric, his earthen skin is healed. No, it is *intact*. Like nothing even happened.

Everything inside me goes as still as death.

No breath, let alone words escape my dry throat.

"What's wrong now, ajnoob?" he sighs in exasperation.

This time I don't answer him.

My High Commander instincts activate instead, throwing me at him in the next second, lifting him up and against the curved stone wall the one after that.

He winces at the impact.

"You know *exactly* what's wrong," I grind out through the gate of my teeth, the words a menacing echo off the empty cylindrical chamber. "You—you're *healed*. You were burned by the iron bars. And now—"

"Is this how you treat everyone you save, ajnoob?" he asks in a casual tone, even as he's pulling at my clenched fist, kicking his feet in the air, trying to break my hold on him. "Listen, I was just offering an exchange and thought it better to show you what it was than tell you. Clearly, I was wrong."

I lower him to the ground but keep a tight grip on his shirt.

"You can heal yourself? How?" I demand through my incredulity. "The Unnamed still having . . . *gifts* . . . that's just a story."

He stares at me as if I'm smart enough to see that obviously they are not.

"To answer your first question," he grunts, trying to pull away one more time. "No. I cannot heal myself. Two, it's not *my* gift, and so it's not my explanation to give."

I let him rip away from my hold and he stumbles back, straightening his rags as if they're the finest silk of Vuor and my touch has tainted them.

"But, like I was saying, I was going to help you meet the one who *does* possess this particular gift, and maybe if you ask him *nicely*," he emphasizes the last word as if it's obvious that it doesn't exist in my vocabulary, "he might be able to gift it to you too . . . for your sick father."

I'm stunned. The ever-shifting sand dunes of this terrible day are making me hallucinate, making me delusional. That must be the only explanation for how the solution to my nightmare is appearing right in front of me.

And then the other part of me—the High Commander part, the future Malika part—warns that all of this is against Order. That I should be taking this shattering revelation of a gifted khasir to the Jirga at once and let them figure out the implications and do what is for the good of our kingdom.

But then I remember the guards' words, the possibility of a coup from within the Citadel, and the thought of involving the Jirga gutters.

"Who is he?" I ask despite my self-preservation warning me not to. Warning me that I am at the precipice of a deep chasm. That any more steps forward will only lead to a fall so great I will never be able to climb back out.

I do it anyway.

The boy shakes his head and turns away.

"I like you, ajnoob. I don't know why, and I definitely shouldn't, but I do." A veil of something resembling sadness flicks over his usual carefree expression. "But I don't *know* you."

"You can lie," he says bluntly. "Your kind don't trust us, but we don't have reason to trust you either." He sweeps his hand in a wide arc in front of him as if to emphasize where we even are right now. How and why we even got here. There's nothing to say to that, so I don't. "What I do know is that you have a need, and he has a way to fill that need. And it sounds like time is running out."

"But why would *he* help me?" I ask, my voice almost shrill as I try to weave together the frayed threads of this incomplete tapestry.

"Because I am in your debt. And whatever you may think about my kind, we take care of one another." I open my mouth to protest once more, but he presses a little finger against my lips. "Save the questions for when you meet him, ajnoob."

I huff at the gall of his assumption.

"How do you know I'm going to?"

"Oh, you will. Find me in the alley where you tried to kill me." I roll my eyes at his flair for the dramatic. "At sunset. And you only have a week to make your decision."

"Why a week?"

"Because I have better things to do than wait for an ajnoob who doesn't know a boon when she sees one."

And with those last words, he throws a stone down the tunnel leading to the sewer, hears it skip and echo in confirmation that it's safe to traverse, then sets off into its wet haze.

"Hey," I call to him one last time, realizing something. "Why did you let me carry you all this sandblasted way if you could heal yourself and walk on your own?"

He turns to look over his thin shoulder, a silly grin plastered across his face, looking, for the first time, like a child of his age should. And Fate, I can't help smiling back.

"Oops." He shrugs, then keeps walking, his giggles filling the air, filling my ears, my heart with a strange sort of ease I'd been missing all day.

Chapter 5

THE BICENTENNIAL OF THE NIHAYA IS ONLY A month away, Your Maj—" Basteel's anxious murmur in the Maliki's ear is interrupted by Mori's loud chanting as she swings her thurible over the king's supine body. The smoky plumes of healing incense emitted from the metal-lattice sphere wrap their tendrils around his lax shoulders, filling his nose and wheezing mouth with their fleeting, numbing comfort.

I kneel on the rug at the other side of his bed, the same rug I've knelt on as he braided my hair and reviewed my lessons throughout my childhood, my eyes landing on his hands crossed over his abdomen. The same once-mighty hands, that could wield not one but two long swords in the training yards and on the battlefield, are now limp and lined with frail, pulsing veins.

When the thurible nearly pummels Basteel's face on the next swing, he sniffs his irritation at Mori and shuffles toward me.

"Before you begin your vigil, Ameera, I would like a word."

My body stiffens.

I look up from Baba's hands to find Mori's keen attention on me from across the bed, her soft smile doing nothing to cushion her cautionary gaze.

But she doesn't have to warn me to be careful. My life has always been one of vigilance. Looking for traps in the most unassuming of places, most unassuming of people. Not only because I am the Ameera, but because my people did not achieve what we have without survival and resilience. By not just finding threats, but *eliminating* them before they became reality.

Except yesterday.

I grind my teeth to shred the errant thought and push to my feet. He leads me into the hall before easing the door shut. I nod at him to get on with it.

"There is much to discuss, Ameera, that I believe the Jirga and your father, in his current state of health, need not be privy to." He seems to consider this before amending, "At least not yet."

I take a moment to observe Basteel. Observe his immaculate silk robes with fine gold embroidery, his portly but rigid stature, his air of wisdom I often suspect is a ruse for guile. Like everyone on the Jirga, he was personally selected by Baba—a token representative of the Janoon sect of Vuorians, or "purity zealots" as the prison guard called him last night. But as the years of Baba's rule progressed, he made himself indispensable, climbing the ranks of the king's Jirga by showing unwavering commitment to the implementation of Order, especially when it meant lessening the population of the Unnamed. Showing overt loyalty to Vuor's Maliki . . . but internal resentment of his heir.

But today, after learning about the possibility of a coup the day before, I don't give a damn.

He clears his throat when I say nothing. If he is here to discuss something with me, reprimand, accuse or shame me, then he has to have the gall to say it.

Maybe I'm becoming not so guileless, myself.

And oddly, something in me feels emboldened by that.

"The khasir boy we discussed last night in the Jirga chambers, the one *you* so ridiculously defended in front of us all, in front of the Maliki," he hisses, pointing to the door separating us from him as if I committed an egregious sin, "was not in his cell this morning."

I'm no fool. I knew this would be an easy discovery. Knew it even as I slipped the key back on Tamir's ring as we left for patrol at dawn and walked the streets of the Burrow for hours in gnawing silence. Even as every cell in my body tingled in awareness as we passed the alley we discovered the boy in the day before.

Even as my mind whispered that I could find an end to my father's misery if I chose to discover him there again.

But I offer Basteel nothing.

He clicks his tongue.

"Pity. But I assumed I would be subjected to one of your defiant moods, so I took the liberty of speaking to the captain of your patrol myself upon your return from the Burrow."

I plead for my tongue to remain still even as my pulse ratchets. It doesn't.

"And?"

His eyes flash with something resembling victory at my predictable impatience.

"And, *Ameera*," he spits the title in derision, "he said he took care of the spy himself. Said he didn't want to worry you further with all the stress you are under about your father, knowing it was the likely reason for your *questionable* judgment at the Jirga meeting yesterday."

I force myself to nod, to paint my face with the same level

of concern as I'd wear if we were only discussing the season's almazi harvest in Canton One or the fishermen's weekly catch in Canton Three.

"He did me a kindness, it seems," I say, managing not to lie, hoping he will leave it at that.

But of course he doesn't.

"Really?" he asks as he stalks closer to me until he is almost pressed to my side. Until he lowers his sweaty face, his hissing voice to a rattling rasp in my ear. "Because to me, it seems what he did was anything but a *kindness*."

I move to leave, done with this conversation, done with *him*, but he grabs my upper arm and digs his fingers in, nailing me in place as he spits, "Because one day, very soon I fear, *you* will be the one on Vuor's throne. And it will not be *kindness* that will make you a fit ruler over these savages, nor will others come to save you from *stress* when your weak heart bleeds for one of them."

I spin out of his grasp, a dagger at his throat right as the last word escapes his lips.

His wide eyes dart to the door, down the hall, everywhere except my eyes, because he knows he will find no escape there. So caught up in my supposed weakness with the Unnamed, he underestimated my prowess as High Commander. Neglected to account for my thinning patience with him.

"Yes, Basteel. One day I may very well be on Vuor's throne," I snarl, pressing the blade against his jumping pulse until a fine dribble of blood skates down its whetted edge. "But what makes you think that *you* will be the one standing behind it—behind *me*? And if you're not there, where will you go? How will you live in the squalor you so detest outside the Keep's wall?"

My dagger slides lower, snipping the threads mooring the gold-plated button to the top of his robe. We both listen to it roll across the floor before circling on itself.

Again.

Again.

Until it *stops*.

"So, maybe have less *concern* for my position here, and more for yours," I whisper, easing my dagger into its sheath. Leaving him fuming as I plow through the door back into Baba's bedroom.

I wait until I am sure of his own rageful exit down the hall before I speak to Mori, who is now applying foul-smelling tinctures to Baba's head and neck.

"Mori, I require the truth. I *deserve* it. How bad is he, really?"

Her moment of hesitation is all the answer I need.

"But he was just fine yesterday! He's been worse than this before, I'm sure of it—and he came back. He even went to war with the Bediyeh beyond the border, and he came back. He always. Came. Back." I insist before she can reply, my shaking voice and rambling words hanging precariously over the chasm of my denial. How could he possibly have deteriorated so quickly? How could he have gone from talking to me, holding me, *loving* me just last night only to nearly *leaving* me tonight.

And how does Fate do this so easily, so carelessly? Why do we expect it not to? Expect it to give us time to figure it all out. Expect it to delay death until we're ready?

I guess it's because if it did, we would never give in to it, never give up; we would never be ready to die.

But right now, I can't look at that thought too closely.

Because the only thought that deserves my attention is how to keep him alive.

Mori beckons me with an open hand.

"Come sit with your father, child. He will want to feel you with him when he—"

I take one step back, and her tired eyes dart from my over-whelmed ones to my selfish retreating feet and back again.

I take another.

Another.

But Mori refuses to look away from me. Her sympathetic smile is a lifeline in her doughy face, but I refuse to grasp hold of it anyway. She's not judging me for leaving, for running from my feelings, my responsibilities.

And though I appreciate her sincerity, her empathy, the truth is, I'm not running *from* those things at all.

This time, I'm running for the sake of them.

THE STARS IN THE CLEAR NIGHT SKY ARE SILENT SENTRIES, the full moon their general, as they bear down upon the empty streets of the Burrow, upon me hooded and slinking in the shadows of the same alley from yesterday's patrol. The Crown's most recent curfew has been in full effect for the past several hours, and anyone, Vuorian or the Unnamed, caught outside their homes is subject to questioning, if not detainment. I cannot imagine what would happen if I were seen, let alone recognized at this hour, in this place.

I also cannot seem to care. Not anymore. Not when Baba is lying on his deathbed and the fate of his kingdom seems to rest on my shoulders like an undeserved mantle.

On my head, like a cursed crown.

The boy told me to meet him at sunset, at the end of the Unnamed's workday, an hour before the start of the Burrow's curfew, and it's decidedly much later than that, so all of this risk may be for naught.

And yet I wait anyway.

Two laughing guards pass not three paces from my

crouched position, and I'm so distracted by the danger ahead that I nearly miss the shadow pooling on the pavers behind me.

I would have yelped at the small clearing of a throat if not for the equally small hand being slapped over my mouth just in time.

"Fate, you always this jumpy, High Commander? Or am I special?"

The boy. He's here.

And then my eyes are widening for a different reason. He must have heard Tamir call me by my title yesterday afternoon. Does he know what it means? Who I really am?

Who my father, the man I told him *everything* about, really is?

Khur.

I rise inch by inch until I'm looking down upon him, into his obsidian eyes' fathomless depths, looking for answers I refuse to ask aloud. Trying to reestablish the power dynamics between us once again. The order of things.

But it's too late.

By freeing him last night, it's as if I'm the one who took his place inside the iron cell—and he's the one with the key to let me out, or to send me to the gallows.

But then he lets out a serrated sigh, and I realize he still seems to be waiting for a response.

"First of all, don't curse. Secondly, you're not supposed to be out here," I say instead.

"And neither are you. Also, I specifically said sunset." He jerks his head to the night sky to emphasize his point. "A *week* from now. You trying to get me killed again, ajnoob?"

I huff.

"Yes, I waited until I could get you arrested, then rescued you from your cell, only to get you killed now." He smiles that toothy childish smile again at my sarcasm and I think—no, I *know*—he likes our banter. And maybe, just maybe, even likes me. "Even *I'm* not that much of a fool."

His smile falters at that. Something sad and almost uncertain ripples across his otherwise steady gaze before he sighs and glances behind me, then behind him.

"Last chance to walk away, ajnoob. My job was to *offer* you an exchange. You're not bound to take it. You could easily forget that you ever met me and pretend that yesterday never happened. And I could easily forget y—"

He bites down so hard that his teeth clack with the impact. I raise my brow as he winces and watch him work his jaw until he can speak again.

"And I could *try to* forget you," he tries again, looking away at last, the tips of his tapered ears reddening with embarrassment at being caught in a lie. Or perhaps surprise at catching himself in one.

And the thing is, I couldn't forget these two days if I tried. Couldn't ever forget him either. But maybe I should.

Both for his sake and mine.

But I don't say that.

For now, we have one more night.

"Lead the way, khasir."

Chapter 6

THE BURROW WAS GIVEN ITS NAME FOR A REASON. Besides referencing the baluur mines it houses, it resembles nothing more than an animal's tortuous underground tunnel: narrow corridors that twist, sow, wind and climb, meant to keep strangers out, secrets in. It's a veritable fortress in its own right, and I would be in awe of its prowess if I weren't so wary of its purpose.

We are mostly silent as we navigate the empty streets, united by one unspoken goal: don't be caught together. The past forty-eight hours have intertwined our paths, risked our lives, more than either of us would care to admit.

Just one more night. Then he can be on his way, and I on mine.

The thought comes more from guilt for the trouble I'm causing him than the relief I'm hoping for myself. Because even though he survived the prison, he is a marked man—no, a marked *boy*. He's just a boy that was supposed to be dead by Tamir's hand, and it's only a matter of time before it's discovered that he was not. I didn't save him from death. I only delayed it. One more failure to weave with the others into my braids.

Into my soul.

And Tamir! What was he sandblasted thinking by lying to Basteel like that? The captain of our forces, no less. He will be made an example of if he is found out.

When he is found out.

I grind to a halt.

Try to prevent my heart from doing the same.

The boy takes three more steps before realizing I'm not behind him and then knocks his chin over his shoulder.

Glares.

"This is a mistake." My voice, though a whisper in the alley, booms in my head. "This—this *exchange*, as you call it, is—is unfair. To *you*. You are risking so much more than I am just by walking these streets at all. Just by—by *living*. You were supposed to be dead, remember? You need to keep low. You need to—"

"You need to stop talking," he hisses back, whipping his gaze around to see if anyone heard my rambling before forging ahead. "Now, c'mon, ajnoob. We're almost there."

I have no choice but to follow him, and not two dozen paces later, we stand in front of a splintered wooden door no different from any of the others.

My mouth opens to object one last time—

But then the door creaks open.

And behind it, a young stranger peeks through the gloom with a cautious but welcoming smile. When our eyes meet, I'm so disarmed by the brightness of his smile against my bleak reasons to be here, that any further protest dies on my lips as he hurries us inside.

The entry room is dark and cramped. A low flicker from

the small hearth in the corner the only light I have to make out a few rickety pieces of furniture and a worktable littered with rolls of parchment, rusted measuring tools, and bits of charcoal. More than a few guttered candle nubs hold the intentional mess in place.

The Unnamed man with the kind smile who shuts the door behind us can't be much older than me. Though, like the boy, there is something just behind his eyes that tells me otherwise. He tosses his white, almost-translucent braids over his shoulder as he glances down the dark hall opposite the hearth, and I can't help but admire how they resemble the precise twists and turns of the Ekoni River as it winds to the Vuor Valley from the Ma'asa Mountains, tied back at the nape of his neck with a simple strip of leather. Can't help but take in his lean form and upright posture, his neat clothes, his sharp bone structure that matches the tapered ears pressed against his undercut. His eyes that are more slate than the boy's pitch-black ones, though—thank Fate— they too hold no edge to them.

"Sifr." He crouches in front of the boy, but keeps his gaze on me. "You know you're not supposed to be out right now." His voice carries both concern and reprimand.

The boy rolls his eyes.

"Sifr. As in zero? Is that your name?" The words spill from my lips before I realize what I'm even saying.

Of course it's not his name. He has no name. None of them do.

"It is what they call me," the boy replies, tasting the truth of the words in his mouth before offering them to me.

"Is . . . er . . . that what I should call you then?" I stutter back. He jerks his head in affirmation before clearing his throat and looking away.

"You can call me Reim," I find myself saying, and am

acutely reminded that my goal right before I came here was to get what I need and leave his life forever—not form further closeness.

He says nothing, his wide black eyes remaining as indiscernible as ever, before he turns back to our host.

Maybe he's thinking the same thing about me.

"You can call me the architect, Reim," the man interrupts my reverie. An apologetic smile hooking up the side of his mouth, which is ridiculous because I'm the one who made the blunder.

"Why are you called—umm, that is to say . . ."

"We are usually called by our work or our role in the cantons," he says, walking over to the worktable. "I help with repairs to the buildings and tinker with making them more efficient—"

"He's being modest," sifr interjects. "The Burrow, the Groves, the Shore are all only still standing because of him."

The architect glares at him.

"He doesn't just fix things—he makes them better."

I want to ask him what he means, but sifr turns his attention to the man.

"Anyway, this is who I was telling you about. The ajnoob who got me out of the prison. Who I promised to exchange something with in return." And for some reason, sifr using the derogatory title he's used countless times before instead of my name picks at me, *pricks* me in countless ways it hadn't before.

"I figured," the architect murmurs as he scours my tired but vigilant face with his galvanized eyes, sliding them over my intricate black braids next, woven just so to cover my strange ears. But he doesn't seem to miss their odd shape despite my expert efforts to hide them.

He flashes me another smile before addressing sifr again.

"He wasn't expecting her for a week."

"Well, neither was I. She just showed up and not at sunset like I told her to." The boy crosses his arms over his small chest.

"*She* is standing right here and can answer for herself," I snip, tired of feeling like there's something crucial I'm missing. Like I'm truly the ajnoob they insist on calling me.

An agonized scream rips through the air.

Before either of the two can stop me, I barge past them into the narrow hall the architect had been peering down earlier, the blade strapped to my back already unsheathed.

But I don't even make it half a dozen steps when my boots stop in their tracks. Because there, below a closed door on the right, a pulsing gold light creeps over the floorboards. Like water set on fire. An impossibility. And though a strong sense of survival urges me to turn back, to get out, to *run*— another deeper, almost primal curiosity tells me to stay right here. To keep going.

That beyond that door is something that has the power to change everything.

Filling my lungs with that anticipation, my heart with that instinct, I rear my foot and kick down the door. The crude wooden plank flies across the floor and comes to a splintering stop under the large boot of an equally large man.

The man, swimming in shadow, whips toward me with murder swirling in his eyes the color of spun gold. Eyes so awful, so riveting as they emit their own rippling radiance, that I am caught between a scream and a gasp under their sudden, relentless attention.

"Get the *Fate* out of here!" the man roars, and I feel rather than see the architect barrel into the room after me, hooking his arms through mine from behind in attempt to haul me back out the door. But not before I see beyond the shadowed stranger's smothering presence, finding an old man writhing on a cot, rasping mindlessly for help.

Not before I watch the large man, his body dipped in darkest night and his eyes dipped in blazing sun, stalk to the side of begging invalid and punch out a fist, grasp the old man by his gasping throat.

And *squeeze*.

The pulsing light from his eyes radiates into the veins lining his face and then charges down the ones in his arm until it shoots into the suffering man's neck, making his thin body arch off the bed with the contact.

When the old man's mouth opens in a silent scream, I snap into action. Using the architect's position behind me to my advantage, I bend forward and let gravity lift his unsuspecting body up and over my back until his arms twist and he lands with a thud at my feet. Once he is forced to let go of his hold, I leap over his splayed limbs and charge my sword toward the glowing stranger in front of me.

But unlike the other day with sifr in the alley, this time, I damn well don't miss.

My blade slices clean and true through cloth, muscle, and sinew, stopping only when the resistance abates and my sword meets nothing but air on the other side of his chest.

I'm still breathing hard as I attempt to pull the saber back out, my mind already cataloging the next steps: pushing the assailant to the ground to bleed out while I attempt to resuscitate his victim.

But the sword won't budge.

I pull once, twice, before shifting my focus from the uncooperative weapon to the uncooperative man it skewered.

And for the second time in his presence, I am robbed of breath. Of thought. Of sense.

His powerful fist that was just around the invalid's throat is now clutching the sharp shaft of my sword, preventing its retreat. His sweltering gaze pinning me in place somehow more deadly than the weapon still buried deep within his body.

Desperate to break his hold on me, his hold *over* me, I break my own hold of the sword's hilt. I stumble back, but something inside still keeps me here. Keeps me watching him as he watches me. He reaches behind his back and pulls the blade from his body on his own, then throws it clattering across the floor until it is mine to claim once more.

But I don't. I can't. Not when what happens next has me riveted instead. The wound on his hand, in his chest, that should have ended his life—from not just the severed arteries, but the punctured organs—starts emitting the same pulsing light as his illuminated eyes. Growing brighter and brighter, taking over the entire room if not the entire world until—it blinks out, leaving my eyes temporarily blinded as they adjust to the sudden darkness.

I rub them with urgency, blinking over and over until my vision returns. But nothing is as it was before.

The man's body no longer seems larger than life, no longer an endless midnight drowning in shifting shadow. He stands tall, lithe and honed like the blade still lying forgotten on the floor at my feet. His eyes, no longer burning stars racing across the desert sky, are at rest but no less arresting with their rings of golden fire encircling pools of black ice. His hair, though not quite pitch like mine, is black with fissures of gold snaking through the braids that curtain each temple and through his cropped beard. The same threads running through the unruly waves of the rest of his mane that he's distractedly tying back into a loose bun at the back of his head.

But none of this is what has me staring. What keeps me here despite my warring instinct to run.

I dart my gaze from his hand to his torso. Like sifr's burns from the prison's iron bars last night, the man's bronze skin is seamlessly stitched back together even though his shirt is not. The torn cloth the only evidence of my assault, the only proof of my own threadbare but still intact sanity.

Meanwhile, the old man swings his wiry legs onto the floor and sits up on the cot, massaging his neck. He clears his throat, clearing the air, relief making the many lines of age and sun on his face disappear for a moment before he flashes a toothless grin at me and then another at the tall man who ignores it.

Who is saving his stony regard all for me.

"You did good, son. Though next time, I could do without the audience, no matter how beautiful. I have my dignity, you know."

The dark stranger only grunts, batting away the elderly man's thin hand as he tries to give him a coin on his way to the door.

"And you." He turns his watery but amused gaze to me. "Try to wait for when he's not healing a decrepit old miner's throat to have your lover's spat."

A final wink at me, and then he's gone.

I frown at the stranger who glares at me right back, both of us still upset by what just happened but for different reasons.

"*Well?*" I finally break the standoff in a tone I reserve for addressing the Unnamed on patrol while snatching my sword off the ground.

"Well, what?" he growls back, either not recognizing that I am a ranking Vuorian warrior, or more likely, not caring.

"What was the old man talking about?"

And then he turns away from me to light a lantern, the soft glow throwing him once again into stirring shadow. I'd rather the blaze from his eyes or the blinding darkness than this. This reclaiming of the space as his, of the direction of the conversation as his.

"You mean calling you beautiful?" he calls over his shoulder in his gravelly voice. "I healed his throat, not his eyes."

"No," I sputter, shocked at his gall.

But then I realize that even without drawing a sword, he's still sparring with me, trying to disarm me with words just like sifr did in the alley yesterday. Using the only weapon the Unnamed are allowed to have.

I take a deep breath.

"No," I say more evenly, "but it's true? You actually *healed* him?"

He doesn't answer, his gaze moving past me to collide with the other two occupants of the hovel. I didn't even realize they were still here with us. So much for my years of training.

The architect moves first, resting a reassuring hand on my shoulder before guiding me behind him, almost as if guarding me. Sifr takes this as cue to do the same from my side.

"This is the ajnoob warrior I was telling you about, healer," sifr begins just like he did with the architect, his voice unwavering, though he's but the size of a mouse in front of this mountain of a man. "Like I told you, she saved my life, and I offered her an exchange for it. Her father is sick—"

The healer holds his hand up to stop him from going further. The architect's shoulders tense.

"Yes, very unfortunate for her. But I'm not in the habit of dealing with ajnoob. How do I know that once I heal her father, she won't send her patrol on me? Have them kill me, or worse, have them *study* me? Poke and prod me in an iron cell for the rest of my life?"

My desperation grows the longer he talks, the longer he insults me and my kind. Sifr opens his mouth to speak only for me to beat him to it.

"I promise I won't do that. My word is my honor."

At first, he says nothing to that. No one does.

And then he laughs, a cold and merciless sound that scuttles up my spine before settling behind my ribs.

"No, it certainly is not," he snarls. "You people can lie. And *enjoy* lying. There is no honor in that."

"Then what would you have me do?" Desperation enters my voice, but I don't care—don't care it's with the Unnamed, or that it's with this stranger who can disarm me in more ways than one. I don't care about anything other than Baba right now. "I will do anything to save him."

His molten gold irises momentarily spark with confusion, his tongue stilling with a hesitation he hasn't shown himself capable of before now.

"You could have her make a blood oath," the architect murmurs from beside me.

The healer and sifr both stiffen. I turn to look at sifr, but he whips his gaze to the floor while the two men stare at each other for a long minute, wordlessly communicating in the way only those who've known each other for a long time can.

"She must be told *exactly* what it entails, then. Or I go no further," the healer grits out at last, and the architect bristles at the caveat.

"Fine," the architect returns in the same steely tone, but by the time he turns back to me, his eyes are as soft, his mouth as kind as always.

"Reim, a blood oath to our people, is more than the mere offer of exchange sifr made with you. It is a new . . . er . . . agreement altogether and can only be made between you and the healer." His lips press into a thin line before he continues, "Once the terms are agreed upon, it is irreversible, except by another blood oath between the two of you. And it prevents either party from hurting or endangering the other."

I hazard a glance at the healer to gauge his reaction, but he is as unreadable as ever with his arms crossed over his tapered chest, a stoic expression across his face—so at odds with his friend, who in person and speech is as fluid as the silver river braided into his hair. The one they call the healer, meanwhile, is all steep cliffs and hard edges. As if carved from the vertical ridges of the Ma'asa itself.

I sigh, lassoing my need to flee once again. To go back to

my life from two days ago. To forget I met any of them. To let it all go . . . let my father g—

No. Never.

"You all already know my ask." I squeeze my eyes shut against the constant waking nightmare I'm living in. "I need you to heal my father. Not like what you did with the other man just now, but whatever way you were able to heal sifr from afar."

At first, the healer doesn't move; he just stares at me with that unnerving quicksand gaze. And then, right as I'm about to repeat myself, he pushes off the wall and prowls closer. Almost as if giving me the chance to run, but only so he can chase.

But I don't.

And then, all of a sudden, he's so close, *so* close that I can feel his warm breath heat my upturned cheeks. Feel his distinct scent of fresh earth after rain fill my arid lungs.

I stumble a few steps back, but it does nothing to lessen my suffocation. "Wh-what can I give you in return?"

No sooner do the words fall from my lips than I become afraid. Afraid of his answer. Afraid of not being able to fulfill my side of the bargain, of somehow being forced to. Afraid of being at a disadvantage for the first time in my life—of someone almost holding my life in their hands for once. And it's a fear like no other.

It's a fear I instill in all of them every damn day I patrol these streets.

But now is not the time for the hot punch of shame that pulses through my veins at the epiphany. Nor is it the time for my own fears.

Gutter that fire. Deprive it of air.

I try to call upon Baba's words, the ones that have served me since I was a youngling, but I just can't. Not while the healer cocks his head to the side and keeps his eyes locked with mine, watching me as if he can see all the anxious thoughts go through my head. As if he sees how weak I really am.

"How badly do you want this?" he taunts, as if he wants me to voice my fears, admit how scared I am, and I *hate* him for that. So, instead of guttering the fire, I find myself igniting it.

"He is worth more to me than my own life," I snarl, "and certainly more than yours." And something akin to surprise flashes across his eyes at my show of defiance, the corner of his lips lifting in a reluctant smirk.

"Well, if that is truly the case, then you will understand why I will need time to think on it."

I snap my head back as if struck and instinctively grab his wrist as he makes to leave.

No. He can't do this.

Spinning, he drops his eyes to where I'm holding him captive, flexing his hand against my tight grip but ultimately letting it stay there.

"No. We have no time. *He* has no time," I insist as I throw his wrist back at him. "We have to do this now."

He has me backed against the nearest wall in the next breath, his fist slamming next to my head in the one after that.

"Then we will do this my way," he rumbles, his face so close to mine that we have to ration the air between us. "I give you what you need now, and *you* give me what I need when I decide."

Whether it's because of his punishing proximity or my refusal to be intimidated by it, I remember who I am, who my *father* is, and especially, who this man is: an Unnamed stranger with unknown motives.

"Fine," I spit. "Ask from me what and when you want. But I have a condition of my own in return."

"What?" he demands through a tight jaw. The gold rings of his irises swirling once more until they're a pair of sparking vortices, ones I'm not sure I'll be able to escape despite my sudden burst of confidence.

I push forward anyway.

"You cannot ask to claim the kingdom's throne."

He stares at me for an endless moment, assessing each word like the open wounds they are.

"A very . . . *specific* request you have there, Reim," he murmurs, somehow feeling even closer than he already is, as if his voice is coming from inside my own head.

Sifr's small body edges closer to mine, watching the healer as if he senses the shift too. The architect does the same. The tension in the room stretches taut in the fragile web of space between us.

Tightening.

Tightening.

Until it *snaps.*

"Deal." The single word reverberates like a clap of thunder as the healer brings his right hand from beside my head to his chest, grabs my sword from my loose grip with the other, and slices his palm clean through. He then snatches my hand as it flies to cover my gasp and cuts it too.

The sting of pain at the wound is nothing compared with the bolt of pressure that pounds into me when he joins our hands as one—our blood as one. Nothing compared with the charge of power and light surging from him to me and back again, over and over, until we must look like twin stars chasing each other's tails across the sky, never quite catching.

And then—

And then it's gone.

He stumbles back as if burned. As if I were the one who cut him open and not the other way around. Stares at me as if I somehow betrayed him.

Lied to him.

Shaking his head as if attempting to clear it, he storms to a crude worktable next to the cot, grabs a small glass vial, and presses its opening against the cut in his palm, letting his glowing blood drip, drip, drip into the container until the wound closes as the others had.

And then, without a single word, he's in front of me again, shoving the stoppered flask into one hand and my sword into the other, dismissing me.

But I'm not done with him just yet. My palm still aching though the cut upon it has also healed, my lungs still catching their breath, my mind still reeling from what just happened. What could happen still.

"Wait," I call as he starts stalking away from me. And miraculously, he listens, though the broad muscles of his shoulders twitch with barely restrained impatience.

But that's not what empties my next thought. It's an emerald phoenix feather peeking at me from a swinging braid that escaped his tie. There's a painful beauty about its shimmering vane, its upright rachis, and I'm overcome with a sudden, aching urge to touch it.

"Well?" he barks, snapping me out of my enchantment, while the other two grunt their disapproval at his tone.

The architect smiles at me in apology for his friend's manners and in encouragement to continue.

"Well, are you the only one? I mean, with a gift?"

The architect narrows his eyes when the healer says nothing.

"Yes, as far as we know," he finally answers, though still facing away from me. "Anything else?"

"Yes. If your blood is able to heal as easily as your touch, why don't they bleed you to death, hoard your blood?" I ask.

And the silence that follows is so deafening that I know I must have blurted something wrong or at least offensive.

"I—I apol—"

"*They,*" the healer repeats the word, giving me an unobstructed view of his severe profile as he looks at me over his shoulder. "If by *they* you mean *your* people, it's because they don't know I exist, or they would try to do just that." My cheeks heat at his poor depiction of us, but I stay my tongue nonetheless. I *did* ask the question, and now I must hear the answer. "And if you mean *they* as in *my* people, it's because they know a gift that is not freely given loses its worth. And they especially know that when it's forcibly taken, a gift can become a curse."

I cross my arms to hide my shiver his cryptic words elicit, words that feel more omen than explanation, that seem to answer more questions than one. Questions that I don't even have yet, or questions I may never want answered.

And then he turns his gaze forward once more. Looks away from me.

"Now, get out."

Chapter

THE RISING SUN IS JUST STARTING TO PAINT THE sky with streaks of pink and violet, smudges of blue and amber, when I notch my boot on a loose stone in the far wall of the Keep. I pull myself up, one crumbling crevice at a time, until my hand finally grasps the shaft of one of the iron spikes that line the top of the serpentine wall like so many venomous fangs.

Hauling my leg to straddle the ledge, I try to catch my breath while keeping an eye out for guards, especially one roughly the size of a boulder and just as unforgiving if I dare lie to him about why I was out beyond curfew.

Why I'm only just returning with the dawn.

"I can't *wait* to hear this one," an exasperated voice calls from one of the Keep's lookouts.

"*Fate*, Tamir, I nearly fell to my death just now," I hiss at him under my breath, scrambling off the ledge and onto the safety of the wall's landing. I dust myself off. "But at least you're not Radnor. I'm already on his khur list."

He says nothing, just stands there with his expression as unreadable as the rest of him.

Was it just yesterday that I allowed myself to daydream of us as something more? Just last night that he tried to, and I used his feelings, used *him* for other selfish purposes?

I sigh.

He's been by my side through so much, has shown integrity and honor at every turn, and my lack thereof is what he has to show for it.

"What I did was a terrible wrong, Tamir, not just because of Order, but because I hurt you." He flicks his gaze to the sky as if to deny my words, but the evasive gesture only confirms them. "I want to tell you why—not because I deserve your understanding, or your forgiveness, but because *you* deserve the truth. *You* deserve a better friend."

His shoulders flinch at the last word, and I imagine his heart flinching in the same way. But friendship is all I can offer him. In truth, it always was. The rest was escape. Fantasy. And I will not ruin this precarious new trust I'm trying to build between us by lying to him about the possibility of more.

"But . . .?" he trails off. I shake my head.

"No buts. What you did for that boy, what you did for me . . . well, like it or not, you're in it as much as the both of us now."

He continues to stare at me, his blue eyes absorbing my words, his mind considering this moment of no return.

"C'mon then," he finally exhales, the tension between us disappearing with the last stretch of night. "I could use a good story." He flashes that dimpled smile one more time, and I can't help returning it with a relieved one of my own.

"Well, that wasn't exactly what I would call a *good* story," he sighs an hour later, rubbing the back of his neck as we walk the balustrade above the empty training yard. I just finished recalling the last time I laid eyes on Baba—lying in bed, death keeping vigil at his side.

"No, it's not, but you can't tell anyone of this, Tamir. Especially not members of the Jirga. I still don't know for sure whether talk of insurrection from within the Citadel is merely court intrigue or an actual truth. I just know that waiting to find out wasn't a risk I was willing to take."

He nods, but I've known him long enough to tell that his understanding is not the same thing as his approval.

"But you're still not convinced about my methods."

"If I'm being honest, Reim, no I'm not. The khasir boy tells you about this—this healing *gift*, and you believe him? And . . . and say it is real, then what? How are you going to get it for the Mali—"

The word dies on his tongue as his eyes widen in sudden realization.

"No! Reim, don't you tell me that's where you were last night. Don't you *dare* tell me you went off into the Burrow after curfew for this—this khasir trickery!"

"All right, I won't tell you that."

"Reim," he groans my name like he used to do when we first started training and I would challenge him to run one more mile, "this is madness! I care about the Maliki's health as much as any Vuorian, but involving the khasir—"

"You're right. You care about my father's health as much as any Vuorian. But you do not, you *cannot*, care about him as much as his daughter does. I will do whatever it takes, Tamir. Whatever it takes to keep him alive. To keep him here with me. To keep *me* from replacing him and becoming a curse upon this kingdom."

I don't even realize that we've stopped walking, that tears are streaming down my face with each subsequent word until Tamir starts wiping them away with the pad of his thumb. Soothing my short breaths with a gentle shushing sound through his lips as he lets me rest my head against his shoulder.

Forgetting all about maintaining Order in the face of my absolute misery.

While I forget to tell him about the deal I struck with the Unnamed healer in the face of his much-needed friendship.

I REACH BABA'S CHAMBERS NOT HALF AN HOUR LATER, ONLY to find them unlocked for the first time in my twenty-eight years under this roof. This incredible break in precedent has me panicking and breaking another by barging through the door without knocking.

Only for my feet to grind to a halt and my pulse to ratchet when I come upon various Jirga members and court nobles taking turns bending down and murmuring prayers and praise into the sedated king's ears. Mori and a few other apprentice healers stand at the foot of the bed, the position that is taken as a sign of respect for someone approaching death's door.

I am filled with the sudden urge to scream, my throat raw from the sheer anticipation of violence yet to be unleashed. I dash my accusatory glare over all the other occupants of the room. Are they here because they truly do want to send Baba safely through death's door while honoring his life and legacy? Or are they waiting like mountain vultures to steal his power for their own the very second he is gone?

My eyes land on Basteel at the head of the bed, rocking on his heels in rhythm with the murmured prayers on his lips, squeezing his eyes shut as if the proceedings are the most painful for him to witness as the Maliki's vizier. As if no one cares for the king—or rather, his kingdom—as much as he. And I can't help but wonder if he's surreptitiously inserting himself, if not overtly, in the minds of everyone present as a viable competitor for the throne.

His eyes snap to mine as if sensing that very competition right here, right now, his chin lifting as though challenging me to do something about it.

"Ah, it's the Ameera. Finally!" His gasped declaration could easily be misinterpreted as one of relief at seeing the princess at a crucial time like this—or rightfully interpreted as one of accusation that she wasn't here sooner. That she doesn't care as much as he does.

I squeeze my fists at my sides to relieve the urge to do the same around his neck.

"Basteel, I see you brought the Jirga to my father since he is unable to attend himself. How . . . thoughtful of you."

His smile is as thin and as angry as the vein pulsing across his temple.

"The Jirga has only the best interests of Vuor and should be *involved* when its leader is readying to leave this world. Especially when he's readying to leave it to his heir."

Some other members murmur their agreement, and I finally see this gathering for what it is: an intervention, if not an insurrection.

They knew they would get nowhere with their schemes when the Maliki was hale and whole, so they waited for this precise moment of incapacitation to vie for control.

"What sort of *involvement* are you suggesting, Basteel?" I snarl, dropping all pretense even if he won't.

He chuckles as if my mere existence is amusing rather than the thorn in his side I know it to be.

"Oh, Ameera, I mean nothing untoward or disrespectful of your esteemed position. I only suggest that since you will be new to your role, it may be beneficial to have a Jirga member serve as a guide, an adviser—"

"A puppet master," I finish for him.

He has the decency to look affronted by the accuracy of my conclusion.

"And let me guess, you would be honored to be the one to pull my strings."

He sputters as other members do their best to avert their gaze. "You stubborn, headstrong—"

"Do go on, Basteel. Once my father takes his last breath, anymore 'compliments' about me will be grounds for treason."

He wisely shuts his mouth, glancing at the king to make sure he is, in fact, still breathing and my threat was for naught before nodding to the others to follow him out of the chambers at last.

It's only when their cacophony of footsteps disappears behind the door and down the hall that my spine folds over in exhaustion. Mori grabs me around my shoulders, calling for an apprentice to pull up a chair and another to fetch me some food and water.

How long has it been since I've eaten or slept? Since I even sat down? Since I've given a single thought to myself?

Soon, I lie.

"You can lie. And enjoy lying."

The memory of the healer's cruel taunts leaks unbidden through the fissures of my fractured mind. He wasn't wrong. But he wasn't completely right either. Some of us lie out of enjoyment, out of manipulation and machination. But some of us, perhaps most of us, lie to survive.

That's what I'm doing right now.

Telling myself I'll rest soon. Take care of myself soon.

Soon as I take care of my Baba. Help *him* survive.

"Mori, please, call off your infantry." I try to smile. "I'll be fine. You were right earlier. I need to be with him. He needs me to be with him right now too. If you would be so kind as to give me that time alone, I will do whatever you want for a whole week."

She huffs, but there is no heat behind the noise.

"A whole month," she barters.

I smile wider.

"Deal."

"*Deal.*" The healer's thunderous voice booms in my head once again as Mori returns my smile and ushers her apprentices from the room.

Deal. It strikes closer than ever as I lock the many latches on the chamber door, pull the vial he gave me from my pocket, and rush back to Baba's bedside.

Deal. It threatens to cleave my mind, my heart, my very soul open as I tip the gold elixir into my father's parted mouth and the reflexive ball of his throat begins to jerk as he swallows.

Deal. Deal. Deal. It pulses over the invisible wound on my palm as I pocket the empty vial once more.

As I wait and wait and wait.

Until traitorous sleep claims me at last.

Chapter 8

HE SKY IS ON FIRE. THAT IS THE ONLY EXPLANATION for the flames that hang from the clouds, chewing the earth until it too is ablaze. The only reason for the screams of the too young, the too old. For the blood soaking the almazi groves instead of the rain.

The world is ending. Or at least our world is. But as we were always taught by our elders, our songs, our stories—everything in the world was made in pairs. Men and women. Mountains and oceans. Love and hate.

Ends and beginnings.

The world may choose to end us now.

But it will also make sure we begin again.

I spring up from my bed, my breath coming hard and fast as I try not to scream, try not to inhale the ash and sulfur that were descending from the blood-red sky but a few moments ago.

The same sky that is now as blue and still as the Sakoon Sea.

I pass a trembling hand over my eyes.

A dream. That's all it was—a catastrophic, exhaustion-induced dream.

Which serves to remind me of my catastrophic, exhausting reality.

The healer . . . the elixir . . . Baba . . .

Pushing the covers away, I attempt to scramble off the bed.

"Not so fast, child," Mori clucks from the open doorway, letting in a few servants carrying trays of tea, broth, and other plain, palatable foods.

I look down at my clothes, noticing that I am in my linen nightshirt, my body washed, my hair redone in a simple braid down my back.

"How long, Mori?" I form the words with a heavy, unused tongue before smacking my dry mouth and trying again. "How long have I been in bed?"

"Oh, a day and a half, I'd wager." She offers me a small smile along with a hand to lift me up.

A day and a ha—

"Oh! How could you let me do that, Mori? What about Jirga meetings, patrol?" I seethe, knowing I'm displacing my anger about *everything* onto her, but not caring anyway.

She doesn't even flinch at my unfair words, my acidic tone, as if she doesn't care either.

"You needed rest," she says unapologetically. "The handsome captain took care of patrol duties, and there will always be meetings. It's been a difficult week for you, dear, first with your father's worsening health, and then with his—"

There's a knock at the door before a guard calls out from behind it, "Er, Your Grace, I was informed that you are much improved."

"I am," I call back before Mori can say otherwise. She shoots me a disapproving glare, which I parry with one of my own.

"Then your presence is required at the Jirga chambers immediately."

"But Baba . . ." I breathe to Mori.

"I must see him first. I don't know how much time he—"

She sighs, knowing better than to wage a war against Vuor's High Commander.

"I'm sure you will find all the answers you are seeking at the Jirga meeting."

Something about the way she whips away from me to rummage through my wardrobe makes me want to demand she give me the answers *now*. But that same something makes me hold back, makes me trust her advice as I always have on countless occasions before.

"I'll be right there," I yell to the guard as Mori rebraids my hair into a simple coronet atop my head and helps me change into my state robes made of gold and crimson silk that cascade from the tips of my shoulders to the tips of my fingers in open sleeves. The robe cinches at the waist with a gold-plated belt that holds my dagger in place before falling in shimmering rivulets to my feet.

It's stunning. Magnificent in both make and mold.

But whether I am wearing it for a coronation or funeral, I have yet to know.

"Now," Mori says, smoothing my sleeves while what looks like tears fill her eyes. "Whatever you may discover in that chamber today, know that it is what was destined. Know that you, Reim of Vuor, are capable of greatness. Maybe even more than your ancestors ever were. Or ever imagined."

No one has ever spoken to me in this way besides Baba— with love, honor, pride. My mind wants to deny her praise, deny her trust in me. But my heart . . . my heart wants to curl around it, treasure it.

Wants to *believe* it.

And before one part of me can lay siege upon the other, tear me apart into tiny, confused pieces, she cradles my face between her warm palms, demanding both sides make a tenuous peace.

"Now, go."

And I do. Without waiting for the guard to escort me, I storm past him down the bustling halls and corridors, past the many courtiers and dignitaries, the open sleeves of my robes whipping in my wake like a banner of war.

But I'm unsure what war I'll be waging once I step past those Jirga chamber doors.

Will it be with my fellow Jirga members for my right to sit on Vuor's throne? Or a war within myself for a throne I am unsure that I even want. One that I *am* sure I do not deserve.

But none of this matters. Not if Baba is gone, and with him the future of the kingdom. All while I was sleeping because I was too exhausted, too *weak*, to do even this one thing: to be with him when he needed me most. To help him. To save him. Another failure added onto my ever-increasing list.

The guards outside the Jirga chambers bow as they haul open the heavy doors, and the deep breath I attempt to fortify myself with as I step across the threshold escapes me in one asphyxiating whoosh.

Baba.

Baba, who is not in his room. Not on his deathbed. Not taking his last breath on this earth, of this air.

Baba, who is *here.* Standing at the head of the table with his spine straighter than the swords he wields on the battlefield, his hands resting at his side steadier than the best years of his rule. His smile upon seeing me wider than the horizon basking over his kingdom.

He allows me to run to him, to embrace him, even as the rest of the Jirga bristle with discomfort—perhaps even with disappointment. At me, of course, but perhaps also at his renewed health, at their missed opportunity to seize power. But I push my nagging suspicions away, at least for now, because nothing, not even talk of treason, can distract me from my joy at the miraculous gift of Baba's recovery.

Gift. That's what the boy called it too. What the enigmatic healer called it as well. *A gift given freely.* But that's just it. It wasn't free. There was a price.

One I have yet to pay.

My hold around Baba's shoulders falters, my pulse doing the same a moment later. A dangerous ripple of panic and premonition courses through my veins as I pull back from him, pretending with my reassuring eyes, my encouraging smile that all is well and we will talk later, before I lower myself into my usual seat.

Baba watches me for a few tense moments longer before he finally sweeps his gaze across the table, commanding everyone's attention back to the discussion they were having before my entrance.

He must have been the one who called for me. He *wants* me here.

Then again, he doesn't know what I did and with whom. What I would do again and again if it meant he would live.

And that is why I'm going to make sure he will never know. That no one will. This was my deal to make. It will be only me from whom the healer will take. The healed wound on my palm pulses hot and heavy at that vow, almost as if in confirmation. In reinforcement of my promise.

Baba clears his throat.

"As I was saying, the debilitating state of my health had prevented me from seeing the true debilitation of our kingdom. I have no one to blame for it other than myself."

Protesting murmurs rise from the table until he holds his fist in the air for silence.

"But now that Fate has chosen to grant me life once again like it once chose us to rule this land and save it from those unworthy, I will be its humble servant. I will atone for my mistakes, my negligence. I will clean Vuor of its cursed filth and bring glory to our home once again."

And then the murmurs rise to a deafening roar of approval. Even those who usually remain stoic and unmoved stand in ovation. I find myself doing the same, and yet something inside, the same undefinable yet undeniable something that has taken root since I met sifr, is *detached*. It's here witnessing rather than participating, wrapping me in slow, suffocating coils of dread as it hears all the things he is *not* saying.

Fate may have brought about this moment, but I am now struck by uncertainty as to what end. To why Fate would choose for Baba's salvation, *our* salvation, to come at the hands of those he just promised to doom.

The extended applause beats like a war drum in my head as I battle for breath, for control. As I try to gutter the fire, only for the embers of alarm to reignite, refusing to burn out.

And just as I think I'm going to burn with them—to *say* something, *do* something that will combust in regret—the moment is over. The members are taking their seats once again and waiting for the Maliki to continue.

"I have been informed since my recovery that the matter is most urgent in Canton Two. That the Unnamed dwellers are becoming more of a liability than an asset. That their contribution to Vuor is minimal, while their willful disruption of Order is increasing by the day. That they do not alter their ways when they are docked their rations like Canton One and Three. Or even when their insurrectionists are punished and executed."

Basteel takes this as his cue to bring a scroll to the head of the table.

"Therefore, we will not wait for further attacks," Baba continues. "We will not be on the defensive. From this day forth, we will show them who Fate has chosen to hold the power in this kingdom. Their rations will be further quartered, and *all* men, women and children of the Burrow will be ordered to work daily in the baluur mines. This will keep their unnatural bodies productive and their conniving minds occupied. It will remind them how thankless they've been for the generosity of Vuor, and how our generosity too has its limits. And if they refuse or are found to fall below expectations, they will be charged with sedition and will have no one to blame but themselves for the consequences."

I swallow bile.

Does he mean execution without trial?

My mind, my body, is shocked into paralysis as Basteel unfurls the scroll, the hot crimson wax he drips onto the parchment resembling nothing more than spilled blood. Blood that was dripping from my father's mouth when he told me he was dying. Blood that was dripping from my own hand when I made the deal with the healer to prevent it.

"*A gift that is not freely given loses its worth. And when it's forcibly taken, a gift can become a curse.*"

The healer's ominous words ring in my ears, pulse through my veins as Baba's signet ring comes down upon the pool of red, sealing a deal, a fate, of his own. One whose outcome we have yet to know.

He lifts his knuckle bearing the ring to reveal the dahaka sigil once more, but the mighty creature doesn't raise its two heads clean of the wax, proud of the decree it committed to law like it always does. It instead takes flight with bits and pieces of red still clinging to its roaring maw, like mutilated viscera, like too many lives torn apart by its callous reign of fire.

I jerk my gaze to Baba once more, trying to catch his eyes, to plead with him to see the sudden, debilitating fear in mine. But he doesn't. The entirety of his attention is fixed on his mangled judgment, his newly resuscitated heart and revived mind focused on a singular purpose: restoring Order.

I swallow, severing my gaze in sharp, shattered increments from this man I know and love with my very soul—and yet have never truly seen before now.

And I cannot reconcile the two. Cannot reconcile my own role in this unveiling.

What have I done?

T HAT'S EIGHTY-FOUR, EIGHTY-FIVE, EIGHTY-SIX, eighty-seven today." The Jirga's appointed marshal double-checks his ledger before daring to look up at me.

When he receives no response, he mistakes it for dissatisfaction with his accounting abilities and rushes to amend himself.

"And of course that does not include the bodies unaccounted for . . ."

"Under the tunnel debris," I finish for him when he trails off.

I pass a trembling hand over my braids when what I'm aching to do is dig my fingers between the weaves and rip. Scream. Cry.

It's been a fortnight since the Maliki signed the Canton Two Workers' Edict into law—or what is referred to in the Burrow as the Death Sentence, for the death toll it has taken on this place is higher than any other sanction in recent history.

From collapses in the mines that cannot evacuate the increased number of workers, to starvation due to the quartered supply of food, water, and fuel, there are too many ways to die. And I was assigned to oversee its implementation.

And now I'll never be able to *unsee* its devastation.

I nod for Jafri to proceed, and the bodies of varying sizes are methodically wrapped in green cloth and laid side by side in the Burrow's market streets. The end of workdays is no longer marked by evening meals with community, but by identification of bodies and final goodbyes. Grief-ridden requests by surviving family members to join the dead are granted with a knife slit across their throats.

And I make sure to witness it all. To look at the face of every lifeless body before it's covered. For sifr. The architect. Even the healer. Yet I can't taste relief, because even if they aren't among the dead, I'm still complicit in all of those who are.

I witness, but I *do* nothing. Just let my eyes, my heart, my lungs drown in their blood—blood that looks no different from my own as it floods their streets.

As the last of the bodies are laid on the dusty road I patrolled only weeks ago, I can't help but conclude the day with one last glance at the alley where I first met sifr. The alley where I *last* met him too, when my desperation to save one life made me attempt to bend Fate to my will. Made me blind to the possibility that by doing so, I would be destroying so many others in its place.

I nod to Jafri again, my face blank, my eyes empty as I turn back to the Citadel. As I turn back to the conversation I had with the Maliki that fateful day after I healed him. That same day *he* destroyed me.

"Baba." I approach him as the last of the Jirga *members filter out of the room. He glances up, dutiful as ever in giving me his full attention whenever I ask for it.*

"Reim." He reaches for my hands, clasping them tightly between his as he hasn't been able to do in years. "Are you well rested, little gazelle? Mori found you unconscious at my bedside when I woke and reassured me that she would personally care for you until you recovered."

He sweeps his concerned gaze over my face, my body, to confirm my condition for himself.

"It is not me who had everyone concerned, Baba. Are—are you entirely well?"

His smile is full, easy.

"Yes, my child. Entirely. You had wished for my 'enduring rule,' and it seems Fate has answered your plea."

My pulse stutters at the unintentional accuracy of his words.

"Yes, Baba. And if I may, there is another wish I would like to make." I swallow. "But with you, not Fate." His smile buckles, his gaze curious but tinged with wariness. He shifts from Baba to Maliki right in front of my eyes as he nods for me to go on. "I ask that we wait to enact this order against Canton Two. That we give them perhaps a warning instead, another chan—"

"Reim." The Maliki's voice booms in the empty room, silencing mine as easily as the flickering wick of a candle. "This is the second time you have argued with my decision regarding the Unnamed, with Order, in the past week. I had forgiven it at first because I imagined you stressed by my illness, by your possible succession to the throne. But that is not the situation any longer. So perhaps it should not be the Burrow that should be given a warning, but you."

My eyes widen and my spine locks. I have never heard Baba speak to me with such unchecked anger before. In the past, he always redirected me with empathic guidance and controlled emotion.

And as if he too notices his uncharacteristic response, he shuts his eyes and exhales through the flare of his nose before addressing me further.

"I am the king, Reim. I am the legacy of my ancestors who survived unconscionable cruelty. Who vowed to never let it happen to us again. Who took this misused land and made it a home. And I will uphold that legacy until the day I die."

"I know, but—"

His hand whips up between us, and for one terrible moment I imagine he means to strike me.

"No buts, Reim!" *he snaps, and the strike of his words is somehow worse than a blow.* "You expressed fear of sitting on Vuor's throne should I pass, and now I understand why. We fear what we don't respect. And you do not respect our pain, our Order, our legacy."

He has not moved an inch, and yet his words, his disappointment, his shame, are in every beat of my heart, every breath of my lungs. In every single part of me.

He turns toward one of the large windows lining the chamber wall overlooking Vuor. Turns away from me. "It seems Fate intervened because it understood too. Understood your lack of conviction. Your lack of purpose and readiness. Understood that you—"

"Understood that I'm the weak link in our ironclad armor, right? That I'm the curse to the kingdom everyone says I am."

His clenched jaw feathers at my conclusion, but he doesn't correct me.

So, I turn away from him as well, from the thought that though my father is here with me like I wanted, I'm somehow still losing him in all the ways that matter. The condemning silence between our backs as I walk out the door louder than his righteous fury ever was.

"Reim . . . Reim."

I shake my head free of the aching past for the distressing present. So lost in my thoughts that I didn't even realize when my feet brought me back onto the Citadel grounds. Didn't even realize that Tamir must have escorted me the whole way.

I look up at him, only for him to sigh down at me.

"Where are you, Reim?"

Where am I? I'm somewhere free-floating. Nonexistent. Somewhere safe from all this sandblasted loss.

"I'm right here, Tamir."

"No, you're not. You're going through the motions. Have been for the past few weeks. Ever since the Maliki—"

He stops walking, whipping in front of me so I'm forced to stop as well.

"You're not . . . thinking about *that* again, are you?" he whispers, referring to the reason for my father's recovery, his eyes darting around the bustling marketplace as if they know what I did. As if it matters more to them than their feverish preparation for the Bicentennial celebration of the Nihaya in two weeks. A full-day annual celebration of the liberation of Vuor from the Unnamed, heightened this year by my father's miraculous healing, seen as a sign of Fate's ongoing favor upon the kingdom and upon any decision its ruler makes.

And since his recovery was due less to Fate's fortune and more to my own desperation, I am absolutely thinking of *that*. Never stopped thinking of *that*, if truth be told.

"I can try to forget you."

Sifr's boyish voice rings in my head just then, and I'm undone. Utterly undone. I crumble forward, clapping my hands over my ears to block it out.

Tamir pulls my rigid arms to my side, forcing me to stand, to look up into his alarmed eyes. Finally, he asks me what he forgot to ask the day I returned with the elixir.

"Reim, what did the khasir make you do in exchange for your father's health?"

With a grunt, I wrench myself away from him, shoving myself through the crowds of vendors and villagers, revelers and courtiers as he attempts to keep up.

"They didn't make me do anything, Tamir. Don't you see? I'm the one who makes people do things. I'm the one who's always making life difficult for others—making decisions I shouldn't, making things happen in a way that only leads to other things breaking."

Including Tamir. I turn around to tell him that—to tell him I'll find a way to assign him to another patrol, to stay away from me for his own sake—but he's gone, swept away in the voracious crowd during my tirade. And now I'm surrounded but so very alone. The laughing people, their world untouched by the devastation kept hidden beyond the Keep. Their carefree words, their pointless celebrations, nothing but blissful, *willful* ignorance.

But I can't reconcile the grief in the Burrow today with the claustrophobic joy here. The safety and ease of my home, even if deserved, with the hardships of others just over a stone and iron wall.

I can't think, let alone smile. I can't breathe, let alone speak.

The repressed fire in me trying to spark to life, begging to be ignited, to be set free.

And I can't do that either.

All I can do is run.

TWENTY-THREE DAYS.

It's been twenty-three days since I spoke with the Maliki of Vuor. Even longer since I spoke with my Baba. The two names, the two identities, forever fractured, never to be healed since the night I healed him.

And today . . . today marks Vuor's Bicentennial of the Nihaya at last. A celebration of its great history and its even greater destiny. My role to play today is not the High Commander patrolling the cantons, implementing Order to those who oppose it, but rather the Ameera—the worthy heir to Vuor's throne, a decorated and paraded symbol of our glorious future. In fact, the cantons are barely monitored today, not because they are also celebrating, but because our warriors and guards are encouraged to join in the Citadel's festivities.

I walk the path in front of his chambers for the first time in a month, my footsteps loud in my ears as I imagine the dahak knocker condemning me with its ruby eyes.

And then past the Jirga chambers, the one place I couldn't avoid him. Where my tongue would report the daily death tolls, the tally of baluur mined that fuels the entire kingdom, while my eyes would watch the Jirga members' satisfaction increase in direct proportion to both numbers reported—even though *he* remained expressionless. But my mind and heart would remain at times trapped within my detached body, and at others, escape somewhere far away.

Somewhere Baba and I still shared secret smiles, sincere embraces. Where I could bask in the unconditional love I could not have imagined living without a month ago.

But when the meetings ended, so did our interactions, neither of us trying to repair this gaping wound in our relationship. Both instead choosing to let it fester, a necessary personal sacrifice to keep the peace.

But whose peace I do not know. Perhaps the peace of the Jirga, or the citizens of the Citadel, or even an ashamed father—but certainly not mine, nor that of the cantons. Cantons One and Three, responsible for harvesting the bounty of the land and the sea respectively, have been subdued. The catastrophic example made of Canton Two a sufficient deterrent to any further dissent there. And the Burrow has become nothing more than an empty husk of what little it already was. The Unnamed population within the canton has thinned, while the pockets of our traders have done the opposite.

My distressed maids, whom I've only ever employed on this occasion, hurry over to me when I round the bend to the throne room at last. Securing my mantle around my neck, they drape the embroidered red train on the floor behind me just before the massive carved wooden doors in front of us are heaved open, announcing my entrance.

The court rises as I walk down a path cleared between them. There will be festivities and revels across the Citadel late into the night, but the celebration formally commences with a staged reenactment of the Nihaya, our ancestors' victory over the Unnamed, hosted within the castle itself.

My father waits for me at the feet of the twin thrones placed for us on the dais facing the performance stage. He is dressed in his iron crown and regal attire of red silk and gold-embroidered battle scenes that complement my gold silk robes overlaid with crimson lace in the pattern of our almazi leaves. He smiles as I approach, and I detect both genuine pride and sincere grief in the tilt of his lips, in the pools of his eyes for the first time in weeks.

Why? I want to scream at him. Why now, when there is a desert so vast between our hearts that it would likely destroy us if we tried to cross it? Why do you even get to feel grief and loss when you're the one who chose to create distance in the first place? To isolate me? To choose to believe, to trust, everyone except me?

But I swallow every barbed word, every poisoned question, and my own grief as I slip my hand into his outstretched one, turn my gaze to the cheering crowd until, at last, he does the same, and we take our seats.

I attempt to pull my palm away when we are settled, but he grasps it tighter and whispers, "Little gazelle." And my heart aches at hearing the familiar term of endearment that has been a stranger for the past month. "May we please talk after this, my child? May we please find a way to set this right between us?"

And the hardened part of me wants to ask for whom he intends to set this right—for him, for us, for the kingdom, or for the Burrow? Wants to tell him that there are too many wrongs "to set this right" again. And yet . . . yet the raw and bleeding part just doesn't care. It just starves for his love, the only love I've ever known.

I squeeze his fingers before folding my own in my lap, neither a yes or no to his questions, but he accepts it nonetheless as we both turn our distracted attention to the massive stage in front of us. The cavernous room's torches dim, and the crimson curtains bearing Vuor's dahaka sigil open, revealing the narrator of the performance in a single flame of spotlight.

"Vuor, in the ancient tongue, means to rise again," he begins, looking to the rafters, throwing his painted face and rotund body into flickering shadow. The audience behind me rustles in anticipation at the familiar opening monologue.

"But one can only rise after one falls. The greatness of our kingdom now is only a reflection of how great the suffering was in our past."

Then the rest of the stage lights are illuminated in unison, making me raise a hand to shelter my eyes from the sudden brilliance. When I am able to look upon the stage again, I am confronted by scenes of poverty and oppression in a foreign land of lush greenery—of tree-lined mountains, of wildflowers and lakes. Of rolling fields of every kind of vegetation under a clear sky of sun and birds. A thriving land that became greedy of its bounty, so it found ways to drive out those it deemed unworthy of it.

I attempt to swallow past my dry throat, unable to look away as Vuorian actors are whipped and corralled by others who look like them, as some are mock executed and others lucky enough to escape into the dreadful unknown offstage.

I'm unable to look *at* the audience, who watch it all unfold with horrified empathy, with tears and anger for their people, yet they cannot *see* what I now cannot unsee: that if we merely changed the scene from valleys to desert, extended the tips of the ears of those suffering, that *we* have become what we abhor.

I have seen this play every damn year since I was a child, and yet I sit here riveted as if I'm seeing it for the very first time.

The scene shifts, and wagons and carts filled with women and children are dragged by exhausted men into the Koora Desert. They battle not only the desert's harsh elements, but also its mythical monsters of lore constructed of metal and wood, horror and imagination, until the Ma'asa Mountains, painted like a beacon of hope on the backdrop, are unfurled, and the land we call home takes center stage. The exiled wanderers finally arrive to our current land, proclaiming to the audience the blessing of it being unsettled or otherwise mistreated by the savages who dwell there.

An adult and child actor take their cue to step out from a decrepit tent, dressed in rags made of hide, their makeup exaggerating tapered ears into horns, teeth into fangs. The Unnamed man snarls in a foreign tongue that is made of barks and gnashing of teeth while the child leaps at the innocent Vuorian refugees, trying to bite them despite their attempts to help them. To civilize them.

"Khasir filth!" the crowd boos. "Ungrateful khur!"

And I stiffen.

My breaths come in shallow, insufficient pants.

My pulse attempts to match their erratic rhythm.

Because I know what happens next—the escalating jeers from the crowd serving as cue, as permission.

"Give them what they deserve!" one yells louder than the rest, and then . . . and then the actors do just that.

A prop sword is thrust to the sky before it appears to ram through the chest of the Unnamed man and then slice across the throat of the boy.

The room erupts, and my heart feels as if it will do the same.

My tongue tastes blood as my teeth hold back a scream.

My eyes can't look away from the still-rising chest of the boy, the subtle adjustment of the man's arm as they play dead.

I remind myself that they're alive, that it's not real.

It's. Not. Real.

But it's too late; my mind doesn't believe my eyes. It exchanges the images of their fictitious corpses on the stage with the actual Unnamed ones lying on the streets of the Burrow.

Just as I think I'll bite through my tongue with the sheer effort to stay seated, to pretend indifference at this unreal reality, the scene ends. The torches lighting the stage blink out to allow the final act to unfold. For this waking nightmare to be over at last.

I feel my father's steady fingers lace through my trembling ones and hear his voice murmur in what he believes is empathy, reassurance, "The Iron Crown we wear is a heavy one, my child, but I hope being reminded of how far we have come will give you hope for how much further we can go."

But it has the opposite effect.

"How much further we can go."

I snap my gaze to his, meeting it directly for the first time in weeks.

In its sandstorm depths, all *further* means is further death, further destruction. And it's not hope that I feel at this future, but *fear*.

No sooner does the thought pass through my mind than what looks like frustration flickers through his eyes.

But before I can examine it further, the torches flare once more, and the pounding of the Vuorian battle drum fills the room, the crowd stomping the floor with their feet in time with its powerful beat.

The reenactment is reaching its climax, and I exchange the war building in my father's regard for the one already raging on stage.

The Vuorian warriors are no longer portrayed as desperate refugees, but an organized army, their armor gleaming and their swords slicing theatrically through the air as they charge toward the rabble of masked Unnamed heathens across the stage.

But something is wrong.

While it is obvious that the Vuorian soldiers are acting—their fighting stylized, their armor and swords of cheap leather and wood—the Unnamed troupe has formed an actual defensive stance. And their swords . . . their swords are the exact make of the ones issued to our castle guards, and they are decidedly *real*.

As are their tapered ears.

As are their looks of fury and determination.

And this time, I do stand.

Do scream.

"Look out!"

But it's too late. One of the Vuorian actors runs straight into the honed blade of an Unnamed's extended sword. His cry of surprised pain drowning out the end of my own warning, drowning his throat, his mouth, in a thick pool of blood.

And then the crowd is on its feet, screaming, scrambling over toppled chairs and one another for an exit.

But not me.

I leap forward, using the decorative dagger at my belt, which is no less lethal than the sword I left in my room, to slash the ankle of an Unnamed assailant at the edge of the stage. His body slams to the floor, his stolen sword sliding toward me as the tendon that kept him standing severs with a sickening pop and gravity does the rest. I don't wait for him to recover before plunging the sword through his heart.

I swing onto the stage, my dress ripping up my leg and giving me the leverage to charge through one, two, three more of them before I yell for Tamir to rally the other Vuorian guards who have joined the fight to prioritize the protection of the performers, the guests, their Maliki.

But no sooner does his title fall from my lips than I realize the king has joined the fight as well, each hand wielding one of his twin swords as he covers me from behind. I take but a moment to admire his agility, his prowess like I used to as a child in the training yards, as he thins their ranks one by one, before turning back to my own battle raging in front of me.

How is this even happening? How were the Unnamed able to get inside the Citadel—let alone procure arms? How did they even learn to fight with them?

It becomes clear in a matter of minutes that what they lack in training, they more than make up for in perseverance and numbers. As one falls, another two seem ready to take his place. All masked from the nose down, they leave only furious, kohl-lined eyes to engage with. Men and women, adolescents and elderly, they keep pouring into the hall from offstage. Some stay to fight the Vuorian warriors, and others jump into the frenzied crowd, corralling them into manageable groups.

And soon, it's clear that there's no way to keep fighting and win. Vuor is outnumbered and outmatched. That this may be *our* home, but we are fighting by *their* rules.

"Some stories end with honorable deaths, little gazelle."

I let my father's soft words from my childhood comfort me as I ready myself for that exact ending.

As I bolster my spine, tighten my grip around the stolen sword. As I attempt to face inevitability with honor and courage.

But just as I inhale, then exhale perhaps for the very last time—everything stops.

Just. Stops.

The horde of Unnamed still surrounds us, their swords at our throats, but the entirety of their focus is on something behind me.

Or rather, *someone.*

My breath turns shallow, my pulse laboring as if underwater. But its singular flow isn't gushing to my overworked heart, or my dizzying brain.

But to my palm gripping the sword.

To the invisible wound cut across it, the vow made in words and blood, which may be out of sight but is *never* out of mind.

The pulsing pressure there becomes so overwhelming that I have to grit my teeth, call upon all my failing strength to keep me from dropping my weapon, from surrendering to this strange hold over me instead.

I whip around to face who every part of me knows is there. Who is behind not only my pain, but also my kingdom's.

Who came to collect what he is owed.

My eyes collide with those of spinning gold.

Eyes that promise no mercy. Only wrath.

No healing. Only death.

"Hello, Reim," the healer rumbles as he pulls off his mask. And that's when I look down. See the edge of his sword stamped against my father's throat.

Right before he pulls.

Chapter 11

No!" I SCREAM, THE WORD RIPPING UP MY throat, tears blinding my eyes as I scramble across the blood-slicked floor to reach my father's fallen body. He's taking futile gulps of air through a throat that won't draw breath, pumping blood through arteries that won't flow. And I'm powerless to stop it.

"Baba," I whimper over and over as I cradle his head in my lap, knowing it will be the last time I will be able to call him that, the last time he will be able to hear it. That despite everything I did to run from this moment, it found me anyway.

"Baba, I'm sorry. I'm so sorry," I cry as I stare into his amber eyes one last time, as I watch them dull from the color of rippling sand to that of the packed earth he will soon return to.

"No, Reim." He smiles, his pale lips mouthing my name. "I— I—"

And then he's gone.

I shift his emptied body to the floor and wail to the sky—to Fate, who everyone was so sure blessed him, blessed all of us. Who was just waiting for the right opportunity to damn us instead.

My grip tightens around the pommel of my sword, and my next rageful yell fuels my body to lunge from the ground and charge at the healer. But I only take two large strides before my limbs lock, my spine contorting backward until it's as if I'll snap in two—the invisible cut across my palm no longer pulsing, but *burning*.

As if it's the head of a match not only set ablaze but determined to spread its fiery wrath to the rest of me.

To consume me from the inside out.

My mouth cranks open in a silent scream as I crumble to my knees. The clatter of my sword upon the wooden floor jars my brain into sudden, painful understanding.

The blood oath. I can't hurt him.

He knew this would happen.

No—he damn well planned for it.

And sifr, who I thought about every moment of every day, dreamed terrible dreams about for the past month, he knew too.

I stare at the sword lying abandoned beside me. A guard's sword. The exact kind I saw the prison wardens carry the night I freed sifr. Sifr must have guided the Unnamed through the castle sewers. The same sewers I led him to during his escape from the prison.

"I like you, ajnoob."

Sifr's words assault me as I pant through a different kind of agony as I push myself to stand. To face the healer with the courage, the dignity he refused to show me.

I may not be able to hurt him, but I vow to find a way to *destroy* him.

"You lying piece of khur. You planned this," I snarl. "You and sifr and the architect. You all knew who I was, who my father was the whole damn time."

He just cocks his head to the side, staring at me from under the hood of his cloak with his firebrand eyes lined in warrior kohl—resembling nothing more than a mighty dahak playing with its meal, discovering all my weaknesses before deciding how best to devour me.

"You used me," I seethe, refusing to go down without a fight. He did use me. Used my love for my father, my helplessness to help him, my vulnerability in ruling in his stead.

His eyes flash at my accusation.

"Just like your father used us, Ameera. Used our land, our bodies, our very lives for your selfish gains. And yet, the balance between what we did and what your people have done for centuries will never be even," he growls. "Just like *your* balance between the two of us is yet to be paid."

A ripple of shock reverberates through the otherwise paralyzed crowd.

"What does he mean, Ameera? What does he mean?!" someone demands.

"How could you do this to us, to your father?"

"Did you see how her body seized just now? She was cursed and brought her curse upon us all!"

My mind whirrs—the deal, the healer, the crowd, my father's empty accusing eyes, all tightening, suffocating until—

"*Silence*," the healer booms. Though his thunderous order subdues the room, his stormy regard remains locked on me.

"We made a deal, you and I," he reiterates as he stalks up to me, his palm where he cut himself snapping open and closed at his side with every deafening step. "An oath sealed in blood. I heal your father, and in return, you give me whatever I ask."

"I have not forgotten, you fateforsaken wretch," I shear through the bars of my teeth as I too take a step closer, closer until there is but an inch of space between us, refusing to be intimidated any longer by this man who once spoke to me of honor but has none himself.

He lifts a brow at my unexpected daring but holds his ground.

"And since you're here now, having *killed* the one you knowingly healed, I can only assume what you'll be asking in return is to take his title, to be made Maliki of Vuor." I sneer. "But, for all your impeccable scheming, you forget you forfeited that very right. My one condition for accepting your deal was that you not lay claim to the throne."

But he remains as immovable as ever, my words of no more importance than the throats he slit, the lives he ruined today.

"You are right. I did accept your condition not to ask for the throne of Vuor," he concedes easily.

Too easily.

But as I scramble to locate the trap in his words, he springs it.

"But I did not say that I would not ask for the hand of the one who sits on it."

The blood drains from my head and limbs as his meaning dawns on me. With Baba killed, I am no longer the mere heir of Vuor, but its rightful ruler. Its Malika. And by asking for my hand, by *marrying* me, he will be its king.

I stumble back, unable to breathe, to *think*, but he grips me by the shoulders, keeping me here in case I run.

But that's where he's wrong. I don't want to run. I want to *fight*.

"Why not just kill me and take the Crown that way?" I rip away from his hold. "And if not you, because of the damn oath, why not have someone else do it for you?"

He sighs, massaging his temple. "Because, if *you* remember, that 'damn oath' prevents us not just from directly harming but also from willfully endangering the other."

"Besides"—he spins, pinning Basteel, held by two Unnamed guards, with his savage glare—"rumor has it, there are those within these walls who would foolishly claim the right to succession with the king and his heir dead and attempt to fight me for it."

Basteel bristles but says nothing.

The healer turns back to me.

"No, a marriage is the best way to keep the peace."

"Who says it will be peaceful?" I hiss at him. And his pupils expand at that, his serrated gaze raking over my face, cutting me open, *seeing* me in a new light.

Then one corner of his lips tips up. In amusement, in challenge, I know not.

All I know is that I don't like it.

Don't like it at all.

"Reim!" Tamir's voice fractures the brittle air between us.

I whip my head around to see him struggling against his own Unnamed guard's punishing hold. "Reim! You don't have to do this! There has to be a different wa—"

Thump.

The guard thwacks the back of his head with the pommel of his sword, and Tamir crumbles to the ground. Alive but unconscious.

Tamir, who I should never have involved in the first place. Whose friendship I abused and betrayed, and now Fate is cursing him by association.

The same way Fate is cursing the entire kingdom.

Guilty tears come unbidden to my eyes once again, but they sting less than the prickling perusal that follows their trail down my cheek.

I turn in its direction, only to find the neutral mask the healer was donning a moment ago has fractured into an obvious frown.

He's angry. That's easy enough to figure out.

But at what? Tamir's insolence? My tears? My grief?

It doesn't matter. I'm done hiding what I feel. Done pretending for the sake of others, especially someone who can't hurt me any more than he already has.

You're angry, khasir? Well, so am I.

And as if not only hearing the challenge in my mind but rising to it, he bellows for Basteel.

"You! Zealot in stolen silk and pilfered gold, you hold some undeserved weight here." The vizier's Unnamed guard shoves him forward until he staggers between me and the healer.

"You will marry us in front of my people and hers. And you." He looks back down at me, whispering so only I can hear. "You have to accept me as your husband, as the Maliki of Vuor, or the pain you felt just now when you tried to kill me will return a hundredfold because of the oath, and this time it will not stop; it will just barely keep you alive until you do."

I say nothing, just glare into his cyclonic eyes with a promise of a lasting pain of my own. Swallowing, he looks away first, but I feel little satisfaction in such a paltry victory. Not when the comparative loss is too great to even comprehend.

"*Now!*" he thunders at Basteel, who scrambles forward.

"W-we are here to bear witness to the joining of our . . . Malika, Reim of Vuor, with . . ."

He trails off. Does he realize this marriage joins a Vuorian with an Unnamed? A blasphemy and high crime in our kingdom? One he, a Janoon purist, of all people, is now sanctioning?

"With the healer of the Unnamed, soon to be Maliki of Vuor," the healer finishes for him, daring the coward to correct him.

"Yes, as you say," Basteel mutters. "May their union be one of peace, love, and glad tidings for us all."

"May it be one of justice, of liberation, of righteous victory," the healer amends the traditional blessing. "Your kind may make a habit of false promises, but we do not."

The Unnamed rebels roar their approval, while the Vuorian captives look on in terror.

"Then make one more, if you are so truthful," I shout above the din that dies upon hearing my words and stays that way until the healer breaks it.

"Why?"

"A wedding gift to your *bride*." I nearly choke on the word. "To secure her cooperation."

I watch him watching me, picking me apart again with his sharp eyes, which I suspect are a gateway to an equally sharp mind.

"Go on."

"Release the innocent people of the court here. Do not take revenge on the citizens of the Citadel. You want justice, liberation, victory? You want to be the Maliki to all of this land? Then be one for *all* of its people."

He continues to stare at me, weighing my words—words that, unlike his, can be untrue. Perhaps he realizes that if he is to agree to them, it cannot be through a mystical oath this time but through something that requires much more vulnerability, but is also much more powerful.

It has to be through trust.

"Done," he says after a long moment, and that single word presses into me with the same authority as Baba's signet ring on hot wax. Never to be undone again.

Baba.

The bludgeoning reminder that we are only even having this conversation because Baba is dead, because he was *killed*, dulls any relief over my people's guaranteed safety. None of this would've even happened if it weren't for me.

Baba. Baba. Baba.

My heart cries out again and again, breaking through the bars of my chest to follow the healer as he walks over to my father's body still lying in a pool of blood and crouches to pick up the iron crown which slipped off his head.

I look up from his unseeing eyes into the healer's too-perceptive ones as his large hands close around the circlet. As they blister, burn, char.

As they then heal.

Blister. Burn. Char. Heal.

Blister. Burn. Char. Heal.

Again. Again. Again.

Faster.

Faster.

Until I am unable to tell the order of events.

Until he places it upon his brow and the cyclical phenomenon continues in such rapid succession around his head that the crown seems to be made of the same molten metal as his eyes, and his skin and hair seem to be in a constant state of horrifying metamorphosis.

Until he has become something awful and awe-inspiring at the same time.

I stare transfixed by this undulating corona of magma and might. By the reminder of the dream I had of the world on fire.

Of the daunting words that jolted me awake.

"The world may choose to end us now.

But it will make sure we begin again."

Is this terrifying ending of our kingdom the inevitable beginning it was referring to?

And what does it mean if it is?

I *see* nothing, though I watch the healer come to stand by my side once more; I *hear* nothing, though I listen to Basteel bluster through the rest of the ceremony; I *say* nothing, though I speak the required words to bind myself to the healer, and him to me.

And then he joins his hand with mine, and though our blood oath is now fulfilled, the pulsing pressure begins anew. He frowns down at them as if he notices it too. But then he grits his teeth. Jerks his gaze back up, wrenching our laced hands to the ceiling in the same motion.

"Victory has come for those Unnamed," he roars to the awaiting crowd.

"Victory has come for those Unnamed," his people answer back.

Chapter 12

THE COLD NIGHT AIR DOES NOTHING TO COOL THE heat of shame coursing through my veins as I press my forehead against the wooden lattice of my bedroom window. The night's darkness cloaks the Citadel as always, but the city's torches don't flare in response. Tonight, which was to be one of celebration and revelry like no other, has become one of mourning and loss instead.

Because of me.

I should be thankful that it isn't worse. That instead of the lack of lights, it isn't a surfeit of fire. That instead of the absence of joyful laughter, it isn't the abundance of terrified screams. I should be thankful that the healer kept his promise of peace for now.

But I can't be.

Because I didn't keep mine. Didn't keep my promise to save my father, to save his kingdom . . . from me.

"You shadeed, you a-abomination, you cursed us all!" a courtier wailed as I was escorted to my chambers after the ceremony. Only one of the few brave enough to do so in the face of the two Unnamed guards flanking either side of me. The same two guards who stand watch outside my room now.

I push off the window seat to look about the sparsely furnished space visible only by a few tired beams of moonlight. The large, curtained bed that takes up the majority of the room, the matching wardrobe, a pair of nightstands, and a vanity. The two abandoned armchairs on a threadbare rug that's spread in front of a massive hearth empty of baluur's soft violet glow and its radiating heat. As are the torches on the walls.

As is the soul in my body.

My room was never much of a refuge. This castle, never much of a home. Just a place I slept and ate. Attended meetings and trained to be heir. My mind and my heart valued the time spent with the people of this castle rather than the space itself. Mori in the healing ward, Tamir in the training yards, Radnor on the Keep, Baba in his—

I squeeze my eyes shut until sparks appear behind the lids. Sparks from the power of his sword clashing in the training yard. Sparks that would burst in his eyes when he was happy to see me my whole life—and when he was upset with me the whole of this last month.

Sparks that blinked out one by one as I held him in the cradle of my own arms, in a pool of his own blood, one last time.

"Little gazelle."

I can still hear the low, almost hesitant cadence of his voice from earlier today.

"May we please talk after this, my child? May we please find a way to set this right between us?"

He wanted to talk. He wanted to listen. He wanted better. And I let my own anxieties, my own inability to follow, to respect Order like he always said, ruin us all.

He was right.

I was wrong.

Yet I am alive.

And he is dead.

"*Khur*!" I scream, snatching my own iron crown I donned this morning from the tangled grasp of my hair and pitching it at the chamber's door. It clatters to the ground just as the door bangs open and reveals a tall, limber shadow standing in its frame.

The healer.

He's here.

My pulse ratchets.

So lost in the what-ifs and sorrow of this day, I forgot the terrible relevance of this night.

Our wedding night.

When the groom is meant to take down the braids of his bride, and she is to take down those of her groom. And by both doing so, they show that they are safe with each other in all ways. In their souls that are unleashed with their unraveled hair. And in their hearts, which are joined by the joining of their bodi—

No.

No. No. No.

With my sword and dagger confiscated earlier, I grab a candlestick from atop the vanity in my instinctual need to arm myself. Grip it tighter even if it's no match for this man with a body made of windstorm, and eyes made of sun flare. A soul made from the very elements of the earth themselves.

But I'll be damned if I give up, give in, to this monster without a fight.

He barrels into the room before slamming the door behind him, still dressed in his bloodstained clothes, cloaked in his thunderous mood, but bearing no crown upon his head.

Not even sparing a glance at my own bloody clothes, my fighting stance, my choice of weapon, he stalks to the cold hearth and starts lighting the baluur.

"Why do you care if I freeze to death?" I call to him in the darkness that was so quick to embrace him. "It would do you a favor."

He grunts as if he would like nothing more.

"Perhaps I'm doing it for me rather than you."

The kindling sparks once, twice beneath his keen effort before the pile of baluur ignites, throwing his severe profile into vivid relief.

And suddenly, I can't seem to look away.

Where most men have scars and lines from battle and age, he does not. His skin is taut and smooth as untouched sand as it clings to the ridges of his cheeks, the cliff of his straight nose. His black-and-gold hair carries a few braids within its folds, including the one intertwined with the green phoenix feather. His midnight brows sit low over his flashing eyes, his full mouth framed by the nest of his neatly trimmed beard. He's not conventionally handsome like Tamir, nor charming like the architect.

But there is something that draws me to him.

That holds me here.

Something that convinces me he is gravity itself.

And then, as if he heard my thoughts, he turns the entire force of his attention to me and only me. Pinning me in place with his honed gaze, he pushes up to his feet from his crouch, stretches his neck, and unfurls his limbs as if he's a beast in his prime—a beast preparing for the hunt.

As if tonight, he's chosen me to be his prey.

"Come here, *wife*," he rumbles.

And though my pulse starts sprinting anew like the gazelle my father always called me, my body refuses to move. Refuses to go willingly to my own annihilation.

So, he comes to me instead.

He takes his time walking in my direction, as if not wanting to startle me. As if he knows how much he already does. Coming closer . . . and closer until he's towering above me but not touching me. Until he's surrounding me not with the stench of the blood and tears from earlier today, but by his own astounding scent of fresh soil and recent rain.

Until he's tugging gently, so damn *gently*, at the candlestick in my hand that I let him have it from the sheer shock of such a harsh man even knowing the meaning of the word.

But then his other hand comes up, and I can't help but imagine him reaching for my braid next, doing that same gentle tugging at the fastening, undoing my hair, my dress—

I gasp.

"*No!*" I object so loudly the room echoes it back in chorus.

"No," I say again, more calmly but no less adamant in my refusal.

He drops his hand but stays where he is.

Waiting.

"I do not want this marriage. And I certainly do not want *you*," I blurt before my courage threatens to fail me.

He doesn't blink, just continues to watch me with that impenetrable gaze until I feel as exposed as if he *had* made me undress.

"Be that as it may, wife," he says finally, that last word sending a shudder down my spine. "We *are* married."

He holds up the hand where he cut his palm, continuing to pin me with his gaze.

"We are joined forever. There's no mistake about that," he

murmurs, and I shutter my eyes, my heart, my soul. Prepare myself for him to take me against my will.

But I'll be damned if I don't at least try to keep one last thing for myself.

"Don't call me that."

"Call you what?" he asks, genuine curiosity lifting his otherwise deep voice. "Wife?"

A pause.

"Like I said, that's what you are." He stretches his words, as if we were playing a game and he's unsure of the rules, the stakes—uncertain of making the wrong move lest he lose. Or worse, lest I win.

"But that is not *who* I am," I snap at him, snapping my eyes open in the same frustrated breath.

Big mistake.

Fate, was he always so close? So . . . so imposing?

I try to take a step back from him, but find the stone wall I took shelter against preventing my retreat. The wall of his chest at my front does the same. How is it that he's still not touching me, but somehow in this moment, he's all I feel?

"So, *who* are you?" he murmurs, but is he asking me or himself, trying to stay one step ahead of me, to figure out the answer before I give it to him?

"I am . . . I am . . ."

He presses a calloused finger to my trembling lips when they fail to deliver a response, delving deep into my eyes with his, trying to find it there instead.

"You are surprisingly brave," he concludes after a while. "But you are lost. Unsure of your past." He traces the line of my odd ears with his eyes. "And even more unsure of your future."

He meets my gaze once again. "You are like us, the Unnamed."

My own eyes widen at that, the thick haze from his proximity clearing at his conclusion.

"I am not," I spit as I slip out through a sliver of space at last. Moving to stand over the fireplace, I pin my stare to its flames while hoping to douse my own.

"I'm nothing like your kind. And as for to-tonight and whatever your *expectations* may be, you were the one who told me that a gift forcibly taken can become a curse."

He turns to face me, leaning against the same wall I'd just vacated, crossing his arms across his chest, cocking a brow in surprise.

"And so, if you don't want to be a hypocrite—or a liar, like you call us—you will not take from me what is not freely given."

His mouth curves up in an annoying smirk as he pushes off the wall.

"I didn't realize my words would have such an impact on you," he murmurs, his large shadow creeping over me again, closing in until I imagine it devouring not only me but the entire room, like I witnessed it do the night I'm referring to.

But then it stills.

"But they aren't relevant tonight. I didn't come here tonight to take anything from you. I came only to offer an . . . *amendment* to our bargain if you are agreeable."

My spine locks.

Why that absolute piece of khur! His vague words, his misleading behaviors were all just ways to intimidate me, to disarm me! To take the upper hand once again like he did the night of the oath and like he did earlier this very day.

Well, not anymore.

"Another deal?" I sneer. "No, thank you."

But all amusement drops from his face as he replies, "Not even one that will free you of this marriage?"

My heart stutters.

What? No. He did not mean tha—

"I mean it, Reim," he says, and I hate how he seems to read me so easily.

"Fate, you're just loving this, aren't you? Just dangling one scrap after another at me? Reveling in it?" I seethe. "Haven't you had enough? Haven't you done enough? Ruined enough? Won enough?"

"There are some things that are more important than winning. Than owning and ruling. But your kind doesn't have to care about that," he spits right back.

"Today was the Bicentennial of the Nihaya. And though your people remember it as the end of your oppression, we remember it as the beginning of ours," he snarls. "And we don't recall a big, glorious battle between good and evil like your damn play, but a brutal massacre of our people by yours. And even more devastating, the stripping of our history, our gifts, of our names that harness them."

And there's something so adamant in his retelling of these events that, despite my anger, confusion, and grief . . . or perhaps because of them, I say nothing so he will go on.

"To manifest our gifts, our names would have had to appear in a book when we were born—*The Book of Names*. But this book was no Vuorian ledger filled with gains and losses, weights of fish and grain, baluur and bodies," he sneers. "It held our complete history, our songs, our poems and epics. It held our hopes and dreams, our very names and identities. And each time a youngling was born, we would open *The Book*, and the child's name would appear on the page. *The Book* bestowed our names and with them, our gifts along with our long lives, our purpose, our sense of *self* . . ."

He trails off, the solid tenor of his voice crumbling, his gaze turning toward the fire but suddenly cold. Distant.

"What happened? To *The Book of Names*, I mean?" I whisper after a while, hating that I'm unable to stop my curiosity from simmering to the surface despite all the boiling reasons not to. But I've never heard anything about this book, not from any scholar or Jirga member. And even if there's no way it's true, it's still . . . intriguing.

He pulls himself from his reverie, peering back at me over the broad breadth of his shoulder as if deciding how to answer the question. As if there are many truths and he's deciding which one to give me. Which one I can handle. Which one he can trust me with.

"It was said to have been destroyed by your ancestors in the Nihaya. And our history, gifts, and our names along with it," he says finally. "But I have recent reason to believe it was not. That, in reality, it was hidden before it fell into ajnoob hands at all. And furthermore, that there is a cipher somewhere that will help us find it again."

I swallow thickly, knowing there are so many more questions that need to be asked but one takes precedence above them all.

"And how does this have anything to do with my freedom from this marriage?"

"Because, Reim of Vuor," he says, tasting every sound of my name, as if he wished he could do the same for his own missing one. "If you help me find this cipher, find this book, find my *name*, I promise I will end this marriage."

My heart thuds to the ground, but my mind takes flight.

"And what of the Crown . . . the kingdom?" I ask, trying not to get too ahead of myself.

"We will fight for it on the battlefield instead of the marriage bed," he says, steady and serious as ever.

Yet my cheeks flare with heat nonetheless at his salacious answer, and I hate that I can't tell if he's goading me yet again or not.

"Will this need a blood oath as well?" I force myself to move past it.

"No. We are not exchanging favors. I am offering you an out. If you help me find the cipher, we end this marriage, I return *The Book of Names* to my people, and we fight for Vuor fairly. Or you don't, and things remain as they are. *We* remain as we are."

I consider the stakes. Nothing could be worse than what is happening now. I have very little to lose at present . . . and even less to love.

But I dash the thought of Baba away. Because love was what got me into this mess to begin with. My desperate love—and my desperate decisions in the name of it.

"No." The word tears past the bars of my teeth. "Not until you tell me why."

"Why what?"

"Why should I believe you now when I lost *everything* because of your lies?"

His body stiffens, his gold irises still, but he says nothing, which only makes me angrier.

"Why *any* of this?" I grab the forgotten candlestick and hurl it an inch from his face, neither of us even flinching when it shatters against the wall behind him.

"Why? Why *me*?" My voice cracks as my knees give out underneath me. "Why did Fate curse me? Why does it keep causing me such pain and then keep dangling impossible ways out of it? Just . . . just . . . why?"

And though I started this line of questioning brimming with hot rage, by the end, it's evaporated, leaving the cold bitter dregs of my earlier grief in its stead.

And worst still, he's seeing it all. Hearing it all. Yet saying nothing.

Just standing there as my entire body shakes with exhausted sobs, clenching and unclenching his hand over and over until the oath cut across my palm starts throbbing in time with his movements.

I cradle my aching hand against my chest when I can't bear it anymore.

"Get out," I seethe, throwing his own words from our first deal back in his face like a dagger I wish I had.

But then, as swift as the lightning bolting through his eyes, he reaches down and snatches that very hand, pulling me to him until I'm flush against his front, another mimicry of that night we first met. My breath hitches at the thought that I went too far, that he's going to force a deal, that he's going to cut me again—

But then he unfurls my fingers that are clenched against his chest, brings his lips to the pounding oath cut at the center of my palm, and murmurs, "As you wish, *wife*." His breath hot against my clammy skin before he releases it.

Then he storms out the door, slamming it with a bang.

And somehow manages to leave me even more angry, lost, and alone than before.

Chapter 13

HOT TEARS FILL MY EYES AS FRIGID DEATH FILLS *his.*

But only when the gold of his irises finally dulls to the color of the earth do I let them fall.

Let them soak the thirsty ground with salt instead of ash and blood. Let them grieve for the life cut too short. Mourn for the life we could have had.

I toss my head to the burning sky, my long keening wail ripping through the rain of soot and embers, joining the hundreds of others in terrible soul-wrenching harmony.

But the strangers' angry shouts and thundering approach cut short my lament, forcing me to get up.

To remember my promise to try.

To live.

For me and my people, those who returned to the earth . . . and those yet to come. Hoping Fate will guide me when my mind and heart cannot.

Hoping it will protect me if my gift cannot.

I jolt awake, my heart pounding so hard, so damn fast, it's as if I hadn't just awaken from sleep, but had been dead and had now been wrenched back to life.

Trembling, I fall back against my headboard, watching the night embrace the dawn through the thin chiffon of my shifting bed curtains. My skin is damp, my breaths shallow as I attempt to breathe through the seismic shift in time, self . . . reality. Never in my life have I dreamed like this—like the indomitable laws that govern the empyrean fracture just for me once I sleep before seaming themselves back together once I awaken.

I've had several such dreams in the past week since my self-imposed confinement. Since my world changed forever. But I'm too damn tired to even curse Fate for stealing my sleep after having stolen everything else.

Rolling my heavy head to the side, I stare blankly at the forgotten spread of yogurt and honey, bread and oil, nuts and fruit on my nightstand, which comes and goes daily despite being barely touched. The full pot of tea that has gone cold, like my body and heart.

I avert my gaze when it lands on Baba's signet ring, left for me by Mori the morning after his death.

"It was always meant for you, albi," she murmured as she set it on the teak wood.

I grit my teeth against the memory of it gleaming on his finger when he would braid my hair or open his arms to me for an embrace. When he sealed the law that would change our relationship forever. When he grasped my hand with his for the very last time. I shove the damn thing into the table's drawer, slamming it closed just to make the memories stop.

I let out a bone-weary sigh. Mori will be here soon with her forced joviality, her mock offense at my lack of appetite, at my unwillingness to *try*. With her demands that I get out of bed and out of this room. She will pretend that everything is the same as it's always been outside these four walls, and when I say nothing, do nothing but turn over in bed, turn away from her, she will brush my open hair in silence until I feign sleep and she leaves again.

She will do all of this, but never during her visits, not even when she gave me the ring, will she mention Baba. Nor the healer.

The old Maliki and the new Maliki.

My father and my new husband.

As if they don't exist. Or as if she worries I'll cease to exist if I think about either of them.

Little does she know that they are all I think about any-way—Baba, whose life and legacy I ruined despite everything I did to preserve it, and the healer, whose victory was built upon the rubble of that ruin.

And yet . . . he hasn't come to revel in it. Nor to discuss his new *deal* about *The Book of Names*.

In fact, he hasn't come at all.

The first two nights, I waited for him from the moment the sun set over the harsh peaks of the Ma'asa to its rise over the lolling waves of the Sakoon, part of me fearing that, with my lack of cooperation in his next quest, he would change his mind about the consummation of our marriage. That he would decide to take what was already his by the terms of our oath and by those of our tradition, my measly permission be damned.

While another part of me waited for him in anticipation, wishing he would just try it, even *daring* him to, so if I had to suffer from the interminable pain of hurting him because of the oath, I wouldn't be the only one. And if I had to die from it, I would at least take him down with me.

And then sometimes . . . sometimes in the deepest, quietest parts of the night, I would hear the deepest, quietest part of me—the part that thought not about ending his life, but about ending my own. That imagined the curse lifting from my land and people as it lifted from my body.

That found complete peace in the possibility.

I exhale as the lulling thought floats over me again just now, settling over all others as gently as a gossamer veil. No, not a veil—because I deserve no such thing—but a death shroud. Like the ones covering the rows of Unnamed bodies in the cantons.

Like the one covering Baba now.

So much damn devastation. All because of me.

Tears slip down my cheeks yet again as I peel back my sheets and bed curtain with an unsteady hand. My gaze drifts to the latticed window where I often sit for long hours each night, watching the Citadel and cantons beyond the Keep. Watch the lights not only return to our city at their usual times but spread across the wall as well—like stars that somehow escaped the suffocating confines of their orbits, now free to scatter their majesty across the sky.

What would it be like to be free like those lights, those stars? Those morning clouds peeking through the latticework now?

I pad barefoot across the warm rug and the cold limestone floor until I see the sky more closely through the carved crevices. Until I feel the soft, comforting sunbeams poke through the openings upon my face, beckoning me to be with them. To join them.

But their warm, caressing whispers are not enough.

Because everything within me is so damn cold.

So I throw the carved wooden shutters open. Gripping either one, I pull myself onto my knees on the seat level with the ledge. Spreading my arms wide, I close my eyes and throw my head back. Imagine myself as a phoenix about to soar up, up, up . . .

And *lean.*

"*Reim*!"

The sound of my name is like a bolt to my brain, and I jerk back, whipping my head toward the voice.

Only to be confronted with a familiar set of quicksilver eyes that somehow hold more concern for me this morning than when I first encountered them in a Burrow hovel many nights ago. The night that ruined everything.

"Reim. Fate, what are you—"

"*Lies*!" I hiss, long and low at the architect, still gripping the shutters. The gentle, welcoming breeze at my front no match for the hostile gust of the storm brewing within.

He halts.

The morning light that was just embracing me moves to circle him instead, turning his neatly braided silver-white hair and shaved undercut into a halo. How I wish it were a noose instead.

"Excuse me?"

"Lies. All lies," I say, enunciating each word, still precariously tethered to the ledge. "Maybe not your words, but your forged smiles, your deceptive kindness, your fabricated empathy. You knew who I was, who my father was the moment you saw me. You all planned this. Planned to lure me into caring about sifr when he was imprisoned, then into letting him out. Into him leading me to you and the healer, and then into making the blood oath—"

"Did we lie, Reim?" he interrupts this time, resuming his careful approach. "Or did you *assume* the Unnamed were too stupid, too lazy to know who governs our lives? Who signs our executions?"

I say nothing, hating that despite my anger, he's right. I *did* assume that. I shift my body back into the room.

"And how about *your* role in this?" he presses, stepping closer. "Did you not get what you asked for? Was your father not healed?"

"Only for him to be killed a month later!" I sputter, letting go of the shutters and dropping onto the seat.

"And how many of our people did he kill in that month, hmm?" he asks. "How many families ripped apart, how many children suddenly without parents—parents without children?"

I don't dare answer him this time. I know the number. I had them counted and documented every single damn day.

"So yes, we knew who you were," he says. "We've always known. But we also knew that ending him was the only way to end his reign of terror."

My heart clenches to the point of pain.

"But you didn't know *him*," I bite back, attempting to stand tall, but somehow feeling smaller than ever.

"And the fact you don't want to face is that neither did you, Reim," he counters, now right in front of me. His eyes take on that familiar sheen of empathy, his mouth stretching into that compassionate half smile I remember so well from the night we met. "Not all of him, anyway."

I squeeze my eyes shut until the hurt there is enough to dull the one in my chest. Until a tear slips down the sharp plane of my cheek to give my bleeding heart some reprieve. I hear his words, I understand them, but I don't know if I can accept them.

Baba, with his integrity, his pride, his sense of honor, he could have listened to reason. He could have changed. He could've—

But he didn't, a small niggling voice reminds me.

He already had the chance to change, but he didn't. He chose Order above everything else. Above everyone else. Always.

And it was devastating.

I snap my eyes open, forcing them away from him so he won't see the confusion—the doubt about my father that's been festering for the past month—spreading within me once more. So he won't see the doubt about *myself* tangled there with it, the same doubt that led to this damn mess.

"I would like to rest now, please," I murmur.

The silence stretches between us, his alert gaze not leaving my exhausted face or my wringing hands for endless seconds before he finally breaks it.

"I'm afraid I can't let you do that," he sighs. "Your healer woman fears for your health and implored me to talk sense to you today. And frankly, being here with you now, I can see for myself the extent of grief's toll on you."

Reaching behind me, he pulls the shutters shut with a decisive thud, then steps back.

"But this is not the way, Reim." He glances at the window and then back at me. "If I can make one more suggestion, it would be that if you can't find a way to live for yourself, then do what the Unnamed have learned to do their entire lives— live for your people."

"I have told your guards to take you about the castle, the Citadel, the cantons, wherever you like," he calls as he starts walking away. "I told them that you are the Malika of this kingdom, and it would be the best for your people to see you among them."

I doubt that greatly.

"How could you do this to us?"

"She has cursed us all!"

I grit my teeth against the memories of the bludgeoning

words. But then again, he's right. This isn't the way. What *would* happen to my people if I had killed myself? With me dead, would the healer's people uphold his promise at our wedding to not harm mine? Would mine exact bloody revenge on them? Would there be endless war and death?

I lock eyes with the architect one more time before he sees himself out of my chambers with a small nod. And then, right as the latch clicks shut, I take a bolstering breath, march over to my wardrobe, pull on my leathers, and start braiding my hair. Prepare myself the best I can for what lies ahead before the past tries to seize me again.

I was willing to die for what I did to my kingdom. But am I willing to live with it? Despite my conflicting thoughts, I know that's the one thing Baba would have done. The one thing he always raised me to do.

Heaving my bedchamber door open, I find my newly ap-pointed guards about to collide into each other in surprise at my sudden appearance.

"*Khur*—I mean yes, Your Grace?" the two of them say in unison before glaring peevishly at one another.

I tie off the end of my braid and whip it over my shoulder.

"Take me to the king."

Chapter 14

AND THEN I TOLD HIM THAT HE COULD TAKE his coin and shove it up his—"

"Oh, Blessed Fate! No, you did not!"

"I couldn't believe it either."

"No, I literally mean you did not do that. As in, that never happened."

"You calling me a liar?"

"Nooo, but I did stop you from being one right now. Stopped you from biting off your tongue to save your face."

"My face is the same as your face."

"Except, I'm not a dramatic man."

It's been like this since we left my room, and I don't know whether to stop my guards in order to save myself from a burgeoning headache or let them keep going at each other in hopes of escaping them—and then . . . and then . . .

Gutter that fire. Deprive it of air.

Baba's mantra to curb my impulsivity comes as readily to my mind as the tears come to my eyes.

He's right. No more escaping. Not this reality and not this life. Not when they're of my own making.

"Malika?"

"Malika!"

I shake my head to clear it and find two pairs of identical gray eyes watching me with concern.

"Yes, er . . . I'm sorry. I don't know what to call you," I admit sheepishly, blinking away the wetness in my eyes.

"You can call me the queen's guard," says the strapping man, whose massive size rivals Radnor's, whose dimpled smile rivals Tamir's, and whose rumbling voice rivals the heal—

"And you?" I whip my face to the woman, slamming the door on the uninvited thought of my *husband*, enthusiastically imagining doing the same to his face.

"You can call her the queen's jester—*Oof!*" the man answers for her right before doubling over in pain. The tall, agile woman, smirking while flexing the fist she just drove into his stomach, gives me a wink.

"My people call me the elder," she says, flipping her long tawny braid over her shoulder. "And this big fella right here"—she shoves a shoulder into the man's giant bicep—"we call him the baby."

He scowls down at her but doesn't deny it.

"Better than being called phoenix-khur sweepers, which is what we did on the farms in Canton One before the healer personally chose us for this job." He puffs up his already large chest with pride.

"You're siblings?" I ask, though apart from their vastly different body sizes, they share the same hair color, the same almond eyes, the same mischievous grins, making it obvious they must be.

"Yes, twins, unfortunately," the elder mutters in confirmation, sticking out her tongue at her younger brother. "Our parents died ages ago during a fire in the almazi groves. And it's just been the two of us since."

"Oh," I say instead of telling them anything about myself in return—about being an only child, about knowing little about my mother except that she died while laboring with me, and especially about how what I thought I knew about my father has only grown increasingly unclear as well.

And besides, these two are not here to become my friends. They were assigned to be my guards—or rather, my wardens—and I, their Maliki's prisoner.

The thought of him makes me turn my attention toward the clang of weapons and the thud of bodies hitting the sand-dusted floor of the castle's vast training room. It's busier, fuller, than I've ever seen it before. Men, women, adolescents, and even children are grouped by age and capability throughout the open-air amphitheater while an Unnamed trainer and a Vuorian soldier monitor, coach and refine each fighter's technique before sending them off to spar with the others.

"Hmm, he's usually here this time of day," the elder murmurs as we scan the oval floor below from the observation balustrade encircling the space.

"If you mean the Maliki, he *is* here," a familiar voice calls from behind. I spin around to find Tamir making his way toward us. "But I didn't expect you to be."

I'm so happy to see him no worse for wear from the cuff to the back of his head on the day of the Bicentennial that I almost forget myself, forget my role in his suffering, and run to embrace him.

Almost.

My arms fall to my sides at the last second as common sense saves me from doing just that.

"Tamir," I breathe instead. "You're . . . you're . . ."

"Alive?" He barks a humorless laugh. "I was able to keep my life and barter for the other warriors' as well because I promised to train the Unnamed in combat."

Then his lips thin.

"However, I highly doubt that our new Maliki will keep us around after our purpose is served."

As his friend, I want to deny it, to tell him not to think like that. But we were soldiers before we were friends, and speaking plainly about the risks and outcomes of any operation is ingrained in our training and essential to the ranks we both carry.

Or rather, the ones we once did.

I am no longer the High Commander, and he is no longer the captain of just a few weeks ago, giving me the daily report. Nor are we two friends seeing each other safe and well for the first time after a life-changing event. Yet we are also not quite a newly crowned Malika and her faithful subject, either.

"I will never let that happen, Tamir," I say instead of the many apologies, regrets, and laments that sit on the tip of my tongue. "I will do whatever it tak—"

"No," he returns instead of the many insults, accusations, and disappointments he could have lobbed at me too.

All of them deserved.

I almost wish he had.

"No, Reim, if anyone is going to do something, it's going to be me. I wasn't able to do a damn thing the day of the Bicentennial. Not for your father and not for you. I failed you."

He hangs his head, and I step closer and grab his hand.

"Tamir, look at me. You're wrong. I'm the one who failed you. I'm the one who dragged you into all of this to begin with. I'm the one who stole your keys, freed sifr—the Unnamed boy. Made you lie for my decisions."

He shakes his head as if he's not buying it.

"Listen, Tamir. As your Malika, I order you to stay safe. To protect yourself and protect the kingdom. I have to sort my role in this for myself. You can't protect me from the consequences of my own mistakes."

But before he can object further, the baby rumbles under his breath, "Er . . . Your Grace."

But I don't need him to say anything more, for a fiery prodding begins between my shoulders before scouring down my arm. Down, down, down until it pools, sparks, *ignites* the invisible scar slashed across my palm.

A type of prodding that can only belong to one person.

Even though I came here to seek the king, in our ongoing game of cat and mouse, predator and prey, he found me first.

"Hello, wife," he says, and the sounds of training, jeering, of the entire world stop. Just stop.

I walk my gaze over my shoulder to meet his, and it's as if I'm staring directly into the sun at its highest orbit. But despite being burned by its blinding attention, I dare not look away.

The healer stands in the central sparring ring, dressed in a combination of chain mail and fighting leathers that mold to every brutal inch of his honed body, watching Tamir and me, his brows buckled, a sharp frown carving across his already chiseled face.

But instead of cowering, it just makes me furious as well.

I mean, what did he expect? That I would just stay locked up in my room like a good political prisoner for the rest of my days? And how would that have helped him with this new quest he thrust upon me to find his damn book? Not that I even believe it exists, but he doesn't know that.

That stupid, insane, barbari—

"Why don't you come down here and tell me what you're thinking instead of just wearing it all over your face?" he booms, turning the simultaneous force of the room's combined attention on me.

My face heats, and I turn away lest he see it, turning my roiling anger inward. *Fate.* How does he do that to me so easily? And more importantly, why do I let it, let *him*, bother me so?

I stand up straighter.

The dahak wants me to come down into his den? Fine.

Spinning, I let my fury overtake my fear and propel me down the stairs into the expansive yard below, the curious crowd clearing a path through the dust and sweat straight to him.

But with every step closer, I am reminded not only of how huge he is in person, but how massive in persona, how intimidating in his mere presence. Reminded of the last thing I said to him on our wedding night. Of how I broke apart, surrendered to my feelings of weakness instead of fighting them—and him—as I should have.

My flaming anger, my blazing courage that drove me down this path are nothing but sputtering embers by the time I'm in front of him. My tongue but a shriveled husk of baluur as it attempts to form the right words.

"M-may we speak in private?" I ask in a raspy voice, instantly regretting it when he tilts his head at whatever he must perceive from my hesitant words, my nervous demeanor. Maybe he's thinking about how pathetic I was that night too.

And then, he glances over my shoulder at Tamir, who must have followed me, and hardens his expression even further.

"You can say what you need to say here," he answers, crossing his arms, though he lowers his voice so only I can hear him.

"Fine." I narrow my eyes. Of course he would make things more difficult. "I would like to attend the Jirga meetings again."

"Would you now?" he rumbles, a little louder this time.

"Yes," I hiss under my breath as I sense the crowd inching closer to hear what's going on.

Fate, I hate him. But at least hate is something I can work with.

"I am this kingdom's Malika, and I have a right not only to know, but also to dictate how it is run. I have been at every single Jirga meeting since I was of age and know every single edict, amendment, and order made within those walls. And there is a lot of change happening right now. I need to be there to make sure it goes as peacefully as possible . . . for both peoples."

He moves his fingers over his beard for an annoyingly long time before looking back at me. "Be that as it may, *I* am this kingdom's Maliki, and *I* have a right to decide whose advice to take."

Then he sweeps his gilded gaze over my body in a way that would have felt suggestive if his disappointed *tsk* at the end of his perusal didn't set my last nerve on fire instead. "And I'm not so sure that scrawny body can stand much longer, let alone endure the fortitude necessary to lea—"

An abandoned sword is in my hand and notched at the side of his throat before he can finish the sentence.

"A deal, then?" I shred the question through my clenched teeth. "I know how much you *love* making them."

He waves off his men who unsheathe their own swords when he sees that I'm in no pain from the oath, so not threatening him, but he cocks his brow as if intrigued by where this is going nonetheless.

"Since you think I'm so weak, so incapable, I'm sure you wouldn't mind if we test that theory." I press the blade into his pristine brown skin a fraction further. "You and me. Sword to sword. The first one to cut the other is the winner."

And then I say, with a confidence I haven't felt in a long time, "And *when* it's me, you will allow me to attend the meetings."

As quickly as the lightning flashing through his eyes, he seizes my sword hand at the wrist and slides the side of his neck along the sharpened steel until a trickle of blood slips from his self-imposed nick, which heals instantly.

I blink and find his rough cheek grazing mine.

I blink again, and now his lips are skating over the tapered shell of my ear.

And he's whispering just for me.

"And when it's me, you will allow me to attend to *you* in our be—"

I gasp, cutting off his lewd words, his audacity at saying them in front of everyone.

And then I rip my wrist from his hold and *launch*.

He lets out a deep, throaty chuckle as he dips and dodges my erratic swings, until I belatedly realize he started the match before I even made the first strike, his words as effective a weapon against me as his sword. Just as they were on our wedding night.

Well, not anymore. Two can play this game. And I've always been a quick learner.

I step back, regrouping my mode of attack.

Then take aim.

Release.

"All of you men are the same. Big talk, little . . ." I trail off, flicking my gaze down his body this time, pausing halfway so there can be no mistake about what I'm referring to.

Though the onlookers jeer in appreciation of my parry, that's not the part that hits its mark with the healer.

"*All* of you men?" he growls as one of his men throws him a sword and he stalks toward me. "Exactly how many are you talking about, Reim?"

I block his next strike and circle his blade down and away from me, the approving din of the room only emboldening me further.

"Oh, you understand what I mean," I tut airily. "One tends to lose count after a while."

More laughs and hoots, but he's quick to recover and comes at me from the other side, while I just spin out of his saber's way.

"You know what I think?" he says as he faces me once again, releasing a flurry of swings and stabs that make my mind and body work to keep him at bay—that make me feel *alive* for the first time all week.

"What?" I pant, my sword at the ready, circling him as he circles me.

"I think I was right the night we first met." He drops to the floor and kicks my legs out from under me in the next breath, straddling my hips in the one after that. "You *do* enjoy lying."

I buck my hips, trying to free myself from the shackle of his legs, only for him to bend closer, pressing his own hips down harder against mine.

I still.

"But you know what else," he murmurs, his face so close to mine that his braids and hair, now loose from their tie, fall into a curtain around us, his phoenix feather stroking my temple, his breath heating my cheeks. "I think I'm starting to enjoy your lying too."

I somehow swallow past the thickening air.

Instead of guttering the fire like I always have, I stoked it.

Teased it.

Played with it.

And now I have no choice but to feel its burn.

Our audience's catcalls bring me out of my smoldering thoughts, and I realize that for all of our back and forth, neither of us has delivered the winning blow.

So I push up until he has no option but to lock his fiery gaze with my icy one. No option but to keep it there as I say, "Well, I hope you enjoy it as much as having me at the Jirga meetings."

And then I slice off the very end of one of his braids. He flicks his confused gaze to it thumping to the ground and then back to me.

"I said the first cut. I didn't mention where."

The crowd raves as I roll out from underneath him and spring to my feet, pushing my own hair behind my shoulder as I look around at all of them, my self-consciousness returning once again.

I look back at the healer rising from the floor, bowing low to me before standing as tall, as self-assured as ever. That damn smirk, as annoying as ever.

Why is he smiling when he lost? And in front of all his people, nonetheless? And why do I feel like I'm missing something crucial, yet again? He told me he enjoys my lies, but the problem is, I don't know what to make of his.

Something tells me to stay far away from finding that answer, that it's more dangerous than I realize, while something else tells me to look closer, dig deeper—that I'm on the precipice of something that has the potential to change everything.

But something has already done that, I remind myself.

No, *someone*.

Someone who has already fooled me, tricked me, *used* me to get what he wanted.

The same someone who is standing in front of me now, trying to do it again.

"Listen," he murmurs when he's right in front of me, dropping his voice, though it still sounds deafening. "I've been thinking about the question you asked the other night. Why I—"

"I don't want to hear it." I hold up a hand between us as a hot punch of shame at the memory of my weakness threatens to overtake my righteous anger once again. "I don't want to know your selfish reasons for why you do anything."

Pressing his lips together, he just looks at me for a long time.

"I see," he says finally, before clearing his throat. "Have you thought over my offer?"

I glance behind him to see that everyone has dispersed, resuming their drills and exercises as before, leaving us in semi-seclusion. I cross my arms over my chest.

"If you mean, have I thought about finding your name to end our supposed 'marriage'? Why, yes. Yes, I have."

I swear his eyes almost glow at my response.

"And . . .?" he says, and his voice gets impossibly lower, curious. Maybe even hopeful.

Perfect.

"Annnd, I have come up with many possible options without the help of your fairytale book. Let's see." I start counting fingers. "There's Wretch, Liar, Thief, Murderer, Monster . . . and oh! How could I forget? My absolute favorite—Heaping Pile of Dragon Khur. Or just Khur for short."

There's silence, just gnawing silence for a long, pulseless heartbeat where I'm convinced that I did it. I won't have to worry about hurting him or myself ever again because he is sure to kill me now and end both our misery.

But then he laughs.

And not just the hooked smile at his lips or amused flashes of gold dust in his irises, but a full, booming laugh that forces his eyes closed, his mouth open. That transforms his entire face.

Anger and awe battle within me as I stare and stare. His stony face that I've only ever imagined as carved from the Ma'asa itself, that I've only ever seen glowering in contempt or smirking in condescension . . . when he laughs, it's arresting. It's striking. It's almost . . . almost—

No.

My shame at feeling anything other than disgust rises just as his mirth calms and his eyes open, falling upon me in the same serious way they always have, filling me with a sudden awareness I've never had before.

And what's more, he looks at me as if he may sense it too.

But it's another lie. Another trap. He needs something from me, my cooperation as well as my knowledge to find this cipher, find this book, and I won't be fooled into thinking it's anything else ever again.

"You're wrong," he says as if he's just heard me. Heard it all.

"W-what?" I say, caught between incredulity and conviction that he somehow did.

"My name. Unfortunately, none of your 'guesses' are right, as amusing as they were."

"How would you even know if it was the right one?" I manage to ask despite my muddled thoughts.

He considers this question for a long beat, all traces of amusement falling away.

"You just do," he murmurs.

And another jolt of awareness charges down my spine. Another sense of conviction that we are not talking about names at all. But about something that perhaps runs even deeper than our individual sense of self.

You just do.

A deliberate cough sounds from somewhere behind us.

I turn to find Tamir standing with my guards, an unreadable look upon his face as he watches the two of us.

"Come, Reim. I'll debrief you on the past week. There's a lot to know before you go before the Jirga."

I nod and make to move around the healer when he stays me with a touch to the crook of my elbow. Gently. Just like before.

My eyes jump up to his.

"I welcome you to spar with me again, wife," he says, his voice rumbling from somewhere deep inside his chest. And just as I'm about to tell him not to call me that, he goes on, "But next time, let's make the stakes even higher."

And then, with one last furtive glance at my reddening cheeks, he slips back into the crowd once again.

Chapter 15

YOUR GRACE, ARE YOU SURE YOU DON'T NEED
us with you—"

"In that room with all those people?"

"Fate, I hate it when you finish my sentences,"
the baby mutters while his sister grins.

What must that be like? The ease of a genu-
ine relationship, the innate trust to be our true selves around
someone, knowing you won't be punished for it?

Knowing that they love you unconditionally.

But that's not fair. Baba loved me unconditionally. Except
the last month of his life, when he said what he did during our
disagreement.

Another thorn of doubt pricks my heart at the memory.

"Yes, I am sure." I give them a tight smile as we approach
the familiar carved wooden doors of the Jirga chambers.

"Besides, the Maliki will be there," I try to reassure them,
though the same words do nothing but unsettle me.

He will be there. There with those eyes that see more than they should. With that impenetrable mask he wears over his already harsh face. That equally rigid armor he wears over his already unyielding body.

"Stay here, please," I say too loudly to my guards as I push open the doors, pushing the unwanted thoughts away in the same motion.

Only for all other thoughts to disappear as well when I see everyone's eyes pivot toward me. And mine pivot out of habit to the head of the table, where Baba would always stand to welcome me with the soft murmur of my name, ground me with the easy spread of his smile, embrace me with the steady strength of his arms.

But he's not there.

"My queen," the healer rumbles by way of greeting instead, and all the attention vanishes from me and surrounds him. It's been almost three decades since that honorific was used in our halls, and the Vuorian Jirga members look perplexed about whom he could even be referring to. While I'm equally shocked that there are Vuorian Jirga members here at all.

"Reim." His voice rolls like summer thunder, long and low, to dispel any remaining confusion on the matter. "Come join us, *wife*."

And just like that, the entirety of my discomfort and surprise evaporates.

Only for my ire to replace it.

Only for my common sense to prevent me from reprimanding him for using that damn word in front of all these people.

Only for him to know my internal dilemma, smile that little half smile, and revel in his unfair victory.

For now.

Letting go of my death grip on the door handle, I walk toward my usual chair two seats down from the head of the table, wringing my empty hands together—hands I'd much rather wring his neck with instead.

"No," the healer calls again. "Your place is next to mine. Basteel may take your previous seat."

Basteel sputters his disbelief for a moment, but with one steely look from the healer, he gathers his parchments and relocates.

I want to demand that the healer tell me what his game is, tell me what he could possibly want from my proximity other than showing off his trophy, his damned victory cup, and my humiliation that fills it to the brim.

But I say nothing. I just lower myself to the vacated seat and decide to appear as unaffected by his torment as possible. For what bigger loss to a tyrant than his victim ignoring his tyranny.

But as I do my best to disregard his keen perusal, his imposing physical presence next to me, I am caught off guard by the architect's own intense gaze from across the table. But where the healer's nearness makes every inch of me feel alert, exposed, and vulnerable, the architect's calms.

Soothes.

And I instantly feel better. He sends me an encouraging smile before turning back to the king, who clears his throat and resumes.

"As I was saying, I promised to rule over Vuor not by using my gift to subjugate any one people, but by creating opportunity for *all* the citizens under the Crown. That is why I have kept members of both people as part of the Jirga."

"Easy words," a Vuorian member scoffs as soon as he's done speaking, "but creating 'opportunity' of any kind for your people will certainly mean lessening it for ours. It will mean diminishing our resources and our lands. All of *our* hard work."

The healer eases back in his chair, the heel of his boot notching on the opposite knee, while his fingers come up to steeple at his lips as he bores his gaze into the man.

The architect frowns at the healer and grips the arms of his chair as if to rise and intervene, but the healer bats a hand at him to stand down.

"*Your* hard work," the king murmurs to himself at last, but the words somehow still crash upon the room like a land-slide. "Right. Because it was *your* people digging for baluur who were crushed in the mines, right? *Your* people who were starved when resisting their poor conditions, right? *Yours* who bled and died so *mine* could have warmth and comfort, right?"

And then he drops his leg back down and leans forward, banging his hands onto the tabletop and making the man jump. "No, it was *our* hard work, and it was *you* who benefited from it. No longer will that be the case. We will find a different way to distribute Vuor's resources. Equally. Fairly."

The Vuorian Jirga member says nothing but wears displeasure on his face just the same.

But then a familiar voice bellows from down the table at him. "Oh for Fate's sake, go take a khur before that entitled stick gets lodged up your ass."

The room bursts in a cacophony of gasps and guffaws.

I peek over to discover the old miner who the healer was helping on the night of our blood oath standing, his spindly arms bracing the edge of the table.

Well, nothing wrong with his throat now.

"I'm older than most of you in this room," he goes on, sweeping his trembling finger over all of us in one long arc, "and that means I've seen the best of this damn place and the worst of it. And these cocky Vuorian khurs, sitting in their filched finery, obsessed with ownership, will never change. Will never be *fair*."

And then he pins his wizened gaze on the healer.

"And you, my boy, have to learn that you can't heal it all. That sometimes you just have to raze it to the ground and start again. That's what they would have done to us if they hadn't needed us to do their labor, and you damn well know it."

The Unnamed members howl their assent.

Surely, he doesn't mean that. Surely, it's just an airing of frustration.

I look to the healer for reassurance, and then quickly look away, shocked by my turning to him for anything, let alone that. Mercifully, for once, his honed attention is on everyone except me.

"*Quiet*," he thunders before pushing back his chair, rising to his feet like a mountain birthing from a quaking earth. "I did not say that I will not do what needs to be done, if it comes to it. But, I will not do unto them what they have done unto us. I will not make them into savages, into animals, into monsters in my mind. I will treat them as the humans they are, and expect them to use their reasoning and intellect to resolve this matter I have put to them."

The crowd starts arguing anew until he slams his fist upon the obsidian tabletop again.

"And if they don't," he snarls, "then we treat them as *humans* who have chosen the wrath that befalls them."

The din of approval from the Unnamed members is now louder than ever, joined by stomping feet and rhythmic grunts that force my heart to match the beat of their war drum.

The rest of the room, the Vuorian members in particular, are uneasy at best, overtly afraid at worst. Oh, how they looked at me only months ago, with tight lips hiding razored words, with eyes narrowed in shuttered disdain. Yet even then, even *now*, despite the horrors and scheming I have witnessed them be capable of, they are still my responsibility. Maybe now more than ever.

My chair creaks as I slide it back and stand.

The room goes still.

"I—I would like to make one request on my people's be-half," I begin, my small voice loud in my own ears, competing with the pulse already whooshing there.

And then I make the mistake of glancing up from my trembling hands, only to be assaulted by the attention of the entire room once again.

My mind blanks, my throat dries.

Oh Baba, how I need your sheltering smile, your steady support right now.

"Go ahead, wife," the new Maliki murmurs, pulling me from my panic, dousing me with irritation instead.

Fate, that word again. I swear he's doing it on purpose. But what purpose, for the life of me, I don't know.

I glare at him.

He smirks at me.

"I ask that you give them time to adapt. To learn." I spin back to address the room, my anger at the healer sharpening my focus as I find my words once again. "This, *all* of this, is a major change. It is beyond anything my people have ever faced. I ask that you approach this with patience, with mercy—"

"Enough!" Basteel leaps to his feet.

"That is enough!" He stabs a pudgy beringed finger in my direction. "Patience? Mercy? For Fate's sake, we shouldn't even be in this position. We are the rightful heirs to this land, and you make us sound weak, desperate, *pathetic* in front of our enemies. You make us sound like *you*."

His face starts turning red, his mouth frothing more and more with every word.

"You, who would embarrass yourself, embarrass your father, your entire kingdom with your outlandish sympathies for the Unnamed in this very room when he was alive. You, who then went against your father's own edict to break out that child spy, then made a deal with this devil. You, who are the sole cause of the king's death!"

The other Vuorians shout in agreement, and instead of blushing at his venomous words, my face drains of all color, my lungs of all air.

The memory of Baba's unseeing gaze, the blood pooling around his body, flashes before my eyes.

I swallow bile. Basteel's right, for once. I did everything he's accusing me of. I'm the reason for all these awful outcomes. Fate, what made me think I had any right to speak just now? Any right to have even come here?

This was a terrible, terrible mistake.

But just as my eyes dart to the door, just as my mind contemplates making a mad dash toward it, my vision starts blurring.

Then fading.

Blurring and fading.

Blurring and fading.

Until I am blinded by such brutal brightness that I swear I am about to faint.

Or die.

Yes, this must be what it feels like to reach death's door, I think irrationally as I bring up my hand to shield my eyes against the all-encompassing light. A light that, without a doubt, can only belong to one person. But when I attempt to look upon its source, upon the harbinger of death himself, I realize that the light isn't just emanating from the healer.

The light *is* him.

From the flaming rings of the healer's irises to the expanding rays of molten sun radiating from him and into him, the light is in every way him.

"It is *you* who embarrasses yourself, zealot," the king's voice booms, severing all other screams, all other sound on its singular shattering path to Basteel.

"It is *you* who brings shame to your people. It is *you* who dishonors your Malika," he continues as slithering shadow begins to leach from his light, swirling with the flaming rays until he is brightest day and darkest night all at once.

Until he is the passing of time itself.

"And just for that, you deserve to be dishonored in return. You deserve to have your skin flayed strip by painful strip off your sniveling body until you can't endure the agony any longer and you *beg* me to heal you," he thunders as I grip the edge of the table, attempting to endure his surging wrath.

"And I will, you piece of ajnoob khur. I will heal you and then I will flay you all over again. Flay and heal. Flay and heal. Until you are as weak and as pathetic as you accused my wife of being."

In the blink of an eye, his massive whirlwind of shadow and light unfolds from his body.

Wraps itself around Basteel.

Squeezing him.

Crushing him.

"And you know when I will finally end your misery?" he seethes as Basteel begins to choke from the pressure around his throat. "When she asks me to show you 'outlandish sympathy.' Asks me to have undeserved 'mercy' on you, even when you have never once shown it to my kind."

And then he lets go.

The lashing tendrils of shadow, the whipping ropes of light, fly back into him once again.

And when my vision returns as well, so does the image of Basteel tumbling back into his seat, coughing and wheezing, while the other Vuorians silently simmer in theirs. And though I cannot feel any pity for him, I can very much feel a surge of embarrassment for myself and renewed anger at the king.

How dare he do this? How dare he use me as a reason to

punish others? How dare he make me look like I need him? Make me look as weak as Basteel just accused me of?

But I wait to unbridle it. This shaking assembly has already been through enough because of me.

I stay silent as the agenda resumes and the topic of my father's burial is discussed. Hold my tears as Vuorian Jirga members confirm that he was buried next to my mother and that our last rites were performed over him with honor.

I knew he had been, as Mori had informed me of the procession days ago, but my heart was too much of a coward to attend in the end.

Not soon enough, the meeting ends and everyone starts filtering out of the chamber.

Until only I, the architect, the healer, and the elderly Unnamed miner are left. The old man pauses next to me on his way out to give me a khur-eating grin.

"Won your lovers' spat that night I came to him to heal me, did you?" He cackles, knocking his knobby shoulder into mine, as if sharing an inside joke. "I knew you would, my girl. Hard to resist beauty like yours, even for an old dahak like him," he says as if he's a spry phoenix himself.

But then his toothless smile drops, his eyes suddenly serious as he snatches up my hands between his warm ones.

"But that being said, your sharp mind and pure heart are prizes in and of themselves. Never let anyone tell you otherwise, especially not these Vuorian khur-bags, you hear me?"

I just nod, shocked by the unexpected adamance of his words.

And then, with a single dismissive wave at the king and architect, he's gone.

I barely wait for the door to close behind him before spinning on the healer standing at his spot at the head of the table.

"How dare you?" I seethe at him. "How dare you threaten someone's life on my behalf? Basteel was only speaking the truth of what I've done. I could have handled it."

But the healer doesn't move a single muscle. He just stares at me with crossed arms until I could swear he's turned into the rocky cliffs I often imagine him to be carved from.

"Answer me!"

"Well, it doesn't seem that I am needed here." The architect bows as he takes his leave, easing the door shut behind him lest he trip an already precarious mine.

"What would you have me do instead, Reim?" the healer snarls once we are alone.

"Nothing," I return in the same acidic tone. "That's the point."

"Because *this*"—I point between the two of us—"whatever this is, no matter how many times you taunt me by calling me your wife, is not real. Will *never* be real. We are not in this together. I don't want you. I don't need you."

He tilts his head and cracks his neck side to side but continues to hold his tongue as I release mine.

"And I *definitely* don't need you to help me or defend me. I've dealt with their cruel words all my life. I don't need you to save me," I snap, stepping closer and closer to him with every word until I can feel the heat radiating from his stiff body and see the spinning gold of his eyes. "Especially since all you've done is trap me in your own way."

His eyes flash dangerously at that final remark, and he breaks his silence at last. "I gave you an out, if you recall."

"Right. How could I forget?" I sneer. "Finding your cipher. Your precious book. You're just setting me up for another failure."

"I can't lie," he murmurs down at me, his cold breath only fanning the flames of my already blazing cheeks.

"Oh yes, you can. And you can murder too," I hiss back, done being afraid in this room, but hating how this courage seems to surface only when facing him.

"For the right reasons," he grits out the words.

"You couldn't have just negotiated?" I ask, unbidden desperation seeping into my voice, tears threatening to fill my eyes. "You couldn't have just . . . just—"

"Just what, Reim? Asked nicely?" he sneers, so easily picking up where I left off. I can't stand it. "Wrote a damn letter? And it would say what? 'Please, Your Majesty, stop killing my people'?"

"No! Of course not. That's—"

"He knew what he was doing, Reim," he snaps. "My people used to tell ourselves for *centuries* that if we just cooperated, or just did as we were told, surely there would be peace. That if Vuorians only knew how bad it really was, they wouldn't do this to us. But it was a lie, because yes, they would. They did. And this last edict wiped away any remaining doubt. We couldn't wait anymore."

"This was the only way, Reim," he says, emphasizing every word. "And I do not apologize for it. Especially not when he so unapologetically murdered my people again and again. My only regret is that I didn't do something sooner."

My hand whips up of its own volition to slap him, only for his to shackle my wrist before it can.

"Let go of me," I seethe, twisting my wrist against his determined hold.

But he just pulls me closer until I collide with his chest. Stares into my wide eyes with his narrow ones for so long, so intently that I imagine him being able to see into me. See that behind my obvious anger, my gnashing defiance, is nothing but paralyzing confusion, petrifying grief.

He keeps staring and staring until he lets go at last.

Grasping my wrist, which still feels the firm stamp of his hold, I scramble back from him.

"Your turn," he finally rumbles.

"W-what?" I manage, cursing myself for always feeling one step behind this man, for always having to play catch up.

"I told you what I want. But I also just said to the Jirga that I strive for a kingdom that is fair. So, it's your turn, Reim. What do *you* want?"

My head recoils.

"What do *I* want? You already know what I want. I want you gone. I want my kingdom back. I want my father b—" I bite my tongue until the taste of blood blooms across it, but unlike the Unnamed, it's not because I was about to lie, it's because I'm telling the truth. To him. Again.

And I hate this. I hate always giving him so many of my truths over and over when he gives me so little of his.

Well, no more. I'm done.

He wants to be fair? I'll give him fair. His lies for a lie of my own.

"Or . . . I should say I *wanted* those things," I begin again after a moment, closing my eyes in what I hope seems like reluctant resignation, only to paint them with false determination when I open them again. "Now I just want what's best for everyone. So, I'll take your deal to help you find *The Book.*"

But instead of finding him joyous or smug with his victory, I find him watching me in that unnerving way that I now know means, though his body is stock still, his mind is hard at work.

Fate. Please, please don't let him see through this. There's no book. I, of all people, would've known about it. But that doesn't mean I can't use his desperation for it against him like he used mine for Baba against me.

"But with one condition," I force my words to outpace his racing mind and my racing heart. "You let me run the kingdom the way I want. With fairness and equality as discussed. But also without your interference."

He mulls this over.

"With trust," he finally concludes, his eyes still boring into mine.

What? Trust? Never.

"Yes," I say instead, the lie easily tripping off my tongue after the others.

He nods. "And to show my good faith, I will take into consideration time and mercy for your people to adjust like you asked."

I try not to show my surprise at this unsolicited addition.

"But, make no mistake," he goes on, "that does not absolve your people of accountability. There will be no privileges afforded to them that the cantons are not also given. There will be equal application of our laws and justice."

And I'm so relieved to have gotten away with my deception that I take it.

"Okay, agreed," I manage to whisper before slowly heading toward the chamber doors.

"But as for your obvious distaste for me calling you *wife*," he calls from behind me and I stop, biting back an exasperated groan. I should have known this was too easy. "I am sure you will agree *my queen* is an adequate replacement."

"As sure as I am that *my fool* is an adequate one for you," I throw back at him as I wrench open the door and then let it slam shut behind me. But it's still not loud enough to drown out his rumbling laugh or his parting words.

"Still not my name, but getting closer . . . my queen."

Chapter 16

WE'RE JUST TRYING TO HELP," THE BABY yells for what must be the hundredth time as another dilapidated door shuts decidedly in our faces.

"It's all right." I squeeze his shoulder, stopping him from knocking again. "Let's keep going."

He curses under his breath.

I understand his frustration, but there is little to do about it. We've been visiting the cantons daily for the past week since the Jirga meeting, trying to speak with the inhabitants and gauge their needs and concerns, but with little success.

"Out with it," I command when the two siblings start murmuring together.

They stare at each other intently for a long moment, as if silently arguing who should be the one to say it until—

"Fine, I'll do it," the elder sighs, glaring at her twin. "You really are a baby."

Her brother grins in victory.

"Well, for one thing, Your Grace, it may help not to carry that sword with you on these visits. It may remind them of when you were the High Commander, and you . . ."

She trails off, but it's easy to fill in the gaps. I patrolled them. Cornered them. Interrogated and arrested them.

And I did that for years.

It seems so obvious now that they would distrust me, avoid me, and fear me when they say it like that. How embarrassing to think they would see me differently just because I say so. Or because I feel so.

I blush, nodding for them to continue.

"Right, you get it. But that's not even the main thing. If we're being completely honest . . ." She pauses, clearly unsure if she should be. "We're here in the Burrow with you, but we don't understand it at the same time. Why *are* you coming here?"

She steels her spine and then adds, "I mean, the healer can take care of us now. Why not, I don't know, help your own people?"

"What she means is, why do you even care?" the baby blurts, earning a smack across his head by his sister.

"*Khur.* You know you were thinking it."

It's not the question that fills me with hurt, but the answer I have to give them. But unlike the healer, they've been nothing but honest with me. The least I owe them is my honesty in return.

"Because of guilt and confusion," I whisper. "So much confusion."

"Because though I'm still not over what happened at the Bicentennial, I also remember grieving for your people that same morning. Because even though I'm angry, so damn angry still about so much of that day, I still can't stop thinking that, despite it all, my people are worried, yet they still have more than enough. And it's because of what I did to the cantons for *years* without question, for the sake of supposed principles, for *Order*, that I benefited while never seeing how others suffered from them, too."

I swallow, looking up at the fluttering phoenixes gliding above when I am unable to look at my guards any longer. "Until the last month before the Bicentennial—when the suffering became too hard to ignore. But even then, I didn't do anything about it."

I pause, consumed by my shame.

"And now, I can," I murmur "I want to. And it doesn't matter that the king can do it. It matters that *I* do. Because I'm the one who committed this wrong."

I take in my surroundings along with their silence, the phoenixes swooping in and out of the dilapidated hovels of the Burrow, stacked too close, too high to be safe. How did I never see the danger of that before? How did I scoff at the dirty streets, only to see them lined with bodies, day after day, in the month before the Bicentennial?

"I can't speak to your anger. Nor do I regret what we did," the baby says at last, his usual easy joviality replaced with stalwart conviction. "But if you're being honest about wanting things to be better for us, I can tell you that before you do anything with your hands, you have to do it first with your ears and heart. You'll have to listen and learn, and that means you'll have to unlearn a lot too."

His sister nods. "And there is no need for your self-pity here."

"And there is definitely no need to *save* us to make yourself feel better."

I had told the healer at the last Jirga meeting that I didn't need him to save me because it would make me feel more dependent, more weak. Yet, how did I not understand that it could mean the same for others?

"You can't have any expectations from people you've harmed. Not their forgiveness. Not their praise. This can't be for your sake."

"This has to be for our sake and our sake only or . . ." He pinches his nose with a sigh. "Or you should honestly stay across the Keep, in the Citadel. Just leave us alone."

I think back on our first conversation, how they seemed proud and happy after our defeat, and I resented them for it while I was in such a state of grief over the same thing. But how many times had I done the same to them and their people? How many times had I walked their streets and felt carefree, and they were suffering?

We are both trying in this new reality: I'm trying to get better and be better, and they're trying to help their people *and* help me—and they didn't have to do the last part. They didn't have to say any of this to me, especially when it's easier to let me suffer, to fail. Maybe I even deserve to, as my own people have told me time and time again.

But they didn't. And I'm humbled by this.

"Thank you, to you both. I—"

But my tongue suddenly stills, my head jerking to the right.

My years of honed vigilance on patrol alerting me that something is watching us.

No, someone.

My pulse skips a beat, then slows, sludges as if it's trying to pull the reins on my thoughts, trying to stop—no—trying to *reverse* time.

Because I swear I've felt this exact feeling of being watched before, in almost the same exact place. Before the siege. Before Baba's last edict. Before the oath. Before everything changed forever.

Sifr. It's sifr.

Now, instead of slowing, my heart starts pumping harder. Faster.

I'm not foolish enough to have thought I'd never see him again, but I was foolish enough to be so caught up in my anger at his betrayal that I didn't plan for what I would do when I did.

My body acts out of habit, out of memory. I unsheathe my sword despite my guards' confused gasps and charge toward the alley I'm sure he's nestled in.

And then I slam it into the mortar next to his head, just like the first time we met.

But this time there is no squeak of surprise. Those fathomless black irises just look up at me as if expecting me to find him. As if *wanting* me to.

"Reim," he says in his soft, boyish voice.

"What do you want this time?" I skip the pleasantries. My heart is cut wide open with hurt, and my eyes fill with tears of relief at seeing him alive at the same time.

"You already took my father, my friendship, my trust—" I choke on the last word. "What more do you want?"

One of my guard's steadying hands lands upon my shoulder. How is this so much harder than so many other hard things I have already done these past few months?

"I am sorry, Reim," sifr whispers, blinking back tears before looking away. "I really am. I'm sorry for making you sad, for worrying you and *lying* to you."

His throat bobs.

"But I'll never be sorry for fighting back. I'll never be sorry for just wanting food, or just wanting to feel safe, or just wanting to live. And I'll never be sorry for doing whatever I could to make it happen."

And though only a few weeks ago his words would have made me so angry, now I just can't be. Not when I just promised my guards I would listen to people, that I would hear them. And especially not when seeing sifr's face reminds me of how wildly I would search for him among the dead. How simply hearing his little defiant voice calms my heart in ways that I haven't felt since Baba issued that terrible edict.

For the first time since Baba's death, I understand. Whatever Order meant to me once, it *never* meant that to them.

I understand. I accept.

"But there was something more important I wanted to say to you, and that's why I looked for you today." He pauses for a moment, like the Unnamed do when they're being vulnerable but are afraid not only of saying but of hearing the truth of their own words. "I thought I knew everything I ever wanted to know about your kind—that you would do anything to put us down, to make life miserable for us. That you use us and then get rid of us. And it's all true. But it's not the entire truth."

He sniffles, crossing his arms over his chest as if anchoring himself for what he wants to say next.

"Because *you* didn't do that. When we were coming up with the plan, it was all a big risk. Sure, it was easy enough to get arrested. We just had to exist for *that* to happen. But for you get me out? To *care* enough to get me out?" He wipes his eyes with the back of his hands. "Then for you to keep caring . . . and then to keep looking for me . . ."

We both take a deep breath, mine to prevent me from reaching out to him, his to *keep* him from reaching out to me.

"I never had anyone do that for me besides the healer and the architect. Never thought I'd care if someone ever did." He starts fidgeting like he wasn't planning on saying all of this, and now that he has, he needs to stop. Needs to get out of here.

Not because he fears for the safety of his life like he once did, but because he fears for the safety of his heart.

"Maybe it's for the best that we say goodbye now." He rubs his eyes, his voice catching. "I just really wanted you to know that. And just wanted to—to see you one last time."

Then he spins and runs back down the alley, disappearing around a corner before I can respond.

I stare after him, paralyzed by his admission. For all the times I've thought about sifr after the Bicentennial, I never thought about the possibility of him thinking about me in return.

Let alone *missing* me.

I've missed so many people in my life. Continue to feel their loss in every moment of every day. But someone feeling all of that for me? Never.

For the first time in a long time, something small and fragile inside feels held, comforted.

"Your Grace?" the baby murmurs from next to me, his sister approaching me from the other side.

"You both have done so much for me today," I whisper through a tight throat. "But can I ask you one more question, please?"

"Of course," the elder answers, a spark of concern flickering between the siblings' gazes.

"Why would an Unnamed be called sifr?"

They say nothing at first, and I swear the already thick air becomes suffocating with their silence.

"Please," I say, closing my eyes against the tears that are building behind my lids.

Leaking through my lashes.

Spilling over my cheeks.

"It means zero or none," the elder murmurs at last. "As in, no family. It's . . . it's what we call Unnamed children that are orphaned."

I put out a hand to steady myself against the alley wall.

He's an orphan.

No wonder he volunteered as bait in this plan. No wonder he was willing to risk his life. He had nothing and no one to lose.

How terrible must living here have been, if it was worth dying to change it?

I wipe my tears with my sleeve before turning back to my guards.

"I have work to do," I admit.

Too much work, that anxious, self-doubting inner voice attempts to discourage me.

But I solder my spine. Bolster my heart.

I have to at least try.

"Are you both willing to help me?"

Their determined nods are the exact hope I need.

Chapter 17

S O WHEN YOU SAID YOU NEEDED OUR HELP—"

"And then had us agree to it—"

"You didn't say it meant to help you deceive the Maliki—"

"By letting you go into the cantons—"

"*Alone.* Remember? Fate, don't forget the most important part!"

"Yes, I was just about to say that if you didn't interrupt me! Letting you go into the cantons *alone!*"

I swing my gaze back and forth between the exasperated faces of my guards.

"I actually have both of you to thank for the idea," I say, attempting to defuse the tension. "How are the Unnamed going to trust me if I always have a sword strapped to my back? And further yet, how are they going to trust me if I always have you both with me, who also have swords strapped to yours?"

They share a look I've come to recognize, the one that means they know they're being manipulated and can't do a thing about it.

"I don't like this, Your Grace," the elder finally groans in a voice that sounds like the beginning of reluctant defeat.

"And I don't like you calling me that. Reim will do just fine." I take the win and then some.

They roll their eyes.

"The Maliki is going to ask where you are. And then what, Your Grace?"

My fingers falter on the buckle of my sword strap.

He asks about me? Why?

And as soon as the ridiculous question enters my mind, a pragmatic answer follows. He's still keeping tabs on me. Sure, he loosened the reins, but I'm still his prisoner. His trophy, his—

His—

"My Wife."

"My Queen."

I want to scream at his insistence on using these names. At how his deep voice rolls over the words, invading my every hollow like sweltering wind and heat, only to quench the fire with cooling storm and rain. At how, despite knowing they must be a part of some sort of mind game, my mind drags me back to them, to *him,* so easily.

But such a crazed reaction would likely not inspire much confidence in me by my guards, and I really need their trust right now.

"You can tell him whatever truth you need to," I tell them, pretending to busy myself with my buckle once again. "That I ordered you to. That I tricked you. Whatever you want. But I will not have you attempt to lie, or to risk yourself for me in any way," I say, meaning every word.

"I need to do this my way for it to be meaningful, remember? I need to try to set things right for me and for the people." I finish unstrapping the sword from my back and push it toward them, imploring them one last time to take it and go.

And with long-suffering sighs, they do.

"Besides, I won't be alone, since that's what worries you the most," I call behind me, already weaving through the bustling streets before the whiplash from what I just said wears off and they change their minds and come after me. "I'll be with sifr."

I hope.

I dare not look back at them as I pull my linen hood over my head and let the wind twist my plain outer robes around my ankles, then head to the alley where I last saw sifr yesterday.

I'm tracing my calloused finger along the divot my sword left in the wall last time I was here, for the fifty-seventh time, when a throat clears softly behind me.

"You know, we don't have to keep meeting in alleys anymore. I'm a free man now."

Sifr shuffles his feet a few paces from me where the shadow meets the light, as if straddling the fine line between caution and hope, ready to choose either if he needs to. But that doesn't stop the smile from blooming across my face anyway.

Of course it would be him who would make me smile for the first time since . . . *everything*.

My eyes fill.

"Hey, stop that," he says, scampering over to me. "Smiles one second, tears the next? Besides, I hear there's a new Maliki and Malika now and things are different."

I wipe at my eyes with the back of my sleeve and sniffle.

"I can't speak to the Maliki's objectives," I say honestly, and perhaps a bit bitterly. "But the new Malika wants things not only to be different, but better."

I look away from him lest I start crying again. "But the problem is she doesn't know how. And she is so afraid of making things worse."

He looks at me for a long moment before shrugging.

"Bah, take it from a kid who's been scared his whole life, fear's not so bad. Let's see." He throws his back against the wall next to me. "It can help you be more careful. It can make you listen and learn, change and adapt."

And then he smiles mischievously. "And I don't know this part myself, but I hear it can also make you humble, which makes you a good leader."

I laugh, hearing the conviction in his words, though I don't know if I believe them just yet. It's hard to believe that living in a constant state of change is a good thing when your whole life you've been told to follow something as rigid as Order so . .. so . . . *blindly.*

"After everything that has happened, are you still afraid, sifr?" I ask, wondering whether he even knows what I mean. Whether he's been thinking about all the things that need to be done, the sense of impossibility they bring, or if it's still just survival for him.

"Yes." He nods vigorously. "But what's different this time is that I have hope too."

"The healer and his gift really mean a lot to you all, huh?"

His eyes light up at my comment, his silly smile stretching even farther across his round cheeks.

"Yesss," he says, stretching the word, "but I was talking about his wife."

"*Me?*"

"Of course *you*," he huffs. "Weren't you listening this whole time? Fate, helping you is going to be harder than I thought."

And now it's my turn to smile.

"Don't curse," I mutter to get the last word.

He rolls his eyes before linking his fingers with mine and tugging me into the bright street.

"Now, come on. We clearly have a lot of work to do."

By the time the sun is dipping over the Ma'asa, I've managed to gather enough complaints and suggestions to fill all the parchment I brought with me. From the safety of the baluur mines, to the dilapidated homes and streets, there's so much work to do here. But at least today, we made one stride forward.

Sighing, I tip my head up to the sunset sky dancing with ribbons of gold and crimson, my mind spinning and tangling within its loops and whirls.

The same way it does when it gets tangled up in the whirling rings of someone's fiery eyes. The same someone who I've been avoiding since the last Jirga meeting, when I told him not to interfere. Who seems to keep finding ways to interfere in my thoughts anyway.

"You okay?"

I blink, and the sky and my mind still once again. And the eyes I'm looking into are no longer the color of gilded sunset but that of encroaching night.

I ruffle a hand through sifr's short chestnut curls as I pack my things.

"More than okay. You did good today."

The streetlights flaming to life are no match for the radiance of sifr's proud smile.

"Again, you're sure you want to stay here?" I ask. "There are plenty of rooms in the castle."

"I don't doubt it," he mutters, looking over his shoulder at the massive limestone and terracotta fortress that's visible from every part of the kingdom. "But the Burrow's home. It will always be home."

I smile.

"And you're sure you don't want to join us for a meal?" he asks, jerking a thumb at the bustling street, each person, young and old, setting up a communal feast in the Burrow square.

"Yes, I'm sure. I should head back home. My guards will be worried about me," I lie which is so much easier than admitting the truth—that I still remember how I was often the one to enforce the curfews, making a gathering like this not only impossible but illegal and punishable. That I don't want to ruin the precarious peace and trust sifr helped me build today by intruding on the canton's precious time together by reminding them of things they'd rather forget.

Sifr watches me for a minute, understanding me like he's always been able to, before nodding and running back into the crowd. And I take my fill of his easy stride, his fuller limbs and fuller smile. Of the mother feeding her child a piece of bread folded over lentils, two men tuning their two-string ouds while another tries to harmonize with a soft beat on his daf drum. Of the aroma of saffron rice, toasted pine nuts, and spiced lamb. Of the sound of open laughter, stories, and song.

With one last look at the boisterous gathering, feeling happy for the joy they now have after so much recent loss, while also feeling an aching loss at never finding that sense of belonging anywhere, I head back home.

To say my summary from the citizens of Canton Two presented to the Jirga was met with mixed feelings would be an understatement.

While the Maliki stayed silent but serious, persuading his advisers by the sheer force of his attention on me to do the same, the Vuorian Jirga members took turns to passively scoff and openly ridicule the ideas put forth.

But despite it all, edicts to better Canton Two's infrastructure were drawn up by the architect and passed to the healer to seal with his own signet ring—an emerald stone set in a silver band, embossed with a soaring phoenix.

One so similar, yet entirely different from the ring I dug out of my bedside drawer for the first time since Mori gave it to me. The one I now roll between my fingers tonight as I stand on the half-moon balcony of my father's room, looking out over Vuor.

Baba's ring.

As the heir of Vuor, it was always meant to be mine to wear, along with the Iron Crown one day—to bear witness to my ascension to the throne, to stamp across hot wax and declare the words beneath it law.

Yet I never once slipped it on my finger.

Don't know if I ever will.

Don't know if I even want to when I always saw it as Baba's and never as mine. Saw this kingdom as Baba's and never as mine. And now I don't know who it belongs to at all.

"You're lost . . . like us."

The healer's words from our wedding night wrap around me.

I clamp my fingers, my palm, over the signet of the dahaka until I'm sure it's burning through my own skin like hot wax. Branding me. Reminding me I'm nothing like the Unnamed, but neither am I anything like the Vuorians. I'm stuck in the in-between. Alone.

Creak.

I spin to see the bedroom door opening behind me, letting in a chill that's somehow colder than the one from the brisk night air out here.

I rush to pocket the ring in my robes, heart pounding with the possibility that it's the healer, that somehow, just by thinking of him, I have called him to me, only for Basteel to slither

M.Ṣ. Maṣood

into a patch of moonlight instead. His long silk robes swish back and forth over the dusty floor, reminding me of nothing so much as an undulating snake on the hunt.

"What are you doing here?" I ask as he closes the gap between us.

"The same could be asked of you, Reim," he replies in what could only be described as a low hiss.

"You will refer to me as Malika now," I tell him like I've told no one else before, not even myself. But I need there to be distance between us in some way, especially since he seems to be swallowing the literal space between us by the second.

Cursing myself for coming here unarmed, I take a step back, then another. But he keeps coming. And now there are no further steps to take, and the back of my legs hit the limestone balustrade.

"No, I will not," he says when he's right in front of me, his putrid breath choking me when he leans in further.

"You are impure. A curse to our blessed bloodline and legacy," he says, piercing his gaze at my tapered ears before looking back into my eyes. "Both on the outside and inside. You were always undeserving of the title."

He's baiting me. Like the slimy snake he is, he's going for my weaknesses, using them against me. But what my mind knows and what my heart feels are not the same right now. He trapped me in my father's room, on his balcony. With his memories surrounding me, his kingdom behind me, and I can't even think of fighting back because I was just thinking the same thing: I am undeserving.

"But perhaps that could change," he muses, and my slick hand slips on the railing before righting itself again.

"What are you blathering about, Basteel?" I return, faking courage I do not feel as the wind starts picking up around us, threatening to take me over the edge with just one wrong step.

164

"Despite your thickheadedness, you must have known that there were many of us in the Jirga dissatisfied with your father's rule. Yes, it was obvious he cared about Vuor and the legacy of his forefathers. But it was also just as apparent that he was so damned caught up in preserving the past, he could not even imagine a better future. A future without the Unnamed altogether."

His eyes gleam despite the darkness.

"Vuor for Vuorians. As Fate meant it to be," he croons. "So, what was Fate to do but take the problem into its own hands? Your father's health worsened and worsened, paving the way for those of us who wanted the best for Vuor to take over once he died."

"You sick bastard! The whole lot of you Janoons. You're just deplorable."

But his lips only stretch farther across his face.

"Bastard?" He laughs. "Oh Malika, it takes one to know one. But deplorable? Right up to this past week, I might have said the same thing about you. A deplorable curse that's spread its destruction to the rest of us. But then"—he leans further into my space, placing his hands on either side of mine on the cold stone—"I saw something extraordinary."

His pupils widen until his dark eyes resemble nothing more than endless, devouring maws. "I saw you getting your law passed, your voice heard. You found a way to take what you wanted."

He laughs, his crooked teeth gleaming, while I just continue to stare, paralyzed.

"And it's ridiculous because you did it so damn easily. You cried just the right amount, fought back the right amount." He looks down between us. "And spread your legs the right—"

"That's enough!" I snarl.

"No it's not, Your Majesty," he snarls right back. "That's the sandblasted point. It will never be enough until all the

Unnamed are gone. From the cantons and from the face of this earth. It's not too late, Reim. You started rebuilding the Burrow as a way to gain the savage's favor, but that's fine. We can have our people settle there once it's complete. Join me, Reim, in taking back what is ours. All will be forgiven, and together we will find a way to kill him since you cannot. And we can return the rightful glory to our kingdom."

"Imagine Reim," he goes on, long lines of spittle hanging from his lips as hunger builds in his eyes. "You'll no longer be a curse. You'll be a *miracle*!"

But I don't let my head imagine it. I pull it back and slam it against his.

"I'd rather be a curse than be the devil you are!" I spit as he staggers away with a pained yowl. "I have not forgotten, Basteel. You wanted me to be a puppet to you before, and you want me to be a puppet to you now. You don't give two khurs about the good of this kingdom. You only care about yourself. And I may have failed my people and my loving father, in more ways than I can count, but I will do whatever it takes to keep this kingdom from the likes of you."

He swipes at the trickle of blood seeping down his ruddy face but doesn't come any closer.

"Your *loving* father? You honestly still believe that? Fate, you are so naïve. He didn't *love* you. He *hated* you. He only put up with your incompetence, over and over, for the sake of Order. Until he finally grew a backbone. Finally put you in your place. But then you found a way to ruin that too."

He throws his head back to the listening sky.

"Fate!" he screams as blood continues to stream down his face. "I offer you power, a place in our glorious history, and here you are looking for love. Always looking for love, first from your father and now from these khasir animals instead of ruling them as you should. But that's Fate's real curse, isn't it? Just like your Baba, no one really loves you. They're all just *using* you."

I clench my fist in response to my clenching heart but say nothing.

"But at least I am honest about it," he goes on. "At least I was offering you something in return. But I should have known your stupid need for love would be your downfall again."

"Get out of here!" I scream when his words not only manage to land a blow but rip me wide open. "Get the Fate out before I—"

"Before you what?" Basteel sneers as if he was hoping for this exact reaction. "Tell your *husband*? You wouldn't dare. Because like I said, you may not care how weak you look to us, your own people. But you damn well care how weak you look to him."

My pulse whooshes in my ears at the truth of his words.

"But guess what? That's your loss. Because whatever may be going on in that frail, bleeding heart of yours, this is *our* land." He sweeps his bloodstained hand toward the sleeping kingdom behind me. "By Fate and by will. Victory will not come for those Unnamed. And I will make sure it won't come to those who align with them either."

And then he slips back into the darkness, retreating like the wounded but vengeful animal he is until he's engulfed by the empty room of dust and memories once again.

I finally gather my wits, place the ring in Baba's apothecary table, and leave before I am swallowed in this night's oblivion myself.

The dahak door knocker still watching me, always watching me, as I do.

Chapter 18

T he sun is high, the wind low by the time I reach
Canton Two the next day. The architect looks up
from the many plans, figures, and diagrams strewn
over his table and gives me a wide smile in greeting.
One I have to force myself to return.

"A big day ahead of us, Reim. A new beginning."

"Yes," I manage to say in a calm voice, though last night's
encounter with Basteel still has me on edge. "I'm so glad you
are here to oversee it. The people know you, and you know the
people and these streets and buildings."

"Yes, that is true," he says, looking around before circling
his gaze back to me. "And it seems you are trying to get to
know them as well."

I lift my eyes from the desk to him. His words create the
type of statement that harbors an unsaid question, but I'm
not sure what it is, let alone how to answer it. I'm about to
ask him to elaborate when sifr bounds over to us, an apple
clamped between his fingers and his teeth.

I quirk an amused eyebrow at him. Lately, every time I've seen him, he's chomping, chewing, or talking about food.

"What?" he says through his full mouth. "I told you the first time we met that a man's gotta eat. It's not my fault you thought I was joking or something."

I roll my eyes.

Waving goodbye to the architect and his team, sifr and I begin what has become our daily routine in the Burrow. First, we visit the storage house to make sure the rations of flour, produce, and meat from the Citadel are enough and accounted for. Then we go to the mines to make sure the Unnamed overseers have tested the tunnels for safety and stored yesterday's baluur for even distribution before the miners begin work for the day. And finally, we go to the orphanage that needs not only to be repaired, but also to be moved to a better location. The same orphanage where sifr spent his childhood scraping by before the healer and the architect took him under their care.

The healer.

The healer, who makes my pulse scatter at the mere mention of him, who has not asked me about the cipher since I told him I would help him . . . but who asks my guards about me, who listens to my ideas, seals my edicts into law. Who hasn't spoken to me since the day I told him that I don't need him to defend me, to save me. But will still insist on referring to me as *my queen* when addressing her in front of others.

Who Basteel claims is only trying to use me.

"Reim!"

I shake my head and snap my gaze toward sifr.

"Fate, you do that a lot." He stares with a blank expression to demonstrate.

"Don't curse," I mutter, elbowing him for his likely accurate depiction of me.

"Anyway," he says, dismissing my reprimand. "I was saying we should probably get back to the Keep. It's getting late, and this place still isn't without its lowlifes." He darts his onyx gaze around the dark streets encircling the orphanage, wrapping his arms around himself with a shudder.

My brows buckle in concern.

"Don't worry, sifr. We will move the orphanage's location as soon as we—"

But just then a great shadow falls over us from behind, the dim torches lining the streets no match for its blight.

My High Commander instincts ignite, my mind calculating the possible attacker's exact location, predicting the likeliest stance and strategy for their strike in a blink of an eye.

I take a breath, my body primed and ready in the one I take after that.

Khur, I had not expected for Basteel to act upon his threat so soon.

Pushing sifr behind me, I reach for the pommel of my sword.

But grasp only air.

My sword! I haven't been bringing it here for weeks.

But before I can regroup, a punch lands hard across my cheek, and I crumble to the ground.

"*Sifr*! *Run*!" I manage to order past the blood pouring from my mouth.

When I'm sure he listened for once, I turn to face the bloodshot glare of my assailant—not Basteel or a Vuorian mercenary, but that of an Unnamed stranger. A glare that holds a hatred so personal, so deep, I'm drowning just by daring to look into its roiling depths.

I shift my leg behind me, pull my arm back as I've done countless times in training and in the field, and slam my fist forward until I hear the sick crunch of his nose breaking.

But he doesn't even flinch, just lets the blood gush down

his face as he swings a punch in return. Ducking underneath, I pivot on my heel until I'm standing behind him, and then I spring up and onto his back.

My arms clamp around his broad neck as he swings his large shoulders back and forth, trying to dislodge me.

"*Argh*," he roars as his massive hands paw at my arms' tightening noose. But the surge of adrenaline is already coursing through my nerves, filling me with the surety that only comes with endless training: it's not about if I'm going to win, but *when*.

I quickly calculate that, considering his large size and lack of skill, he will lose consciousness in seven . . . six . . . five . . .

Crack.

"Ugh." I fall back hard onto the ground, my spinning head and blurry vision telling me he must have slammed his head into mine.

But my pounding confusion is quickly replaced by the sharp pain of my long hair, braids and all, being yanked up as I claw at the cobblestones, until I'm not only on my feet but lifted into the air.

"You," the large man slurs, rank spittle spraying across my face. "You ajnoob bitch. You got some damn nerve showing your murdering face here again."

He grips my scalp harder, and I grit my teeth against the pain, trying to keep my hazy mind on my next mode of attack.

"Three younglings! A beautiful wife! *Gone!*" he snarls, shaking his fist that's tangled in my hair. "Buried alive in the mines!"

And suddenly I stop struggling, the fight draining from me like the blood draining from my face. The pain lancing through my head and neck competing with the one now wrenching my heart and soul.

His eyes start brimming with tears, and then he lets out a quaking sob.

"My whole family," he wails, his cry echoing down the abandoned street. "My whole world! Because of your father! Because of *you*! Wasn't it enough to starve us? Throw us in prison? You had to throw us into our graves too?"

With one hand still wrapped in my braids, he yanks out a strand of shimmering silver from his pocket—a wedding anklet that swings like an executioner's noose in front of me.

"This," he whimpers in a mournful trance as his glazed eyes follow the chain's pendulum swing, "this is all I have left of her."

"I'm sorry," I whisper to him, meaning it, but also knowing my words are meaningless now. "I'm so sorry."

And for a second, he's so enraged by my apology that I begin to accept my inevitable death by his hands, almost welcome it. A deserved end.

But then . . . he looks at me, really looks at me, and the intoxicated anger in his eyes shifts, a profound grief revealing itself just behind its haze. And then he loosens his grip, lowering me to the ground.

But just as my feet find stability once again, his legs give out from underneath him.

His eyes roll back, his lips mouthing something unintelligible as his massive body crashes to the ground in front of me. Gasping, I look up from his unconscious form to the architect standing above him, a bloodied cobblestone in his hand, sifr at his side.

"Damn idiot," he murmurs, looking down at the Unnamed man, his usual affable expression replaced with a disappointment, a disgust so deep it's almost chilling.

"No. No. He . . . he . . . lost his children, his wife. He was grieving," I say, shaking my head. "He was grieving because of me. Because of what I let happen to his family. Fate, I'm so stupid. How did I think I could just come in here and fix this?"

The Unnamed

The architect snaps his gaze to my face, his grim expression unshifting, while sifr runs over, wrapping his arms around me and burying his wet face into my chest as I stroke his hair.

"Nevertheless, he attacked you, Reim. Could have killed you," the architect says at last.

"And he *failed*," I emphasize, tired of the endless cycle of violence. The tit for tat. The obsession with *justice* when all we really mean by that word, all we ever meant by it, is revenge.

"And he failed," the architect repeats, looking me in the eye.

I break his gaze to look at the unconscious man on the street, and all I can think is I'm the one who failed him. Just like everyone else. I told the healer I didn't need him, could do this on my own, yet—

"Will my husb—" I cut myself off, shocked my mind would refer to the healer in such a way ever, but especially when it's so vulnerable. I squeeze my eyes shut and try again.

"Will the Maliki be able to heal him?"

The architect looks down at the oozing gash across the back of the man's head and then back to me.

"He should be able to, yes."

"Good. But please don't tell him what happened." Fate, first the run in with Basteel and then this poor man. The things I'm keeping from the healer are growing by the minute. "And if he's too busy, I would like this man to be seen in the healing wing of the castle."

The architect's jaw ticks, but he doesn't say no.

"I don't want any more action taken against him," I plead again, sensing the architect's reluctance. "I don't want him punished. In fact, I want him to receive compensation for my father's last edict. Perhaps it is something we should consider for others as well over time."

But the architect still looks angry, and I'm not used to anything but his calming presence, his easy pragmatism in the face of so much distress and uncertainty. But it's not fair of me to expect that of him all the time.

He sighs, dropping the cobblestone at last and pinching his nose.

"Why don't you go see your own healer as well. I need to think. Need to take care of . . . *this.*"

He shakes his head when I start to protest.

"Please, Reim. Just go."

Sifr starts tugging at my hand, and I finally notice him, his puffy eyes and pale cheeks, his trembling hands and uncharacteristic silence.

I bend down, kiss the top of his head, and squeeze his hand.

I may be no worse for wear than after any other scuffle in my past life, but sifr could probably use the healing ward. Or maybe the comforting distraction of its head healer.

I nod at the architect in thanks.

"Come, sifr. There's someone I'd love for you to meet."

THE HEALING WARD IS BUSTLING WITH ACTIVITY, EVEN this late in the evening. But the patients are no longer seasoned soldiers blindsided on canton patrol as in the past, nor only citizens of the Citadel with various bumps and bruises, but are now also regular Unnamed citizens—nicked and cut, punched and bludgeoned during training in the castle and injured while rebuilding in the Burrow. I think back on my visits here prior to the Bicentennial and am shocked to realize I had never seen any Unnamed here at all before.

Was the healer taking care of all these people—for all these years?

The citizens of the cantons outnumber those of the Citadel three to one, and if they only ever had one healer . . .

"Well, aren't you a sight for sore eyes?" Mori calls out as she straightens up from bending over a patient two beds down. "Or a sore back, or a sore shoulder." She winces, massaging each in turn. "I'm sure you understand, my dear."

I do, and she does too because she's tended to all those injuries for me.

I smile. "Hi, Mori."

She walks over to me, assessing me from head to toe in a way that's loving yet instinctual to her profession at the same time.

"Hi, Mori," she mimics, bracketing her full hips with her fists. "Hi, yourself. Haven't seen or heard from you in several weeks, and all you have for me is a measly 'Hi, Mori.'"

Now it's my turn to wince. She's not wrong. The last time she saw me was when I was catatonic with grief, and then after that, I made sure to leave for the cantons before she could make her rounds on me.

"You're right," I say, throwing my arms around her shoulders, stuffing my nose into her cap that smells of cinnamon and cloves. "Forgive me, please. I . . . I wasn't myself. I'm still not . . ." I trail off, struggling once again to describe the upheaval of the last few weeks—the charged meetings with the Jirga and Basteel, the confusing ones with the Maliki, and the overwhelming ones in the Burrow.

Like the one I had with sifr today.

My head shoots up.

Sifr. Where's sifr?

I spin around, my heart racing, but he's not behind me. He's not in front of me or to the sides of me either.

"I see you brought a visitor . . . an old friend perhaps?" Mori murmurs as she joins my frantic search, her astute gaze landing on him across the room, visiting with an Unnamed boy not much older than he is.

"Yes," I say, relieved yet hesitant, knowing what everyone is saying about the siege—how the Unnamed managed to access the heavily guarded castle so easily. How an Unnamed child prisoner led the way.

But if Mori has an opinion about it, she doesn't voice it. Instead, she nods at me as if my one-word confirmation gave her all the information she needed, and now the subject is closed.

A shaky exhale slips past my lips.

"I brought him here because we had an . . . *incident* earlier in the Burrow, and I wanted to make sure he's all right," I say, swallowing past the sudden tightening of my throat at the mere mention of what happened. "He was pretty shaken up by it."

"An *incident*?" She whips her gaze to mine, homing in on the slight swelling of my cheek, the coloring that's starting to change there.

Her eyes flash dangerously. "Should've known this wasn't a social call. Now, you better elaborate girl, or I'll—"

"What? Make me clean the bedpans like when I was young?"

"Worse," she hisses, long and low enough to make me forget I'm the Malika now and not a petulant youngling who would spit out her horrible concoctions she would try to shove down my throat every time I got a fever.

I sigh to hide my gulp.

"A man who had lost his family in the mines during the final edict was just airing his frustrations and—"

"He attacked Reim!" sifr interrupts from next to me, and I nearly jump.

Fate, he really has a talent for showing up when you least expect it.

"He *what*?" Mori screeches back, and now half the ward is staring at us in alarm.

"It honestly wasn't—"

"He punched her in the face, yanked her off the ground by her hair," sifr cries, and Mori ushers me into the nearest examination room, slamming the door behind the three of us. She begins moving my face, turning my head this way and that, then lifts my eyelids to check my pupils and runs her fingers through my hair to feel my scalp.

"Ouch," I mutter despite my need to reassure her and de-escalate the situation.

"Go wet this towel in that bucket of cold water, young man," Mori orders, and sifr hurries off to obey as if he's known her all his life and I'm the stranger.

Traitor.

Mori pushes the cold rag against my face as she continues her relentless examination . . . and her complaining.

"Should have known this would happen. Should have known that becoming Malika wouldn't change your awful penchant for finding trouble. If the Maliki finds out about this—"

"No! Mori, no." I grasp her hand, forcing her attention to my words. "This has nothing to do with him, do you hear me? This is not his fight. I am not his concern. I am not his—"

"Wife!" A deep, cavernous voice blasts like a mighty thunderclap over the room, stripping the air of all conversation, all sound.

I feel him before I see him, his fiery ire pulsing through my veins, charging through my nerves, until every channel, every capillary running under my skin seems to converge at the invisible cut scoring my palm. I drop the rag to clutch my paining hand with my other one. To raise my hardened eyes to clash with the healer's molten ones.

"Out," he growls at Mori and sifr, keeping his eyes on me, and I hate how the sound rumbles through me, like the inception of a storm, the crashing of waves. Like the quaking of the earth and the howling of the wind. Like a command of the earth and all its elements combining into one devastating blast.

And even though the impulsive and rebellious part of me wants to lift my chin, brace my heart, ready my tongue for a fight, another deeper, more vulnerable part of me that's just so damn exhausted from fighting and failing wants to accept its primal call.

Wants to submit to its promise of strength.

Wants to submit to *him*.

If he notices my inner turmoil, he doesn't show it. His churning rage seeming to overshadow his usually accurate intuition about me. He waits until he hears the door shut behind them.

And then lets me have it.

"When you said you didn't need me to defend you, didn't need me to save you at that first Jirga meeting, I listened," he clips out as he stalks over to me. "When you said I *trapped* you—"

"I—"

"No, Reim." He puts up a single finger in front of him. "No. I. *Listened*. Now, it's time for you to return the favor."

My lips press together with the effort to still my tongue.

"When you said I trapped you, I listened. I *heard* you. I made sure to give you the freedom to do things your way. To not interfere. I didn't look for you, didn't make sure you were all right. Even let you leave your guards behind. And I did it for *weeks*."

I open my mouth once again to remind him that he only did it because I promised to help him find his damn cipher, but—

"No!" he snaps once again as he starts pacing, looking nothing more than a caged beast stuck in this tiny room, trying not to rip into its meal. "I don't want to hear any of it. Not anymore. I already know what happened tonight. The entire healing wing—Fate, the entire *castle*—already knows what happened tonight."

If this is how he's reacting to what happened tonight, I'm really glad he doesn't know what happened the night before, too.

He stops his infernal pacing and whips his wild gaze back to me once again.

"You accused me of trapping you once, Reim. But you're the one trapping me now."

His chest heaves with shallow breaths as I buckle my brow.

"What does *that* mean?" I ask, bristling with genuine confusion. "Is my putting myself in harm's way and you letting me do it hurting you? Activating the oath between us somehow? Is that the same as you endangering me, causing me harm?"

I give his face, his body, a quick once-over.

"You don't look like you're in any pain."

He pauses for an endless moment and then murmurs, "Not all pain is apparent, my queen."

My oath mark pulses, warm and heavy, at his words, and I instinctively close my fingers over it.

He watches keenly as I do.

I clear my throat, linking my hands behind my back, away from his quick mind, his knowing eyes.

"Then I'll take my guards with me from now on. Surely that will remedy the situation," I offer, instead of demanding he tell me everything about this . . . this *tether* between us like I should. About why the scar still pulses despite the completion of the blood oath. About why he seems to know exactly what I'm thinking, yet his mind, his motives remain inaccessible to me.

And most confusing of all, about why he seems to actually care that I was hurt.

I should ask all of this.

But I don't. Something inside me warns me that I can't. That I'm not ready to hear the answer.

"I'm afraid not," he says, suddenly calm. Too calm. "I've given them permission to visit their people in Canton One for a few weeks. They've been working very hard, and they take care of a particularly difficult and frustrating charge."

I narrow my eyes at him, while an inadvertent blush at his teasing stains my cheeks once again. *Damn it.*

His eyes spark in amusement at my expense as usual, and then . . . then in something else too. Something I've never seen before in his eyes—or anyone else's.

Something serious.

Something *dangerous.*

"A very frustrating charge, indeed," he burrs under his breath, and my own breath hitches in response.

His eyes snap to my mouth at the tiny noise, until they catch my tongue peeking out to lick my suddenly dry lips.

His gaze whips back up again, and he swallows.

"No, not your guards," he says, his voice slowly returning to his usual obstinate tone. "I will be joining you on your daily visits from now on instead."

My sluggish pulse starts pumping again, my heart feeling lighter by the possibility of his presence and help—

No, how could I think like this? That would mean I'm a failure.

I push off the examination cot and march up to him until there is no more than an inch of space between us.

"Let me guess," I snarl up at him, "For my protection. Because you think I need your help. I told you, I don't need . . ."

But I trail off as he shakes his head, keeping his eyes fixed on mine, my gaze transfixed on his, until he finally murmurs, "No, Reim. Not for your protection. For *mine.*"

And there it is again, that urge from deep inside to ask him—just ask him—what that means . . .

But it's all suddenly too much: the events of the past few days, the assaults these past two nights, Mori's and sifr's overbearing concern, their underlying love. And now this—this overwhelming man and his offers of half-truths that wait for me to ask for the whole of them. It's too much. Too soon. Too—

His large hand presses into the small of my back, followed by a tender, soothing heat climbing up my spine as he guides me back to sit on the examination cot once more.

"*They're all just using you*," Basteel's voice echoes through my mind. But I'm just so damn tired, and the hand at my back so damn comforting that I just can't seem to care right now.

And then the healer sighs as if he's tired too, and I'm so caught up on the idea, no matter how ridiculous, of him sharing how I feel that I just watch his giant limbs bend until he's crouched on the ground in front of my knees. I let his sure hands pull off my boots, lift my legs in that unexpectedly gentle way of his, then tuck them under the starched sheet of the bed before pulling it up to my shoulders.

And maybe it's the fatigue settling in, or the thought that he may actually hear me even though he doesn't say nearly enough, but I give up. Give in.

"Fine." I yawn into the pillow. "We'll go together, you stubborn brute."

His low chuckle falls like the first heavy drops of desert rain on my drooping eyelids.

"Still not my name, my queen . . . but not wrong either."

Chapter 19

THE SUN FLICKING ITS BEAMS OF LIGHT THROUGH THE *leaves of our almazi tree feels akin to the spattering of gilded ink upon my upturned face, my fluttering eyelids. Sleep is unable to keep its hold on my consciousness in the face of such a warm awakening.*

I stretch my stiff limbs on the soft grass, starting from my tingling arms that served to pillow my head, working my way down to my folded legs that served to cradle my growing middle. My muscles feel both rested and exhausted as I manage to pull myself up inch by inch to lean against the trunk of the ancient tree that bears the fruit that has sustained our people's appetites and trade caravans for centuries. It's not gathering season yet, but it will be in a few months.

I yawn, covering my mouth with the back of my hand.

Yes, so much will be happening in a few months.

Resting my head, my back, against the soft, sweet-smelling bark, I sweep my still-tired gaze down my nose, down my embroidered robes, all the way to the delicate silver chain encircling my right ankle, its cascading links lined with bells that chime with each step. My cheeks heat for reasons beyond the warm afternoon's caress. My heart races from the memory of Adami's strong, steady fingers slipping it on as our village's ululation rose to the stars in celebration of their Maliki's marriage to me a year ago. As did my gift of light.

As did the strangers' screams right after.

They claimed to have never seen such "trickery," such "sorcery" before. Adami did his best to explain that it wasn't either. That they are gifts from Fate to care for the land and one another, as the land is not a thing to possess or own, but a responsibility to protect and love.

They did not understand any of this then . . . and they certainly do not now.

Shielding my eyes against the bright sun, I look over at their camp that we had helped set up for them at the edge of our grove when they first arrived—one that has only grown and grown since . . . along with their fear of us.

Yet their leader came to speak with Adami last night. I assumed he just wanted to learn more about how to cultivate the land as he always does, but he said he wanted to learn about our gifts instead. How we received them and how we use them.

But why? Why, when they only ever talk to us, tolerate us just enough to learn how to work the land, take from the land, but not love the land? Why do they want to know more about us now? About the most sacred, most important part of us, now?

Why do they now want to understand what and who they do not love?

I shiver despite the sun's attempt to wrap me in its warmth.

A few more months.

We just have to get through a few more months, then they will leave like they promised.

Using the trunk of the tree, I heave myself to my feet and stuff my unfinished needlework into my basket. The sheltering shadow of a familiar spread of wings and the rhythmic jingle of my anklet offer me reassuring company as I head home.

Ting. Ting. Ting.

Ting. Ting. Ting.

Knock. Knock. Knock.

Ting. *Knock.* Ting. *Knock.*

Ting.

Knock. Knock. Knock. Knock.

I groan as my brain tries to harmonize the jarring knocking of wood with the gentle chiming of the anklet and fails. As my heart urges it to stay in a sweet dream so unlike the usual bitter ones for just a bit longer, but my eyes ignore it, slowly blinking awake.

Only to squeeze shut again at the bright beam of morning sunlight filtering through the latticed windows facing the bed.

Judging by the earliness of the day, it has to be either Mori or one of her healer apprentices coming to check on me.

"Mori," I groan into my pillow. "I already told you yesterday, I'm feeling better than ever."

I roll my face toward the door but still keep my eyes closed. "I've been through much worse, as you very well know. And I really need you to just phoenix-peck—I mean—*care* about someone else for a change."

I yawn wide, smacking my lips at the end of it. "But wait, if you come bearing a fresh pot of almazi tea, please do come in."

But no sooner do the words of admittance leave my mouth, than a furious gale bangs the chamber door open, forcing me to sit up in sudden alarm. The bedcovers drop to my lap, the dagger I found placed on my bedside table since I returned from the healing ward instinctively clutched in my hand.

"No tea, I'm afraid. We do have a long day ahead of us, my queen, so we'd best be going without it," the healer booms, stalking into the room, and I'm so shocked to see him here at last—after the many nights I've imagined his presence, dreaded it, anticipated it, in this very place—that I raise my dagger higher.

"What are you talking about?" I hiss, wide eyes darting from the emerald phoenix feather that waves shyly in greeting from between his freshly braided hair, to the simple black tunic and pants he wears underneath his black outer robe, to the sword slung across his back and the dagger tucked into his belt.

A veritable blot of shadow in the brightest sun.

But as hastily as I take in his appearance, his presence, his existence in my space, just as leisurely does he take in mine.

As if insisting on sipping scalding tea, despite the high likelihood of being burned, he sips past the swirling tea leaves of my wild eyes, only to then linger, *savor* the ripples of my open hair, and then finally drink his fill of the dagger's handle pressed between my white-knuckled fingers, pressed against my heaving chest.

My chest.

Gasping at the sudden awareness of how I must appear in my thin linen nightshirt, I pull the covers up to my neck, severing his bold perusal of my body.

Only for it to land on where I am seated.

The bed.

The same bed that stood as a beckoning testament to the nature of our relationship the only other time he was here.

The same bed that he suggestively asked to "attend to me" on if he won our sparring match in the training yard when I saw him a week later.

His eyes snap from the empty side of the bed back to me as if I said the thought out loud.

Half of me wonders if I actually did, as my entire body seems to flush under the force of his heated gaze.

While the other half wonders if it's not his knowledge of my thoughts, but my body's innate understanding of his that is keeping our eyes anchored even as both of our thoughts are at risk of becoming unmoored.

"Us, Reim, together," he murmurs, his voice the low rumbling calm before the storm. A storm I'm irrationally considering running into instead of away from.

And now the heat enveloping my body is not behaving as a blanketing embarrassment, but a thick, heavy, primal awareness of him. An awareness of myself that's pooling at the very center of me.

The very core of me.

I readjust my hold on the sheet within my clammy hands.

"To-together?" I manage to rasp through a throat that is simultaneously thirsty and drowning.

He sweeps his golden gaze over me one last time as if preserving this exact image, this exact memory forever.

And then takes a resolute step back.

And then another.

"Yes, in the cantons," he says, his voice returning to his usual steady yet seismic cadence. "Like we agreed upon in the healing ward."

I close my eyes, knocking my head back against the headboard in sudden understanding.

Sudden . . . disappointment?

No. How can I even think that?

A familiar harsh self-loathing overcomes me.

"Right. For your protection, as I recall," I spit, and his eyes flash at my sudden vitriol, right before his own body stiffens, his own impenetrable armor coming up to shield him, defend him against me.

"Reim—"

"You may wait for me *outside* my doors." I stab my stare ahead, away from him and the timbre in his voice when he says my name that reminds me of the chiming tinkle of anklets.

I wait for the expected flame of his gaze against the side of my face, pricking me with questions, prodding me for answers . . . but it never comes. And its absence leaves me colder in more ways than one as I force myself to get up, to move on.

THE WAY THE FARMERS AND FARMHANDS OF CANTON ONE look at us is unlike anything I've encountered in all the days I've come out here thus far. Or more accurately, the way they look at the Maliki. Some with easy smiles, some with awe, with pride. And others with barely concealed attraction, with open yearning.

Though, if he's affected by their obvious admiration or overt flirtation, he doesn't show it, keeping his expression serious and his responses courteous and respectful. And while it's easier to have him here with me in some ways, it's harder in others, because even as the heir to Vuor, the High Commander, the Ameera, I never received admiring looks like this from my own people.

But how much was that really their fault? How much can I really blame them when I kept myself apart, kept to myself? Kept my days busy pursuing an ungraspable goal of what I believed they wanted from me? Of what would please them as a leader, what would make them stop seeing me as a curse, and instead as someone they would come to respect?

Someone who, one day, if I wanted it enough, tried enough, they would finally come to love?

A familiar, guttural ache forms in a deep, abandoned chamber in my chest, one I tried and failed to cauterize from the blood flow of the rest of my body a long time ago when I realized the loneliness, the sadness that festered there had the power to infect, to ruin the rest of me.

"No one really loves you."

I swallow past a sudden wave of nausea, my legs wanting to sway the same way as the willowy branches of the almazi trees we stand beneath. But large, sure fingers fold around my waist, pulling me into an equally solid body before I do.

"Everything all right, wife?" The healer's low whisper moves like a reviving breeze in my hair, against the sensitive, peaked shell of my ear.

I discreetly lean away from his side, carefully breaking away from his hold.

"It's just . . . I was hoping sifr would be joining us," I say, not lying, but not telling the complete truth either. Being alone with the healer makes it so much harder not to think about the healer. He seems to know I'm hedging too, silently assessing me as I attempt to suppress a telling shiver that climbs up my spine despite the oppressive heat.

He nods a goodbye to our hosts.

"Sifr has taken an apprenticeship of sorts with the castle's head healer," he explains as we continue our walk along the Grove.

I jerk my gaze up to him.

"Really?" I ask, though it makes sense. Sifr seemed surprisingly comfortable in the healing ward and took to Mori's commanding nature readily.

He offers a vague hum in answer, and now it's my turn to possibly catch him in a lie.

"I see," I say, raising a brow. "And who . . . *facilitated* this convenient arrangement?"

That slow smile hooks one side of his lips, tiny embers of mischief and joy sparking in his eyes. And I can't seem to find my usual annoyance at the sight of them today, can't help but feel the little cinders float over to me, catching and sparking on the bed of empty husks inside my heart, setting them alight into a small, joyous flame of my own.

I hide my own smile behind a clearing of my throat.

"Thank you," I whisper, willing my heart to pump its blood anywhere but my cheeks.

He huffs, the deep, guttural sound only blowing more air onto my internal kindling.

"Don't thank me just yet. They both have to survive each other first."

And my own smile breaks through at last, my whole body shaking in suppressed laughter at the shared joke, shedding its earlier anxiety in this moment of genuine ease.

I'm so caught up in allowing myself this freedom to just *be*, that at first I don't catch him allowing himself the freedom to watch me undisturbed. But when I finally do, it's as if instead of emitting light as he usually does, he's absorbing it.

Absorbing me.

All of me.

And Fate help me, I let him.

Let him look at me.

Let him *see* me.

See me free.

And I don't know why—why I've let *him* in when I've kept so many others out—but the moment doesn't care about why. And I'm slowly unable to care about it either.

And that's why I have to stop this.

Now.

"Those women in the field we visited this morning seemed to want you to taste more than the first almazi of the season," I blurt, surprised at my brazenness on a subject I'm always keen to avoid, especially with him. But I'm overcome by an urgent need to remind him where he belongs.

With *whom* he belongs.

To remind *both* of us now, more than ever, that it's not with me.

But despite my trying to create that safe distance between us once more, it only ends up drawing him closer.

It only ends up making his eyes darken, his blazing irises thin, his midnight pupils expand until his gaze resembles nothing more fascinating, more dangerous, than the eclipsing sun.

Until, instead of reminding us of all that we do not have, *should* not have, between us, it reminds us of all that we could.

"And?" he murmurs, cocking his head and towering over me once again in the way that reminds me so much of the da-haka of legend. But right now, surrounded by a vague memory of someone's love that took place somewhere exactly like this, surrounded by the clear reality of his scent that belongs to the earth as much as his gaze belongs to the sky, I don't want to cower in front of his might.

I want to bask in it.

And it's wrong. So very wrong.

"And since this marriage isn't real," I say to him, to myself, desperately trying to find right in all this wrong, "you can be with whoever you want."

But again, instead of his gaze blinking out like I'd hoped, the ring of fire in his eyes only spins faster.

Faster.

"Whoever I want," he repeats, tasting the three words as if they were sweeter than the juice of the fruit I just spoke of. "Is that a promise, Reim?"

And whether he understood me or not, I understand him perfectly, and the blush that I insisted on caging minutes earlier escapes its shackles, and dances freely over my cheeks once again.

But he doesn't smile in victory at its appearance, doesn't tease, doesn't shift a single muscle at all this time. He only continues to watch me as if he's as confused, as hopelessly intrigued by me as I am by him.

"And what about who *you* want?" he murmurs at last.

I nearly trip over a jutting root on our path.

Who I want? What? I—I mean I guess it's a fair question since I just asked it of him, but no one has ever asked me something like that before. I hadn't asked it of myself, either. Well, maybe except about—

"The Vuorian captain, perhaps?"

My head snaps back.

"Tamir? F-Fate, how do you keep getting inside my head?" I sputter.

But he ignores the question, hearing an answer in it instead. "So . . . you *do* have feelings for him, then."

And that strange, chipped note in his otherwise granite voice tells me this is it—this is my chance to close this door that's cracked open between us once and for all. To use the one weapon he'll never have access to. To do it. To lie.

So I stand up straighter, wet my tongue with some fable of forbidden love I once read somewhere and—

"It's not that simple," the traitorous flap of flesh begins instead. "We've never . . . That is to say, we just . . ."

I let out a frustrated huff.

"No, not in that way. Not anymore," I blurt.

But just as I realize what I've done and try to take it back, to pull another libelous arrow from my arsenal and try again, the taut set of his shoulders loosens, and he breathes out long and low. And I am lost in what it could mean—what any of this means, especially since I was the one who started this entire conversation with the intention of making it clear that there could be nothing between us, but ended up blurring the lines even further.

And how my world only seems to be blurring along with it.

"I'd like to show you something," the healer finally breathes down at me. "Will you come with me?"

And once again, I should hold my breath, stop my lungs from gorging on his simple words, his baffling behavior.

I should demand he just tell me exactly what he wants from me. Should tell him to stop playing with my shattered mind, my shredded heart. Should remind myself that part of my soul died the same day he killed my father and that nothing will change that, no matter what this tether is that keeps tightening between us.

I should say all of this.

But once again I don't.

"Yes," I breathe, from somewhere close yet far away. Somewhere safe yet lost within me. "I'll come with you."

He absorbs my answer within him as he did my earlier smile, my laughter, my light. My recent desperation, my confusion, my guilt.

And then he nods for me to follow.

Chapter 2

THE LATE AFTERNOON SUN ACCOMPANIES US ON our silent walk, an ever-watchful chaperone peeking through the lush, full branches of the almazi trees on its homeward journey behind the Ma'asa. Though we walk side by side, the healer's hands locked behind his back and mine clasped at my front, with not a foot between us, our minds may as well be miles apart.

I should be readying myself for what lies ahead. Should be questioning his motives. Should be planning for his attack. In truth, I should never have agreed so *foolishly* to work with him yesterday and then to follow him today, knowing how capable he is of destroying me.

But like all my recent decisions, I followed my impulsive heart and curious mind instead of my cautious sense, gave in to my need to know more about him despite knowing it will only tie me to him further.

Like, did he have a family? Does he still?

How does he have a gift while others don't?

Our books described the original Unnamed tribes as having long lives due to their gifts. If that's true, how old does that make him?

And most frustrating of all, why does any of it matter? Why do I want to know now?

"To know the enemy, will only teach you how to overpower him." That's what Order always taught me.

But is that really what I'm trying to do?

Not a moment after the question forms in my mind, his footsteps stop. The well-worn path of the almazi grove ends, leaving only an untended thicket ahead of us and not another soul in sight.

My heart throws itself against the bars of my ribs.

Wait, does he know I lied to him about trying to find *The Book of Names*? Or that I was going to lie about my relationship with Tamir as well? Did he bring me here to kill me for it?

No. The oath—it won't let us hurt each other. I can still feel its charge rushing through my whole body when I remember trying to stab him at the Bicentennial.

But what if he found a way around it?

But then why let me in the Jirga chambers to begin with? Why trust me with his people for weeks, people he champions and who love him back? Why trust me with sifr? Why consider mercy for my people? Why not make an example of me in front of everyone instead of doing it secretly in an abandoned field?

And why is my heart so damn desperate for a single drop of closeness and compassion that it's willing to lead itself to its own execution?

Why?
Why?
Why?

"Reim," he calls, snapping me out of my thoughts and back to him, to his serious gaze scouring my face. "Your sword. You will need your sword."

I honestly forgot I had it on me after so many weeks without it. I look down at his hand clutching the hilt of his own, and I don't know whether to laugh or cry that he still has honor. That he's willing to give me a fair chance to duel with him instead of killing me outright.

With a resigned sigh, I unsheathe my blade from down my back and hold it with both hands in front of me. He nods, raising his own above his head.

And just as I prepare for its downswing, he spins away from me and takes long, pendulum-like swipes at the thick foliage and tall grass ahead, again and again, until a rough path opens in front of us.

Then he tips his chin over his shoulder and jerks it forward, a silent order for me to follow his lead.

The sudden coolness of twilight settles over the field and over my ashen heart, which is always preparing for the worst, even as it foolishly hopes for the best.

I sigh, watching the steady rhythm of his hypnotic swings, as if he's been clearing brush his whole life, watching the powerful muscles of his shoulders, his arms, his back ripple and stretch. Ripple and stretch.

And then I raise my sword and do the same.

The hum and buzz of night fill my ears as we at last arrive at a crude four-walled structure made of bleached wood, clay, and stone, a far cry from our modern limestone bricks, terracotta roofs, and latticed windows, all secured with strong mortar. No, this place has been built and rebuilt so many times and in so many different ways that its layers remind me of the age rings embedded in the trunks of felled trees, a chronicle of so much more than meets the eye.

A story begging to be told.

The healer steps next to me, and even though his tall body blocks the awakening light of the moon and stars, I don't feel submerged in darkness.

"What is this place?" I whisper, my eyes jumping from the new layer of palm thatch upon the roof to the ancient cracks weaving up the far wall, no matter how many times they've been spackled.

"It's somewhere I come when I need to think," he murmurs. "When I need to be by myself . . ." I feel him hazard a glance at me rather than see him do it. "And *be* myself."

He clears his throat.

"I've been coming here almost every night since we took the kingdom, though admittedly by a less strenuous route," he says as he shoves the door open with a nudge of his shoulder, then ducks under the frame to let me in. I settle my surprised expression as he busies himself lighting the baluur in the small hearth and setting a kettle of water over the flickering violet blaze. I know he doesn't occupy my father's room, but I had assumed he slept somewhere else in the castle. And now, knowing he doesn't, knowing he comes all the way out here, I—I just don't understand it. Don't understand him at all.

"Is this . . . your home?" I grasp at the new piece of yet another puzzle he has laid at my feet as I sweep my gaze over the sparsely furnished room: a small, thatched cot on one side and a large worktable with various vials and instruments, drying herbs, and a single pot on the other. It's not large enough for a family, and there's not one sign or scent of a woman's presence.

I grit my teeth at the ridiculous thought.

He adds a handful of tea leaves, dried almazi fruit, spices, and herbs to the bubbling water before lowering his huge frame onto the creaking cot, nodding at a worn armchair opposite him for me to sit.

"What would you say if I said I don't know?" He chuckles to himself, shaking his head. "It's the only place that's been a constant my whole life. Walls went up to divide the land, people came and went, the years and kings and edicts passed and passed. But this place . . ." His voice drops as he sweeps his gaze over the snug space. "This *stayed*."

And there's something in the cadence of that last word that makes my overworked mind still. Something in the way he rests his forearms on his open knees, his shoulders relaxed, his head knocked back against the wall, that forces it to imagine someone else entirely.

Not a king. Not an enemy. Not even a stranger.

But then he seems to find more words, and I lose mine once again. "So, I don't know about a *home*. I'm still figuring out what that means. But this was where I was found as an infant, wrapped in a cloak, clutching an emerald phoenix feather in my hand."

My eyes dart to the one secured to a single braid at his right temple, the rest of his shoulder-length hair braided and loosely tied back at the nape of his neck.

"I mean, have you ever seen an emerald phoenix?" he asks the ceiling. "I haven't. And neither had the tribespeople who found me. They took it as a sign that I was special and took me in and raised me."

He continues to look at the ceiling as if it's as fascinating as the star-studded sky, and I hold my tongue about the emerald phoenix. I have, in fact, seen one. More than once. I can still see the effervescent spread of its verdant wings as it flew above me, can still see into the wise crimson of its eyes.

But then he drops his wise gaze back to meet mine, and I drop the memory back into the recesses of my mind where it belongs.

"And it turned out they were right." My words spark out of me like the fire in the hearth. "About you being special."

Special. Gift. Not a curse for killing my mother in child-birth, not an abomination for looking and acting different like I was made to *believe* about myself my entire life.

What a difference a word makes, I think, hating that I have once again reopened this bleeding wound that is always so damn hard to close up again.

"Hmm," he hums, tracing my ears with a gaze that is somehow so much warmer than the fire he lit, as if he's consid-ering every syllable of my said and unsaid words. "In a way, yes, they were right. I was able to heal by mere touch. Even as a child, if I sensed someone was hurt, my hands would glow, and I would be overcome with a need to reach for them. To *heal* them. And also, as you know, even more 'special' was that I was able to do it without a name."

He leans forward on his knees and holds my stare as se-curely as if he were holding me.

"But perhaps what you *don't* know is that even though my people value my gift, value me,"—he pauses when he sees my knuckles going white where they clutch the arms of the chair, but then pushes forward anyway—"when my gift prevents me from growing older with them, *living* with them . . . they move on with their lives. Eventually, move on to their deaths. Move on without me."

And now I'm the one who can't look away from him, even if I tried. Who doesn't even want to.

Without me.

In his two words, I hear myself.

Without me.

See myself.

And what's more is that for the first time, it seems that someone truly sees me too.

And then he rises from the cot, and I can't seem to see any-thing but him either. Can't seem to leave this chair. Can't seem to even think, to breathe, to *exist,* as he walks, as heavy as a shifting mountain, as light as the clouds at its peak, toward me. As he drops to his knees in front of me and folds his warm hands over my frigid ones on either armrest.

As he looks at me and *into* me and murmurs, "And yes, Reim, whether by being gifted or by being cursed, it's lonely, so very lonely."

Forbidden tears fill my eyes, yet I still can't look away.

"But at some point, it doesn't change the work that needs to be done. Doesn't change that you know you will do it. Whether people praise us or not, stay with us or not, *love* us or not, we will still do it."

Because it is what is right.

He nods. "Because it is what is right, my queen."

And now that the aching loneliness, the gnawing isolation that we've both felt for so long seems to have found understanding, *compassion*, in the other, it's threatening to never return to what was before again.

My heart suddenly takes off like the beating of a phoenix's wings, faster and faster until it threatens to break through the cage of my chest. To take flight.

"Reim," he goes on, turning my hand, finger by finger, over in his, so focused on the invisible scar at the center of my palm that he's oblivious to my rising panic, "There's something more you should know. Something about our—"

I rip my hands away from his before he can finish his sentence, shooting to my feet so fast the chair crashes to the wooden floor behind me.

"Sor-sorry." I begin backing away from him, though he hasn't moved toward me at all. "I—I . . ."

But the words die in my throat because all of a sudden, it's not him, or this moment, or even this world that has me overcome.

It's the far wall that from the outside was cracked and fissured, patched up countless times . . .

But from the *inside,* it's obvious why.

The clay surface is as black as the night watching over us. It clearly has been burned, charred—

I blink, and thick flames climb behind my eyelids.

"Ugh," I groan, clutching my head in pain, squeezing my eyes tighter.

"*Reim!*" The healer's yell is muffled by the roar of a fire. Not the small one in the hearth, but another one—one large enough to engulf an entire home.

I snap my eyes open. *This* home.

Panting and coughing, I spin. There's no cot, no armchair. No tea. No healer.

No, it's this home, but it's also not.

And it was my eyes I was looking through, my legs I was standing on . . . but now they're not. I was just myself and now . . . now I'm someone else entirely.

The woman from my dreams—I'm somehow in her body, her *reality.*

The creak of burning wood rumbles from above like approaching thunder.

Once, twice, before a large piece of the ceiling crashes into fiery splinters right in front of me, blinding me with a torrent of smoke and cinders, making my lungs blister, my heart stutter.

But there is no time left. No choice, either. I look over my shoulder at the gaping doorway. The strangers will be here soon. Despite the fires they started, the devastation they caused, they will come.

Because they did it all for one thing.

My hand shelters my burning eyes as I sweep my gaze across the room. Searching, searching, until I find it—a leather-bound tome, thankfully unscathed—on top of the corner table.

I leap over the blazing wreckage and manage to snatch it from its perch, clutching it to my chest before it too is swallowed by the hungry flames.

Whipping back around, I watch the fire climb higher up the far wall, the roof above moments away from caving in.

I bite back my wail. The home Adami and I built together, the love we filled it with, I have no choice but to leave it as I had to leave everything and everyone else.

But then I remember my promise, my purpose, and my grip on The Book *tightens.*

All that matters is what I carry now.

But then another crash from above takes the rest of the ceiling down. And before I can recover, something hard and unforgiving shoves me to the ground, The Book *sliding across the wooden floor into the curtain of smoke.*

And now, it's not the world that's ending.

It's me.

Because The Book *. . . our final hope . . .*

It's gone.

Strong hands grab my shoulders and pull me against an equally solid chest, trying to pry my arms apart where they're wrapped across my body. But my fingers dig into my flesh. Refuse to let go.

No. No. The Book. They can't have it.

"Reim!" the healer thunders my name, the hearth threatening to blow out with the force of his gift coming to life, and I gasp, taking great pulls of air into my parched lungs as he moves his glowing fingers from my arms to either side of my face, forcing my vacant eyes to meet his full ones and my mind to calm, to ease, to return to itself under the throbbing light emanating from him.

And it does, but my pulse ratchets in its stead when he presses his forehead to mine.

His expression wild.
His breath heavy.
And *growls*.
"Now, what the *Fate* just happened, wife?"

The Book of Names. *The lost piece of your people. I saw it. It's real. It's sandblasted real.*

That's what I want to tell him. What my heart and soul are screaming at me to tell him and the whole sandblasted world.

But despite this Fate-shattering revelation . . . I can't. I shouldn't. Especially not to him, and definitely not right now.

Not when I'm at a loss more than ever before. Not when I still remember his lies, but now they're impossibly muddled with his truths. Not when I don't know what this could mean for the future of Vuor.

And especially not when he's still holding onto me like he is, his large hands cradling my small face like I might slip away if he lets go. Like he's afraid of it happening.

Like he may actually care.

Because I can't, *can't,* think like this. Can't let myself believe he feels anything for me besides ambivalence because then that might mean . . . it might mean . . .

Fate.

I lift my trembling hands to his that are clamped along my temples, cheeks, and jaw. And once the cold tips of my fingers touch the burning ones of his, he relaxes.

Seems to breathe again. The fiery whorls of his eyes cool with confusion, but also with . . . with that new something else as well.

"Nothing," I whisper into their fathomless depths. "Nothing happened. I'm fine."

"Don't lie to me," he growls, his eyes roaring to life once again.

"I'm. *Fine*," I growl right back, digging my heels into this perilous path I've chosen.

"Reim," he warns again, but this time it sounds almost like a plea, and it nearly makes me give up. Turn back.

I squeeze my eyes shut. It's the vision. It has to be. This *thing* I'm feeling between us is happening because of whatever happened to me just now, and it's making me struggle with separating the emotions of the ghosts who once lived here from my own.

Taking a deep breath, I wrench his fingers from my face. And at first, he continues to hold onto my hands as they drop between us, before finally, *finally*, letting them go.

I exhale.

"I just want to go home." I force yet another lie past the knot in my tongue, which is so much easier now that he's not touching me. "It's been a long day, and I must be more tired than I thought."

He just stares at me in silence, as if he knows I'm lying but he's holding back on calling my bluff—like a dahak holding back his fire—and I suspect he's holding back in more ways than one.

But why? And more inexplicably still, why, for the first time since meeting him, do I wish he wouldn't? Why don't I want him to hold back at all? Why do I want to see him the way he saw me, the real me, earlier? To see him *free*?

But then he rumbles, "Then by all means, we should go." He douses the raging fireplace with the forgotten tea, before storming out the door without any further word, any further look, any further touch.

Leaving me to burn alone with the ashes of my indecision.

I OPEN MY HEAVY EYES THE NEXT DAY TO THE EARLY AF-ternoon sun trying to murder me with its pestering cheer. Peeling my face off the sticky surface it was pressed against during sleep, I smack my lips and blink at my bleary surroundings.

Books, at least a hundred of them, are strewn about every-where. I groan through a parched throat as the previous day comes back in one battering memory after another.

A cautious walk through breezy groves, a home filled with warm feelings that had nothing to do with the hearth's heat, a vision of destruction, a life-changing discovery, healing hands followed by harsh words.

And then returning to the castle not to sleep, but to race to the moonlit library, pulling every book on the shelves that even mentioned the Nihaya . . . only to find poems, illustrations, story after story of Vuor's valiant conquest, but nothing, not a single thing, about *The Book of Names*, as if it had been wiped clean not only from our pages, but from our memories as well.

Also, my mind was unable to think about *The Book* with-out also thinking about the terms of the deal he proposed on our wedding night. About how in exchange for helping him find it, he promised not only freedom from marriage but a fair fight for the kingdom. And though at the time it felt just and right, after working with the Unnamed in the cantons, after listening and learning from them for weeks, it feels wrong. So very wrong. It feels like a betrayal of our tenuous peace. It feels like war.

But worst of all, I couldn't separate any of this from thinking about the one who told me about *The Book* in the first place. About the ease in his usually stiff body and face as he walked about his home. The vulnerable cadence of his usually firm voice when he told me about his loneliness and held my hand before the vision.

"There's something you should know. Something about our—"

"Damn it! What was he going to say?" I ask the empty room.

And why couldn't I keep my fracturing emotions together long enough to hear him? And then I damn well did it again after the vision when I demanded he take me home, when he had gone to such lengths to host me in his.

Only for me to reject it. Reject *him*.

I snatch the book lying open in front of me and stuff my face into its pages, scream my frustration at him, at myself, at the whole damn situation into its thick, useless folds.

This—this confusion within me is exactly why I couldn't ask the healer about *The Book* back at the hut. Why I can't ask him about it now. Because the only thing we can ever be to each other is a means to an end. Because these feelings, no matter how overwhelming, are just that— feelings. Because, in truth, he is still as much a stranger to me as I am to him, what brought us together was my fear of being alone, and in truth, whatever happens next, I must do it alone.

Because the biggest truth of all is that I am destined to be alone.

The aged parchment is wet where it presses against my eyes.

Knock. Knock. Knock.

The book crashes to the ground as I almost do the same from my chair.

Khur. The healer. We're supposed to be going to the cantons together.

But then Tamir's voice comes from the other side of the door. "Reim, are you in there?"

And I hate that I don't know whether the breath I take when I hear it is from relief or disappointment. I shake my head.

"One second, Tamir," I call back as I straighten the chair and books as best I can. "But what are you doing here? Is my husb—*Fate*—I mean the Maliki looking for me to go to the cantons?"

Once again, I can't believe I almost called the healer my husband, despite literally just telling myself all the reasons to maintain distance from him.

From the blaring silence beyond the door, it seems Tamir can't believe it either.

I slap my hand against my forehead.

"Tamir, I—"

"The healer asked me to tell you that he will not be accompanying you today."

A beat.

"Oh," I manage to say before shaking my head.

"Al-all right. Well, let him know I will take my sword and dagger with me, and he need not worry—" I bite my tongue as if I am an Unnamed attempting to lie. But this is worse. My need to reassure the healer came from a place of truth.

What the Fate is wrong with me?

"No, Reim," Tamir interjects. "He said you're not to go today either."

I push a stiff hand into my tangle of hair.

Not to go today. Did he find out what I'm doing? That I found out about *The Book*?

"He's holding his first court this morning in the throne room for the people of the Citadel. He wants you there with him."

And I nearly pull a patch of hair right out of my skull in surprise.

He wants me there? Especially after how I acted last night? Why?

"Umm . . . I don't know?" Tamir answers, and I realize I've asked the question out loud. "Maybe to deflect some of the vitriol he's sure to receive onto you."

And though there is so much I still don't know about the healer, I do know what Tamir is saying isn't true. He never used me to shield himself from anyone's weapons or venom. In fact, he stepped in the line of fire so I wouldn't fall victim to them, like with the Jirga.

I hasten to rebraid my hair, pinching my cheeks to bring some color to them and chewing my lip until I fear they're bleeding instead of just plump and bruised.

"All right, let's go," I huff, out of breath when I finally open the door on Tamir's shocked stare.

"Reim," he breathes, his eyes skating over me in a way that makes me feel as if I'm wearing a gown of the finest silk, not yesterday's travel robes. A look I would have welcomed from him a year ago. The same look the Unnamed women wore for the healer yesterday.

I try not to flinch when the unseen mark on my palm throbs at the memory.

"You . . . you look—"

I hold the pulsing hand up in the pulseless space between us.

"Stop, Tamir. Please."

And he does, though I don't know whether it's in response to my harsh first word or my soft last one.

I shake my head.

"I just don't see you the same way you see me. And I told you once I can only offer you sincere friendship—"

Now it's his turn to stop me.

"Then that's all I will accept," he says, a sad smile curving up his face. "It just takes time for emotion to catch up with reason sometimes."

My shoulders drop, and I look away at his answer. Not because I dismiss his struggle or his words, but rather because I know exactly what he means. It's what I've been trying to do all morning about someone else.

"Thank you," I murmur, meaning it. He nods in return.

But then his eyes light up.

"Oh no. I know that look, Tamir. It's the same one you used to have back when we were younglings and you would convince me to sneak honey cake with you from the castle kitchens in the name of reconnaissance."

"Ha!" he barks. "You're acting like you weren't the one who created a scene to distract the scullery maids while I got the goods."

I roll my eyes.

"Anyway." He looks up and down the hall. "I was thinking court doesn't start for another twenty minutes, and . . . the training yard is probably empty right now. So, what do you say? A bit of sparring for old time's sake?"

"I don't know if that's a good—"

"C'mon. I'll even go easy on you . . . to make up for what I said earlier."

And now it's my turn to laugh. "All right, all right. But *I'll* be the one going easy on you."

"Yeah, yeah," he says as we race toward the amphitheater, the smiles on both our faces staying with us all the way until we're geared up and facing each other in the familiar ring.

"You know something," he begins, spinning his saber in slow oblong spirals as we circle each other. "I'm surprised the healer sent me to get you. I've never hidden my mistrust of him, and he certainly hasn't hidden his for me."

I take two leaps forward before bringing my longsword down on his. *Clang.*

I was surprised too, but I say nothing. It's hard enough to talk about my complicated thoughts regarding the healer with myself, let alone with someone who detests him as much as Tamir.

He grits his teeth as he pushes me back and regroups.

Swing.

Clang.

Swing.

Clang.

I exchange thrusts and parries with him, which is so much safer than exchanging words, when he finally rolls away from one of my strikes and bounds to his feet.

"But that must be it then," he says, slapping the broad side of his sword against his plated chest. "This isn't about whether he trusts *me* or not, is it?"

His blue eyes widen, and then he points the weapon at me. "It's about him trusting *you.*"

My palm aches at that, forcing me to readjust my hold on my own sword. "What are you talk—"

"He trusts you, Reim." He slaps his free hand against his head. "Fate, of course he does. I mean, *I* trusted you enough to lie for you, so I know the feeling."

I grimace. "And I still feel terrible about that, by the way."

He waves off my words as if I'm missing the entire point.

"The healer trusts you, Reim," he enunciates. "And perhaps . . . perhaps even something more than that."

Perhaps even more than that.

"What are you trying to say, Tamir?" I snap, lunging at him to avoid reading too much into his words, but also knowing it's too late.

But he circles his blade over mine before nudging it away, chuckling at my usual impatience. "Well, *Reim*, what I'm trying to say is that trusting you may be the first thing he and I agree upon."

My mouth drops open, my blade sagging. Tamir softening to the Maliki was not something I thought possible.

He takes the opening to thrust his sword.

"That's a stupid thing to base anything on. And it's all theory." I spin out of its way, dismissing his words, even as all the memories of the healer threaten to cut me open worse than any weapon.

"No, it's not," he says seriously. "Trust is the foundation, the fundamental need of every relationship."

I huff a short laugh.

"Well, there you have it then. There's no 'relationship' between the Maliki and me."

Dragging his blade against the sand-dusted floor, he slows to a stop in front of me, until he's looking down at me fully, a gleam of sunlight breaking through the canopy of clouds above the massive empty room to witness whatever we say next.

"Maybe not," he concedes. "But you trust each other with the people the other cares about, and that amounts to the same thing."

"Who?" I ask, giving into my curiosity instead of suppressing it like I should.

"You with the Unnamed of the cantons, with the architect, with sifr. Him with Mori. With *me*. Now with the people of the Citadel." He jerks his head toward the exit doors to remind me of the court I still have to get to.

I groan, Tamir's words confusing me even further than I was this morning.

"I don't understand you, Tamir. You just hated him an hour ago. Hated the Unnamed for much longer than that."

He looks at me, his cerulean gaze rocking me like the gentle waves they resemble before sending me out to sea.

"And I *do* still hate him," he says, drinking in my features as if this will be one of the last times he'll be able to do so. "But perhaps the reason why is changing."

And I want to tell him he's wrong. That whatever he's implying about what's between me and the healer is wrong.

But I can't.

Because I'm feeling the change too, and I've spent all morning trying to stop it. And instead of making me certain of my decision to do so, Tamir's words only further my struggle.

Tamir tugs the gilded handle of my sword from my slack grip.

"And Reim."

I slide my uncertain eyes up to his sure ones once again. "Yes?"

"I just want you to know, whatever happens next, whatever you choose, I will always be on your side. I will always choose you."

THE HEAVY WOODEN DOORS OF THE THRONE ROOM close behind me like the sliding of a coffin lid. The deafening silence greets me, like the welcoming of death itself. Which is fitting, since the last time I entered here, just like this, it was for an execution. And today, the executioner stands waiting for me on the same dais my father did that day.

Except now, neither his face wears the mask of a murderer, nor his head the crown of the king. And my mind can't make sense of it, especially after everything that happened last night.

Who are you?

But no sooner does the question form than it fades— because though I smooth my donned crimson robes with sweaty palms and force my leaden feet to complete the short journey up the dais with my crowned head raised high, though I try to force my shoulders to shrug off the mantle of my heavy thoughts, they are weighed down by the congregation's stares instead.

I can guarantee they haven't forgotten the last time I was here either. Or the role I played in the complaints they have gathered to present today.

But Fate has made me their Malika, and the time for trying to prevent it from happening, for wishing it weren't so, is buried forever with my father.

And yet, knowing this still doesn't stop the first sparks of panic that ignite within me as I turn to face them for the first time since the Bicentennial and receive the full affront of their anger and hatred.

I swallow, trying to grasp Baba's words.

Gutter that fire. Deprive it of air.

Gutter that fire. Deprive it . . .

Gutter . . . that . . . fire . . .

Gutter . . .

But it's not working. And now my lungs, not my panic, are the ones being deprived of air.

And just as my heart, my mind, threaten to follow, threaten to gutter out themselves, I feel warmth.

Pulsing warmth, starting in my palm, then spreading, covering, *embracing* every part of me until my overwrought mind is cocooned in ease.

In relief.

My eyes lift to what has to be the source of this relief, but the Maliki's head is bowed slightly toward the ground in front of me.

"My queen," he murmurs to me, his low tone rolling like a landslide over the room, a clear command to the assembly to follow his lead.

Some do while others don't, but at this moment I can't seem to care about them or about what they think of me. My mind caring only about one thing.

One person.

And what he just did.

How he just . . . just *healed* me without blood. Without touch.

"*He trusts you, Reim. Perhaps something even more than that.*"

But that's the problem that wouldn't come to my tongue earlier. Even if the healer does trust me, how can I trust him when every time we're together, I find out something new about him like this? No, not just new, but incomplete. A clue, a hint. Perhaps neither.

And what if they're all just misdirection? Just different ways to get what he wants?

He lifts his face to mine, and his molten eyes only reflect my own confusion.

Fate, did he even realize he did it?

And all the pent-up tension from last night, from right now, threatens to snap.

I want to scream my frustration at him.

I want to beat my fists on his chest.

I want to grab him and demand at knifepoint that he tell me what is going on right this instant. About *The Book of Names*. About him. About this obvious but also obscure thing between us.

I want to pull his face down to mine like he did to me in the hut, but this time I want to—I want to—

"Reim, whatever is on your mind right now, we will discuss it after Court," he murmurs as we take our seats.

I blush in mortification.

No, that's the one thing I do *not* want to do.

Tamir brings the first petitioner before us, nodding to me with a small smile before addressing the man, "State your name and your need from the Crown."

"My name is Saqeib," a muscular man in silk robes and sour spirits introduces himself. "I own one of the largest baluur trade caravans. Or I should say, I used to," he spits.

"Then what is your need?" the healer snaps back, his lip curling in disgust. "It seems you may have more coin in your coffers than even the Crown."

"And I earned every last one of them, and now my income is more than halved. The majority of the shares are going to your savages," the man says, escalating. "You stole our kingdom, stole my—"

"Do not dare speak to me about stealing," the Maliki booms, bounding to his feet, his eyes flashing as his gift and righteous fury flare to life.

The crowd starts jostling against each other, shouts punctuating the agitated murmurs.

Oh no. I snap my attention back to the healer, but his attention is fixed on Saqeib.

"You who stand so proudly, so insolently, in a castle built on the backs of my people, raised on top of their graves. You, who stole their very lives in those mines that you now profit from."

And then they're no longer sparks. His bright irises are no longer distinguishable from the rest of his eyes as light bursts from them, shooting through the veins in his face until it illuminates every capillary of his covered chest, of his exposed neck and hands, until he is so blinding that anything outside of him disappears into shadow.

The luminous hall fills with screams of terror, and my mind is pulled back to a similar scene of chaos in this very room at the Bicentennial. And just like before, I lunge at the healer to stop him. But this time, not for my sake, or even for my kingdom's.

But for his.

I grasp his hand with mine and hold it tight.

We both look down at our joined palms in shock. His glowing gaze instantly sputters before whipping up to my face. He holds my gaze as securely as I hold his hand.

Why? it seems to ask me.

I don't know, mine replies back. Yet neither of us lets go.

And only when his molten eyes cool completely and his gift's light dims until it's but a shy flicker nuzzling the twin scars of our joined palms do I let go.

"I will answer for the Crown. Please take your seats," I say, turning to address the still shaking assembly. "In our first Jirga meeting after the siege, I asked the members for time for us Vuorians to adjust to the many changes that would inevitably come. I asked for fairness and equality for our people. For mercy. And I thought that would be enough."

I let go of the healer's hand, and though his honed attention remains on me, mine turns to the petitioner. "But now, Saqeib made me realize that we require more."

The caravan owner dusts off his silk robes as if what has just occurred were nothing but a strong wind through an open window, tilting his chin haughtily as if he were the victor in some imaginary duel with the king.

"Clearly, for there to be meaningful betterment of our kingdom, there must be accountability as well," I continue, as Saqeib dares to smile a dirty, ugly smile at the Maliki, confident in my ruling in his favor.

Overconfident.

"Therefore, Saqeib, master of the Kubra Caravan, you will be accountable to pay the same dividends to the miners that they have been receiving for the past month, now back-dated for the past *year*. You will also be required henceforth to pay an additional maintenance tithe for the safety of your mines and any other expenses that may incur if there are collapses."

His smile sours, his face turning the bright crimson of my dress.

"And furthermore, the same accountability will apply to those trading almazi and those overseeing the fish trade in Canton One and Three, respectively. You can thank Saqeib for bringing this matter to our attention. You are dismissed."

"You-you shadeed bitch." The petitioner sputters at me, attempting to rush the dais, but Tamir and another guard shackle his arms from either side and start dragging him toward the door instead. "I came here today to give you a chance to prove your loyalty, and you proved it all right. But you'll do well to remember this—you may have whored yourself to this khasir animal, but it still won't save a traitor like you. You think we're just going to sit here and take this khur? There are people in your very Jirga that hate you and are plotting to ruin you. And there are many here who will join them. We will take back what is ours, and when we do, we will tie you to his bed and take turns—"

His tirade is cut off by a sharp whistle renting the air.

Then a piercing scream.

My eyes widen as blood pools hard and fast where a dagger protrudes at the juncture of Saqeib's thighs.

I glance up from the carnage to find Tamir shouting orders to keep the Court in check before spearing his shocked gaze on the space next to me. Or rather the *person.*

"What did you do?" I whisper to the king while staring, horrified, at the macabre scene.

"Showed him the mercy I promised you I would," the healer growls low from beside me as the guards drag the screaming, writhing man away. "I told you, Reim—I respect your decisions, your leadership, but that doesn't mean I won't do what I must to run our kingdom. And that includes what I do when someone disrespects my queen, my *wife.*"

My breath catches, not only at the adamancy of his words, but at *how* he said the name he's called me countless times before. How this time it bore not a single teasing syllable. How it was, in fact, deadly serious. An undeniable truth.

And I wait for the anger that usually follows the healer's use of that word to overtake me. I wait and I wait for the fury I once felt at him fighting my battles, defending me, to fill my head, my heart, with irritation if not hatred.

But it never comes.

And I'm prevented from thinking further about what that could mean because a guard calls for the next petitioners—a Vuorian man, woman, and child a little younger than sifr—to take the stand.

"State your name and your need from the Crown," the young Unnamed guard announces.

"I am Bashem, and this is my wife, Salwa and my d-daughter Rukhsar," the man stammers. And after what just happened, I don't blame him, but I also can't bring myself to blame the Maliki either.

"I-I come before the Crown to-to . . . you see my daughter, she-she." The man glances at his daughter who is clinging to her mother's rigid arms.

"For *Fate's* sake," the woman curses at the cowering man. "You're so pathetic."

And then turns to us. "My foolish husband has dragged us all the way here with an idiot's dream. He spawned this child here who has a bum leg."

She shoves the girl in front of her. "Go on, show the useless thing to them."

The girl's chestnut braids fall in a gnarled curtain over her face as she hurries to do as her mother demands, curling into herself with embarrassment as she trips a few times in the process. Though she is dressed in the usual Vuorian finery, she lacks the expected social graces that are taught in our schools and society. She must have been kept at home because of the disability. And from the way her mother is treating both her and her father, who knows what she was taught about the world. About herself.

She lifts the hem of her robes just enough to reveal her inturned foot and a flash of the thinned leg above it before dropping the cloth over it once again.

"We heard of the Maliki's . . . er . . . ability to heal, and we wanted to ask if he could help her," Bashem finds the strength to say.

"*He* wanted to ask. Not me," his wife corrects him, staring daggers at her husband as if she were the most unfortunate person in the room.

"And you, Rukhsar?" I lean forward from my seat, smiling at the quiet child caught in the barrage of her parents' tumultuous relationship. "What do *you* want, albi?"

Two wide lilac eyes peek through the fringe of braids, looking between her parents before turning their sad gaze to me and the Maliki.

"I want to play with the other children," she admits with a raspy voice that gets stronger with every word. "I want to run. To go to school. I want to see—"

"That's enough, stupid child." Her mother cuffs the back of her head. "Wanting to do silly things like play when you are needed at home to cook, clean, mend, and wash."

"So, you have come here to ask for a servant then?" the healer thunders sarcastically at the woman, who has the sense not to respond to the king. But that doesn't stop her from displacing her ire onto her hapless husband.

"Are you satisfied now? He's ridiculing us in front of our people. And from what we all have just seen, his supposed 'gift' is not healing but intimidation and fear." She starts pulling the quiet, hobbling girl toward the exit. "I will not have it. We are leaving! Now!"

The healer doesn't say anything, nor does he move. He just sits, steepling his fingers at his lips, watching them leave with his gilded eyes.

While I wring my hands.

"Aren't you going to stop them? That poor girl," I whisper under my breath as the crowd begins to murmur among themselves. "The mother is cruel and hopeless, but you can help the child. I know you can."

He turns his serious gaze to me at that.

"If you truly believe that, Reim," he murmurs, "then I ask you to trust me."

There's that word again. *Trust.* So easily falling from Tamir's lips earlier and now the healer's.

And I want to tell him that it's anything but easy for me. That I don't know him enough to trust him. That he betrayed the trust I already placed in him the first time we met. That though he told the truth about *The Book*, saw the truth about me like no one else, I still wonder if he's lying in other ways. If he's just feeding me enough truths until he once again gets what he wants.

No. Any further trust is a weakness I can't afford to add to the others already growing where he's concerned.

But I say none of that.

I just look away. Just look at the girl, who is looking back at me one last time before the throne room doors close behind her.

Chapter 23

B Y THE TIME I REACH MY ROOM, NIGHT IS SETTLING over the castle, its many inhabitants settling into the night in return.

Having taken a bath and changed into my usual linen nightshirt, I walk barefoot to the bed, brushing my unbound hair as I think about Court—how seeing the healer again, seeing us defend each other, seeing us work together only confused me further.

I think about Tamir and his words, his slow change of heart toward the healer, about his thoughts on trust.

I sigh, setting the brush down on the nightstand, and my gaze falls of its own volition to the hidden drawer beneath it. The one that once held Baba's signet ring, the one constant I had left of my previous life. My fingers itch to hold it one more time. Ache to feel the familiar sense of blind obedience, of "Order" it symbolized, which is so much easier than feeling and dealing with all this change.

I bunch my fist to crush the urge to charge through the hall, the sleeping castle, to my father's room and hold it again.

Yes, Order would be so much easier to navigate than all this uncertainty I'm drowning in. But easier would never have led to the people of Canton Two having safety and community. It would never have led to Canton One having control over their crops, trading them and living off their work. It would never have led to meeting sifr and the architect, learning about empathy and justice from my guards. It would never have led to meeting the—

Molten eyes filled with concern and strong hands filled with healing flash across my vision.

Ugh, why does my mind always circle back to *him*?

I pull my hair back into a single braid, tie a cotton robe around myself, and slip barefoot into the hall, not going to my father's room, but knowing that I can't stay here either.

That I need to *move*.

That I need to wander.

To avoid looking too closely at the possibility that I'm not wandering at all.

That I know exactly what I am looking for.

Or rather, *who*.

That I am looking for the healer, not to demand my right to sit at the Jirga table like I did the first and only time I sought him out in the training yards, but to talk to him, to hear him. To know if he's been feeling differently since last night too.

Last night formed a crack in the impenetrable wall between us, more jarring than the crack in the burned wall of the hut. A crack in both of our defenses that led to everything that came before that to fall apart. That led us to understanding each other, building something together today.

I sigh, digging my bare heels into the cold stone floor, forcing the blazing energy coursing through me to snuff out.

What am I doing? He likely isn't even in the castle. He said he goes to the hut most nights.

Leaning my elbows on a nearby windowsill, I look out at the full moon above, then stare at the shifting stars, the restless desert sky that reminds me so much of my own restless heart.

"Good evening, Reim."

I spin, my surprised gaze colliding with a familiar slate one. I fall back against the window ledge.

"Oh, hello." I smile at the architect, who readily returns it. "Can't sleep either?"

"You could say that," he says with a shrug. "May I join you?"

"Of course," I say, sliding over to make room for him on the ledge too.

"How was Court?" he asks, leaning back against it while I turn to the undulating empyrean.

I scoff. "As if you don't know. As if the whole kingdom doesn't know."

"You mean your father never castrated a man in front of the entire Court for insulting his wife?"

I turn my head to meet his amused gaze.

"No." I laugh with a shake of my head. "But please don't mistake me. It's not because he abhorred visceral punishment or something. It's just that Vuorians prefer to carry it out behind iron bars, away from the oblivious eyes of the common folk."

I think of how I found sifr in that exact situation in the castle prisons and swallow back bile before continuing. "Appearance of civility was more important than actual civility. Plus, without witnesses, it's easier to lie—to others, yes, but also to *ourselves,* about what actually happened."

All this time he says nothing, just continues to rest against the stone ledge with loose limbs, and an empathetic smile.

"Besides, the Maliki didn't do that for me. He did it for his particular definition of justice."

The architect raises an eyebrow. "If I tried to say what you just did, my tongue would be cut clean through."

I groan, shoving his shoulder with mine. "Please, enough. Things are confusing as it is without your meddling."

His brows dip.

"Confusing . . . why do you say that?"

I think about his question for a moment. Answering him, talking through my thoughts regarding the healer would in one way give me relief from the restless emotion that brought me out here, maybe even some direction. But I've never talked about these things with others. Not even truly with myself.

But the architect? Can I talk to him? Can I trust him? On the one hand, he is one of the Unnamed who orchestrated the siege of the kingdom. He is the chief adviser to the Maliki and is aligned in many ways with him. On the other hand, he was the one who encouraged me to live after the Bicentennial, after my grief over Baba threatened to be the death of me. He was the one who saved me from the man who attacked me in the Burrow. He has always been consistent in his support and kindness to me.

I take a deep breath.

"I just mean I can't comment on the reasons behind anything the healer does or doesn't do, let alone attribute them to myself. But I can say that things seem to be . . . changing between us."

I feel the architect's astute gaze cut across my profile as I keep my lost one pinned to the sky.

"Is that a bad thing? For things to be 'changing' between you two?" he asks after a moment, his expression open, listening.

"I . . . I'm not sure." I give a wry smile. "When it comes to ruling the kingdom, we seem to be finding compromise, common understanding, more easily. . ." I trail off.

But when it comes to ruling our hearts, things seem to be getting more difficult. At least for me. And that reminds me of another difficult change I've been preoccupied with. One the architect, with all his pragmatism and knowledge, is actually the perfect person to discuss it with.

Turning to face him fully, I wave my hands in front of me.

"But never mind all that. Can I ask you about something else, please? It's something I don't know who else to turn to with. And . . . and you have always been so helpful to me."

His eyes clear, and he smiles that easy smile once more.

"Of course. I would be happy to listen."

I smile back, bolstered to say what comes next.

"What do you know about *The Book of Names*?"

His eyes go wide before he does a quick sweep of the hallway and then ushers me into the castle library at the end of it.

"What do *you* know about it, Reim?" he asks once we're behind closed doors and he's sure the room is empty. "Most Vuorians have never heard of it."

"Well, nothing from these books, I assure you." I flick an accusing hand at the stacks upon stacks of books still taking over the tables from this morning. "Most of what I know is from what the healer has told me."

He raises both brows before guiding us to sit at a window seat bathed in moonlight, as the hearth and torches were doused hours earlier. "All right. Go on."

I nod. "Well, on our wedding night, the healer told me he would let me out of this marriage if I help him find *The Book of Names*. He said it was an ancient tome that not only bestowed names on your people but also their gifts."

"I see. And did he say what would happen to the kingdom if you did, in fact, help him find *The Book* and were released from this marriage? He would no longer be Maliki."

There's an overwhelmed edge to his voice that wasn't there before. But about what? That the healer told me, a stranger, about something so important to their people? Or that he didn't tell the architect that he did? Or is it that the stakes of this endeavor are the loss of the kingdom? The kingdom they worked so hard to conquer in the first place.

Fate, maybe I shouldn't have said anything. But it's too late now.

"Well, his ultimate hope is that the names and gifts would be restored to the Unnamed, and then . . ." I swallow, looking away. "And then we would go to battle for the kingdom."

Just saying it out loud makes my heart pound to the beat of a Vuorian war drum. Gritting my teeth, I power forward.

"He told me *The Book* is widely believed to have been destroyed, but there's reason to believe it was hidden and that a cipher reveals its location"—I wave my hand in a wide arc—"*somewhere*. He wants my help finding that cipher."

Or he did.

He hasn't mentioned *The Book* to me since the first Jirga meeting, though my mind seems to bring it up constantly.

The architect rubs the bridge of his nose as he considers all of this.

"So, for you, finding this supposed cipher would be the only way to deal with this marriage. The only way to win back your kingdom."

I sigh.

"And therein lies the problem. I may have believed that at one point, but not for some time. The thought of war after so much loss then so much hope makes my heart ache. I also admit that I saw all of this as a fool's dream—at best, a way for people to have hope amid their suffering. And even if *The Book* once *did* exist, what was the likelihood it survived for two hundred years intact. And what was the likelihood that, even if it did, it would still work as it once did?" I finish, breathless and twisting my hands.

But then he reaches over, clasps them between his, and tugs them toward him. The silver of his eyes glints in the moonlight as he nods.

"Yes, these were our thoughts on it as well. But something has changed this, hasn't it?"

I nod back.

"But then I started having dreams," I say out loud for the first time.

His hold trembles.

"I've been dreaming of an unknown woman during what I assume is the Nihaya. First, she seemed to just be trying to survive it, to grieve her loved ones lost during it, but then . . ." I swallow. "Then, just last night, I dreamed of her again . . . but this time I was awake."

"A vision," he murmurs, rubbing his fingers over the back of my knuckles in soothing circles, as if his mind is spinning in the same motion.

"Reim, this . . . this is . . . incredible. This changes *everything*," he breathes. Then drops my hands and runs one of them over his neat braids. "But wait, does the healer not know? About the dreams? The vision?"

"No." I shake my head, getting up and walking away from him, the nervous energy from earlier starting again at the mention of the king—my husband. "I told you, things are confusing between us."

He lets out a low whistle at my dilemma.

But all I hear is the whistle of the dagger. The screams of the man. The healer's violent threats to Basteel.

But I also remember his sincerity with the people in the cantons yesterday, his confusing yet real concern for me after I was attacked, and then again after the vision in the hut.

Yes. Confusing is the correct word for his behavior. For the feelings it inspires in me.

And then, of course, there is the other problem.

"Besides, he promised a fair fight in exchange for my help in finding *The Book*, and though I want the best for your people, I don't want war."

"Hmm. Well, why don't we take one step at a time for now. Let me look into this cipher, and these dreams." The architect's rational, decisive voice breaks through my anxiety. "And if you learn any more about *The Book*, about its location or the cipher's location from these visions, you can always tell me."

I nod rapidly.

He squeezes my hands once more.

"Reim, I know this is a lot to deal with, but you have given me so much hope, to so many of us just now."

And I cannot lie.

After causing so much suffering, hearing I've given others hope . . . it gives me a sort of hope too.

I SMOOTH THE BRAIDED CORONET I WOVE OVER MY long, loose hair for what must be the fifth time in as many minutes. Which is only marginally better than the hour I spent prior to that, picking out my clothes for the day. I finally donned the jade chemise and shalwar I'm wearing now, after the gold embroidery on the black one I'd originally chosen stupidly reminded me of the gilded strands of someone's hair.

Someone who's still not here.

I steal one more look at my vanity mirror before turning to the bedroom door haloed in the warm sunlight instead, my heart fluttering like the wings of the phoenixes delivering their morning missives outside my window.

Is he even coming?

I throw up my hands with a huff. This is ridiculous. I've been doing work in the cantons before him and am perfectly capable of doing it without him now.

I spring to my feet, march to the door, and swing it open.

Only to slam it closed and spin around.

He's here. He came.

Of course he did. I knock my head back with a thump. He said he was going to, and he can't lie. That's all there is to it.

Closing my eyes, I take a deep breath and open the door again.

Only for our gazes to collide this time instead.

There's no teasing at what just happened. No explanation for being late. Just a stillness in the air that is both loud and quiet at the same time. Just his overgrown beard and his hand-combed hair. His clothes that are different from the ones he wore to Court, but unkempt.

Almost as if he rushed here. Or . . . or as if he had been here this whole time . . . the whole night?

My palm throbs in answer. And both of us stretch out our hands at our sides just before he breaks the silence.

"Did you sleep well?" he rumbles, and it's only been less than a day since I last heard his voice, but it feels like it's been longer. So much longer.

"Yes." I force the lie past my parched throat. "Did you?"

And the moment after I ask the question lasts so long, I wonder if he heard it. But then his throat bobs, lips part.

"No. Not at all."

And there it is again: his half-answer, his deliberate opening for me to ask more about him. But instead of frustrating me as it usually does—making me believe he's intentionally keeping things from me to fool me, to lie to me—it makes me start to wonder if it's something else entirely.

If it's him giving me the choice, the freedom to determine my next steps when it comes to knowing him. When so many choices have been taken from me, perhaps this one remains mine. When he has power over me in so many ways, perhaps this is his way of giving me power over him. His way of telling me I'm safe with him.

And today, or at least in this infinitesimal moment, I take it.

"Why?" I whisper, hoping he understands what I'm doing, that with this one small word, I'm taking a leap of faith.

His eyes flash at the question as if he *does* understand and he's waiting for me to take it back, to look away, to walk away like I've done before.

But I don't.

So he takes a step closer.

Bends closer.

"Because I—"

"Ready for the day?" a jovial voice calls from behind him. The healer turns in its direction, hinging his body away from me until I can see the architect and Tamir approaching.

"I didn't realize you were accompanying us," the healer says simply to the architect, not a hint of frustration like I surprisingly feel at being interrupted in the middle of . . . of . . . whatever this was.

"Yes, today we will begin breaking ground on the new orphanage in the Burrow, and I will oversee the construction while the captain here will supervise the Vuorian guards as they build the frame."

I whip my gaze to Tamir.

"Really, Tamir? What about . . . I thought, well, you never liked the Un—"

He places a reassuring hand on my arm and shakes his head.

"I told you, Reim. I will always choose you." I swear a sudden flare of heat at that last sentence emanates from where the healer stands at my side. "I trust you, and know this is important to you, so I went to the architect and offered my services."

"I don't know what to say. Thank you. Truly."

He drops his hand then and the temperature of the air mercifully drops with it.

"Shall we go then?" the architect calls to us, already heading toward the staircase that leads to the front courtyard.

And it isn't until we are well on our way on horseback, guiding the carts of building materials, that I remember I asked the healer a question.

And that he has yet to answer it.

The architect pulls his horse up next to mine. "I wasn't interrupting anything important earlier between you and the healer, was I?"

Apparently I'm not the only one who has been thinking about it.

I keep my gaze on the healer riding his black steed at the front of our small caravan.

"No, of course not," I lie.

He follows my gaze with his and hums.

"What?" I ask him.

"Just take care of your heart, Reim. If your marriage is truly destined to end when you find *The Book*, it's perhaps advisable to maintain distance."

And I know he's right. And I appreciate his logic. But . . . the new feeling in my heart from two nights ago won't leave me alone either.

Until we reach the gates of the Burrow, and my heart is preoccupied for a completely different reason.

I gasp.

The Burrow is transformed. The dilapidated streets and buildings are in an active state of repair, while the people are no longer milling about aimlessly with empty bellies and empty purpose, but are readily partaking in the revival of their homes, their community, their lives.

"Oh, you have done so much since I've been here last," I breathe to the architect. "I scarcely recognize it."

His smile is filled with pride. "And it's just the beginning."

I laugh in happiness, my traitorous eyes turning to the healer for his reaction. But his attention is all for the citizens crowding his mount, celebrating his presence, his leadership, with sincere joy and praise, and for the first time, I don't measure it against what my people never gave me.

But I do think about my father. About how he didn't care at all for the Unnamed's happiness. How he didn't think them capable of feeling joy except at his expense. I also think about how I shared that view for so long as well, though I'm starting to forget why.

But that still doesn't undo what I did here myself, and I'm struck once again with that feeling from a few weeks ago: that I don't belong, that I'm intruding on something joyous and therefore not meant for me.

I'm about to pull the reins to guide my horse back to the castle when someone jerks at the straps to stop me.

I look up only to stare directly into the centers of twin suns. Big mistake.

"Where are you going, my queen?" the healer murmurs as I jerk at the reins.

"Back to the castle. There is much to do there and—"

"Dragon khur."

"Excuse me?!" I bristle more at being caught in the lie than at the expletive itself.

"I said, you're lying, Reim," he enunciates, but without any anger. If anything, it's with a distinct note of empathy, of something perhaps even resembling sadness or pity . . .

And I hate it.

"How dare you? You think you're so—"

"You are not unwelcome. You are not a burden. You are not a curse."

He lists and negates each and every one of my self-doubts so easily, as if they weren't buried deep within me but plastered over all these walls for everyone to see. My anger fizzles out.

"I know you believe that to be true," I say, rebellious tears filling my eyes. "That's why your tongue is still in your mouth."

He shakes his head but continues to hold fast to the reins and to me.

"But you don't know all the things I've done. Here, worst of all," I admit, staring at his steady hands.

"You're right," he concedes. "I don't know it all. But I know plenty. And yes, it was pretty terrible."

My head snaps up.

Ugh, this frustrating man.

I want to jump off this saddle and pull him down with me. I want to fight him, make him fight me, unleash myself on him so much harder than the time in the training yard. I want to beat him and make him admit how contradictory his words are.

But then he smiles that slow, hooked smile, leans further into my space, and whispers next to my ear, "Later. I still need to come up with the stakes for our rematch."

I let out an annoyed huff to hide my ratcheting pulse at his teasing and try once again to pull away from him. "How can you jest about all of this?"

"Simple, my queen," he says, still holding fast. "Finding joy, no matter how small, is a type of resistance. It was all we had at times. It was something that couldn't be taxed, stolen, or deprived."

And now I can't look away from him even if I wanted to. Happiness or joy was never a factor in Order. Nor was any emotion.

Except fear.

Fear, which we made sure to address and pay homage to in every conversation since childhood, in every law we passed as adults.

Fear, which we would never name, would never admit to feeling, yet readily accused the Unnamed of causing.

Fear, which we then passed down to our children to justify and continue the sins of our forefathers.

"I know you're scared, Reim," he says, sliding his fingers up from the leather straps until they cover mine. And once again I don't know what to do with his ability to know me so well, to see and hear me so easily. "But you have to keep going. You have to face it. Live it. Live through it. It's the only way to be rid of it and conquer it."

I silently watch where his hand lies on top of mine. How huge it is, how intimidating. Yet also how careful it is, how gentle.

So I decide to try out his way, letting out a mock sigh while raising my chin haughtily.

"But it would be so much easier to beat you in the training yard again."

The corners of his eyes crinkle as a rumbling chuckle powers out of him.

"If it makes you happy, wife, I'll let you try to beat me right here, right now."

"No. No. No. I was just-just *jesting* like you. I don't think—"

"But this time, in a race across the Burrow." He ignores my bumbling protests. "I saw your swordplay, High Commander, but I have yet to see your horsemanship."

And now it's my turn to let out a laugh.

"I'm afraid your view won't be very good though, you trickster."

"Still not my name," he returns, but his smile only widens. "But why do you say that?"

"Because." I lower my voice, leaning in until we're nose to nose, waiting for his golden irises to expand to the shape of the twin eclipses that almost engulfed me in the almazi grove a few days ago, before saying, "All you'll see is my horse's ass."

And then I'm off, another one of his deep laughs chasing my heels until it's overtaken by the telltale gallop of his horse's hooves.

My own laughter fills my ears as I lose him by veering past street vendors, barreling through narrow alleys, nearly tumbling down stairs. It drowns out the memories of my father's patient reprimands to slow down, to always look for dangers and threats.

Amplifies the memories of equating his fears for me with love.

Fears that were a product of his own terrible actions against others, a product of inherited trauma of his ancestors' fears. Too often, I equated them with love for his kingdom, with love for me.

Oh Baba. I wish you could have tasted this freedom from fear I feel right now.

Tasted this freedom of simple happiness.

But Fate determined it not to be, so now I am determined to taste it for both of us.

A few more near collisions and I'm almost to the other side of the canton. I can feel the sun beating down just a bit harder with each raging step, can feel the wind fighting its scorching assault from where both are permitted to roam free in the vast space beyond the sentries of buildings and canopies.

I kick my booted heels into my horse's side, pushing him to go just a bit faster, just a bit harder. Just a bit farther.

The open land where the mines begin, where this race ends in my victory, looms closer and closer.

Until with one final leap over a wagon of baluur crates, we finally do it.

We sandblasted win!

At a sharp pull on the reins, my horse stands on his hind legs, whinnying while I whoop my victory to the clear sky, never having felt more alive in my life.

But then someone clears their throat from behind me.

"Not to interrupt this premature celebration, but . . ."

No. *It's not possible.*

I loosen the reins until my horse lands back on all four legs, then glance over my shoulder. The healer is lounging against a palm trunk, munching on a date while his steed drinks water from a trough nearby.

I trot over to him, dismounting before my horse has even fully stopped.

"How?" I screech as I leave my horse to find his way to the trough as well.

"Easy. I never challenge people to things I can't win," he answers, flicking the date pit away and walking over to me.

My mouth pops open and then closes into a thin line as the full extent of what he's saying dawns on me.

"So that day in the training yard . . . you let me win?" Even if I'd wondered as much, I hadn't dared say it then.

"No, my queen," he says, now so close I have to tilt my chin up to look at him. "I *wanted* you to win. There's a difference."

He moves his hand carefully, almost reverently, to one of my braids whipping in the wind and tucks it behind my ear, letting his touch linger there.

"I knew you were in your room grieving your loss," he murmurs, drinking in my face, looking into my eyes. "I knew you weren't eating. Knew you weren't sleeping . . . weren't *living*. But most importantly, I knew I had a role in it."

He glances at my odd ear, and his warm fingers twitch behind it.

"So when I saw you actually caring about something, asking for something, *wanting* something that I, who had only taken from you, could finally *give* to you . . . I wanted you to win."

And suddenly, I can't breathe—not with his body so close to me, not with his words surrounding me, embracing me.

"And now that I've lost?" I find myself asking despite it all.

"Hmmm," he rumbles, the sound feeling like it's coming from the earth itself. "Then, I have no choice but to claim my prize."

And then he steps impossibly closer.

Closer.

Until the entire world seems to be made of nothing more than his hard planes and my soft curves and the tides of our chaotic breaths that threaten to force them together once and for all.

So I rest my pulsing hand against the heaving expanse of his chest. Against the throbbing muscle of his heart.

And then slowly, oh so slowly, I push him away.

"We need to get back to the build site," I murmur to my still-outstretched hand, ignoring its disordered rhythm beating at the oath mark despite it not touching him any longer. "It's getting late, and I'm sure there is still much to do."

Then, turning away before he responds, before I do something I'll regret further, I swing myself back onto my horse and race back into the convoluted streets that resemble the state of my soul once more.

Chapter 25

T LEAST I DIDN'T LIE.

It *is* late by the time I return, and there is still much to do. But there was already so much done.

I climb off my horse and walk over to Tamir and the architect.

"This is truly amazing." I clasp my hand over my mouth at the sight of the foundation of the new orphanage taking shape.

"It truly is." Tamir smiles as he wipes the sweat off his brow. "We'll be heading back to the castle now, but will return in the morning."

He nods at the architect, who returns it, and then he's gone.

"I'm just sad that sifr didn't have this as a youngling," I muse aloud.

"Don't be. Sifr has a whole castle now," sifr says from behind us.

"How do you always sneak up on me?"

Sifr raises a proud brow.

"Seems like a weakness you have to work on, my queen."

I smile, shaking my head.

"But didn't you say once the canton is your home?"

"Of course. That's why I'm here, isn't it? It's dinner time. That stuff you Vuorians eat at the castle is disgusting." He makes a gagging sound. "You all had access to all the best ingredients of this kingdom, and yet somehow the food is still so damn bland."

"Don't curse," I mutter absently as the community sets up the tables and lights, as has become tradition. Musicians start tuning their instruments, signaling the end of the day of work. Food that is clearly not "bland" is brought out in great big pots to the cheers of the workers and neighbors alike.

The twinge of sadness at the prospect of eating alone in my rooms returns.

"Where's the Maliki?" The architect looks around while I stare straight ahead.

"I honestly don't know. I came back alone," I tell him the truth. I even made sure not to look for the healer as I rode back to the build site. But that didn't stop me from feeling his familiar prickling perusal every few minutes from the shadowed depths of the streets.

"Enjoy your meal." I force a smile to my face. "I will see you at the next Jirga meeting."

He nods, walking into the crowd with sifr as I tighten the saddle straps more securely on my horse before attempting to climb back on.

But two strong hands grab me around my waist and lift me easily back to the ground instead.

I whip around to find the healer and the elderly miner, now an elder Jirga member, standing behind me.

"What are you doing?" I ask the Maliki. And though I want the question to come off as angry and controlled, with him standing so close that I can smell his scent of earth and rain and still feel the stamp of his hands tingling around my waist, it comes out shaky and vulnerable.

"My wife and I insist that you both feast with all of us tonight," the miner responds instead, as demanding as ever.

I smile at the old coot.

"That is quite kind of you, sir, but I must de—"

"Did you hear a request in my words, my boy?" he cuts me off, turning to the king who is already rubbing his temples in exhaustion from the conversation that is yet to happen.

"It is to be a wedding feast," the old man says, stretching the words, his ashen eyes darting between the two of us as if we were the dumbest people he has ever had the displeasure to know. "*Your* wedding feast."

My eyes widen as the king's clamp shut in barely restrained mirth.

"Well, in that case, I don't see how we could refuse—"

"So kind, but I am not dressed for the occasion—"

We both speak at the same time. I shoot a glare at the Maliki, one he astutely pretends not to notice.

"I have just the thing, my dear. Don't you fret." An old woman scurries over to us from up the street, joining hands with the miner as she arrives.

Little does she know that the dress is the last thing I'm fretting about right now. This happiness, this celebration, this joy, having it with others—it's not for someone like me. It wasn't before I became Malika, and it's definitely not now.

"You are not a curse."

The words are so loud, so adamant, in my head that I look to the healer as if he were speaking them into my ear. Into my damaged heart once again.

And he's looking back at me as if he did.

"Save the longing looks for the wedding night. Or I guess this is the second one." The miner cackles toothlessly as his wife shakes her head, taking me by the hand and leading me away.

"Oh, don't mind my husband. He's been talking about you constantly since he met you. He thinks you're the best thing that has happened to the kingdom, to the healer, to all of us."

My heart squeezes with old doubts.

"He's kind, but he's wrong." I wrap a hand around myself. "I have too much to atone for."

"Yes, as do we all in our own ways. But I'd rather have a leader who has regrets and then changes because of them than one who believes they are beyond reproach."

We enter a small mud-and-stone dwelling, which is well kept, warm, and inviting. She walks into a back room, while I stay in the front, taking in the cozy comfort of the space.

"Besides, my husband was once of the mind to do unto the Vuorians what was done unto us, and you have shown him there is another way."

Oh, I remember.

She comes back into the room with a draped package over her thin arms. And I'm scared all over again—of sitting with people, of breaking bread with those who think ill of me, who have reason to. Of trying to belong, only to be ultimately rejected.

"I'm scared," I admit in a small voice I have only ever let speak in my head.

The woman's worn face softens even more, her wrinkles deepening around her eyes as she extends her laden arms toward my empty ones.

"Courage is not the absence of fear, albi. It is being afraid and doing the right thing anyway."

She pushes her arms out a little bit more. "Here, it was my daughter's. She and her husband live in Canton Three now."

I take a deep breath and take the package.

Take her suggestion and try to have some courage with my fear.

I'm thankful for the old woman's sure hand holding my trembling one as we both emerge from her home, because the street in front of it is completely transformed. Torches and lanterns flicker over low seating areas piled with multicolored floor cushions and pillows, and a massive fire burns at the center of the gathering. The lamb roasted over it is being divided among the guests with scoops of fragrant rice cooked with nuts and vegetables, while they pour hot tea infused with dried almazi into mismatched teacups.

The night air is filled with the sounds of children playing, women tittering, and men guffawing. Sounds of joy. Of peace.

Until they see me.

And then there is complete silence.

I try not to think of what I must look like to them, dressed in their traditional green robes that flare at my arms and my ankles, embroidered with the reds, browns, and greens of the earth, the blues, yellows, and violets of the sky and sea. My head is adorned not with the crown of Vuor, but with a silver wedding diadem of their people, embedded with unfinished rubies and emeralds, from which tapered strands of beads, tinkling coins and bells fall across my forehead and frame my ears.

I try not to think that I must look like the impostor I feel— the desperate ajnoob pretending to be one of them.

But then the ululation begins.

Low at first, sporadic, like the hum of cicadas. And then picking up in both volume and cadence.

The telltale rhythm of the leather hand drum and clapping joins in welcoming harmony.

And then the crowd starts pounding their feet, parting in synchrony like wind parts the fields of wheat when it blows, like lightning parts the earth when it strikes.

Like a kingdom parts for its king.

And then as if merely thinking of him, *he's* here. There. Everywhere. Walking through the pounding pulse of music and people. Walking to the pounding pulse of my heart.

Walking to me.

He's dressed in his usual black tunic and shalwar, but his onyx-and-gold threaded hair is freshly braided away from his kohl-lined eyes, and his tunic is cinched at the waist by an elaborately tied leather belt that sheathes his dagger, the bronze pommel shaped like a screeching phoenix—the twin to the one I found on my bedside table the morning after the attack in the Burrow.

The old woman slides my hand into the healer's, pressing them together with hers, then turns to me and mouths, *Courage*, before walking away.

Keeping my eyes on our joined hands, I release a shuddering breath, the courage she just spoke of threatening to escape my lungs with it.

I attempt to sneak my fingers from his grasp, but his grip only tightens, beseeching me to look away from them, to look up at him.

To look into his gilded gaze behind shadowed lashes, to trust the truth shining there, even though I don't know what it is. Even though I am afraid to find out.

"Have courage . . ."

"Trust me . . ."

"I wanted you to win . . ."

Another bolstering inhale, and then . . .

I look up.

And he smiles.

And that's all the crowd needs to roar its approval as it sweeps us into its raucous festivities. We're hauled into the middle of the gathering, the communal fire blazing next to us as the drummers form a wide circle around it and start beating a new tune while the growing crowd gathers around the periphery at the quickening tempo. I'm unsure of what this means and am about to ask the healer when a new stomping joins the beat of the drums, coming from all around us, louder, closer.

A row of Unnamed men steps forward from between the drummers into the center. They link arms and begin orbiting the healer and me in synchronized stomps while the drums pound a faster rhythm. Another man with a reed pipe joins them, stirring the crowd into even more cheers.

They're dancing.

For us.

The crowd starts clapping and shouting as the dancers' footwork becomes more intricate, each showing off their happiness for us in their own special way.

Soon, I'm clapping along with everyone else, the muscles of my cheeks stretching from my smile and laughter, the muscles of my heart doing the same from something I haven't felt in a long time—my own happiness.

And I don't know why, but I suddenly want to turn to the king next to me, to share it with him. To share *in* it with him.

But he's not here.

And before I can figure out where he went, I'm not here either. Sifr tugs me insistently toward a raised chair someone must have brought over and settles me onto its plush cushion. He points for me to look forward while he keeps stomping and clapping at my side.

And when I do, it's as if my heart starts beating to the beat of the drum too.

For there in the center of the circle of dancers and drummers, in the center of this night of courage and joy, in the center of my entire world, is the healer.

Dancing.

And when he locks his gaze with mine, I know he's not just dancing.

He's dancing for *me*.

Each powerful stomp to the ground, each skip in the air, each kick of the sand—it's for me.

And then he pulls something that resembles a silver chain from his pocket, spinning it high above his head while continuing his mesmerizing footwork, and the cheers and ululation become deafening in their approval.

My body, my heart, my soul, sit rooted in place as if they do not belong to my will at all but to that of this night, to that of these people.

To the will of something as elemental, as *primal*, as this land beneath us.

I dare not look away from his body as it stalks and stomps toward me.

From his hungry eyes as they take me in.

From the whirring chain as he offers it to the sky.

Nor do I dare move away when he finally gets down on one knee in front of me, lifts my left foot onto the perch of his thigh, and fastens the silver chain around my ankle.

Or when he lowers my foot to the ground and drops his forehead to mine. And then whispers, low and deep, like the depths of the earth itself, "I have now claimed my prize."

And I feel his claim to the depths of my soul.

Feel its truth.

Feel it being written across a book of old.

And then it is I who eliminates the sliver of space remaining between us. It is I who returns his claim with a claim of my own, a claim of his lips. I, who closes my eyes and wraps my arms around his broad neck, tangling my fingers into the plaits of his thick braids and soft tendrils of open hair until it's impossible to tell if the loud beat drumming in my ears is from our cheering audience or from the deafening pulse of my own heart.

He hoists me easily into his strong, sure arms and carries me away from everyone's gaze but his, drinking from the spout of my mouth in long, thirsty pulls.

He sets me down but keeps me molded to his body's embrace while I dig my fingers into the deep groove of his lower back, and he drags his warm, open lips from my swollen ones. Feathering them against the curve of my slack jaw, nipping them down the slope of my bare throat, stamping my name over and over against the fluttering pulse there in that desperate way that makes it sound like he's reciting his own.

"Reim . . . Reim . . . Reim. My queen . . . my wife . . . my m—"

My moan drowns his words, my neck arching to give him better access, my throat aching to say his name back. My heart, to know his in return. But though I can't give him that exactly, there is something else I *can* give.

Courage, I hear the old woman tell me as I let his ravenous mouth, his hungry hands move over me faster. Harder.

Courage, I tell myself, as I imagine finally letting his solid and insistent hips take me. Here. There. Everywhere.

So, I open my eyes, whimper it in my mind.

Husband . . . husband . . . husband.

Open my mouth to release it to the world.

"Husb—"

But just then a tiny tinkle from the anklet he gave me rents the charged air between us. Incinerates it.

And the word turns to ash in the back of my throat.

Scorchingly reminding me of the Burrow man who attacked me, waving the one that belonged to his dead wife in my face due to my failures. Reminding me of the other one in my dream, encircling the woman's ankle as she woke under an almazi tree. Reminding me that the healer doesn't even sand-blasted know about the dreams or visions—that if he did, he might not be doing this right now.

That I may be drawn to him, that I may even *want* him, but I still don't really *know* him or his motives outside of wanting *The Book*.

But what I do know is that he manipulated me in the past to get the kingdom. So, what's stopping him from doing it again to get this powerful book?

From preying on what he now knows is my fear of loneliness.

My pathetic need to be loved.

Maybe that's why he insisted on accompanying me to the cantons, why he took me to his home. Why he gave me the words, the confidence, the affection I need, so he could ulti-mately get what *he* needs.

I drop my hands from around his neck and raise my guard once again.

Am I so starved to belong, to be loved, that I'm willing to pretend that I do? To pretend the lips stilling on my neck belong to someone who actually cares about me? Pretend the celebration happening a little way from us is meant to wel-come me? Embrace me?

"They're all just using you."

I take a large step away from him, the cool night air searing a fiery trail along all the places his mouth laid claim to me. My oath mark throbs as if I'm hurting him, when he's the one backstabbing me.

"Reim," the healer rumbles my name once again, but his tone has changed. Instead of desire, of need, it is one of confu-sion, of warning. "Please. Just talk to me, albi."

But I don't want to look at him, let alone talk to him. Don't want to hear whatever confusing half-truth he's going to spin next. I *can't* hear it. Can't *bear* it.

So I don't.

I run.

Chapter 26

I RUN AND RUN. RUN FROM THE PEOPLE. RUN FROM the healer. But the constant company of my tinkling anklet won't let me run from myself. With burning muscles and burning lungs, I find my horse tied with the others and climb on, the beautiful wedding dress given to me with such sincere kindness tearing as I do. A piece of my threadbare heart tearing with it.

But I can't stay here.

Not when I can't trust what I'm thinking, let alone what I'm feeling right now.

I kissed him. I let him in.

The man who murdered my father, who took my kingdom, who took so much more from me than I ever imagined.

The man who saved his people, who did not destroy mine when he could have, who gave me so much more than I ever imagined though he didn't have to.

How can one person be made of so many opposing truths? And how is it possible to know which ones matter most?

I kick my heels into my horse's side, and we're off through the gates of the Burrow and then under the raised iron portcullis of the Keep and soon back at the castle stables. I don't dare look at the stable hands staring at me, judging my state of mind and my state of dress as I rush past them into the courtyard. Under the intricately carved castle entry, up the wide staircase, and down the abandoned corridor that only leads to one place.

And finally . . . *finally* I burst into my father's room.

I don't look at anything until after the door shuts behind me, shutting the night behind me in the same motion. And it's only then that I let the tears finally fall along with my borrowed wedding diadem. Let my body that's still burning from his touch fall to its knees. Let my fragile heart shatter and bleed all over the cold stone floor.

But even that is not enough. Will never be enough to cope with the betrayal I experienced tonight. Because the real betrayal was not by the Maliki, the Unnamed, or anyone else. But by my own heart.

I betrayed my own definition of right and wrong—my own logic and sense of what I know and have seen of the healer—for what I can only wish for, hope for. I betrayed myself by knowing all of this . . . and still not caring, still wanting them.

Still wanting *him.*

Gutter that fire. Deprive it of air.

Baba's words speak clearly within my mind despite the murky darkness of his room, and suddenly I know what I need to help me feel grounded in this quicksand of desperation.

I need control. I need clarity. I need order.

And I know just where to get it.

Taking a deep breath, I push off the dusty floor, wipe my angry tears from my swollen eyes, and approach the apothecary table that's still by his bedside.

But instead of the countless vials of tincture and bowls of incense cluttering its surface, there is only one remedy, one poison, atop it now.

I hold my breath as a single beam of moonlight reaches tentative fingers across the gloom, as if aware how fragile this moment is, how utterly weighty at the same time. Until it finally wraps itself around the signet ring that I left in this tomb not too long ago.

Until it then wraps itself around my wrist, urging my fingers to move. Beckoning them to reach for it like a miner for baluur, like a farmer for almazi . . . like a king at his wedding feast for his queen.

I squeeze my eyes shut, hot tears tearing past my lashes as I snatch up the ring at last.

But when I open them again, I am no longer in his room. No longer in this time. No longer in my own body.

I am myself. But I am not.

I am once again, just behind the surface of the woman of the past.

The Book is far away but The Book *is safe, I tell my heart as I trip and scramble, trudge and stumble over the fallen debris and smoldering remains of my home. As I bracket my ears to shut out the piercing screams that continue to rain down upon me like sizzling ash, realizing I don't know whose screams they even are. That despite all the differences between my tribe and the strangers', our screams are the same. Our tears and horror, the same.*

Then how can they be doing to us what was once done to them?

But I can't think of their betrayal now. I can't think of how they demanded we share our land, our gifts, our Book with them, only to then punish us when we did and The Book *did not bestow its bounty on them. And I especially can't think of* all those who are no longer with me now. Not if I want to survive. Because thinking of my murdered loved ones is enough to kill me as surely as a strike from the sky.

No, I must keep going. Must make sure that one more thing survives along with me. Not just tonight or the next, but for generations to come, until the world deems it the right time to right itself again.

I must make sure that it is found by those who will see it as a symbol of conquest, of victory. But will not see their defeat lurking just behind its powerful facade.

This is why I stayed back in our destroyed village, instead of running away from it.

This is why I steel my grieving heart for what I must do next, despite the immense pain I'm about to cause myself again.

Why I lift the Maliki's—my mate's—hand from where it lies rigid and cold beside his black-veined body on the floor and slip the ruby signet ring off his finger.

Why I then carefully pry off the gem bearing the two-headed dahaka emblem of our people, and slip the tiny, folded parchment I ripped from The Great Book into the groove behind it, bearing the last words I wrote on its hallowed pages before The Book was safely hidden away.

Why I then push the gem back into place and weld the seam shut with a concentrated blast of my gift of light and return it to his finger once again.

More shouts sound from outside the hut. The strangers will discover his body soon. Just like I discovered it earlier. Like I discovered other members of the Jirga as well. No sign of injury, no pool of blood.

Just empty eyes.

Rigid limbs.

Empty eyes. Rigid limbs.

I tear my eyes away from the terrifying sight. I have to

focus. I have one more thing I need to do to sell the lie. To keep our truth.

I storm to our bookshelf. Pull a random tome roughly the same size and shape as The Great Book off of it, and with one last look at the door, I tear a blank page from its spine before aiming my gift upon the cover—

And set it alight.

I blow on the tendrils of flame until they engulf the book and leave it nothing more than a block of cinder and ash. Then, stamping out the blaze with a nearby blanket, I place the charred prop upon the table.

Make it appear as if the Maliki destroyed The Book to keep it from them.

Make the strangers who love to take and take want to take something more from him too.

So I grab the emerald phoenix quill from the table, smooth the ripped page upon the desk and write the first part of the message I hid in the ring:

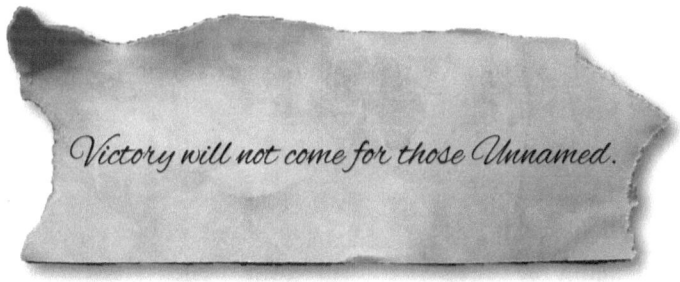

Victory will not come for those Unnamed.

And then I slip the parchment into the clutch of the Maliki's hand for all of them to see. For all of them to falsely believe as prophecy.

A half-truth that the ajnoob will want to believe as the whole truth, so they will preserve it for the rest of their time. But really, so they will preserve it for the ones destined to find us again. Revive us again. I caress my be-

loved's knuckles and then turn away before I give in to the wild urge to lie down and die with him now that my final task is complete.

Because dying is not an option after so much that has happened and so much that is yet to come.

The shouts are coming closer. Yet I am hopeful for the first time that this plan will work.

I bend down to close Adami's eyes, to kiss his forehead one last time, to vow to live on, to hold my grief for an eternity if I have to, if it means our story, our legacy, will also have a chance to live on too.

I gasp as I am shoved back into my own body and mind once more. Losing my balance, I catch my knees on the edge of the apothecary table, and crash to the floor with it.

I stare and stare, with both the woman's and my tears swimming in my gaze, at the ring made of gold and crimson between my trembling fingers that has crossed time and space to be here today. To be here *with me* today.

No. It's ridiculous to think any of this has to do with me. I am but a vessel for this vision. For its relevance to the Unnamed. I am not their hero. I am not their savior.

But the healer is.

The healer, who I left with bruised lips but took for myself a bruised heart.

The healer, who doesn't know anything about my visions, despite being the only one to ever witness one.

The healer, who *did* know the most about the cipher, about the fate of *The Book of Names*—until now.

My heartbeat whooshes in my head, forcing me to focus on the ring once again. My left hand holds the circlet steady while my right thumb and forefinger skate along the seam where the ruby signet meets its gold setting. Where the woman in my vision twisted them apart and welded them back together with a secret pressed between.

A secret that is calling me to reveal it. Reveal it for myself. Reveal it for the world. To never let it be hidden again.

My thumb and finger carefully pinch the stone, gently rocking it, then twisting it.

Again, and again.

Back and forth.

Until finally . . . finally . . . it loosens.

And then gives way.

The red dahaka signet falls into the palm of my hand, igniting the oath mark that lives just underneath the skin's surface, until its pulse is not the shy and fluttering one I have come to associate with the healer, but one that is bone-deep and aching. One that seems to be the composite of thousands of lives cut too short. One that's begging for such devastating loss not to have been in vain.

I lay the flat circular stone on the wooden baseboard at my feet as my gaze shifts to the gold setting the stone has revealed. The setting that is decidedly not empty, as anyone would have assumed for the past two hundred years. As I had assumed myself until a few minutes ago. With the barest of touch across the tiny, folded piece of parchment pressed into the oblong hollow of the metal, it comes away upon my pointer finger.

Could this really be happening? Could this really be the cipher the healer was talking about, the last remaining clue to the existence of *The Book of Names*? To the return of the Unnamed's gifts, their history? The return of their very identities?

I glide the pad of my thumb across the parchment clinging to my finger with care, hoping it will open intact and not fall apart before anything even truly begins.

The thin, worn paper slides with the delicate movement, the very air seeming to take its first breath of life as it starts to unfold in front of my eyes.

And as I had witnessed in the vision just now, there is, in fact, faded writing on it. I squint at the script, foreign only to those not versed in the language of the first Unnamed tribes, but thankfully one I was tutored in during Baba's insistence on Vuorian history lessons. The same lessons that taught me nothing about the people who spoke the language, but only that it might help me understand coded talk of an Unnamed uprising in the kingdom.

And ironically today, it is helping me do exactly that.

With a shallow serrated breath, I begin to read.

"Victory will not come for those Unnamed." I slowly decipher the seven words and pause. Those words are the same words that the woman had written on the parchment she pretended was ripped from *The Book* and then wedged into her Maliki's hand. The same words my people have recited as prophecy for generations without discussing its source. What my people had seen, or rather *wanted* to see, as an undeniable truth about their right to rule over the Unnamed.

Saw it as their absolute destiny, just as the woman predicted.

And yet, she had called it a *half-truth*.

So does that mean this parchment contains the *full truth*?

My palm pounds with that same ancient energy from before in reply. The intense pulsing spreading to my heart, my brain, to my very *existence* as it compels me to see with my eyes the answer I already know in my soul.

I barely breathe as I unfold the rest of the paper. Barely exist when another line of script appears below the previous one, and I then read both of them together.

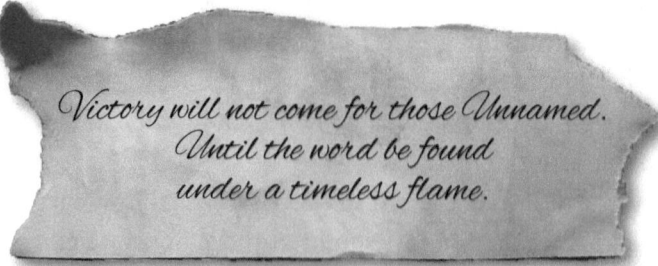

Victory will not come for those Unnamed.
Until the word be found
under a timeless flame.

My mind spins, dissecting each word, its meaning, its placement, its relationship to the others.

The first words of each line stand out foremost.

Victory . . . Until . . .

A temporary victory for Vuor.

A temporary loss for the Unnamed.

And if I'm honest, my people must have known our victory to be such. Because we certainly acted like it. Or why else would we always be so damn afraid of losing it? Why would we have built walls, divided our kingdom into sections to keep people apart, to stifle dissent, if we truly believed in our right to victory. If we truly believed we were doing the right thing.

Victory will not come for those Unnamed.

We repeated that first line, wanted so badly to believe it, but in the end we must have known something about it was incomplete.

A half-truth.

But that second verse, that second half of that half-truth . . . I don't know what to make of it. After everything that has happened today, I'm not sure I even have the fortitude to try.

I only know that it has the power to change everything once again.

I push to my feet.

Folding the paper carefully before pocketing it, I pick up the signet stone and push it back into its gold setting, using tweezers I find in the drawer of the apothecary table to create a loose hold on the stone once again.

I take a moment amid this overwhelming discovery to see the ring like I never saw it before. To see it no longer as a symbol of my father's esteemed position, or Vuorian greatness, but of another's greatness that we stole yet again. One we literally stole off the hand of a dead man. Of a good king. Of a beloved husband.

With a history like that, how can our legacy be anything but a curse?

"*You're not a curse.*"

I pocket the ring and stagger back into the hall, the healer's adamant yet gentle words from earlier echoing through my razed mind and wrecked heart once again. As surely as the memory of his bold touch branding itself around my ankle, my back, my arms.

Across my jaw, my neck, my lips.

Making me want him here with me right now instead of his phantom memories so we can figure this incredible revelation out together.

I stop outside my door. Just stop.

But there is no together. Can never be a together. Will never be a together now that I found the cipher.

There will no longer be an alliance between the healer and me, no more of this joined leadership that has led to so much change and good. No more of his support, his encouragement . . . even if it was all a lie.

No more of his teasing, his smiling, his *presence* in my life . . . even if it was all a lie.

And yet lying is what everyone in my life has ever done to me anyway, even my own father . . . so why does the thought of *him* doing it hurt so much more?

I pull the heavy door open, then let it thud shut behind me before undoing the dress's fastening around my neck and down my back until the beautiful cloth falls to the floor in a *whoosh*. My misplaced hopes, my scattered thoughts, falling with it.

I slip the cool linen of my nightshirt over my head to soak up the hot, unbidden tears sluicing down my cheeks. I fold the wedding dress, gather the diadem, and place both of them upon the vanity stool, vowing to repair and return them as soon as I can.

And then finally I gather the Maliki's ring, the cipher that fell from it, and tuck both into the hidden compartment in my nightstand once again, not needing to look at the words to see them fixed behind my eyes.

"Victory will not come for those Unnamed.
Until the word be found under a timeless flame."

I douse the wall torches as I consider the last line again and again, becoming more confused the more I do.

Yet I force myself to continue as I climb into bed at last, even as I dream of a different flame entirely—one that flares in someone's eyes as he jests and teases, dances and spins, as he finally claims his prize.

A prize that remains securely clasped around my ankle despite every reason for it not to be.

A prize my heart is not ready to part with even as my mind is trying to part with its gifter.

THE NEXT WEEK PASSES IN A BLUR OF ACTIVITY AND emotion. The long days spent in the cantons overseeing their ongoing revival, and the longer nights spent twisting and turning the cipher's words while I do the same with my restless body, my exhausted mind in my bed.

But the mornings . . . the mornings are somehow the worst of them all. Because each one starts with a bludgeoning anticipation of seeing the healer, only to end with a shame-filled disappointment when he never comes.

When, in fact, he has never come, has never spoken to me since the night of the wedding feast.

The night of the kiss. The night of the cipher. The night that changed *everything* all over again.

And this morning seems to be no exception.

"You know, your hair isn't completely black," the elder observes as she braids my long locks into a similar weave as hers as we sit under a palm tree on the beach in Canton Three. "When it catches the light, you can see deep greens, even blues and violets run through it."

I lift my gaze from my folded hands in my lap to the Unnamed men readying their boats in the lapping waves of the Sakoon Sea in front of me. The twins were back at my door the very next morning after the feast, a few days earlier than their expected return. "The Maliki thought it best," the baby had carefully offered by way of explanation. Almost as an apology.

"Thought it best." His platitude has since become yet another cipher to solve along with the one still tucked away in my nightstand.

Thought it best for whom, I wanted to demand immediately. For the Maliki, so he could have a break from pretending to care, now that he sees he can't use me so easily? Or for me, so I could more easily pretend that I don't?

"Talk to me, albi." Those were his last words to me. And I didn't. But now it seems that he's choosing not to talk to me either.

"No," I snap at the elder, flinching at my harsh, misplaced tone as her fingers do the same across my scalp.

"I never noticed it before," I add in a quieter voice, smiling too brightly. "It looks great, thank you."

I run a hand over my scalp to show my admiration of her handiwork of making the plaits resemble the ebb and flow of ocean waves, though it's been so hard to truly care about anything outside the cipher, the healer, and all that they imply.

All that I haven't told him yet.

It's a good thing he hasn't been accompanying me any longer. I have time and space to figure out what all of this means without his overwhelming presence. It's a welcome reprieve from all of the confusion about his behaviors, his words, his intentions. And it's likely the same for him—a reprieve from having to pretend kindness, pity, desire toward me as well.

A low ache builds behind my chest at that last conclusion, its twin pain doing the same beneath the palm of my hand. I ball that hand into a fist to prevent it from pressing against the hurt in my heart and trying to comfort it.

Because none of that matters now.

The only thing that matters is the cipher and what to do with it next. Because even though I can't share with the healer, I can't do this alone. Or rather, *shouldn't* do it alone.

For this is not my identity to be discovered, my victory to be had. Not my destiny to be unfolded. This cipher—this revelation—is for those who have been deprived of all these things for their entire lives and across generations.

What about the architect? I confided in him about the cipher before, but like the healer, he seems to be busier recently as well, often leaving the supervising of the canton projects to Tamir in his stead while attending to other matters. He would, of course, make time for something so important as the cipher, but the work he already does has so much immediate importance as well.

For now, I need someone with knowledge, with consistent availability. And most importantly, someone I can trust.

My eyes widen.

Or maybe not someone.

But *someones*.

Someones who are always with me, who have, more importantly, shown empathy even when I haven't deserved it and harsh insights when I did.

I whip around on the palm trunk I'm perched on. The elder at my back and her twin one tree over straighten at my sudden movement.

"I have something I desperately need your help with," I say, as they warily look at me and then at each other.

An hour into my explanation of the wedding night and the healer's second deal, the dreams and the eventual discovery of the cipher, my guards seem as exhausted as I am.

"So"—the baby collapses against a tree trunk as he stares stunned at the sea—"*The Book of Names does* exist?"

The elder looks just as perplexed as she plops down on the sand next to me. "It was always just a legend for us, you know? I mean, we always knew about the healer having a gift, but the answer to why and how he did changed from family to family, generation to generation."

"Yeah, until he became as legendary as *The Book* itself."

"He knew the cipher existed though," I say, becoming more confused than when I started this conversation. "Or at least wondered about its existence."

"You should tell him," the baby blurts, pushing off the tree. "He's the only one that could even come close to figuring this out."

The elder nods seriously. "I think so too."

"I can't." My tongue stays firm even as my heartbeat stutters. "Yes, helping him means getting out of this marriage, but it also means war. That's what we agreed upon. What we decided was fair."

"But wait!" I jump up and face them, the sea breeze catching my newly tamed braids and tangling them once again. "The terms of the deal were if I *help* him find *The Book*, then we end the marriage and begin war. But what if I find it myself? Or with the help of someone else, like you both? Maybe then we can avoid it."

The twins look at each other skeptically. "I don't know, Reim. Maybe if you just—"

"Look." I grab their hands between mine. "There has

been so much good in our kingdom, despite how we got here. Imagine how much better it could be if we find *The Book and* evade war. Your people would have their history back. Their names back. Their gifts back. I just ask that you trust me."

"Trust me."

My palm pulses slow and heavy at the memory of the healer asking the same of me. I dig my nails in to make it stop.

They look at each other again for a long beat before nodding.

"Well, I don't know how much help we are, but we do know of those who could be," the baby says.

Hope suddenly blooms in the desert of my chest, and I throw my arms around both of them. "Oh, thank you. Thank you. Who?"

"Well, that's the harder part. They live outside the walls of the kingdom," the elder adds with a wince. "But the woman in the vision said that *The Book* was safe but far away or something, right? I don't know much about what's beyond Vuor, but they do."

But I refuse to let that deter me. "Then we will prepare to leave as soon as possible. In one week. The work in the Burrow will be lessened by then, and the healer can run the kingdom until my return."

The elder shakes her head. "What if he comes after you?"

And I think about the night of our wedding feast, the week after that. How he didn't come after me then and still hasn't come for me now.

"I doubt it," I murmur, before giving them what I hope is a reassuring smile. "But what about you both? Will you come with me?"

"Yes, Your Grace," they both say without hesitation, shooting each other a glare at the simultaneous response.

And then I do genuinely smile at that.

Though the sun is setting when we reach the Keep, my spirits are lifted. We finally have direction.

"You should both go get dinner," I say, turning my horse around to face them when the baby's stomach grumbles again, though he's been eating constantly all day, the Unnamed of the Shore being more generous hosts than necessary, treating him like the moniker he bears.

The elder presses her lips in that way I've come to know means she disagrees with me.

"I'm not sure that's a good—"

"I'll be fine," I say with a chuckle, pleased to have guessed right about her. "I'll go straight to my room, I promise."

"It's just that last time we didn't come with you, you were attac—" Now it's the baby's turn to protest. I roll my eyes. I swear it's as if every decision I make requires double the work with these two as my guards.

I try to remind myself that it will also mean half the work figuring out this cipher.

Besides, by the way this colossus of a man is looking as tiny as a mouse right now at his perceived failure to protect me, I can't stay upset even if I wanted to.

"Last time was the consequence of my own actions," I rush to reassure him. "That is all."

Another growling rumble from his stomach rattles the air.

"Fate, go already!" I laugh. "Before people start thinking a creature of the desert has breached our walls."

The elder reaches over and slaps the backside of her brother's horse, causing it to rear up before galloping back into the cantons once again. Causing her brother to curse her to the twilight sky and back as she cackles, nodding at me before following his lead.

I shake my head in amusement as they ride out of sight, and I'm still giggling at their antics by the time I've returned my own horse to the stables and start walking down the empty hall that leads to my room.

"A word if I may . . . Malika."

Not empty then.

I whip around at the familiar sarcastic hiss of my title.

"It is late, Basteel," I say, reminding him but also reminding myself, my hackles rising in sudden caution. I've been doing my best to avoid him since he cornered me in Baba's room. "Whatever you wanted to speak of will have to wait until the Jirga meeting tomorrow."

My hand brushes over the phoenix-headed dagger tucked into my belt's sheath as he steps forward from the alcove he was occupying for Fate knows how long waiting for me.

"Yes, it *is* late, isn't it?" He continues his slinking approach. "Far too late to undo the many wrongs you have done. The curses you have cast."

"You've said as much before." I try to appear unmoved, despite my racing pulse, my tight chest. "So either get to the point, or get out of the way."

When he doesn't do either, I make to step around him, only for him to block my attempt.

"Is this what it looked like?" He mirrors my steps, blocking me twice more. "The heathens dancing at your wedding feast they had in your 'honor'?" He snorts at the last word, as if the joke were that it was used in reference to someone as dishonorable as me.

"Poor Reim," he mock-pouts, "Couldn't find honor with her own people, so she degraded herself to find it with the enemies."

If only he knew how stupid he sounds. How stupid he has always sounded in his demeaning of the Unnamed. How clearly I can see it now.

Despite my own panic, I am done with tolerating it.

I have the dagger unsheathed in the next second.

Have it poking under his collar in the one after that.

But unlike before, he doesn't cower like the coward he is. Instead, he just chuckles as if this were nothing but a planned stage performance.

My grip on the knife falters.

"My, another wedding gift? I saw your husband carrying its twin. Or rather throwing it through someone's co—"

I dig deep enough to draw blood at his boldness, but he doesn't flinch.

I don't like this.

Don't like this at all.

"I will say this one last time, Basteel. What do you want? I already told you I will never work with you and your Janoon zealots to take the throne."

His mouth stretches into that slow serpentine smile I remember from the night in Baba's room, and I imagine it becoming so wide that it will swallow me whole.

"Well, it's a good thing I no longer need you then. Not anymore. But despite everything you have done, I am still generous. So I will give *you* something instead."

I wait for him to continue. He may be at my knifepoint, but I am the one baited on the hook of his words. And he knows it. *Revels* in it.

"A warning. You may continue to beg for the love of the khasir, even wear the savage's shackle around your ankle like a bought whore, but you're a bigger fool than I thought if you think it will protect you. Save you."

Save me? Save me from what?

But I dare not let on to any more of my uncertainty and unease than I already have.

"What are you planning now, Basteel?" I snarl at him, trying to keep the desperation out of my voice.

He chuckles again, and the movement causes drops of blood to escape his nicked skin and skate down the edge of my blade, yet somehow it feels as if I'm the one bleeding out.

And then he stops.

"Revenge."

He releases the word as if unleashing some ancient beast of old, and a terrible shiver races down my spine. Because for all of Basteel's lies, there is no doubt that this time . . . this time, he is telling the truth.

Chapter 28

I DROP MY KNIFE FROM HIS NECK, BACKING AWAY from him a step at a time, while he remains exactly where he is, his victorious smile remaining exactly where it is. And then, when I round a corner, I pivot and pick up my pace.

And then I begin to run.

Not truly even knowing where I'm going until I'm bounding out of the castle's courtyard and heading toward the stables I left not an hour ago.

The healer. I need to warn the healer.

Throwing a saddle over my horse, I curse myself over and over for not telling him the first time Basteel did this—for not believing the conniving vizier, for thinking I could handle him myself.

But regardless of what we may or may not feel about each other now, there is no denying the healer cares about his people and kingdom. And I don't want to be so caught up in avoiding a war in the future that I risk the brink of one happening any day now.

"Reim!" a voice calls just as I grab the reins and hook my foot into the stirrup.

I cast my gaze over my shoulder to find the architect running toward me.

"I've been calling your name the whole way here." He smiles as he catches up with me, only for it to plummet when his eyes scan my face. "Fate, what's wrong?"

I drop back down and turn to face him. "There's something I need to speak with the healer about. Now. It can't wait. Something bad is going to happen. I don't know when, but it's-it's-"

"Shh," he murmurs as he takes a step closer to me, his hands out in front of him to calm me down. "Now start again, please."

I take a deep breath. "Basteel was threatening me and the Maliki just now."

"What?" the architect growls.

I've only seen him this mad when the Unnamed man attacked me in the Burrow. And now it's my turn to calm him, laying a hand on his arm.

"This isn't the first time he's done this. In fact, he's done this so many times I've just stopped believing him. But this time . . . this time it was different. He didn't get mad, nor did he cower. He was so sure of his threat, so sure of it succeeding, that I—"

"Needed to tell the healer," he finishes for me.

"Yes."

He sighs, his usually immaculate bearing off, his usually reassuring expression distant.

"You don't think I should." I say the question as a statement.

He drops his gaze from mine. "It's just . . . it's obvious you both haven't been the same since the . . ." he trails off, and my mind rushes to fill in the blanks.

Since the wedding feast. The kiss. The cipher.

But he doesn't know that last part. And I refuse to burden him more than I already am now.

"You're right. It shouldn't be me." I shake my head. "But perhaps you could. Please?"

He meets my pleading gaze with his now-calm one before moving past me to climb onto my saddled horse. "All right, Reim. Now go back to the castle. I will see to the healer."

Relief fills every inch of me.

"Thank you," I call up to him as he sets off into the night.

I FLIP AND POUND MY PILLOW FOR THE UMPTEENTH TIME tonight as sleep fails me, just as pacing did earlier. Did the architect find the healer? What did he say? Did he ask about me like my mind can't stop asking about him?

Groaning, I roll over and reach for the handle of the hidden compartment in my nightstand. If I'm awake, I might as well look at the cipher again. See for the hundredth time what I may be missing.

But then loud voices boom from the hall outside my bedroom, and I drop the handle, having just enough time to wrap myself in my outer robe and grab my dagger before the door bursts open and three large shadows barge in.

My dagger-wielding hand is already pulled back into a throwing position to take down the largest intruder in the middle, my mind already strategizing how to use the pockets of shadow throughout the room to get to the other two, but right as I'm about to fling the blade, my hand and arm contort in a searing pain I've felt only once before.

The healer.

I drop the dagger, the pain dropping just as quickly with it as I scramble toward them.

"What's wrong?" I almost scream but he's barely even conscious, his long arms draped over the shoulders of Tamir on one side and the architect on the other, while his head droops onto his chest—his chest, which is thankfully still rising and falling, though quite erratically.

My guards rush in, shutting the door behind them before they all lift him onto my bed.

I stare down at him, my heart threatening to break free from the cage of my ribs to find a way to break into his—to pump him with my own blood, with my own *life* if I have to.

His eyes are closed but fluttering violently, as if fighting some terrible internal battle. His muscles, twitching in sharp jerks as if he's being held back somehow. His skin, overrun with black, tortuous veins.

He's dying.

I whip toward Tamir and the architect.

"Someone better tell me what the Fate is happening to my husband *right now*!"

Tamir lifts his broken gaze to mine. I can see the words floating on his tongue, but he seems unable to find air to speak them before he finally gives up and looks away into the dying hearth.

"I went to speak to him like I promised you." The architect's gentle but firm voice draws my attention to him.

The elder brings me a chair, and I pull it underneath me until I'm tucked into the side of the bed, until my hand is reaching for the healer's of its own volition, until my trembling fingers are intertwined with his contorting ones and our palms are beating together even though our hearts are struggling to beat at all.

"And?" I whisper, keeping my eyes on the healer.

"And I went to his hut . . . and . . . I-I-"

The architect stammers, running a trembling hand over his ashen face, too distraught to describe what he witnessed next.

And I squeeze my eyes shut to stop myself from imagining it.

"And you found him . . . like this," I conclude for him.

Now it's the architect's turn to look away.

"Someone did this to him, didn't they?" I force myself to ask, though I already know the answer. "And . . . and he's dying."

"Yes, it was most likely an attempt on his life. His place was completely ransacked." The architect swallows, starting to pace. "And we brought him here because if he was seen by others in such a state, it would throw the kingdom into panic. His enemies would have the perfect opportunity to attack, and his supporters would lose faith in his ability to protect them."

And then he jerks to a halt. Looks back at me.

"And I can't lie. I brought him here because . . . he should be here with *you* when he . . ."

And everything inside me absolutely hates how he says that. Like the healer's already gone. Like the architect is trying to make his dying easier in some way. Like he wants me to just accept this. To just let him go.

And I may not have all the answers when it comes to knowing my husband's heart, but I have enough when it comes to knowing mine, and I'm not one to give up on anything or anyone. Not when it was my father. Not when it was my kingdom.

And not when it is my husband. Not like this.

"Find who did this. Start with Basteel," I order the architect and Tamir. "I want them brought to justice. And as it was the Maliki they dared harm, it will be *his* form of justice that will be brought upon them."

They look at me as if seeing me for the first time, then nod and hurry out the door.

I turn back to the man on my bed who has never been anything but larger than life, who is now *fighting* for his life, and all the furious courage I just built on his behalf mere seconds ago threatens to abandon me, threatens to leave only doubt and fear in its paralyzing wake once again.

He's getting worse. His hands—limp when he was brought in and then jerking—are now contorted and rigid in mine. His eyes, squeezed shut as if fighting the way he fights with me, are now wide and blank, his beautiful golden irises dimming of their luster, emptying of their life.

I gasp.

Emptying.

I clutch his fingers tighter with sudden revelation, causing his phoenix signet ring to press into my fingers like a similar ring pressed between someone else's hundreds of years ago.

Empty eyes.

Rigid limbs.

Empty eyes. Rigid li—

I whip to my guards standing behind me.

"We need Mori. *Now.*"

Chapter 29

I<small>T'S TAKING AGES FOR</small> M<small>ORI TO COME, AND MY</small> heart and mind battle over what I should do while I wait. My heart screams at me to pace and cry, to scream at Fate for punishing the healer instead of me, who actually deserves it, while my mind tells me to stay here, hold his hand, watch him breathe. Watch him live.

But I can't do either, because I'm too damn paralyzed to cry and scream and too frantic to just watch and do nothing. Because to me, I'm not watching him live. I'm watching him die.

A gust of wind bangs one of my latticed windows wide open, blowing out the wick of my warring thoughts as I shield my eyes with my arm against the storm I hadn't even realized was agitating the night sky, mirroring the agitation brewing within me.

I let go of the healer's hand and fight my way to the window to shut it, but then my breath is stolen for an entirely different reason. Because it is not a storm born of sky and water that is calling for my attention, but that of feather and might. The emerald phoenix I'd seen twice swooping above me is now perched upon the ledge of my open window.

Blessed Fate, has it always been this massive? Or is it because he has his majestic wings spread to their full breadth, spanning half the room, the very apex of either side curving inward toward his head. And I would have likened his pose to a king crowning himself, since the current one is incapacitated, but his round crimson eyes are not on the Maliki at all.

They're on me.

Surrounding me.

Calling me.

Telling me to come to him. That he has all the answers that I've been searching for. All the answers that I want and need.

So I do. My unsteady hand that was just intertwined with the healer's, that bears the hidden mark of our blood oath, reaches for the space between the phoenix's eyes. The plumes there, a spectrum of viridian and jade, grass and palm—the colors of our land and of our sea. The same colors that often wink shyly at me from the feather tied to the healer's braid.

The same braid that now lies limp and lost within a tangle of his sweat-soaked hair upon my pillow.

I swallow, not understanding this sudden compulsion to touch the strange creature while the healer is dying on my bed, yet knowing it has to be done. Now.

The phoenix's midnight pupils widen until the red irises are but thin rings as I extend a single finger. The phoenix, for his part, pushes his head forward to meet me halfway. And I am entranced, not only by the mysterious yet intentional presence of this beautiful animal, but by my own reflection, so clear in the orbs of his eyes, as if I've never truly seen myself before this very moment.

Like I may never truly see myself the same way after it either.

But then my bedroom door slams open once again, and I spin away from the phoenix and toward my guards, who accompany the two new arrivals.

"What the Fate is happeni—" Mori exclaims as she shoves her way inside the room, only for me to tackle her once she does.

"Mori. Oh, Mori. Look at him! He's *dying*, Mori. Please. You have to do something. You have to save him, please," I ramble, finally bursting into tears when her arms return my embrace, holding me at her side as she moves us toward him, sifr hurrying behind.

"And then this great green phoenix came through the window and wanted me to-to-" I turn toward the ledge where it was perched . . . only to find it gone.

"It was just here. I-I swear it!"

Sifr puffs up his chest and marches toward the open lattice window like a warrior charging into battle, searching behind the curtains, then outside to the sky until he finally looks back at all of us and shrugs.

Mori shifts her gaze to me, but I don't care. It was here.

"Reim, my child . . ." Mori begins in her usual voice of concern, but I don't want it for myself right now. I want it for the healer.

"Forget the phoenix, Mori. Forget my words. Forget *me*. I'll be fine. Just . . . the Maliki." I swallow past a wave of premature grief. "Please."

She looks at me for what feels like an eternity of indecision before finally nodding and taking my previous place next to the healer's bedside.

And then she gets to work. My guards light the wall torches, fetch hot water and rags, while sifr sets out her various tools and vials on my vanity and nightstand.

I retreat in direct proportion to the increasing movement around her and her patient, realizing how useless I am to him—how foolish it was to think otherwise.

"Oh no you don't, Reim," Mori calls without looking at me. "I'm not letting you run away this time like I did with your father. You come over here right now. He needs you."

He needs you.

My heart jerks as if it's a fish caught on a line. But I foolishly fight its pull anyway.

"I don't think that's a good—"

"Fate! Less thinking, more doing!" And this time she does turn over her shoulder to glare at me. Sifr does the same over his as if to emphasize her inherent rightness—my obvious wrongness.

I have the decency to look away from both of them before nodding.

"Now, I need you to undress him so we can see the extent of what's going on. Then get behind him in the bed, lean his body back against yours, and maneuver him as needed."

My cheeks flare at the intimacy she's assuming we have as husband and wife but actually don't, but I do as I'm told anyway.

I unbutton his sweat-soaked shirt and let out a long exhale when I cannot only see but feel his clammy chest rising and falling beneath my fingers, only to jolt as the black veins become more pronounced, almost slithering over his otherwise pristine bronze skin.

I bite the inside of my cheek until I taste metal to keep from crying out at the sight and peel the rest of the shirt off. I make quick work of his pants next, fastening my eyes on the puddling fabric and not on the expanse of diseased skin and rigid muscle it reveals, before jerking the sheet over him again.

When I finally step away, I notice Mori watching me, likely having seen my darting gaze, my awkwardness as I undressed him, likely drawing conclusions about the real nature of our relationship . . . or lack thereof.

But whatever she must now suspect, it doesn't deter her from snapping her head for me to get on the bed behind him as she ordered before. And something snaps into place for me too. Because none of the unresolved things about our relationship matter anymore. Not the cipher, not the marriage, not the said and unsaid things between us. Not one damned thing matters except him surviving this.

I pull the sheet back enough to climb into bed behind him and breathe deep. Together we pivot his much larger body onto his side, then lift him until his torso rests against the headboard and his lolling head against my shoulder and chest.

"It's important you keep his airway as open as possible, Reim. As long as he's breathing, we have a chance." Mori peels back his eyelids that have fallen shut to observe his empty eyes, then grabs his hand to discover the viselike rigidity of his fingers.

"I've never seen this," she murmurs to herself, "let alone treated it in my years of healing. But I may have read about it in some old healing book once. Looks like—"

"Iron poisoning," the twins and Mori conclude together.

Mori whips toward them.

"How did you know that?"

"Just remembered." The baby rubs his chin. "Happened to a youngling in the almazi groves several years ago. One of the ajnoob overseers had lost his iron rod he used to keep us in line, though I think one of the people likely stole it because it ended up in the well and must have rusted over time. A child drank from the water and looked just like this before . . ."

The twins look meaningfully at each other.

"Before what?" I screech.

"Before she died, almost immediately." The elder's eyes fill with tears.

No. No. No. No.

"Be calm, dear." Mori cups my hand that must have unconsciously grabbed the healer's. Squeezes it until I am forced to meet her resolute eyes. "The child died. But your husband, he is still here. Still fighting, you hear? Will you fight with him?"

I swallow the bile rising in the back of my throat, feel his shallow puffs of warm breath against the skin of my collarbone. I will myself to believe he can fight this. Survive this.

I take a deep breath for both of us and nod firmly to Mori.

She squeezes our hands once more before turning to sifr. "I will need the small knife, my boy."

He spins to the makeshift apothecary on my nightstand and snatches up the sharp blade, sanitizing it over the low flame of the candle.

Handing it with care to Mori, he makes sure to send me a reassuring smile.

One that I am thankful for, but cannot return, as Mori's steady hands make a small, shallow incision in the healer's upper arm, and a tiny trickle of inky, putrid blood seeps through the opening.

"Now, the glass cup, sifr. Just like I taught you," Mori instructs, and he is quick to obey. A small glass cup is heated in the hot-water bath and pressed over the incision until it forms a secure seal, until the skin enclosed within its circumference rises as if being suctioned and the black blood flows from the cut faster.

She then repeats the same procedure twice more on the same arm before moving to the other arm and doing it three times there.

"I admit, I do not know if this will work," she tells me, or the others, or maybe herself. "His unique healing ability may close the incisions before enough blood is let to rid him of the poison. But then again, that same ability may be what has kept him alive for so long to begin with."

I nod, but then a sudden thought occurs to me.

"If he survives, Mori," I manage past a throat that feels as cut open as his arms with the terrible words I just sliced it with. "Wh-what could it mean for him?"

Her eyes soften in compassion when she looks at me, even as she continues her brisk pace preparing more cups with sifr.

"If you're asking about the lasting effects of the iron poisoning, I don't know for sure. But I hope it will be minimal and that he fully recovers, like he does from everything else."

There's that word again. *Hope.* Despite my few attempts at it, it continues to be a hard concept for me to grasp, much less believe in. It relies too much on what can't be controlled. It relies too much on what someone else told me to have while dressing me in her daughter's wedding dress—courage.

And I am too new to these ideas and feelings to trust myself with them. What happens if I ruin them too, like I'm ruining everything else? Like I ruined the healer?

A lone tear falls from my eye, landing on the healer's closed lid, trailing down the sharp cliff of his cheek as if my grief is his own. It slips off his bearded chin and splashes onto his collarbone.

He takes a shuddering breath in my arms, and I look at him, really look at him, for the first time since this all began. And yes, he's still rigid and unconscious, but his breathing is a bit more even, his skin looking less gray, feeling less cold. The black, diseased veins slightly less pronounced as the glass cups along his arms leach the poison, drop by terrible drop, from his once-powerful body.

He is fighting, like he always has—for himself, for his kingdom, for a better Fate for all. So even though I don't know how to have hope for myself, I vow that I will try my best to at least have hope for him.

T HE ELDER THROWS ANOTHER HANDFUL OF BALUUR crystals from the bucket next to the hearth into the sputtering fire.

"That should keep it going for the night," she mutters to the room. Mori and I nod even though she's already done and said that twice already.

"Listen," I say to her and the baby from my seat next to the fireplace. "It's been a long night, and it's only going to get longer with everyone on edge like this. Why don't you both get back to your stations, make sure he stays safe. We will do the same here."

"Yes, Reim," they murmur in unison, and with one last look at the healer, they leave.

Sighing, I let my head fall back against my armchair and watch sifr, who after much argument, finally succumbed to sleep and is now snoring gently, limbs askew upon the tufted bench at the foot of my bed.

While the healer . . . the healer continues to fight on. To live. For now.

I look up at Mori's beloved face as she sits in an armchair across from mine in front of the fireplace, her tired gaze fixed on the crackling flames. I take in her age-lines, which have only deepened and journeyed much farther over the dunes of her temples and cheeks in the past year than in the last twenty-eight combined.

Mori, who was there for me every time I broke a bone, or broke one in someone else. When I needed an embrace to laugh within and a shoulder to cry on. When I was a child and when I became a woman. When my mother couldn't be there for me, and then . . . when my father couldn't either.

Mori, who was there and there and there . . .

And who is here for me *now*.

"Mori?" I wring my hands together, steeling myself to ask the question that often dies on my tongue but lives forever in my mind, about the two people who died on this earth but live forever in my heart.

She turns her knowing eyes to me but makes me voice my anxious thoughts anyway. "Yes, my child?"

"Can you . . . tell me about my parents?"

With a soft smile, she leans back in her chair, silently encouraging me to do the same in mine. To settle in. To listen. To hear.

But I can't. I remain leaning forward, almost rocking in my restlessness about the unstable state of the healer, about where my question came from, about where her answer could go.

And she sees it all with her kind eyes.

"What do you want to know, albi?"

Anything. Everything.

But time right now is but a broken hourglass, with the sand tumbling faster and faster, so I must ask what is most urgent.

"Did my parents love each other?" I ask before I can think any more on it. "And-and did my father love me?"

Mori looks at me for a long time. The baluur crumbling in the hearth under the weight of the question I took off my shoulders at last. Under the weight of her scrutiny of the many questions behind the ones I just asked.

"Yes," she says finally, as if stating a fundamental law of the universe. So obvious. So indisputable.

Yet, why does my heart still scream that it's not enough?

"How can you be so sure?" I plead. But even though the words are directed to her, my eyes stray of their own accord to the healer on my bed.

She sees it, a sad smile thinning her lips, and then she grunts, rising heavily from her seat and goes to check on the healer. I join her, my curiosity about her answer distracting me from my panic when I see his condition again.

"Well, to understand something as complicated as love, you first have to know that there is no one definition of it. And theirs, my dear, was no exception."

My shoulders slump. "Oh Mori, what kind of nonanswer is that?"

Mori sucks her teeth in mock exasperation, replacing the cups full of his black, viscous blood with newly warmed ones after reopening the incisions that have scabbed over.

"None of that defeated attitude, now. Listen to what I'm saying. Your parents *loved* one another for the sake of the things they already loved as individuals. They both *loved* and believed in Order. They *loved* serving their people according to it. They *loved* the legacy of their ancestors that they inherited."

Her fingers pause in their work upon his chest for a moment, and she looks up at me.

"And they *loved* dreaming of—and then creating—a way to continue it together. So in that way, they loved you."

But no sooner are the words spoken than my heart plummets into my hollow chest.

Her answer is exactly what I've been telling myself for years. Exactly what I've been trying to run away from for years. And ultimately, it found me anyway.

"But that's not love," I murmur, keeping my sad gaze upon the healer. "That's not true love."

Mori's warm arms pull me into the cradle of her soft chest, press me against her strong heart. I close my eyes.

"Yes. It. Was," she says, kissing the top of my mussed head with each adamant word. "Aren't you listening?"

"To them, what they had for each other was very real, because it was based on mutual truths. That's what makes it *true* love. And to your father, having you, raising you, wanting those same things he loved but wanting it for you, despite losing your mother, his wife, was *truly* love for you."

"But then why did I always question it? Why do I still question it now?"

"Because your father made one major mistake." I pull back from her arms to look into her galactic eyes. "Not about loving you, but about not seeing that you may define love differently than he did. That you had your own mind, your own heart, your own version of the truth and of love. His mistake was not wanting to see it. Being too damn scared to see it."

She tucks me back into her embrace, and I stare tearfully at the healer until I can hear her next words straight from her heart itself.

"Now don't you dare be too damned scared to see it, too."

She squeezes me one more time before walking over to sifr and shaking him awake. "Let's go, young man. You need some proper rest. The healing ward isn't going to run itself, especially now, you know."

"*Ugh.* Don't remind me." Sifr groans, stretching his lanky arms before standing up. "Should've known something happened to him when he didn't come to the healing ward at his usual time tonight."

"What?" I march over to him. "What are you talking about, sifr? The Maliki's been coming to the healing ward? Why?"

He smacks his head with the heel of his hand.

"*Khur*, he didn't want you to know." He darts his gaze between Mori and me, but Mori just rolls her eyes. "Umm, at least a few weeks. Since that day with that Vuorian girl, Rukhsar. He healed her foot. Healed everyone there, actually. He's been coming ever since. Doing the harder stuff, while Mori and the other healers take care of the easier ones. Doesn't matter whether they're my kind or your kind."

I thump down onto the settee sifr just vacated, my eyes welling with tears once again.

"*Trust me*," he told me that day in Court.

"*Talk to me*," he told me that night after our kiss.

And I did neither. I pushed him away.

I grip the cushion so I don't lose grip on myself.

"Oh, Mori, how could I have been so wrong?"

"Well child." She sits next to me and tilts my chin up to look at her. "If I've learned anything these past few months, it's that it's never too late to make it right."

Mori EVENTUALLY LEAVES WITH SIFR WITH EXPLICIT orders to call her if the healer's condition changes, and somewhere in the quiet between their leaving and dawn, I dream.

Not a dream like the ones that have been plaguing and enlightening me about the mysterious woman and the equally mysterious book, but a dream that is entirely my own.

I dream of lying under a star-speckled sky in the vast open desert past the river. I dream of unbound freedom, of untethered happiness. I dream of realizing the stars are not stars at all but familiar flashes of light and fire igniting in someone's eyes. And not only am I basking in their magnificence, but they seem to be also basking in mine.

"What do you want, my wife?" the healer's voice rolls over me just as a cloud rolls over the sky. His soft lips, his warm breath, striking the vein running down the length of my neck with each word just as lightning strikes the dune we lie on, striking my heart with a sense of power. Power in being asked such a question, in having him beholden to my answer, instead of fear.

My eyes shutter and I moan as his large body lowers impossibly closer over my smaller one. My fingers rise to tangle in his hair, finding the phoenix feather tied to his braid, and caress its smooth vane, which makes him shudder before he presses deeper into my neck, into my embrace.

"You," I say finally, truthfully, for the very first time, bracketing his sharply tapered ears, his brutally beautiful face with my hands and pushing it up until he can see the truth in my words, in my eyes, for himself.

"I want you, my husband. I want you to live and for us to rule together. I want you to love me. And . . ." I bring his forehead to mine like he did on the night of our wedding feast. Breathe once, twice, before uttering the most fragile truth of all. "And I want to love you in return."

He looks at me then, cocking his head in that way that always tells me he is thinking before speaking. A trait I usually admire about him. But now, as I bare myself to him in both body and soul, I don't want him to think. I want him to feel. I want him to—

"That's unfortunate." He shakes his head, and the very

earth beneath us seems to shake with him. "Because I don't want any of those things."

With a weary sigh, he rears all the way up and rolls off me. His sudden absence exposing not only the gaping cold emptiness of the Koora Desert surrounding us but also my heart within me.

He tosses his shirt at me from somewhere, and I slip it on, hating how his scent of soil and rain embedded in its fibers rushes to hold me even as its owner does the opposite. Hating how I allow myself its forbidden comfort anyway.

Crouching in front of me as the clouds continue to pile on top of each other, his eyes shift from the deep golden hue of his earlier desire to charged flashes of his disappointment and disgust.

I try to look away, look for a way to escape him and my growing shame, but there is only emptiness stretching as far as I can see in both the restless desert and the storming sky. In the starless vortices of his eyes.

Another bolt of lightning strikes the sand next to us, and I no longer feel powerful by its presence, but utterly helpless. But that's the thing about helplessness—it leaves you with nothing left to lose. It leaves you with a bravery forged of survival. And if I am to survive this man, survive this impossible love, then I have to forge a bravery of my own.

"What do you want, then?" I yell above the whipping wind of the inevitable storm as another bolt glasses the sand on the other side. And then again behind me. Caging me in with my impending doom.

Again and again until it's not just lightning that is striking out, but the healer's hand to grab my hair. To pull my neck toward him until I am unsure whether he means to kiss me or destroy me.

"Isn't it obvious, Reim?" he snarls. "I want the cipher. I want our names and history returned to us. I want to stop *pretending I feel anything other than hate for you. And most of all. . ."*

And then he lets go as he rises, and I fall back onto my elbows in the sand.

"I want you gone."

And as if the rumbling clouds above have heard him, one last bolt strikes from right above me.

And I look up just as it meets its mark.

I jerk awake, suddenly sure that the blinding light surrounding me is emanating from the veil that separates life and death. That I found the final escape I was looking for in a lightning strike in the midnight desert, and that no one can hurt me ever again now that I am at death's door.

But, like the end of all dreams, reality slowly but surely intrudes, negating what I perceived to have happened with what's truly happening. And what's truly happening right now is that I'm not dead. That the light I'm clinging to in my heart as my final escape from the healer and my burgeoning unrequited feelings for him, is no escape at all.

Because the light emanates from the cause of my pain— from the healer himself.

I scramble up and off where I must have fallen asleep on his chest. Pulling my long hair back with one hand, I stare at the red circular bruises the glass cups left on the healer's body after Mori's removal, swallowing my gasp when I find them filling with white light. And then the light pulses past the bruised rings, into the diseased veins. Pumping, pumping, pumping light after light until the darkness that filled them is overcome at last.

Oh, Blessed Fate, he's healing.

Mori. I must get Mori.

I run a hand through my unruly hair and pull my nightshirt closer to my chest as I start to shuffle off the bed without disturbing him.

But then a large hand lands on top of my retreating wrist. Wraps its strong fingers around it and keeps it there.

"*Stay*." A serrated rumble powers out from the head of the bed.

I snap my head up toward it even though I dare not move my shackled arm.

The healer's eyes remain shut even as his long black lashes flutter with consciousness, his parched lips rubbing, smacking against one another with words that have yet to find their voice.

I want you gone.

Stay.

I want you gone.

Stay.

He's far from well, but he's alive. And I'm far from anything resembling wellness myself, with the whispers of rejection from my dream still floating through my ears, his disgusted look still flashing behind my eyes. Yet somehow, despite everything unresolved between us, my sabotaging heart feels nothing but relief—even a bit of hope, as Mori hoped for me—in that one soothing word from my reality: *stay*.

So I tell myself that the world and its many complications and contradictions can sandblasted wait for a bit longer. That they can just *stay* for a bit longer.

That I can too.

That he may not be feeling the same way soon enough, but until then I can pretend he does.

So I climb back into the nest of soft sheets and pillows of my bed, back into the warm rays of light from the morning sun tangling with those pulsing from his healing body. So I let him pull my wrist farther toward him until he places it above his heart and then pulls the rest of me by the soft dip of my back into the hard planes of his chest.

Thë Unnaměd

I bury my face into his neck like he did into mine after our one and only kiss. Cry my fears and hopes to him like I would never have dared to before.

And . . . just . . . *stay.*

Chapter 3

HE WOKE UP? WHY DIDN'T YOU CALL ME like I told you to, girl?" Mori squawks as I shimmy into the black-and-gold embroidered chemise and shalwar set I was so opposed to wearing a few weeks ago.

"I'm sorry, what was that, Mori?" I ask, pretending not to hear as I pop my head out through the collar.

"I said—"

"Oh look, the elder and baby are here with food!" I snatch the tray from their hands and dip my head, making a great show of inhaling the aroma of the hefty spread.

"You know what? I'm going to have some now." I stuff a honeyed fig into my mouth.

Mori narrows her eyes at me for an endless minute before throwing up her hands in resignation and marching over to the bed.

I take her indignant muttering readily as I finish getting ready, because it's better than admitting to her what I was doing instead.

Because I'm not sure I'm ready to admit it to myself either. Admit that I was allowing myself to look at him, to touch him, to just *be* with him in a way I never allowed myself to before.

"It would be of great service if you both could report on my behalf to the Burrow and the Groves today. I have an entire list of items that need to be taken care of, and it is already noon." I pass my guards a parchment each, one for each canton, with a grateful but tired smile. "I would like to be nearby if I am needed here."

They nod gravely at the mention of the king's condition, but when their furtive peek behind me reveals Mori and sifr packing away the bloodletting instruments and materials, their solemnity sheds into visible relief. The elder steps closer to me, lowering her voice.

"Reim, I know there's a lot happening, but what does all of this mean for our . . . *plans* we discussed yesterday?"

The baby nods as if he were thinking about the same thing. "Those who may help us shift their camp as easily as the sand dunes they live among. I sent a phoenix yesterday to scout their location, and he returned this morning. The fact that they let it live is amazing enough, but we would have to leave as soon as possible for us to catch them before they move again."

My heart pounds. I knew what I needed to do just yesterday morning, but now? Now that the healer has proved he isn't as invincible as I believed? Now that my heart has proved the same about me and my feelings for him, despite my not trusting his for me at all?

But the uncertainty of our relationship is no match for the certainty of the wrongs I have to right for the Unnamed.

"You're right," I say at last. "Time is of the essence. We will leave in three days, after the next Jirga meeting. Will you help me tie up loose ends before then?" I tap the parchments I gave them.

"Of course, but who will be guarding him while we are gone today? He is still too unwell to be left unattended."

"I will."

I turn around to find Tamir walking up the hallway, still in his disheveled clothes from the previous night, hair messy, eyelids swollen with lack of sleep and an abundance of worry.

My heart clenches when the captain steps in front of me but refuses to meet my eyes. And that could only mean he sees himself as having failed somehow—in this case, failing *me* somehow. And though the first thing I want to tell him is to go to his chambers and get some sleep, I know he won't be able to with his guilt weighing so heavily on his shoulders. He needs to do something, anything. And I have to admit, I need him, too.

"Thank you, Captain." I smile at him with genuine gratitude. But it only seems to make him stiffen further.

"Tamir, what's wron—" But he's already heading toward the guards, and before I can follow him, the architect's desperate voice calls from down the hall.

"Did I just hear the Maliki is getting better? Thank Fate. Can I visit him?"

I turn, taking in his clothes that are the same from yesterday, wrinkled and powdered with soot, his white hair unbraided and unkempt for the first time ever since I met him.

Poor man, to be the one to discover his leader, his *friend*, like he did.

"Yes, he is recovering. But he's not speaking yet."

Liar, I reprimand myself. But how do I explain that the one word he did speak seems too personal, too precious, to share with others? I can't, especially when it's so at odds with what's true. He doesn't care about me or want me. He wants what's best for his people. And if I somehow factor into that goal, then that's the only reason he wants me to *stay*.

My heart and palm ache together, and I force myself to focus on the man in front of me and not the one in my bed.

"Any word on who did this?"

The architect shakes his head with a frown. "Basteel was here all night. If he hired someone, it would be difficult to know. Because honestly, there are too many people with the motive to do this. But we can keep looking."

"Thank you." I smile at him, linking my arm with his. "Come, let's take a walk."

"You seem to be in better spirits, my queen," the architect says as we move down the hall, and my heartbeat stutters at being addressed that way by anyone except the healer—even though it's the architect, and there's nothing inherently wrong in his use of it.

"Oh, please call me Reim as you always have. We're beyond such formality," I say, relieved to voice the correction. "And yes, I am trying. The healer had once told me finding happiness in difficulty was an act of resistance . . . so I'm trying."

He is silent at that for a long moment. Too long.

"I'm sorry, did I say something wro—"

"No. Not wrong, Reim," he clarifies. "Just surprising. I was remembering how you once told me you were looking forward to the marriage ending, and though you cannot do anything to harm the healer . . . well, to be blunt, I had wondered if his dying by another's hand would solve the matter and perhaps even be a relief for you. Yet you were the one who insisted on justice on his behalf and did everything you could to save him last night."

Let the healer die?

I'm irritated with him for supposing this, but do I have a right to be? Wanting the marriage to end is *exactly* what I had told him. But our conversation feels like it was from a different time. A different mind and heart.

"Yes, you're right. I had wanted that once."

"And now?"

I remember the dream.

"*You . . . I want you . . . I want you to live . . . to love me . . . I want to love you.*"

Remember his response.

"*I want you gone . . .*"

And then . . . "*Stay . . .*"

I blink away a threatening tear.

"Now, I want joy," I admit, cutting myself off before saying two more words, not because they'd be a lie, but because they'd be the undeniable truth.

With him. I want joy with him.

The architect's brows buckle as if he's trying to understand me but failing, and he drops my arm, his fingers urgently, almost roughly, braiding his messy silver hair. "And what about the cipher? *The Book of Names*? The very history of my people?"

My smile is small.

"Don't worry, I have not forgotten. I want to find *The Book* above all else. I want your people to be free once and for all. It's their deserved destiny."

While pain and loss are mine.

I FIND MY GUARDS BACK AT MY DOOR BY THE TIME I RE-turn from holding Court, my first time without the Maliki at my side.

"No public castrations today." I huff a short laugh, which they return.

"That's too bad." The baby shrugs as his sister rolls her eyes at him.

But what I don't tell them is that the subdued proceedings and quiet petitioners were somehow even more unnerving than the wild spectacle of a month ago. And stranger still, the Maliki was not mentioned at all except by Bashem and his daughter Rukhsar, who ran over to me afterwards.

"We have been telling everyone of the gift the Maliki shared with my daughter," Bashem had said, beaming at Rukhsar who had demonstrated a perfect spin on her healed foot to make his point. "We've been encouraging other Vuorians to consider the good in your joint leadership and compromise. To hope for a future without fear."

And though I felt that hope in my bones at his words, I also felt the fear. Because for all of Bashem's efforts to soften the hearts of Vuorians, I know others who are doing their utmost to keep them impenetrable. And I can't help but wonder if one of them was in the audience earlier today, if that same someone attempted to kill the king, my husband, the day before.

The elder clears her throat, bringing me back to the present.

"On our side of things, Tamir told us the Maliki's been sleeping most of the day."

I nod. "Good, he needs his strength."

She nods back, but then lets out a long breath.

"But." She glances at her brother. "When he was awake, he denied remembering . . . the incident."

My pulse whooshes in my ears. "*Just* the incident?"

"Yes. He remembered everything else."

"All right," I murmur, urging my heart to calm down. "Thank you both."

"Anything for you, Reim." We smile at each other as they return to their positions and I let myself into my room.

Let myself shed the mantle of Vuor's Malika. Let myself just be Reim. And let the man resting in my bed, beneath my sheets, beneath my *ribs*, shed his too and just be the healer.

Reim and the healer.

Easing the door shut behind me, I slip off my shoes and pad across the floor so as not to wake him.

Ting-ting-ting.

I cringe as the tiny bells of my wedding anklet start jingling, happy to be free of the confining boots I wore all day.

Khur.

I shoot a nervous glance at the previously dormant mountain of a man taking over my bed, watch him slowly shift like a landslide at the noise until he comes to rest on his back.

I hold my breath until it feels as if I'll need somewhere to lie down too. But when he appears to be in a deep sleep once more, I let it out and bend down to undo the clasp on the sabotaging jewelry.

"Don't you dare," the mountain rumbles, and I hear myself—the damn Malika of Vuor—squeak. Actually squeak in surprise.

Snapping my attention back to the bed, I narrow my eyes, trying to see through the dim.

"Just come closer if you want to see me." The healer chuckles, then yawns. "I don't want you to hurt those beautiful eyes."

Tingling heat rushes up my face at the unexpected compliment, and though I can't quite see him, I'm thankful the low light prevents him from seeing me too.

Or at least I think it does.

"I-I was just going to gather some things for the night and find somewhere to sleep in the castle . . . let you rest here," I toss in his general direction as I continue walking toward my wardrobe, using the light from the low fire in the hearth to guide my way.

But then I hear him rise rather than see him do so—a shifting mountain no longer, but an erupting volcano.

"You will do no such thing, Reim. This is your room," he booms.

And him saying my name again after so long, even in such an asinine way, as if I'm the invalid and he's the epitome of health, almost makes me give up on my vow to keep distance between us. Almost makes me march over to him and dare him to stop me.

Almost.

But instead, I ignore him, ignore the light fluttering in my stomach, the heavy aching in my heart, and open the door of my wardrobe.

Only for it to shut with a resounding bang not one moment later.

A large hand barricades the wooden door, the light pulsing so brightly from an unseen cut in its palm, the twin to mine, that it's visible even on the back side of it.

And then I feel the heat of his skin, smell the earthen musk of his body behind me, and know he's making good on his unsaid threat to stop me from leaving the room.

Catching me between churning desire at his defiant disposition and sparking anger.

I choose anger.

I whip around to face him.

"Have you lost your damn mind? You were at death's door not one night ago. You should be . . . back . . . in . . ."

My tongue stills, my mind stuttering to a halt when I realize he's standing in front of me with no shirt on.

His unyielding hand and corded arm brace the door behind me as my sabotaging gaze travels over his powerful shoulders, tracing each flicker of firelight licking his honed chest before free-falling down the sharp taper of his rippling abdomen to his—

I jerk my head back up so fast I nearly bang it against the wardrobe.

He smirks.

I scowl.

"You think this is another game or something?"

He steps impossibly closer, his left hand coming to bracket the other side of my face, forcing me to look up at him until his warm, sweet breath spills into my parted mouth.

"Or something. Told you the stakes would get higher." His smile grows wider, his eyes filling with curious wonder as he runs his big toe along my anklet, making my pulse mimic the teasing rhythm of the bells in response. "You're still wearing my anklet, wife."

And whatever reason, whatever ridiculous excuse I was preparing to launch at him, fizzles on my tongue.

Wife.

How I thought I'd never hear him call me that again. Not when he wouldn't speak to me for excruciating weeks after our wedding feast, and not when he wouldn't speak for terrifying hours after being poisoned. How I missed it so much . . . How I missed *him* so much.

And suddenly I can't breathe for an entirely different reason, my fraught heart remembering how close I was to losing him last night, how close I am to losing him still.

So I push one of his arms out of my way and run for the door.

But I make it less than a dozen steps before those same arms scoop me up against his bare chest and hold me tightly as I buck, trying to wriggle free.

"Put me down! You-you-overbearing, arrogant—"

He presses a tender kiss onto one corner of my mouth and then the other, stealing my weaponized words, my violent thoughts. But just as I move my lips to meet his more fully, more deeply, he pulls away.

"Not my name, Reim. And you sure as Fate are not running again." He stalks back to the bed, laying me down on the covers, knowing I'm too frustratingly proud to run now after he has challenged me on it. Smirking when he sees I'm staying in place, he shrugs on a linen shirt left for him on the bench at the foot of the bed.

"Though I don't remember a thing about how I ended up here"—he climbs into the warm covers next to me—"I do remember what happened after I woke up."

Then he tugs my crossed arms away from my chest, pulls my pliant body to him the same way he did earlier this morning. But instead of me burying my face in his neck, he buries his into mine. Inhales.

"I will never forget your relieved tears, your soothing whispers, your shy but bold touch," he murmurs into my skin, walking his fingers lazily over my body in the same way I explored his earlier. I bite my lip to keep from humming. "And I will never forget your heart caring for me, your soul *healing* me, for the rest of my life."

And I don't cry this time, don't say anything, but I also don't leave.

Couldn't even if I wanted to.

I just stroke his hair, his back, his face until his tired body grows heavy with sleep again.

And my heart grows empty with our borrowed time slip, slip, slipping away.

Chapter

STILL NO MEMORY?" MORI HUFFS AS SHE SHOVES
a spoon of lentil soup at the healer's tight-lipped
mouth the next night. The night before I leave.

He shakes his head while growling at the utensil
as if it's a dagger, but she's not having any of his
posturing and stands her ground.

Sifr and I watch the impasse with rapt attention.

"My coin is on the healer," sifr mumbles around his own
spoonful of soup.

"I don't know," I whisper back, still cradling my bowl.
"Mori's dealt with a lot of obstinate patients in her time."

Namely me.

"Bah, she's not so tough."

"Less talking, more eating, boy," Mori calls to sifr without
moving her eyes from the king, and he nearly drops his bowl.
"I don't need you falling asleep on the job today like you did
yesterday."

I giggle into my spoon, winking at him. "Not so tough, huh?"

"Fate," he mutters under his breath.

"Don't curse," Mori and I say in unison.

"Now, are we going to do this the easy way or the hard way?" She turns the full force of her intimidation back on the healer.

"I'd like to see you tr—"

She stuffs the spoon into his mouth before he can finish his sentence. He chokes it down as I choke on my laughter.

"If you think you can heal others without your own health, then you're not deserving of the title of healer," she declares imperiously before setting the bowl on the nightstand with a dramatic clatter. "I want you to finish all of that before I check on you tomorrow."

He grunts.

She glares.

And I yawn.

"All right, both of you, that's enough. Mori, I'll make sure he eats."

"And?"

"And sleeps."

"I'm right here and can speak for myself. I am not some defiant youngling," he pouts, looking exactly like one.

My smile is wide, but then a sudden punch of sadness causes it to collapse.

Because this simple scene of real affection, joy, and ease I was just a part of . . . it's not real at all. It's a cruel tease of what could have been had this been a different life, had we been different people. It's a fantasy of a life I didn't know I wanted, but definitely don't deserve. A life I will be saying goodbye to tomorrow.

Because even though this morning I woke up in his arms,

the night before was plagued once again by dreams of his rejection—his cruel admission that he only ever played at love to
hurt me, to destroy me, as I did to his people. That he was kind
to me, loving toward me, only to *use* me because it was easier
to rule with my complacency and stupidity.

That, in truth, I'm anything but lovable.

In truth, I'm nothing but a curse.

In truth, he *"wants me gone."*

And him wanting me gone would have been painful enough,
but now it's becoming harder for me to let him go. And if he
knew about the cipher tucked away in my drawer right next to
where we sleep, letting him go would be inevitable.

I go through the motions of helping Mori and sifr pack
away their supplies and wishing them a good night, and after
the door shuts behind them, I busy myself with dimming the
torches and dousing the hearth, with organizing the various vials and bottles on the nightstand, with anything except dealing
with these feelings with this man, who is silent but watching
me all the while.

"Reim, look at me, albi."

And my glass heart that has been fissuring this whole time
finally shatters at the term of endearment, the shards ricocheting inside its cage of bones and sinew until I'm broken and
bleeding from the inside out.

"Don't call me that." I try my best to make it sound like a
rebuke, but it comes out more like a plea.

His arm darts out and wraps around my waist in the next
second, dragging me across and on top of him in the next. My
hair falls in a thick curtain over both of our faces as I brace my
hands on his broad shoulders.

"What are you—"

"Then what should I call you?" he asks, his eyes glowing,
stubborn and serious. "Habibi, my love? Hayati, my life?"

I beat his hard chest above his heart with my frustrated fists to make him let me go, but he only grunts, flipping our positions instead, his strong hands shackling my rebellious wrists above my head, his thick thighs doing the same to my churning legs, his toe caressing my anklet—*his* anklet—again, while his nose and mouth nuzzle the tapered rim of my ear.

"Rouhi?"

I knit my brows. "What does that mea—"

But then he nibbles the soft fleshy tip, blowing warm air on the blissful hurt, and I lose his words along with all the others.

"Don't you see?" I whimper, trying so damn hard to focus. "This isn't real. You don't feel any of these things for me."

He pulls back and meets my gaze, his eyes not yet returned to their usual molten gold, but sparking, nonetheless.

"Is that right?" he asks slowly, dangerously. "Then do tell me, what is it that I feel?"

"Pity," I answer right away. "At the very least. Guilt, maybe gratitude, at the very most."

But I can't get myself to say the feeling I fear he holds so deep down that he may not even realize it: hate.

His grip tightens further. As do the swirling rings of his golden irises.

"Reim, listen to me."

And I really shouldn't. Should just leave him now, leave the kingdom with the cipher and my guards after the next Jirga meeting as planned, but something deep within me cannot. Will not. Not yet.

"You're right," he murmurs. "I did feel those things."

I stiffen at the words, but his free hand has already found its way underneath my nightshirt and starts soothing the taut muscle there. Keeps me from leaving. Keeps me listening.

"At first, on our wedding night," he breathes. "But then they changed."

My breath hitches.

"I felt respect when you challenged me in the training yard." He brushes his lips across my forehead.

"Then impressed, when you advocated for our people with the Jirga." Another one across my right eyelid.

"Awe, when I saw all the fruits of your labor in the cantons." Then my left one.

"Desire, every single damn time I see you, but especially when you wear this ridiculously transparent nightshirt." He drops his gaze suggestively to my chest before dropping a kiss on each furiously blushing cheek.

"And most of all, I feel love. A deep, unquenchable love for you," he whispers, dipping his chin until his hot breath skims across my parted lips, until inhaling his words feels more necessary than air itself. "Love for your sharp mind, your clever wit, your willingness to look for and act upon truth, even if it's against yourself. And yes, even your impulsive courage that worries me to the point of madness, but is also the reason for us ever meeting . . . for us ever kissing."

And it's everything I've ever wanted him to say, everything I ever wanted to hear. And he may believe he's speaking the truth, but in reality, he's saying it only because he doesn't know what his life will be like once the gifts are returned. He won't want to spend it with me once they are. My purpose will end, and he won't say any of this anymore.

He will just want me gone.

But what we have right now, in this very moment—this false confession of love, which for him is only born of survival, comfort, and convenience—is the best we're ever going to have. And I'm so deprived, so aching, so desperate for his love that I'm willing to take anything he's willing to give me.

Just for one night, I want to live like we have forever.

So, slipping a hand free of his hold and around his neck, I pull him even closer. Pass him a truth of my own.

"And it's also the reason for it happening again."

His pupils widen just before I crash my lips to his. And then it's as if he's everywhere. In the molten core of my body, the trembling chambers of my heart, the very essence of my soul.

The world falls away, and the sky collapses. The moment writing itself for eternity without pen or ink, thought or reason, but with blood and breath, nerve and flesh.

I moan low into his mouth, and it makes him dive deeper, his confident tongue sweeping up mine in a dance I don't know the steps to but somehow feel as if I've done with him my entire life.

He slides one hand from my waist to the top buttons of my nightshirt, tearing them off one after another until my trembling shoulders are bared to the cool night air, before dragging his fingers down my arm until he laces his fingers with mine, pressing, joining our twin scars together the way our bodies yearn to. Until I am unable to tell where he begins and I end. Unable to tell whether it's his hunger, his need for me, pumping through my blood or mine for him.

My free hand reaches for the bottom of his tunic, tug, tug, tugging it until it tears in my effort to free it from his pants. And then I'm skating the tips of my fingers over the hard peaks and sharp valleys of his hips, abdomen, and chest underneath it.

He groans low and deep, breaking his lips and hands away from mine to rock back onto his knees and whip his shirt off over his head, his breath heavy as he looks down at me. Devours me with his eyes.

"Beautiful." He swallows. "So damn beautiful. From the first time I saw you."

I resist the urge to say it back to him, to cover myself as his eyes take their time wandering over my splayed hair, swollen lips, heaving chest.

"Then why did you make fun of the elder Jirga member when he called me that?" I tease to hide my rising panic at remembering this is but a charade of love we're playing once again.

The healer groans as he settles himself on top of me again, kissing down my neck and collarbone until that anxious thought disappears with all others. "Please don't mention other men, especially that old curmudgeon, while I'm trying to love my wife."

There are those words again. *Love. Wife.*

"He's a sweetheart," I manage through a shiver at his ministrations.

"He's a menace."

I try to stifle a giggle with my hand, but he pulls it away.

"No," he says, kissing the invisible oath mark on my palm. "I want it all. I want your secret smiles, your mischievous laughs, even when they're at my expense."

He reaches for one of my intact braids, strokes it reverently with the back of his finger before grasping the band and then crashing his eclipsed gaze into mine.

"I want *you*, Reim."

My smile plummets, and I look away. Not because I don't want the same, but because I do. I want it so damn much. But playing at love, at marriage, is one kind of lie. Letting him undo my braids, undo me, and join with me for eternity when we only have one night is another. It's the kind of lie I would never forget, the kind I would never forgive myself for once he finds out the truth. That he's been lying to himself. That he doesn't love me after all.

He wraps his arms around my back and sits us both up until we are on our knees, facing each other. But I still can't look at him, so he hooks his finger under my chin, tilts it up, making me.

"I want you too," I whisper at his concerned expression, tears spilling from my eyes at this living dream that, despite it all, can't come true. "But I-I just can't."

He wipes each tear away with the pad of his thumb.

"Then I'll wait," he says in a low rumble, as serious and sure as the blood oath he made before. "I'll wait for your love for as long as it takes, Reim."

He doesn't even hesitate, doesn't even question me, and I wish he did so I could end my torment. So I could tell him about the cipher and watch his supposed love for me bleed out from his eyes. So he could leave me for the ones he does love. So I could grieve what I never had.

But I don't, like the damn coward I still am.

Instead, I nod, even though I don't believe him, letting him wrap me up in his arms, lay us both back in the bed we made, and rock me into a restless sleep, while I spare myself the inevitable heartache for just a little bit longer, while I refuse to look at the hourglass of our relationship, refuse to see that the sands of time have now run out.

Chapter

ARE WE READY?" I ASK THE ELDER AS WE WALK to the Jirga chambers the next morning.

"As well as we can be, Your Grace," she sighs. "My brother let Mori and sifr know about the cipher and our plans last night."

"And?"

"And they were upset. Insisted you rethink this. But knowing how damn stubborn you are—" She pauses to glare at me. "They said they trust you and would follow your lead."

I let out a withheld breath. "And I will inform the architect after the meeting."

She nods, and just as she's about to turn around to leave, I throw my arms around her and squeeze. "Thank you, friend. Thank you both so much."

Only after she squeezes me back do I let go. I steel my spine and throw open the doors.

"She has finally arrived." Basteel's sniveling voice is the first to greet me as I step into the room. "I had hoped—

I mean—*wondered* if something terrible had happened to you."

A few of the lesser Vuorian Jirga members chuckle at his joke as I walk to my chair at the head of the table, noting the Maliki's empty seat, but also that the architect's seat in his corner is unoccupied as well.

I take my seat and turn my attention to Basteel.

"Once upon a time, a comment like that against the ruler of Vuor would have been enough to send you to the gallows."

He leans back into his chair, a careless grin stretching his cheeks to hide the fury reddening their surface.

"Simply wearing the crown or rutting with that beastly savage does not make you our ruler. This position was once reserved for those who were both pure in honor and in blood."

He pulls at his round ear in emphasis, and half the table stands in violent objection. But I do not. There is something that has been making this coward bolder than ever, and I mean to find out what before I leave. I motion for the Jirga members to sit.

"Your extreme views and your personal attacks will no longer be tolerated here, Basteel. From this day, you are removed from the Jirga, and the king will decide if further action will be taken against you."

But his insipid smirk only grows wider, as if he thought I was going to say something like that. As if he were hoping I would.

"As you wish, of course. But speaking of the king," he says, wrapping his tongue around the last word, as if wanting to strangle it, "where is he? I know I am not the only one of us who has noticed his absence this past week."

But I've prepared for this question. "The Maliki is visiting the cantons, while I manage Court. It's as simple as that."

But there is a lengthy pause at my words, meaningful looks passing between Jirga members.

A chill races down my spine.

"What is the mat—"

Clap. Clap. Clap.

Basteel ascends from his seat as if at the end of a performance, slapping his hands together in mock applause as if he's imagining slapping me instead.

"Bravo, *Your Majesty*," he says, sneering at the title. "How easily you lie. How easily you think you can make us fools— the people you supposedly trust and who are only trying to guide you and help you. But we are no fools. So as a vizier of this Jirga and its most senior member, I took it upon myself to do some scouting of my own and have learned that the Maliki has, in fact, not been seen in the cantons for several days."

He draws his brows together in a mask of concern as he shifts his gaze from me to scan the entire table. "In fact, he has not been seen *anywhere* at all."

And this time, no one—not the Vuorian or Unnamed members—objects to his terrible implication. No one dissents or speaks.

No one even moves.

And suddenly I am done playing this game with him. With all of the Vuorian Jirga. Tired of asking mercy for them, covering for them, and especially tired of caring what they think now, when they never gave a damn about me all my life. I am Malika of this kingdom. And I am in the right. And I will defend it with my life.

"Speak plainly, Basteel," I enunciate each sandblasted word. "*Now.*"

A flash of fury overtakes the smugness in his eyes, but I don't give a khur.

"The Maliki is dead," he spits, his nose flaring, his eyes narrowing. "And not only do you know it, but you are the one who did it, you abomination, you cursed bitch. You killed him."

He starts shoving past chairs and Jirga members as he stalks toward me.

"We thought you were too stupid, too incompetent to lead when your father was alive, but you proved us wrong, didn't you? You were no victim of the siege on the Citadel." He leans toward me, his expression wild. "You were the mastermind!"

Some of the Vuorian members take this as their cue to pound their fists on the table in raucous agreement, while others among them hesitate, and the Unnamed members decry the very notion.

He ignores all of them, circling me like a monster of the desert circles its prey, considering how to best strike next.

"You were no victim of a khasir scheme. You made *sure* the khasir spawn was arrested—the same one you keep in this very castle as a damn pet to taunt us! Not only did you release him, but you also showed him how to access the castle through the sewers. You knew they would come. You knew they would take the kingdom, take your father's life. But that wasn't enough for you, was it, Your Majesty?" He laughs, but there is no humor in it.

Only vengeful rage.

"You then entrapped the new savage king as well, didn't you? Sold your body, your dignity, to him for the crown, and then when you had everything you wanted—" He stabs a finger at the empty seat next to me. "You. Killed. Him. Too."

Everyone's eyes turn to me, some hungry for confirmation, some pleading for denial.

But my heart doesn't care for their schemes or intentions, only for the safety of the man recovering in my room upstairs. I need to get to him before what Basteel is accusing me of becomes a reality at someone else's hand.

But how? The architect isn't here to subdue this, and neither is Tamir. I'm alone.

"Guards," he calls to the soldiers lining the chamber walls, without taking his wide eyes off my face. "Arrest this woman for treason and murder of the kings of Vuor."

They march toward me as if they were waiting for this signal, and it dawns on me that this was all part of a calculated plan.

This was a trap.

But Basteel is more of an idiot than I thought if he thinks I'll just surrender myself, my husband, or our kingdom without a fight.

I take what could be my last breath of this life and draw the dagger from my side. But this time, I'm not going to gutter my fire. I'm going to *ignite* it.

And as if hearing that vow come to life within me, the room does the same; the Unnamed Jirga members, as well as some of the Vuorians, draw their swords on Basteel and the guards, while others scream and scramble to escape the impending carnage.

But just as we are about to charge, the massive, heavy double doors slam open, splintering as they smash against the walls, the sharp wooden shards raining down on all of us as we brace ourselves in place.

"Basteel." A voice made of smoke and shadows pierces through the sudden blinding light engulfing the entire room, a voice and a light that could belong to one person alone. "Your reckoning has come."

And then Basteel screams.

Chapter 34

1 HAD WARNED YOU," THE HEALER'S THUNDEROUS voice booms through the blazing glow, coming from nowhere and everywhere at once. I keep my arms at the ready, but since I cannot see myself—let alone my opponents—I freeze where I stand.

"I had made no uncertain terms of your punishment if you threatened the Malika again. And yet, despite knowing I cannot lie, you decided to test it."

Basteel screams in prolonged agony once again before finding breath to plead with his tormentor. "Please- *please*!" he cries. "I only thought you-you—"

"That I was dead? That you had found someone to actually kill me?" the healer asks before another awful howl rents the air, something hot and wet spraying across my chest a moment later.

"*No!* No-no-no," he stutters. "I wouldn't *dare*! You-you have to believe me!"

"I don't have to believe anything, you lying piece of khur," the healer growls, and the whole chamber reverberates with his fury. "I only have to do as I promised."

And then his light funnels into a fulgent vortex, spinning and spinning until I'm afraid we will all be pulled into its powerful cyclone.

When it starts to pull away from the walls, my sight returns to my exhausted eyes, and the plane of brightness narrows into a singular column. Tightening its edges again and again until the funnel is so taut it resembles a honed blade.

And then the luminous sword finds its mark in a bloodied Basteel, circling him tighter and tighter until he is caged within its blazing prison, like the prison he threatened to cage me in just now.

But unlike the screams of pain and violence hidden behind the curtain of glaring light when the healer first entered, now we are given no such blindfold.

The long vertical blade of light circles Basteel so closely, it starts slicing his clothes into thin shavings.

Basteel screeches, grabbing at his bare arms and then torso, trying to pull his limbs into himself, trying to make himself smaller—ironic, as he spent so much of his life trying to make himself bigger than he actually was.

His skin starts to sliver off next, and the guards throw down their weapons and begin vomiting at the grisly sight unfolding before them.

"Do as I promised." I clasp my hand over my mouth, finally remembering the healer's promise to Basteel for threatening me.

He's going to flay him alive.

Basteel catches my eye with his wide, panicked ones, as if he just had the same thought.

"Please, Malika. Please. Mercy."

And then I remember the caveat to my husband's vow: If Basteel were to beg for mercy, I would be the only one in a position to grant it.

He screams again, collapsing onto his knees only to be pulled into a taut vertical suspension as more thin slivers of skin and sinew slough off his bloody body.

I turn from the macabre vision in front of me to face the king behind me. But he's focusing the entire brutal force of his attention on his victim, his anger raging in a storm cloud of swirling shadow and flashing light unlike anything I've ever seen before.

I whip back, watching Basteel's skin flay, then heal. Flay, then heal—just like the healer said it would at the first Jirga meeting—and I can't look away.

But, despite everything, I can't let it keep happening either.

"Please. Show him mercy, my king," I yell above the shrill whirring of the blade of light.

And at first, I'm not sure if he heard me, as I strain to hear myself, but then everything stops. The screams, the flaying, the entire room . . . just . . . stops.

Only the pulsing sword of light continues to hover an inch from Basteel's suspended form.

"Mercy?" The healer grinds the question past the clench of his teeth, sending an unnerving shiver down the length of my spine at the feral sound.

I edge closer to where he's still standing at the destroyed entry, wild-eyed and bare-chested, as if he came straight from my room. As if he came because he sensed I was in danger. The pulse in my heart and the one in my palm beat together in confirmation.

I stretch my hand out to take his like I did at Court, to make him look at me, be with me. But he flinches when I do, so I fist my hand and drop it, confused by his behavior.

No. Now is not the time to think about this.

I swallow and answer his question instead.

"Yes, mercy. I ask that you grant him mercy."

"Very well," the healer says, and then Basteel, bloody and nearly naked, drops to his knees on the floor.

"Th-thank you, my king," he gasps. "Thank y-you, my queen. You will not—"

A strident sound slices through the air, and Basteel's eyes bulge in his shocked face, his tongue halting upon the lie he left unsaid.

And then his head slides inch by inch off his neck and rolls onto the ground, his body crumbling into a lifeless, bloody heap after it.

My hand slaps over my mouth.

"There you have it. My mercy," the healer bellows to the room. "Let this be a warning to anyone else who would dare test it. The Jirga is dismissed."

And then he spins, storming back down the great foyer without even a backward look at me.

I push past the trembling Jirga members, past the architect—who has just arrived on the scene and is angrier than I've ever seen him—as he directs the guards in the removal of Basteel's body. I race after the healer, a dread somehow worse than watching the vizier's grisly execution surging through me with every step.

The healer's about to round a corridor after ascending the grand staircase when I finally catch up to his punishing pace.

"Wait, healer! What's wron—"

But his hand is at the center of my chest and I am shoved against the wall before I can finish the sentence, his other hand coming to cradle the back of my head right before it meets the unforgiving stone.

"How dare you even think of asking such a question?" He stamps his forehead to mine as the hand at my chest slams into the wall next to my face and the one behind my head tangles in my hair.

Pulls.

I stay silent as my chin tilts up with the motion, watching his fiery irises, attempting to read all the words he's not saying, all the feelings he's not expressing.

Frustration. Anger. *Hurt.*

And as if he knows I saw that last one but didn't want me to, he drops his face to my neck, inhales as if it's the last time he'll do so.

Exhales the same exact way. "How dare you ask me such a question when you already know the answer?"

But I don't know the answer. And right now, I don't know *him* either.

"Is—is this an unexpected effect of the iron poisoning, or perhaps of your gift?" I venture, scrambling to understand his brusque behavior, his cutting speech toward me. Unable to reconcile his declaration of love last night with such overt antipathy today.

Unless . . .

"No," he spits, whipping his head back to look me in the eye, letting me see the unadulterated anger sparking there once more. "It is the fully expected effect of *your* betrayal."

My barely tethered heart plummets.

The cipher. He knows about the cipher.

"Yes, Reim. I know. I found it this morning when I was looking for a salve and opened the drawer of your nightstand."

"You don't understand." I rush to explain, but he stamps his finger to my lips.

"No," he snarls. "I understand you perfectly."

And he looks so much like he does in my nightmares I nearly pinch myself awake.

"Fate, how could I have been so stupid?" he whispers, searching my eyes as if he'll find the answer there.

"Thinking of you night and day after that time in the Groves." His granite voice cracks, yet I feel the fissure climb my own heart. "Allowing myself to imagine leading and loving our kingdom together after Court, of you feeling the same way. Of what it would be like to not be alone anymore. Thinking of being with you so damn much that I stopped thinking about *The Book*. Told myself that building this life with you came first. That we could find it together after . . ."

He slides his finger down my lip until he lets it drop at his side. "But it was all a lie. You had your own goals. You didn't want my love. You wanted revenge."

"No. You're wrong." I grab his wrist and tug it. "When I discovered the cipher, I was scared. It was right after our wedding feast, and I was so sandblasted *scared*."

But even as the words leave my tongue, I can tell they aren't reaching his ears. He snatches his hand away and sneers. "Yes, scared to lose your kingdom. Lose your throne. Lose your *damn* crown."

"I was scared to lose you!" I scream the truth out loud for the first time, clutching his face with the same ferocity as he's clutching my hair.

And for the most infinitesimal of moments, his eyes clear of their anger, become filled with hesitation instead. I scramble ahead.

"I was scared you were going to leave me. That once you had the cipher and then *The Book of Names*, you wouldn't have a need for me anymore."

I swallow the rising bile in my throat before I admit the words that have been plaguing me since I discovered the small piece of parchment.

"That once you had what you needed from me, you would want me gone."

But instead of softening, his eyes, his jaw, *everything about him* seems to harden further.

"That I would want you *gone?*" he seethes, jerking his head back. "After telling you how much I respected you, admired you . . . *loved* you, I would then want you *gone?*"

"I told you already. You didn't mean those things. No one ever means those things," I whisper.

His broken laugh that once filled my ears, my heart, my world is now nothing more than the sound of stars collapsing, dying, in the watchful sky.

"You lie so easily, Reim," he murmurs, withdrawing his hand from my hair even as the inky locks attempt to curl around his fingers to keep him there. "Not to others, but worse—to yourself."

He closes his hands over mine where they cradle his face and draws them down, just like I did the night in his hut. "And it stops you from trusting yourself. Trusting the thoughts in your mind and the feelings in your heart. And if you can't trust yourself, then you sure as Fate can't trust anyone else."

Then he pushes my hands away, the burning in my palm so intense at his sudden absence it's as if he's cutting me open all over again. "And there is no love without trust."

How many different times, in how many ways, did he ask me to trust him? And I didn't. Tears start pooling in my eyes. "Wh-what are you saying?"

"I'm saying perhaps you were right from the start," he murmurs. "That there was never going to be anything more between us. Perhaps it's better we return to our original conditions of this . . . deal, dissolve this farce of a marriage, and settle the matter of the kingdom more justly when I return with *The Book of Names.*"

"O-on the battlefield?"

"If that's what you'd prefer."

No, that's not what I'd prefer at all.

What I would prefer is to eliminate this charged space between us at last—to grab him by his beloved face and kiss him until he's forced to swallow my apologies, breathe my love. Until I'm the one healing the terrible wounds I just caused him from the inside out. Until he has no damn choice but to give in to my feelings, to return them, to return to *me*. No damn choice but to take me back to our room, undo my braids, and love me, and let me love him back for the rest of our lives.

But I don't say any of that, *do* any of that. Because it's too late. I've ruined everything once again.

He takes another step back and nods, the everlasting fire in his eyes somehow doused, and I resist shivering at its devastating loss.

"I will be leaving as soon as I am able. Now that my assassin was brought to justice, I am hopeful that his followers will be duly warned and that you will be sa—" He cuts himself off, squeezing his eyes shut. When he opens them, they're hollower than ever, and my heart can't help but feel the same. "That the kingdom will be safe. I discussed the cipher and my plans with the architect and am leaving him at your side as you continue to rule in my absence."

Then with one last unreadable look, he bows. "Goodbye, Reim."

And then he's stalking away from me.

And I am left, left by him, but also left with the heart-wrenching realization that, despite everything I did to prevent this exact nightmare from coming true, I only have myself to blame.

Chapter 25

THE AFTERNOON WIND WHIPS THE SCENT OF BLACK-wood incense and dead flowers and whirls my emerald robes around me as I race along gravel pathways lined with beautiful shrubbery and dotted with ostentatious statues and gravestones of Vuorian nobility and royalty, all carved from polished, glassed baluur.

I run past the various graves of lesser viziers and the more ornate markers of ancient Ameers and Ameeras, Malikis and Malikas, past families come to mourn. All of them, stone and flesh alike, watch me with judging eyes as I collapse in front of the largest grave in the center of them all.

But I don't care what they think or say or do anymore. I only care about one person.

Catching my breath, I tip my head back and drag my gaze inch by labored inch up the monument I've never dared to visit before now. A monument that is half finished, started in life as death loomed closer because of his illness, but was never destined to be completed. The perfect representation of a life cut too short, despite my desperation to extend it.

Baba. Oh, Baba.

Above, the overcast sky crackles and rolls, flashing and thundering with a stormy grief that mirrors mine, building and building before breaking apart. The rain mixing with the tears that run down my upturned face until they are one. And his monument—with its half-rendered face, the missing hand and signet ring, even the unfinished crown—seems to be sobbing along with us.

"Oh Baba, I'm sorry," I begin, crying out above the burgeoning storm. "I'm sorry for not coming to see you before. But please don't think it was because I didn't miss you. I miss you so much, Baba. I miss your smile and your patience with me, your kindness and your hope for me as a leader of our kingdom."

I take a breath.

"I didn't come before because I was a coward, because I blamed myself like everyone blamed me—for your end and the kingdom's. But I was wrong. I wasn't to blame for the fall of something built on lies and fear. That fall was terrible, but inevitable. That fall was destined."

And I close my eyes, strengthen my heart for what I say next.

"And you were wrong too, Baba. Not only about the treatment of the Unnamed or the blind allegiance to Order. But most of all, you were wrong about me."

I snap them open again.

"My dissent was not a sign of weakness. It was the mark of a thoughtful leader. And it was damn hard, Baba." I let out a tearful laugh.

"You knew it would be. You warned me against it even. But what you didn't know was that paving a new path, my *own* path, was worth it. For me *and* for my people. I am proud of myself as a ruler, Baba. Proud I can trust my training, yes, but most of all, my own mind and my own heart. I wish you could see me now, Baba," I say, letting the rain cleanse me of old hurts, even as I grapple with new ones.

"I wish you could see how much I love your kingdom." I press my hot cheek against the cold, wet hem of his carved baluur mantle. "But . . . also, how I love it *differently*."

Just then the torrential rain starts to ebb, as if the sky were listening.

As if Baba were listening.

I pack my lungs with the scent of earth after rain, the very scent of the different love I'm trying to tell him about.

"It was love that drove me to try to save you. But it was also fear—fear of change, of not being enough. But I don't want to be scared anymore."

I draw back from the statue and stand, tilt my chin up to the sun that's hacking through the clouds to reach me, warm me, hold me. Smile as I imagine the beam being Baba's spirit loving me from beyond the veil between life and death, seeing me, understanding me, encouraging me.

"I love someone Baba, and today I realized he loved me back. Really loved me back. And I'm here just to say that I'm going to him now, even if he no longer feels that way, even if I've lost him forever. Because I don't want to be afraid any longer, Baba. I don't want to be afraid to lead, but even more importantly, I don't want to be afraid to love, even if I'm not loved in return," I say, as if I'm back in the embrace of his arms, loving him one last time.

And then letting him go, once and for all.

I hike the stairs two at a time into the castle and round the corridor to my room, recalling every time I felt something fluttering, then leaping, and then *soaring* between the healer and me, and how I still denied it. Remind myself of the first time I felt it in the training yard as our bodies moved in easy synchrony while sparring, in the Jirga chambers as our palms pulsed at even the barest hint of proximity, of possible partnership. In the cantons, in the hut, the Burrow, my room.

I shake my head. Is it any wonder he now occupies my heart the way he fills every other place in my life?

How did I possibly think I could run from him when he was everywhere around me?

When he was *within* me all along?

No more. My palm pulses not with the hesitant anticipation I always feel before seeing him, but with a surging need I've never felt for anything before in my life. I grasp the door handle.

And *shove.*

But I don't have to wait for it to swing all the way open to know he isn't here.

Don't have to note the missing guards to see there's no trace of him here either—not his clothes, not his scent, not his imprint on the bed.

He's gone.

I clutch at my chest that shelters my hammering heart. He can't be.

And then I see it: the plate of half-eaten almazi on the nightstand, and my mind leaps to laden branches in the Groves, to tea simmering over a cozy hearth.

He may have left me and *my* home, but—

I spin, my boots thundering back through the halls and down the stairs like the cadence of his barreling voice, past the ongoing ruckus in the Jirga chambers like the lightning in his eyes, across the grand courtyard and into the stables like the shadows that cloak him.

Once inside, my gaze snaps to the largest stall. The Maliki's jet-black steed is gone, and my heart is galloping with hope before I even mount my own.

And then I'm off, so similar to the last time I rode with him, and yet so different. The breakneck pace, the internal need to move, to *go*, is the same. But this time, I'm not running from myself, or from the healer. I'm running *to* him. Running for the possibility of us.

I just hope it isn't too late.

My horse huffs as though he feels the same urgency, then lengthens his stride once we're clear of the Keep's gate and into the Groves. By now, the stars are high in the sky. The farmers have long since gone home to their families, and the phoenixes that live in the almazi groves seem to be settling in for the night as well.

I pull the reins, trying to slow us down enough to find the Ma'asa and the farthest almazi grove that seems to thrive under its shadow despite the distance from the others of its kind. That seems to love the harshness, the loneliness, the firmness of the stubborn mountain, enough to forsake its own kind to be with it. The same almazi grove where the healer brought me when he told me that he wanted to show me something—his true self.

I didn't trust him then, but I was still willing to hear him, see him.

I can only hope he'll do the same for me now.

The moon is but a thin crescent, lending only a sickle of light to my search. I dismount and decide to walk the horse from this point onward, the land so lush with growth that I'm beginning to doubt I can find the exact path the healer and I cleared less than a month ago.

I close my eyes, strengthen myself with my newfound but still very fragile hope, and tilt my chin to the sky. Inhale.

But instead of crisp, clean night air, I smell smoke. Terrible, noxious smoke.

And where there is smoke, there must be fire.

And I already know, without a single doubt, where it's coming from.

"No. No. *No.*" I plunge into the blinding thicket, my sword thrashing back and forth to clear my path, my horse trailing by my side despite the obvious danger I'm hurtling into.

"Healer!" I cry as the sky veers from pitch-black to blood-red, the thick cloud of soot and ash choking me with every labored breath.

And all at once, I feel like the woman from the visions, running into her own fiery death, knowing she couldn't live with herself if she didn't.

"Husband!" I scream again as his burning hut looms through the roaring flames.

As the broken and cracked, rebuilt and repatched wall that has stood for centuries collapses in front of my eyes.

And then the roof follows behind.

LEAVE MY HORSE UNTETHERED AND RUN HEADLONG toward the escalating inferno, the sabotaging wind pitching burning debris and whipping ash into my face as I do.

"*Help*!" I wail into the open grass fields surrounding the hut. "Can anyone help me?"

But this place is too far removed from the nearest village or farm for anyone to be out here, especially so late.

I run until my legs feel like they are on fire themselves, the dress I've worn since the Jirga meeting ripping as I shove through brambles and bushes my blade couldn't clear in my haste to get to the hut. Get to *him*.

Crash.

I throw an arm over my eyes to protect them from the new explosion of embers and splintered wood hurtling from the wreckage.

The small hut seems so much larger in its fiery death than it ever was in its simple life, and the longer I run around its gnashing perimeter, unable to find a way in, the more my heart fears for the worst.

I wedge my fist between my teeth to prevent my mind from going there just yet. But right as I'm about to scream my frustration into my muzzle of flesh and bone, something moves in the small, collapsing entry.

No, not something.

Someone.

With a surge of renewed hope, I run toward the bulge of shadow as it hobbles toward me.

"Healer! Healer! Husband!" I scream above the fire's roar. "Oh thank Fate. Thank—"

But then I halt, because as I come within a few paces of the figure, I realize the frame is too slight, the gait too upright to be the healer's.

Who would be in the healer's home during a time like this? And *why?*

My heart can only imagine one damn thing.

"Reim," a familiar voice wheezes, "is that you?"

I shield my eyes against the smoke, just enough to make out tawny Vuorian warrior braids matted in soot, cerulean eyes peering through streaks of ash painted across an uncommonly handsome face.

"Tamir," I gasp, but my legs make no move to go closer. The fire, his presence here of all places, forcing my calculating mind to piece together a terrible puzzle. "Wh-what are you doing here?"

"Get out of here, Reim." He coughs, swirling his unfocused gaze around us. "It's not safe."

I shake my head and unsheathe my sword, aiming it straight at his heart.

"No," I snarl. "Not without my husband. And not until you tell me what the Fate is going on."

But he just stares at the sword and then drags his sad gaze back to mine. "I'm sorry, Reim."

Sorry? Sorry about what? No. No, he couldn't possibly mean—

But I can't let my heart shatter into a thousand pieces at the possibility of his betrayal. There's still too much unsaid, too much I need to know.

"What do you mean, Tamir?" I shout as I charge, my sword slicing left, then right. He stumbles and dives out of the way, barely keeping ahead of me. "How could you do this? To him? To *me*? I thought things had changed."

He parries one of my swings at last, but his sword trembles as it knocks mine away.

"They did, Reim. They did, and I had accepted your choice," he rasps as he holds his sword out in front of him. "But then . . . the architect. I started working with him in the cantons and—and he made me believe the healer was using you. That he was manipulating your feelings with his gift. He convinced me the only way to save you from him was to end him. So we went to his hut and poisoned him that night."

My already breathless lungs threaten to stop altogether.

"What?" I gasp, unable to believe it. First, Tamir, who I'd trusted unconditionally for so much of my life. And then the architect, who I was starting to trust unconditionally too.

The man who stopped me from ending my life, and then stopped the Unnamed man from doing the same. Who was always so calming, so encouraging. Who sandblasted knows about *The Book of Names*.

Tamir lets his sword drop and raises his shaking hands in front of him in surrender. "But then I saw how struck you were by it all, and I realized it wasn't anything that the healer did—it was what I did that hurt you."

He sways on bent knees before collapsing to the ground with a groan. I sheath my sword and drop to the ground beside him, once again feeling powerless in so many ways and knowing I can do nothing more until I have answers.

"Tamir." I elevate his lolling head into my lap while my horse nudges my hair. Grabbing my water bag hooked to her bridle, I unscrew the top and pour some water onto his lips. It takes a few attempts, but then he starts to sip, and then to swallow.

I use the moment to look at him, really look at him. Take in his clammy brow, his trembling body.

The blood seeping drop by drop through his clothes from a gaping wound in his side.

No.

I slap my hand over the wound, but the blood only seems to pool faster.

"No-no—Tamir! We need to find someone. You're hurt."

"No. Li-listen to me, Reim. We don't have mu-much time." He starts to shiver, his eyes unfocused yet fixed on mine as his words bore through me. "I was wrong Reim. I told you I would trust you, and I-I didn't. You loved him, you trusted him, and he trusted you. I f-failed you."

His breathing turns erratic and blood begins to leak from the corner of his mouth.

"The healer loves you. Be-believe me, I would know what that looks like." He smiles, sadly. "He trusts you. Cares for the whole kingdom t-too." He winces as he shifts his body.

I bite my tongue, hating every single thing about this, needing every detail of this shocking revelation, but knowing time is running out, and if he's speaking the truth, he may be my only hope in saving my husband.

"Shh, okay, Tamir, but what happened *tonight*?" I glance up at the smoldering ruins of the hut—the healer's favorite place, his home—and tears escape my eyes once more at the growing possibility that I'm going to lose the man in my arms while the one in my heart may already be gone.

Tamir's beautiful blue eyes roll back in his head.

"The architect . . . he tried again . . ." He clutches my hand as a faster rivulet of blood bubbles over his chin. "But this time . . . I got in the way . . ."

And a nauseating surge of hope climbs up my throat.

"I got the healer out . . . for you, Reim . . . always for you . . . forgive me, Reim. Forgive . . ."

And then—nothing. His lungs release a final breath; his body releases its repentant soul.

"I forgive you, Tamir." I press a trembling kiss to his still brow, choking back tears I cannot afford to free lest I never stop. "Go now. Be at peace, my dear friend."

Resting his head and body onto the earth, I force myself to get up, turn away, and renew my search for the healer.

He's alive.

He's alive.

He's alive.

I vow it again and again until it becomes the very beat of my heart, the very breath in my chest, refusing to even consider the alternative.

The raging fire is beginning to die out with very little left of the small, precious hut to devour, and I'm able to see beyond the smoke at last.

And there, only a few paces from where I first saw Tamir, lies what looks like a large boulder that wasn't there the only other time I came here.

The healer.

My horse neighs after me as I run.

Tripping over a charred piece of wood a few paces from him, I tumble hard to my knees and crawl the rest of the way, not caring that my hands and knees are being sliced open as I go. My due penance for what I've put him through.

Grabbing the jut of his shoulder, I roll him toward me until he collapses onto his back, and even without looking further, I can already see that this is so much worse than the first time.

My hands raise the flaps of his torn shirt while my eyes trace the wounds. There are obvious signs of a confrontation—swelling, scratches, and bruises from his formidable body being slammed into corners or objects—but there are also stab wounds, so many, in fact, I cannot believe he hasn't succumbed to them.

But most alarming of all is that they are still there, still oozing, still open.

Not healing.

Tamir admitted to poisoning him last time, but this—the flesh wounds, the fire—I can't even begin to understand it. But I don't have to. Not right now. I just have to get him better. Have to get him out of here. Have to keep him safe.

But how? It took several hours of bleeding him before his gift came back to save him last time, and he still hadn't fully recovered when this happened again. And here, in the middle of nothing but fire and darkness, I have no such time or such equipment.

And the architect—the one behind it all. How could he do this? *Why* would he? My head jerks up, my wide eyes sweeping the tall grass for movement.

He could still be out here somewhere.

I hook my arms underneath the healer's from behind and heave his head and shoulders up onto my chest, my mind spinning over how I'll get him onto the horse, when the hand pressed to his chest above his heart starts to ache.

Starts to pulse.

Then to *glow.*

To radiate light like I've only ever seen his do.

I flip my trembling palm and find the brightness blazing not only from the invisible oath mark, but also from the fresh scratches and cuts from when I crawled my way to him.

His blood glowed just like this when he filled a vial for me to heal my father.

Then could it maybe . . . maybe—

The phoenix-hilt dagger sings through the air as I draw it from my belt and reopen the oath mark on my palm. But instead of the searing pain I felt when he did it the first time, a deep, unfathomable need overtakes me. *Drives* me to lift my hand to his parted lips, tilt his chin up and tip my cupped hand down until the blood drips, drips, drips into the still-warm well of his mouth.

But that's not good enough. I need him to swallow. I massage the column of his thick neck where it meets the back of his throat until the muscle there shifts at last, the ball of his throat bouncing as the blood makes its way down.

And then I wait. I wait as the fire at our back recedes and the fragile frame of the hut emits apologetic creaks and groans, as if it feels regret for its own inability to protect the healer, its own betrayal and failure of him when he did nothing but love it the entire length of his long life.

I wait as my mind whispers that it's too late, that I have no such gift for healing and I've given him not strength or wellness but my own frantic desperation.

But then he lets out a shuddering breath, and I immediately hold mine in case Fate has decided to allow only enough air for one of us. And if that be true, then I want it for him. I want it all for him.

When he takes another shaky inhale, I tear my clinging eyes from his broken face to sweep them over the rest of his body until they land on the stab wounds in his side. I close them in grateful disbelief when at last the blood stops weeping, the skin gradually stitching itself back together again.

He groans so painfully from somewhere deep inside his chest that it rattles mine. I smooth back his knotted hair, then the deep crease digging into his brow, and whistle for my horse. We're still far from figuring it all out, but we've come such a long way. And despite the conflicting loss I feel about Tamir and the new torch of fear I hold for the architect, I look at the healer and carry a flicker of hope too.

My husband then opens his eyes, his breathtakingly beautiful eyes, now more precious to me than the precious metal they resemble, their radiance more necessary to me than sunlight to this very earth.

"I love you." I laugh softly, relieved as they attempt to focus on mine. "I love you so much, my king, my husband. And I trust you. With our kingdom, with my heart, my soul."

I swallow the salt of my tears before stamping my lips to his forehead.

"I'm so sorry, habibi. So very sorr—"

But the fragile word shatters in my throat as he slams me to the ground with one fierce surge of his body, one powerful shove of his hand. The same hand that then comes to shackle my neck.

Squeezes it.

Right before he bares his teeth and snarls in my suffocating face.

"Who the *Fate* are you?"

The Architect

BLOOD. SO MUCH BLOOD.

Fate, how I hate it. But not because of its color, nor its smell. No, nothing about its physical appearance or intricate natural properties. Those, I can appreciate. I can value its perfect balance, its calculated, precise flow *through* our bodies.

It's when it is *out* of the body that I cannot tolerate it. Its adamant unpredictability. Its impulsive decision to drip, splatter, *spray* over anything and anyone in whatever damn way it wants.

Uncontrollable.

Just like the person it came from.

I scowl and snatch the blazing torch off the wall as I descend the remaining stairs to this part of the castle. *My* part. For now.

The gushing of sewer water greets me as I round one corner and then another before finally shoving open a door at the end of the hall and slamming it behind me.

I let the back of my head thud against the creaking wood.

Fate, how I despised him—from the first time I met him as a boy after being whipped within an inch of my life for stealing almazi, when he had healed the shredded flesh of my back without even looking at me. So easily, so thoughtlessly. The way he did everything. While all I ever do is think and think and sandblasted think.

But of course he didn't give a khur about any of that, a khur about me. He, who actually had a gift and not just the delusional dream of one, who lived longer than all of us thrice over, whose body healed so easily, who didn't have to *suffer* like the rest of us.

Well . . . perhaps he did tonight.

Good.

But even in death he clings to me, his now useless blood soaking my robes, my hair and skin, my roiling soul. I swear I can feel it seeping into my every pore, contaminating me, infecting me, instead of healing me.

I use the torch to light the others lining the walls. No hearth in this underground labyrinth, but no people either. Just like the day I found it, while the rest followed the healer to fight the ajnoob and take the throne.

I splash my face with water from a small basin and look up into the cracked mirror above it. Small rivulets of the healer's tainted blood trickle down the planes of my face.

Why couldn't he just have listened? Just done what he was told?

Why couldn't he have just died when I bludgeoned his head, as that drunk fool I set on Reim did in the cantons?

Why did he always have to *fight* me?

Fight me when I orchestrated this whole plan to begin with. When I did every single thing to make it happen and all he had to do was make the deal.

Fight me for every single piece of information, not even tell me about the sandblasted cipher.

Fight me when he should have been fighting the damn ajnoob. When he should have killed every last one of them. When he should have burned their whole kingdom to the ground. When he should have flayed them alive like I encouraged him to do to that damn vizier so lost in his fanatical lust for power that he played his part of the scapegoat to perfection and earned his grand finale of an ending.

He should have.

But he didn't.

Splat. Splat. I frown at the drops of blood splattering the stones at my feet, resembling nothing more than little sunbursts like his unnerving eyes. I can't have it getting on anything else in here, though. On all my hard work.

Off. Off. I yank until the ties on my outer robe snap. Shrugging it off, I start to ball it up to throw in a corner when the sharp clink of glass rents the muggy air.

Fate, I almost forgot. Reaching into my inner robe pocket, I wrap my fingers around the three stoppered bottles and march them over to my workstation. Shoving aside the many plans and prototypes of the explosive I used at the healer's hut, I set the bottles down. Holding one of them up to the torchlight, I watch the red-gold contents swirl. The healer's blood, uncontaminated by the aerosolized iron, unlike that which stains my clothes.

But more importantly, *contained*. Mine to study and pick apart. Mine to control.

Now only one person left to do the same.

I fling the bloodied robe into the corner at last.

Reim, Reim, Reim. Three times. My mind needs to say it three times. For the three times I was wrong about her, of course.

One—when I thought she was just a weak pawn in my plan, but then she fought for her naïve convictions instead.

Two—when she told me about her visions of *The Book of Names* and gave me a better path to power. Gave me hope of being rid of the healer for the first time. Gave me the possibility of also having a gift, so I could rule this place as it should be ruled, once and for all.

Three—when she saved the healer's life instead of letting him die, collapsing the plot I made with Basteel to blame her in exchange for power and leading to this bloody mess.

I admit, I underestimated her ability to strategize, to calculate, to manipulate. She is my equal in every way—except her disgusting lineage, of course.

Pity.

Yes, Reim, Reim, Reim. She has gone from being like iron in my blood to the only thing I do not tire of thinking about.

But I will not have her at my side like the traitor did.

I'll let her freely roam in my head—but she'll stay shackled in my room, where I will give her no choice but to think of me too, until she forgets how he *loved* her.

Because that cocky piece of dragon *khur* did. He actually loved her. As did that idiot captain. And now they're both dead because of it.

No, I won't repeat their fatal mistake. I won't love her.

I will *own* her.

But first, I will find *The Book*. Take my rightful gift. Make the world bleed with regret for what it did to us.

Hmm. The thought of blood doesn't seem to bother me as much anymore.

Excerpts from The Final Chapter of
The Book of Names
Entered 200 years ago.

H BOOK THAT ALLOWS ONLY TRUTH TO BE written and loves truth to live on, I, Maliki of the honorable Haqqi tribe, bear witness that what I enter now is from what you allow and what you love.

The strangers have discovered that iron burns our flesh, bewilders our gifts, befuddles our minds. They think it only fair to be able to use it against us, if necessary, to protect themselves. However, they are the ones who decide what is considered necessary. And what is considered protecting oneself.

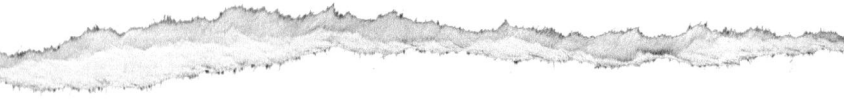

ONE OF OUR VILLAGE WELLS WAS POISONED YESTERDAY. Many of the younglings died well before the healers could reach their rigid bodies. But even though the adults kept their lives, they lost their gifts because they could not remember their names.

Only when they read *The Book* were they able to recall them once again.

The Jirga called upon the strangers to account for this assault on our people. But they refused, saying they now have their own form of justice, of "order," and that this was just a taste of what they can and *will* do if we do not surrender *The Book* to them. There can be no peace between our peoples, they said, as long as we have our gifts.

But what they don't understand is that our *Book* is us. We are our *Book*.

Or perhaps they understand perfectly and that is why they seek to destroy it.

In order to destroy us.

We refused.

THEY DECLARED WAR.

There is no clean water anywhere. Not in the river. Not in the wells. They poison us by increments, enough to keep us alive, keep us afraid. If only rain could suffice for us, our herds, our crops. It does not. But I collect it for Noori anyway, for our unborn child who continues to grow in her womb.

Most of the Haqqi have surrendered to their thirst and have drunk the ruined water. Some don't survive. Some do. But each time it is harder to remember, to return to ourselves, even after reading *The Book*.

We are forced to choose between living as who we are and living at all.

And now we are prevented from traveling beyond the wall they raised around us, built from our own almazi trees and topped with iron blades.

With no water, no ability to move, to live, the Jirga has decided that this is enough, that we have no choice but to fight the strangers. But our weapons are only farm tools and fishing spears. Our soldiers, only farmers and fishermen.

Our gifts only weaken, along with our hearts and our hope.

TOMORROW.

We will ambush the wall tomorrow. Those of us gifted with strength will charge it with all our might. Then those gifted with agility will attempt to climb over and let the rest of us in.

We made a promise to each other—we will fight only those who fight us. We will demand that they stop poisoning our water. Stop killing us. Stop encroaching any further on our home, our minds, our lives.

That they leave us alone.

THE VUORIANS HAVE CONVINCED THEIR PEOPLE THAT WE are attacking them, just like what happened to them in their homeland. That we are the aggressors, the villains. They are stoking fear like never before, because they know fear will motivate them far more potently than thirst and starvation have motivated us.

I reach deep within the pages of this *Book*, deep within myself, for my gift of empathy.

But it is as terribly lost as theirs.

In this, at least, we are equals.

I FEAR THIS IS THE LAST TIME I WILL WRITE IN THIS *BOOK*. That perhaps anyone will ever write in it again.

There is something terrible in the water, but also in the air. Something that makes it hard to think, to breathe. I see fire. So much fire. From above and from below.

Our enemy is here.

But so are they.

ACKNOWLEDGMENTS

The Unnamed wouldn't have been possible without the help of my amazing team and the generous support of my family. But first and foremost, I want to thank God for His mercy and guidance in every step of this process. From the very inception of this story to carving out the exact path that led me to its conclusion, He was with me always.

Then to my husband, Jawaad—my alpha reader, my interior illustrator, my anchor in so many storms, my number one fan, the love of my life. You picked up my broken pieces again and again and taught me to love and respect the cracks, to not only keep the faith when it came to this story but to make it rock solid. Thank you, Jaan. "I was blessed with the rizq of your love."

To Farook and Khadija, who believe in me loudly, confidently, and unconditionally. I am so grateful to be your Mama.

To Nuha, who listened to my tirades of self-doubt a thousand times and was still willing to listen to them a thousand more.

To Hana, who was the first person I shared my love of books with, and to Mom and Dad, who would often turn the other cheek when I'd forget chores because "one more chapter" turned into "several more chapters."

To Alex, my incredible editor, who understood the beating heart of this story, its characters, and its themes from the very beginning and made it her mission to make sure my readers understood it too.

To George, whose developmental direction got me believing in my story again.

To Allison, who never hesitates to remind me exactly who I am whenever life makes me forget.

To Kim, who literally told me I had to write this story, then metaphorically made me take an oath to publish it.

To Chinah, who just had a knack for saying exactly what I needed to hear exactly when I needed to hear it.

To Joyce, thank you for adding your magical finishing touch to this book and giving me the final encouraging push across the finish line.

And finally, to Sarah and the Bloomers, who reignited my love for reading and writing. I love you, Milajes.

ABOUT THE AUTHOR

AUTHOR. PSYCHIATRIST. SOUP ENTHUSIAST.

M.S. Masood can be found overstaying her welcome in bookstores and cafes around the world, judging soup but never people. A humble listener and enthusiastic teller of stories, thanks to the encouragement of her ever-patient husband and children. Lives in Philly, but is a Tar Heel for life.

You can follow her here:

WWW.MSMASOODBOOKS.COM

Instagram: @msmasoodauthor

www.ingramcontent.com/pod-product-compliance
Lightning Source LLC
Chambersburg PA
CBHW030235120726
47903CB00005B/1492